AN ARDENT MOMENT

His hands were gentle on her shoulder. "How long have you cared what I thought about you?"

"Too long." She raised her head defiantly, but her eyes softened when she saw the look on his face.

"Not as long as I have," he confessed.

He stared down at her glowing face like a man mesmerized by a miracle. "You've certainly led me a merry chase. It'll take me years to recover."

Then he abandoned conversation as his mouth came down over her parted lips. The kiss started in light exploratory fashion but changed abruptly to a hard, possessive embrace that left both of them breathless when they drew apart. . . .

THE
ROMANTIC
SPIRIT

by

GLENNA FINLEY

A SIGNET BOOK
NEW AMERICAN LIBRARY
TIMES MIRROR

SIGNET TRADEMARK REG. U.S. PAT. OFF. AND FOREIGN COUNTRIES
REGISTERED TRADEMARK—MARCA REGISTRADA
HECHO EN CHICAGO, U.S.A.

SIGNET, SIGNET CLASSICS, SIGNETTE,
MENTOR and PLUME BOOKS
are published by The New American Library, Inc.
1301 Avenue of the Americas, New York, New York 10019

First Printing, August, 1973

3 4 5 6 7 8 9

PRINTED IN THE UNITED STATES OF AMERICA

For "Ook" and his friends with thanks

Love is a spirit all compact of fire.

— SHAKESPEARE

Chapter
ONE

The apartment building at the end of the narrow San Francisco street looked perfectly normal.

Maggie Rome let out a soft sigh of relief as she stared at it. What an idiot she'd been—to worry about an address! She searched on the car seat beside her for the notice to check the building number again . . . 727 Spirit Lane . . . just as the real estate man had written it.

She dropped the paper on the dashboard and shook her head ruefully. Not a ghost or a goblin in sight, despite her premonitions. This neighborhood looked as staid as Nob Hill and Number 727 fitted smoothly into the landscape. It was a two-story brick building with majestic old shade trees solidly anchored in a narrow parking strip. The four wide windows facing the street were neatly shuttered, as was the big front door whose brass fittings gleamed in the sunlight. Even the white marble steps looked as if they'd just been scrubbed by a Baltimore housewife.

Maggie frowned in confusion. The real estate man must have been imagining things! Either that or he was trying to save this sublet for a friend of his. Certainly there was nothing about the outward appearance of Spirit Lane to warrant such caution.

Spotting a convenient space just ahead, she pulled her car over to the curb and turned off the ignition. Automatically her hands went through the San Francisco hill-parking routine; cramp the wheels against the curb, shove the gear shift lever into "park," make sure the emergency brake was all the way on, now take out the key. There! That should satisfy the most critical Bay city policeman.

She got out of her car and locked it, then stood beside it for a minute to get her bearings.

A passing delivery truck driver almost collided with a parked car as he stared at her. His attention had been drawn like a magnet to a pair of trim ankles and gradually worked up to appreciate the delicate profile framed by shining brown hair which curled at collar level. Maggie's gray eyes widened in alarm at the sudden screech of tires beside her before smiling at the embarrassed driver as he drove off.

Absently she buttoned her red raincoat against the whisper of wind. Although it was mid-March, the breeze was balmy . . . promising spring in the offing like a courtesan intermittently offering her favors. The morning fog had burned off earlier but a salt tang still lingered, leaving the streets with an antiseptic air and the buildings with gleaming, still-wet facades.

Maggie took a deep breath and smiled happily, enough of a visitor to be thrilled with the obvious charm of the Bay city. Subconsciously she noted the mournful blast of an ocean liner as she turned toward Number 727 and went up the steps. Probably it was hoping for too much that Miss Jarvis's apartment would have a view, she told herself. But since it was perched up on the top of Russian Hill, she'd keep her fingers crossed just in case.

She paused for a moment to glance at the row of five brass mailboxes by the door. Evidently there were only four apartments in the building plus the manager's. A calling card bearing the name Miss Agatha Jarvis in fine italic script was inserted under the slot for Apartment **B**.

Since there was an absence of intercoms, Maggie

turned and tried the front door gingerly. It swung open at her touch and she stepped inside, thankful to have avoided the usual shouting match on the steps through an inadequate speaker.

The shadowed foyer made her pause long enough for her eyes to accustom themselves to the gloom. A graceful stairway on the right led to the second floor. She peered up it, wondering if Apartment B was on the second level.

The sound of a door closing nearby made her turn in relief. She walked purposefully through the foyer and saw a half flight of stairs leading down to what was obviously the manager's apartment on the basement level. As she stared, the door opened again and a man in worn gray coveralls, carrying two plumbing wrenches, emerged from the apartment.

She waited until he put a foot on the stairs before she cleared her throat self-consciously and said, "Excuse me, I'm sorry to bother you, but . . ."

He gave a startled glance upward at the sound of her voice, stubbed his toe on the next step, and sprawled up the steps at her feet.

"God damn it to hell!" The words were muffled by his broad shoulders, but Maggie winced at their vehemence.

She struggled with an instinctive impulse to flee out the front door. Instead she knelt down by his side, reaching for one of the wrenches which had slithered under the banister. "Here . . . let me help you. Honestly, I didn't mean to startle you."

The caretaker had pulled himself together by then. He was younger than she had thought, somewhere in his early thirties. Under a layer of greasy smudges, however, his jaw was tight with irritation.

"I don't need any help. For lord's sake, give me that wrench. Your hands will be filthy," he snarled.

"They'll wash," she stood up, clutching the greasy tool

defiantly. "Did you hurt yourself when you . . . lost your balance?"

He was upright by then, and even standing two steps below her, managed to look her squarely and balefully in the eye. "No, and I didn't lose my balance. I fell flat on my face. Don't gloss things over." His mussed dark hair suffered even more as he raked a hand through it. "Now—could we change the subject?"

"Of course." The effect of that devastating glance made Maggie feel as if she'd been the one to go sprawling. "What do you want to talk about?" she asked in some confusion.

His hand tightened on the wrench he was holding as if he were keeping his temper with difficulty. "*I* don't want to talk about anything. *You're* the one who came barreling in here. Exactly what did you have in mind?"

"Nothing subversive." She was stung at his insinuation. "I merely wanted to ask you which apartment belonged to Miss Jarvis."

His eyes narrowed, and his glance swept over her five-foot-four frame deliberately. "Why?"

"It's none of your darned business. All I wanted to know was whether Apartment B is upstairs or down. But I'll find out for myself," she informed him. No wonder the real estate man had been cautious when he told her about Spirit Lane. He probably knew this cretin of a caretaker was on the premises.

Evidently the man in front of her realized he'd gone too far. "I'm sorry," he muttered finally. "Aggie's apartment is right through the arch behind you."

"Thank you." Maggie's chin went up. "I'll tell *Miss Jarvis* how helpful you were." She swung around on the step.

"Hey there . . . just a minute!"

"*Now* . . . what?" Sarcasm dripped from her tone.

"The wrench." He was leaning on the banister. "I'd like it back . . . unless you're passionately attached to it."

"Oh!" Maggie had forgotten she was still clutching it. Unnerved, she thrust it toward him . . . and let go before he was able to grasp it.

The wrench naturally followed Newton's theory on gravity . . . and went down. Precisely on the toe of the caretaker's polished brown shoe.

"Ow! Damn it to hell!" came his anguished shout. The other wrench hit the floor as he clutched his injured foot.

"Oh, my lord! I'm so sorry . . . are you all right?" Maggie's solicitous inquiries were cut off abruptly as the manager finally focused on her white face.

"Just go," he told her. The words grated out.

"But if I could help . . ."

"Get out of here, or so help me, I'll belt you . . ." His voice trailed off as he watched her scuttle through the archway out of sight. Then he limped down the stairs into the apartment behind him, his face pale with pain.

Maggie heard the slam of his door just before she rang the buzzer of Apartment B, and her body sagged with relief. It had taken all her courage to keep from dashing for her car after that fiasco with the wrench. Even now, she'd have to tell Miss Jarvis that she couldn't possibly rent the apartment. If the manager discovered her as a tenant, he'd probably turn off the heat and electricity for pure spite. It was a pity, too, she was thinking, because otherwise the apartment's location would be perfect for a sublet.

She heard the clatter of a chain being drawn on the other side of the door before it was opened just far enough for one bright eye to peer out at her.

"Yes?"

"Miss Jarvis?" Maggie softened her voice after hearing that breathy, whispered monosyllable. "My name is

Margaret Rome—I've come about the apartment. Didn't the real estate man call you?"

"Oh, Miss Rome . . ." There was patent relief in the old woman's tone. "Do come in, dear. Just a minute until I undo this other chain." The bright eye slid down to knee level and there was more rattling of metal against wood. "A woman living alone can't be too careful these days. There we are." The door was swung wide, and the tiny, gray-haired lady motioned her in.

It was hard for Maggie to guess Agatha Jarvis's age because every cosmetic aid that had ever been invented was applied in layers on her face. Her skin was parchmentlike under magenta rouge dabbed on in clown circles on fragile cheekbones. Sagging eyelids were camouflaged in frosted blue shadow and thin lips were disguised under a carefully drawn cupid's bow of Jean Harlow vintage. Even her hair was two distinct shades of gray caused by an inexpertly applied blue rinse on the ringlets over her ears. She wasn't merely dressed, Maggie decided, she was costumed in mauve chiffon with skirt panels which quivered with excitement.

Maggie was left the choice of hovering on the threshold or following Miss Jarvis's trail of flowing chiffon through the hallway into the living room.

"I didn't expect anyone so soon. Those real estate men never tell a person anything," the quavery voice complained.

"Yes, Miss Jarvis," Maggie responded automatically, still stunned at her surroundings.

It was like entering a subterranean tunnel filled with billowing silk hangings and pungent incense. The only illumination came from a Tiffany-shaded fixture on the high ceiling, and she half-expected to see a bust of Ramon Navarro in the corner. No wonder the real estate man had looked uneasy.

"I don't really know how I'm going to do without my things, even for a month." Miss Jarvis settled on a mohair sofa that looked like a prop from a Laurel and Hardy movie and patted the cushion beside her. "Of course, it's such a relief to know a nice girl like you will be looking out for everything. I won't have to worry about your taking care of my belongings." She made them sound like the British crown jewels.

Maggie perched gingerly on a rocklike cushion. "I don't think I'm going to be able to live here, Miss Jarvis." She wasn't quite able to keep the relief from her tone although she was sorry to start the apartment-hunting all over again. "I just met your manager in the hall and, frankly, we didn't get along at all."

"Mr. Malone?" Agatha said. "How very strange. Usually he's so obliging. But that's all right, dear . . . you don't have to worry. He's taking his vacation any day now. I believe he'll be away a month at least." She leaned over and patted Maggie's hand. "You won't have any worries on that score."

"You're sure?"

"Of course." She tilted her head and cackled—there was no other way to describe the sound. "If you knew me better—you wouldn't question my word," she told Maggie. "I have the power."

"I beg your pardon?"

"The power, dear." Impatience crept into her tone. "I'm psychic, you see."

Maggie edged away warily. What was she supposed to say now? Clearly the old lady was expecting something. "That must be very nice," Maggie managed finally.

Agatha's laughter trilled again. "Well, it's certainly handy. The minute you came through the door, I said to myself, Here's a sweet girl with an aura of friendly spirits surrounding her. It's so helpful to have a congenial atmosphere. I know you'll be happy here, Margaret, dear. It's all right if I call you Margaret, isn't it?"

Maggie started to say that nobody had called her Margaret since she was born and then shook her head hopelessly. "I don't really think I'm the type of person you'd want . . ." she started to say carefully.

"Oh, you *are,* dear. One doesn't fight the spirits." Agatha bounced on the cushion happily, causing the chiffon panels of her dress to quiver again. "In fact, I'm willing to forget about the rent just to have you here."

"You can't mean it!" Maggie's clear gray eyes widened with surprise. "Honestly, Miss Jarvis—I couldn't let you. The price people want for sublets in this town is fantastic."

"Oh, I know all about it. Just because I share things with the spirit world doesn't mean I'm unworldly, Margaret, but at my time of life it's important to know that someone trustworthy is caring for my most priceless belongings. Besides, I can afford it." The last words were accompanied with a shy smile. "And I only plan to be gone one month."

Maggie tore her thoughts from the budget figures which were flashing through her mind. "That's all I need, Miss Jarvis. You see, I'm on leave from my job. This is my chance to find out if I'm any good as a sculptor or painting in oils. I've been doing commercial art for three years and saving my money for this holiday. If you really mean it about the rent, it will be a tremendous help. My budget is pretty limited."

"I do mean it, dear." The blue-shadowed lids blinked as Agatha stared at her. "I shouldn't think you'd have to worry about money . . . you're so very pretty. Can't you get a young man to buy your dinner now and then?"

Maggie grinned. "All the ones I know are a thousand miles away. Unfortunately, not one of them suggested coming out here to buy my dinner. Besides, most of them are artists and they're broke all the time."

"Maybe Tony can help." Agatha sounded as if she were thinking out loud.

"Tony?"

"Our nice Mr. Parks on the second floor. I understand he's a photographer, so you'd have things in common . . ."

"I don't quite understand."

"You're both artistic, dear." Clearly artists and photographers were placed in the same creative cubbyhole in Agatha's mind. Her thin hands fluttered as she went on to explain. "Actually I don't think he has to work, so he'd be just the type of man to help with your budget."

"Wait a minute." Maggie felt she'd better nip the matchmaking in the bud. "I won't have any budget problem if I don't have to worry about rent. Let's not bother Mr. Parks."

"Whatever you say, Margaret." Agatha was obviously disappointed. "Perhaps it's just as well . . . one month wouldn't give you much time."

"Hardly any at all," Maggie agreed. "Now I suppose we'd better be businesslike—is there anything special you'd like me to do for you while you're away?"

"We-ll," Agatha drew the word out for two syllables, "if you'd take care of Banjo for me—I'd be ever so grateful. He's my canary and doesn't like to be moved about."

Maggie frowned slightly. A rent-free apartment in exchange for merely furnishing birdseed. It was too good to believe. Her forehead smoothed as she said, "Of course . . . I'll be glad to watch over him if you'll leave a list of instructions. It will be nice having a bird for company."

"I knew you'd feel that way." Agatha bounded to her feet as lightly as a ten-year-old. "Come out in the kitchen and meet him now. Then you can see the rest of the apartment."

Banjo turned out to be a molting, pale yellow canary clinging apathetically to the perch of an elaborate brass cage. He refused to show any animation as Agatha fluttered about, looking like a faded bird herself. She pointed out his water dish, a special saucer for bathing, and the holder for his imported birdseed.

"He loves greens, too," she added, chirruping at the canary fondly. "Don't you, sweet-ums?"

Banjo's disdain was obvious. He leaned over and pecked dispassionately at his toenail.

Agatha chose to ignore this lapse of manners. "Such a fine influence in the morning . . . he sings for hours."

Maggie wanted to ask how early the concert started but thought better of it. "I'm sure we'll get along just fine." She turned to admire the rest of the room. "I like your kitchen . . . it's so light and airy."

"Mmmm," Agatha wasn't enthusiastic. "I don't think it has much character," she complained waving a thin hand at the walnut cabinets and gleaming beige tile. "Mr. Elliott had all the kitchens in the building remodeled last year. The tenants weren't allowed any say in the decor." She sniffed. "Frankly, I would have preferred purple with touches of black. That would have signified supreme power . . . majesty. Besides, my horoscope calls for darker colors."

Maggie felt instant sympathy for the unknown Mr. Elliott. "Perhaps he thought the neutral shades were easier to live with," she said tactfully.

"My dear, he just didn't care. Owners never do." Agatha gave the top of Banjo's cage a sharp, birdlike tap with her nail. "Well, let's see the rest of the apartment."

It was easy to see the obvious tug-of-war between landlord and tenant in the apartment's decor. Mr. Elliott had won in the bathroom—the tile and fixtures were a sunny, pale yellow with overtones of white. Agatha had triumphed in her bedroom. The spread and heavy drapes were purple velvet, the furniture gilt and spindly. "So restful, my dear," the older woman said with satisfaction.

Maggie surveyed the beaded lampshade hanging from

the headboard and nodded, realizing she'd need to carry a flashlight to find her way across the room at night.

"And I always keep the bedroom window partway open," Agatha said, drawing back a blind to illustrate. "This is very important."

"For the ventilation, you mean?"

The older woman looked astonished. "Oh, no, dear. It's for the spirits. Those of us on earth have to show our desire to receive them. The open window signifies a willingness to let the friendly forces invade our hearts." She gazed soulfully upward as she clasped her hands to her bony chest.

Maggie glanced up instinctively, too, and then shook her head slightly as if to clear it. Plastered on the ceiling directly over the bed was a red and yellow poster showing a Dali-like eyeball surrounded by flames. "My God!" she exclaimed.

Agatha followed her gaze. "No, not God, my dear," she corrected gently, "but the sign of the Inner Being. The real you."

Maggie looked back toward the living room hastily. There was no reason she couldn't sleep on the sofa in there. Far be it from her to argue with her hostess but that inflamed eyeball certainly was not food for *her* soul.

"And this is the dressing room," Agatha was continuing the tour, through a spacious closeted area with a bank of high windows which provided excellent light.

"Oh, this is wonderful," Maggie said happily. "Would it be all right if I used this for a studio? I promise to be very careful with my paints and clay over the rug."

"Make yourself at home, my dear. The real estate firm told me about your excellent references so I won't worry. Mr. Elliott can do that," Agatha finished smugly.

"The owner?"

"Exactly. Fortunately, he's an absentee landlord most

of the time." Agatha was surveying her nail polish. "That makes it better for all of us."

"There isn't any trouble about subletting, is there?" A sliver of doubt crept into Maggie's mind. Agatha Jarvis was being extremely offhand for a tenant.

"But you're *not* subletting, dear. This is an arrangement between friends. Let's go back into the living room and be comfortable," she added fretfully. "I don't like this glaring light."

Maggie followed her. "Actually I am subletting . . . in a way."

"Nonsense. There's nothing in the lease that says I can't have a house guest. My apartment is filled with friendly spirits most of the time." Agatha bent over a cabinet and unearthed a key from the drawer of it. "You'd better take this now before I forget. It fits the master lock on the front door and my apartment, as well."

"All right." Maggie reached out hesitantly. "If you're sure it's acceptable to everyone."

"Don't shilly-shally, Margaret, dear. This arrangement was preordained. I even talked it over with Alfred and I have complete confidence in his judgment." She turned her blank gaze towards the fireplace. "Don't I, dear?"

"I'm sorry . . . were you speaking to me?" Maggie asked as the older woman settled on the sofa again.

"No, dear." The old lady rested her head against the cushions and closed her eyes. "You haven't admired my greatest treasure . . ."

Maggie frowned and looked around, half expecting to see Count Dracula reposing in a glass case. She glanced back, puzzled. Eccentric wasn't a strong enough word for Agatha Jarvis. The poor soul must be barmy as a crumpet, living in another world. "I'm sorry . . ." she faltered as Agatha waited expectantly, "you have so many lovely things . . . I don't know which one you mean."

"The fireplace, dear . . ." Agatha hinted.

Maggie's eyes swung obediently toward the wood-burning fireplace on the far wall. It was pleasing with its Roman brick facade and carved wooden mantel but hardly spectacular.

"Very nice," she murmured. "I think they add a lot to the comfort of a room . . . especially in the spring or fall."

Agatha's laughter interrupted her hesitant praise. "No, no . . . I meant my urn on the mantel. Lovely, isn't it?"

Maggie moved over to survey the piece of porcelain that she mentioned. Its warm white glaze was decorated with a group of mythological figures exquisite in design and detail. One of the figures of a warrior god was enlarged to form graceful handles on either side of the urn. "It's perfectly gorgeous," Maggie said truthfully. "My goodness, it looks like an original Capo di Monte piece, but they haven't been made since the early eighteen hundreds. Would it be all right if I checked the markings on the bottom?" She was reaching out for the urn as she spoke but stopped immediately as Agatha drew in her breath sharply.

"No! Don't touch that!" There was nothing of the frail little old lady in her voice now.

Maggie's hand dropped as if she'd been winged. "I'm sorry, I didn't mean to be rude . . ." she began, only to have Agatha come swiftly to her side.

"You silly girl. Don't look so stricken. I didn't mean to frighten you, but Alfred's very fussy about that piece." Agatha's tone took on its fluttery nuances again as she smiled apologetically. "I forgot to tell you about him, didn't I?"

The younger woman was still unnerved. "Yes, you did. Why is he important? Does he live here, too?"

"Hardly." Agatha bridled visibly. "I've never married. Not that I didn't have the chance, you understand, but that was long ago. I don't know what I would have done without Alfred's help these last years. Every time I have a problem, he's given me such good advice."

Maggie smiled sympathetically. "I'm glad. Is he your lawyer?"

Agatha's fingers were twisting the end of her crocheted belt. "You could say that. Really, he's remarkable—last year he even told me when to sell some of my mining stock. It was before the market went down."

"Alfred sounds pretty versatile." Maggie took another look at the old urn on the mantel. "Does he like all porcelain or does he just specialize in Capo di Monte?"

"Porcelain?" Agatha frowned, then her forehead cleared. "Oh . . . you mean my urn?"

"Yes, of course. I don't blame . . . Alfred . . . for being fond of it. That piece really belongs in a museum."

"Nothing's too good for Alfred," Agatha agreed, nodding.

Maggie glanced at her watch. "I really should be going. You're sure that it's all right if I move in tomorrow?"

"Anytime in the morning will be fine," Agatha confirmed as they walked out to the foyer. "I'll leave my list of instructions by Banjo's cage in the kitchen."

"And your forwarding address, too? I don't believe you mentioned where you were going to be."

"Oh . . . around." Agatha's hands fluttered in a graceful circle. "Perhaps down by the shore . . . I find such inspiration at the ocean. There's something clean and spiritual about the action of the waves, don't you think?"

"Ummm, I suppose so." Maggie was making sure that Agatha's apartment key was safely zipped in her purse. "But in case of an emergency, it would be handy to have someone I could call. Especially since the building manager will be on vacation. Is Alfred . . ." she paused delicately, "I'm sorry, but I don't know his last name . . ."

"Master, my dear."

"Thank you. Would Mr. Master be available if I had to call someone?"

Agatha frowned. "It's hard to say. Occasionally even I have trouble getting in touch with him. I'd planned to have him accompany me on this trip for at least part of the time."

Maggie felt an instant's sympathy for Alfred. Even a weekend with Agatha, she felt, would be a shattering experience. She managed to smile reassuringly as she reached for the doorknob. "Well, I hope things work out and that the two of you have a fine holiday."

"Thank you, Margaret. I know I can depend on you to look after my things . . . dear little Banjo . . ."

"And the Capo di Monte . . ." Maggie gave Agatha's skeletal fingers a comforting squeeze. "I'll be very careful with them. Have a nice rest and call me if you remember anything else. The real estate man gave you my number at the hotel?"

"Yes . . . yes. Don't forget about the bedroom window, will you?"

Maggie was trying to peer down the hallway to make sure that obnoxious building manager was out of the way. "I'll remember," she promised absently. "Good-bye, Miss Jarvis. Thank you again."

"You're welcome. Oh . . . Margaret!" Agatha's hail caught her halfway through the entrance hall. "I've almost decided to not take Alfred with me. You might need him more than I do."

Maggie looked over her shoulder, hesitating. "Well, if you're sure . . ."

"I am. Call him if you have any trouble."

"I will, then—and thanks." Maggie gave her a friendly nod and then hurried on through the hallway to the front door. There wasn't a sign of the building manager, she noted thankfully, as she tugged it open. This time his apartment door had remained firmly closed. Once out on the sidewalk, she took a deep breath of relief. Tomorrow he'd be gone, Miss Jarvis would be gone, and she would be free to discover if she had any real artistic talent in the month ahead. Things were definitely looking up!

Maggie's lips curved in a delightful smile, and she reached out to happily pat one of the shade trees on her way to the car.

Her morning's good fortune prompted her to seek a tasty lunch down in Ghirardelli Square and spend the rest of the day with her sketchbook on colorful Fisherman's Wharf.

When she returned to her hotel, the absence of any messages in her box made her sigh with relief. The interview had been so unusual that she was afraid Agatha would have to change her plans for donating the apartment once Alfred had been apprised of her intentions.

Now she could relax, she told herself, and look forward to moving into 727 Spirit Lane tomorrow. Her lips quirked with amusement when she visualized her parents' reaction to the new address. Probably it would be better to call them tomorrow night after she was safely installed rather than telling about her introduction to Agatha in a letter.

By the next morning, San Francisco's unseasonably sunny weather was merely a fond memory. Raindrops were pelting against the hotel windows when Maggie opened her eyes and a radio news commentator gloomily confirmed her fears as she dressed. "Precipitation will continue all during the day and evening," he said. "Coastal storm warnings will change from small craft to gale proportions later this afternoon. Currently, there is a traffic tie-up on the Golden Gate Bridge in the northbound lane. Motorists are asked to exercise caution approaching the area. . . ."

Maggie twisted the radio dial, cutting his warning abruptly in the middle. It was a good thing she'd done her sketching the day before, she decided. Today, she'd finish the picture under cover.

It wasn't until she was driving to Spirit Lane later in the morning that she remembered she had forgotten to ask Agatha if the apartment had a view. The heavy velvet draperies had effectively screened the living room and bedroom windows so she couldn't even tell day from night. The first thing she'd do once she got in the apartment would be to draw those curtains wide open.

She pulled her car into the loading zone directly in front of the apartment, ignoring the "No Parking" instructions. It shouldn't take more than three or four trips to get her bags and art paraphernalia inside. After that, she'd look for a permanent place to leave the car. She frowned momentarily as she opened her door. Why in the world hadn't she asked Miss Jarvis if there was a garage connected with the building? She grimaced, then shrugged, and picked up her first load of belongings. If worst came to worst, she could always go upstairs and knock on the photographer's door. The obliging one that Miss Jarvis had mentioned.

Maggie managed to unlatch the big front door and then shove it farther open with her hip as she struggled into the hall. Really, she should have left the bag of groceries for another trip, she told herself.

As she went through the foyer, she noticed that the manager's apartment door was ajar and her spirits sank. Damn! The man hadn't left yet. Miss Jarvis must have gotten the date confused.

She edged stealthily through the lobby, careful to keep her heels from tapping on the waxed tiles. Once in front of Agatha's apartment, she quietly deposited her load on the floor and felt in her jacket pocket for the key. All she needed now was to find that her landlady was still on the premises!

The door lock opened smoothly under her touch and she was relieved to find the apartment hallway in Stygian darkness. Today though, the darkness was a welcoming sight; it meant Miss Jarvis had obviously left town. Maggie felt a thrill of possession as she hastily pulled her belongings over the threshold, turned on the foyer light, and happily closed the door behind her.

Then, still pleased with her "landed gentry" status— even if it was a temporary one—she picked up her bag of groceries and made her way to the kitchen. A strangely quiet kitchen, she realized belatedly, as she pushed through the door. Banjo must have postponed his concert to wait for an audience.

Obviously the bird had suffered a change of heart over several matters. Maggie thought she had never seen a more unhappy-looking canary than Banjo's listless form as he sat on his lowest perch and stared fixedly at his feet.

Maggie immediately felt a pang of remorse as his unhappiness registered. She put her groceries on the counter and moved, frowning, over to his cage. Did people talk to canaries? Dogs, yes . . . cats, certainly . . . even goldfish liked a friendly finger waggled at them occasionally —but birds . . . darned if she knew. She chewed on her lips as she stared at the other inhabitant of Apartment B. He, grudgingly it seemed, eventually stared back at her.

"Good morning," she said finally. It wasn't original for an opening gambit but it was the best she could do.

Banjo continued the staring session.

Maggie tried to recall any helpful dialogue from the Dr. Doolittle series of her youth. The Doolittle ménage, she remembered vaguely, had encompassed a London sparrow and an ancient parrot. The only thing they had in common with Banjo was feathers. Other than that, there was no similarity at all.

By now, the canary had stopped staring at her and was glumly surveying his toenails again. Maggie wondered if she should take him to an animal hospital. Or bird hospital? Or did owners take sick canaries out in the rain? Perhaps Agatha's instructions would say. Of course, the instructions! She'd been an idiot not to look for them in the first place.

Her glance swept the tidy tiled counter and lit on a grubby envelope with "Margaret" printed in wavering capitals across the front.

"Half a minute, Banjo," she told the canary over her shoulder. "Help is on the way . . . I hope." She ripped open the envelope and surveyed the brief cryptic message inside. "If you have any questions," it said, "ask Alfred for guidance. Otherwise, don't disturb him. Leave bedroom window open. Love and kisses for Banjo." There was a scrawled "A. J." under the writing.

"Damn!" Maggie slapped the paper back down on the counter. So much for her desire for a balanced bird diet. She could only hope that Alfred Master knew more about Banjo or canaries in general than she did. At least she could call him and ask. She moved to the end of the counter and thumbed through the telephone directory which was kept under the wall phone. Martin . . . Marvel . . . Mason . . . Master. Her finger traced carefully down the column; Master, George, or Master, Sybil. That was all there was once she had ignored Master Body Works and Master Fine Laundry. Not a Master, Alfred, anywhere. She closed the directory with a frustrated thud. Trust Agatha to have a friend who lived out of town.

Maggie gave another despairing glance at the silent Banjo and rubbed the back of her neck. She'd just have to look around the apartment and see if she could find an old address. "Take it easy," she instructed the canary. "I'll be back in a minute. You might try some birdseed in the meantime."

She made a whirlwind tour of the apartment, raising shades and pushing back drapes in the bedroom as she went. The half-open window was letting in quantities of fresh air as well as considerable rain on the carpet. Maggie lowered it hastily, leaving a discreet half-inch for the thinner friendly spirits. The double bed was stripped of linen but Agatha had left a pile of clean sheets and blankets on the mattress.

Maggie poked her head around the dressing room doorway and then withdrew it. People, even eccentric people, didn't keep address books in closets. She turned back to the living room and tugged at the heavy velvet drapes smothering the windows there. Next came the opaque glass curtains under them. She let out a gasp of pleased surprise when she finally glanced through the wide window itself. Below lay an artist's dream; a panorama of San Francisco Bay that was breathtaking even under sodden skies. To the far left, she could see part of the Golden Gate Bridge, although it was barely visible in the driving rain. To think that Agatha Jarvis had deliberately hidden a sight like that! She must be crazy, Maggie decided.

A pathetic peep from the kitchen reminded her of Banjo's plight and she turned to survey the faded furniture of the room behind her. Evidently Agatha didn't believe in owning a desk to handle her business affairs. Maggie moved hopefully to the cabinet where the older woman had stored her keys, but the drawer had been neatly emptied.

Maggie frowned again. She hadn't realized her landlady would be so tidy. The chance of finding Alfred Master's address seemed more remote than ever. Her glance played over the other side of the room, lighting finally on the fireplace. The antique porcelain urn still sat squarely in the center of the mantel.

"All I need to do now is to drop that darned thing. I wish Agatha had taken it with her," Maggie muttered, moving in front of it and surveying its graceful lines without pleasure.

Then, defiantly, she reached up to grasp it. Agatha or no Agatha, it was going in the hall closet where it could be safely stored for a month without fear of breakage. After that, she'd go on searching for Alfred's address.

Her hands tightened on the handles of the urn as she carefully clutched it against her breast. It wasn't until she reached the closet and she had lowered the urn so she could open the door that she noticed the hollow interior of the antique piece. The sight startled her so much that, for a minute, her fingers lost their strength and the urn almost slithered to the tiled foyer floor. Maggie was breathing hard as she staggered back into the living room and deposited the porcelain like a bottle of nitroglycerin on the first table she saw. Then she peered in the urn again while the sentences of Agatha's letter danced in her mind. "Ask Alfred for guidance, but otherwise, don't disturb him."

Maggie's hand went shakily up to her cheek. How in the hell was she supposed to know that when she disturbed the urn she was disturbing Alfred as well?

She stared down again at the antique vase which was full to the brim with ashes. Gray, innocent-looking ashes. Resting on top of the ashes was a black-edged card with Agatha's spidery handwriting on it. Unfortunately, this time Maggie had no trouble deciphering the words:

"Alfred. My dear, *dear* Alfred.
May he rest in eternal Peace."

Chapter
TWO

Maggie wasn't exactly sure what happened in the next minute or two. She *did* know that her heart was thudding against her ribs so hard that it sounded like a jungle tom-tom, and Agatha's elaborate furnishings closed around her like a suffocating canopy.

She had to get out of the apartment, she decided. Escape out in the fresh air until she could think logically again. Think logically about a landlady who left her beloved's ashes around to keep her tenant company.

Maggie shook her head, trying to clear it. Someone would help her . . . even that irritating manager would have to tell her where Agatha had gone.

Her lips were trembling as she darted back to the hall and pulled open Agatha's front door. Banjo was momentarily forgotten, her purse was left lying in full view as she scurried out to the building lobby. She was still breathing hard as she pounded on the manager's door which was now firmly closed.

When there was no response, she jabbed at the buzzer by the door knob. Her lips tightened in frustration. She should have known that the creature would disappear the minute he was needed. When a second tattoo of pounding proved ineffectual, she stomped back into the hallway and looked around uncertainly. He must be around somewhere!

He was, she discovered about ten seconds later.

He was standing outside the front door with his hands on his hips, staring angrily at her open car door. When she lunged precipitously through the doorway behind him, he glanced around, startled at first, and then obviously madder than hell.

"I might have known. You again!" His eyes swept over her disdainfully before he went down the steps to slam her car door. "It's a good thing you finally remembered to come back. I was about to call the police and report an abandoned and illegally parked vehicle."

"Don't be ridiculous," her scorched tone matched his. "It hasn't been there more than ten minutes."

"That's ten minutes too long in this loading zone," he pointed out. "Parking is expressly forbidden."

"Loading . . . unloading . . . what's the difference? That's what I'm doing." As she spoke, Maggie was wondering how a man with a temper like his ever managed to hold a manager's job. Obviously he must be good at other things to compensate for his inability to get along with people. It wasn't that he was unattractive. To give the man his due, she'd have to admit that he was quite a splendid hulk of masculinity. Well over six feet of muscle, she estimated with her artist's eye, and those muscles were nicely distributed. That was more than apparent even under his greasy white coverall. The prominent cheekbones in his lean face, that firm jaw line . . . even the way his thick dark hair was combed away from his forehead would have been fine for sculpting. What a pity his eyes were narrowed so unpleasantly and that his lips were pressed in a nasty straight line . . . her thoughts broke off as his words finally penetrated.

"What the devil do you mean . . . unloading?"

"It's not unusual," she replied with flushed cheeks. From his sardonic look, her appraisal hadn't gone unnoticed. Probably he was used to women making fools of themselves over a bulging bicep. She'd set him straight on that right away. "Right now, I happen to be unloading my car. Then I'll unload my belongings in Apartment B. Or at least, I will as soon as you tell me——"

"Agatha's place?" he interrupted, his dark eyebrows in an ominous line. "In a pig's eye!"

Maggie narrowed her own eyes. "Look, Mr. Malone or whatever your name is . . . if you'll get your mind out of the farmyard . . . I'll put it to you squarely. My car, my things"— she pointed to the objects in question as she slowly, nastily named them—"and, thanks to Miss Jarvis"—her forefinger pointed directly at the building behind them—"my apartment—for one month."

"Subletting is forbidden in the lease," he said just as grimly.

She shrugged. "Who's subletting? I'm a friend of Miss Jarvis and I'm taking care of her canary. Not one penny of money is changing hands." Her determined tone evidently got through to him because his stare was slowly thawing.

"It would have been more . . . considerate . . . of Agatha to let me know," he said.

Maggie was happy to aid the melting process. "I didn't know that she hadn't," she admitted. "Perhaps since you were going on vacation, she thought it wouldn't matter. I'm Margaret Rome." As she introduced herself, the reason for her headstrong flight from the apartment suddenly zinged back into her mind. "Actually I'm terribly glad I caught you before you left, Mr. Malone . . ."

"No." He was definitely amused now.

"You're not leaving?" Gratified surprise gave her features a lovely glow. "I'm so glad. Frankly, Mr. Malone, I was scared to death. If you wouldn't mind taking care of the ashes for me, I'd appreciate it. Just until Miss Jarvis gets back," she added hastily as his scowl returned.

"Take care of the ashes!" The words grated out. "My God, what a morning! Two hours with a pipe leaking behind the tile and now you want me to carry out the ashes."

"What's so terrible about that? Presumably you get paid for such things, Mr. Malone."

"No."

"Well, really . . ." Maggie's voice lost its usual contralto qualities and went up in pitch. "If you insist on being paid extra——"

"I'm not Malone," he interrupted her ruthlessly. "He left on his vacation two days ago."

"Oh, I see." Her eyes were hopeful. "You're not Mr. Parks?"

"Hardly. How do you know about him?" he asked with sudden suspicion.

"Miss Jarvis told me."

The suspicion changed to amusement. "She would. Well, you can try, Miss Rome, but at the minute Tony has other fish to fry."

"You're back to animals again and on the wrong track besides," Maggie informed him coolly. "Mr. Parks can rest easy. I plan to work this month."

"Once I take the ashes out."

"Well, yes . . . if you don't mind."

"Would it make any difference if I did?" He leaned over to reopen her car door. "I guess I can help you in with your stuff. Do you want all of this?"

"Just that box and the other case for now. It's very kind of you. Oh, look out! Don't tilt the box—I have a head and a hand in there."

He straightened so suddenly that his head smacked against the steel edge of the car roof. "Damn it to hell!" He rested the box on the back of the front seat and rubbed his head gingerly with his free hand while he stared over his shoulder at her. "What are you—a medical student on holiday or the newest thing in axe murderers?"

"I'm an artist," she told him meekly. "Sorry—I didn't mean to startle you."

"If you keep it up, I'll be a solid mass of bruises," he informed her grimly. "My foot hasn't recovered yet. You don't have any plumbing wrenches in this stuff, do you?"

"Nary a one." She pulled a small case from the trunk and followed him to the door. "I'm terribly sorry about yesterday."

"So am I. Get that latch, will you." He watched her push the door open and hold it with her shoulder. "I suppose Agatha furnished you with a key?"

"Yes, thanks." She trailed him down the hall. "Actually I'd be in pretty good shape if it weren't for Banjo and the ashes."

He gave her a puzzled frown. "Damned if I can figure why you're making such a big thing of a few fireplace ashes. And if you're worried about musical instruments . . . well, don't. We're a pretty placid group here and the atmosphere's quiet most of the time."

"You've got it all wrong," Maggie said as she watched him unload in the apartment's front hall. "Banjo is Agatha's . . . I mean, Miss Jarvis's . . . canary."

"It's all right," he straightened after depositing her box on the floor. "You don't have to be formal. Agatha does very well. Especially since you're such a good friend of hers," he added sardonically.

"I met her for the first time yesterday," Maggie admitted.

"That's a relief. The old lady's batty as they come."

She frowned in reproach. "I should think you'd get in trouble talking about the tenants that way. If the owner heard you . . ."

"He's even worse."

"That's what Agatha said," she confessed. "Utterly ruthless so far as people go."

"You're a fine one to talk about being high-handed.

[26]

Walking in—dropping wrenches on people and giving orders to remove the ashes. *After* you take over an apartment where subletting is specifically forbidden in the lease."

"Look, if I'm going to spend my forenoon arguing with you, Mr. . . ." She sounded impatient. "What *is* your name?"

"Elliott."

"I meant your last name . . ."

"Elliott is my last name," he said patiently. "I'm John Elliott."

"Oh." Maggie took an involuntary step backward. "I see."

"Now, what's all the fuss about the canary?" He was walking over to the thermostat as he spoke. "Maybe he's just objecting to the temperature. It's colder than Siberia in here. Don't you believe in heat?"

"Of course, I do." Since he'd mentioned it, Maggie became aware of the cold draft around her ankles. "Probably it's cold because Agatha left the bedroom window open so long."

"She would." There was bitterness in his voice as he strode through the living room toward the bedroom.

"You needn't bother," Maggie trailed in his wake. "I closed it most of the way."

"After you shampooed the rug?" He was staring disagreeably at the wet patch on the carpet where the rain had poured in.

"Surely it will dry." Maggie caught up with him. "After all, if Miss Jarvis chooses to ruin her things . . ."

"The carpeting was furnished by the owner," he said succinctly.

"Oh . . . that disagreeable man . . ."

"Name of Elliott."

"The same as yours," she said with an air of discovery. "What a coincidence!" Then her eyes widened.

His glance was laconic. "Exactly."

"Oh, lord!" Frantically she tried to remember what she'd said about Agatha's missing landlord.

"Don't go into a decline over it." He reached over to close the window completely.

"Don't do that!" she gasped, clutching at his arm. "I promised Miss Jarvis I'd keep it open for the friendly spirits." She felt his muscles tense under her grasp. "Stop looking at me like that . . . they're *her* friendly spirits . . . not mine."

"Well, that's a relief." Grudgingly he left the window as it was. "For a minute there, I thought you were a left-over from one of her séance sessions."

"I *told* you that I saw her for the first time yesterday." She stared at him as his words sank in. "You really mean it . . . about the séances, I mean?"

"That's what Holly and Tony tell me." He put a hand on her shoulder to urge her toward the living room. "Come on, let's go back where it's warmer. I hope Aggie's friendly spirits aren't prone to respiratory trouble."

"I forgot to ask," Maggie mumbled. "Who are Holly and Tony?"

"Holly's my sister . . . she lives in the apartment above this one. Tony Parks is the other tenant on the second floor."

"The photographer who would help with my budget," Maggie said, remembering Agatha's words.

John Elliott evidently could fill in the missing conversational gaps. "That sounds like Agatha's idea," he said shrewdly. "Better check with Holly first. She and Tony have an 'off again, on again' relationship and I'd hate to see you carried out of here in pieces."

"Don't worry . . . I don't have any ideas along that line. Holly can relax." Maggie looked at him curiously. "Do you live upstairs with her?"

"My lord, no," he grinned. "In that case, I'd be carried

out in pieces within a week. I have Apartment A . . . practically across the hall."

"Oh, I see," she said faintly.

John had moved over to peer in the fireplace. "Why all the flutter about ashes? There aren't enough here to bother about."

"It's Alfred," Maggie took a deep breath and started to explain. "He isn't in the fireplace . . ."

"Alfred?" John straightened on the hearth and wiped his hands on his coveralls. "Alfred who?"

"Alfred Master. An old friend of Agatha's." Maggie's voice dropped as a horrible suspicion suddenly floated through her mind.

"A friendly spirit, eh?" John was inspecting a glass candlestick at the other end of the mantel.

"Exactly." Maggie's expression was ominous. "That's why you're looking in the wrong place for him. Afred isn't in the fireplace . . . he's in that urn on the table."

The glass candlestick suddenly shattered on the hearth.

"I should have taken it away from you before I explained," Maggie told him sadly.

John's dazed glance moved up from the glass shards at his feet to her resigned face. "I liked it better when you just dropped the plumbing wrench on my foot. Are you sure you're not a fugitive from the nearest nut factory?"

She shook her head. "Take a look at that urn on the table if you don't believe me." Then, hastily, "For heaven's sake, don't pick it up. I can't afford any more breakage."

John peered in at the top of the urn. "My God!"

She nodded resignedly. "I'm afraid so."

"This isn't some kind of a joke . . ."

"Don't be ridiculous," she added forcefully. "You'll just have to do something with those ashes. I don't mind sharing this place with some wandering bands of gypsy spirits, but I can't take Alfred, too."

"Now you're getting hysterical!"

"Wouldn't you? I'm not surprised Banjo won't sing . . . he's probably in a state of shock, as well."

John winced. "I'd forgotten about that damned canary."

"Well, I haven't," Maggie said, "and we have to do something about him. If he keeps on this way, he isn't long for this world. Oh, lord, what have I said?"

"Take it easy." John came over and pushed a clean handkerchief into her hands. "Mop up the tears—then we'll go into the kitchen and have a cup of coffee. We could both use one."

"All right," Maggie agreed between sniffs. "I have a pound of coffee in my load of groceries. But promise me you'll store Alfred someplace. I'm sorry if that seems silly but he's more than I bargained for."

"Cross my heart and hope to . . ." John stopped, exasperated. "Damn! I didn't mean to say that." He turned back to the living room. "This is getting out of hand. I'll find a resting place for Alfred while you're making the coffee. Okay?"

"Wonderful! I'm sorry to be such a nuisance. No wonder you can't stand sublets."

"In this case, the new tenant's a definite improvement over the old one, despite your tendency to throw plumbing tools around." Before she could reply, he'd jerked his thumb purposefully in the direction of the kitchen. "Coffee, madam. I'll leave the door ajar so I won't have to ring when I come back."

"You *will* be careful with . . ."

"Alfred? You bet! But just wait until Agatha gets back . . . I intend to have words with the old girl."

"Then you'll have to stand in line. I have a few things

to say to her myself. How did you get her as a tenant in the first place?"

"It's a long story. I'll tell you over that cup of coffee."

"Okay." She looked at her watch. "Ten minutes?"

"Make it nine."

Maggie heard his footsteps disappear into the hall. She went on into the kitchen and started to search for Agatha's coffee pot, when a tentative chirp reminded her to go over and check Banjo's cage. The pale yellow canary had shed some of his lethargy and sidled up to his seed container.

"That's the boy," Maggie told him encouragingly. "Have some breakfast and you'll feel better."

One black beady eye stared up at her.

"I mean it," she assured him. "Later on, I'll go to the grocery and buy some lettuce for you."

"You needn't bother going out," a feminine voice said behind her. "I have a new head in my refrigerator."

Maggie whirled to see a striking green-eyed brunette dressed in tartan slacks and a white pullover standing in her kitchen doorway.

"Sorry," she told Maggie with an amused expression, "I didn't mean to startle you. Actually I did knock but when you didn't answer, I came on in."

Maggie pushed her hair back from her face. "I was holding a monologue with my friend, Banjo, here . . ." She gestured toward the canary.

"That's what I gathered. If you need lettuce for him, I'm your girl."

"You're very kind," Maggie said, surveying her more intently. Something about her visitor's assured manner was vaguely familiar. As the brunette moved over to inspect Banjo's cage, she smiled with recognition. "You must be Mr. Elliott's sister."

"That's right . . . I'm Holly Elliott," the other said absently. "Where is John, by the way? He's the reason I barged in here . . . except that I thought I was barging in on Agatha and I knew she wouldn't mind." Her smile warmed. "You look too normal to be a relative of hers."

"I'm not." The denial came hastily. "I'm Maggie Rome. Miss Jarvis asked me to take care of her apartment and baby-sit for Banjo while she's away."

"I *thought* she was planning to leave," Holly said in a tone of satisfaction. "She must have slipped out in the middle of the night."

"Oh, surely not. Look . . . sit down, won't you." Maggie pulled out a dinette chair from the table by the window. "I'm supposed to be making coffee. Will you stay for some?"

"Thanks, I'd love to. I can hunt for John later on."

"That won't be necessary," Maggie said in a slightly embarrassed tone. "He's coming back here in a minute."

It was Holly's turn to look amazed. "When did you meet my brother?"

"We sort of . . . ran into . . . each other yesterday," Maggie said vaguely. "He's been helping me move in."

"John volunteered for that?" Holly subjected Maggie's features and figure to a more thorough going-over. At the end of it, a mischievous smile transformed her expression. "I'll be darned. Agatha must be part witch, after all."

Maggie spilled some of the coffee she was spooning into the percolator. "Don't *say* that! Things are bad enough already." She brushed the scattered grounds into the sink with the side of her hand and glanced apologetically at Holly. "Sorry . . . I'm a little unstrung. The moving . . . you know."

"You don't have to find excuses." John's sister had turned and was looking out the kitchen window at the rain-soaked landscape. "You're brave to even stay in this apartment. Do you know, it's the first time I've ever seen the curtains pulled back in these rooms. I swear, that Agatha lives like a mole when she's here."

"I noticed that. It's strange she didn't find it depressing." Maggie settled the lid on the coffee pot and plugged it in.

"Not Agatha." Holly turned on her chair and stretched long legs out in front of her. "She didn't let earthly things bother her. Her mind was on a different plane."

"You sound as if you know her pretty well."

Holly shook her head, amused. "Not really. Agatha wasn't interested in living people. Just the dead ones."

"Oh, for God's sake!" John exploded from the doorway. "Don't *you* start."

"What's eating you?" Holly stared at him with sisterly amazement before turning to Maggie. "He's been an absolute bear ever since he dropped a wrench on his foot yesterday."

"There's nothing wrong with my foot," John protested, avoiding Maggie's glance.

"That's not what you said an hour ago," Holly told him severely. "You told me . . ."

". . . to forget it." He moved over and yanked out a chair beside her. "Miss Rome isn't interested in our aches and pains."

"*I* feel fine," his sister said austerely. "Besides, she isn't Miss Rome—her name is Maggie. Aren't you better acquainted than that?"

"Holly . . . for pete's sake . . . just be quiet for a change." John's gaze focused on Banjo's cage. "I thought you said that canary wasn't eating," he accused Maggie.

"He wasn't," she insisted, moving over beside him to peek into Banjo's cage. "I'll be darned! He's certainly tearing into that birdseed now."

"Well, he looks normal to me," Holly announced, "but I'll bring down the lettuce in a few minutes."

"Wonderful!" Maggie beamed. "I don't know what happened to him. One minute he was drooping on his perch and the next minute he was rejuvenated. It was right after you left," she told John. Then she frowned at the thought.

John noted her disturbed look. "Don't search for trouble. Probably the bird just suddenly felt like eating breakfast."

"But you did take the . . . package . . . away?" she probed.

He nodded, "It's stored in my apartment. And from now on, it's my responsibility."

"What *are* you two talking about?" Holly asked vexedly.

"Agatha left some of her valuables behind," her brother told her. "Miss Rome . . ."

"Maggie, please," the other insisted.

"Maggie," he agreed with a slight smile as he leaned back in his chair, "didn't want to be responsible for them."

"So I asked your brother . . . er . . . Mr. Elliott . . . if he'd store them for me," Maggie said to Holly.

The brunette was patently amused. "His name's John."

Maggie peered hesitantly at her landlord. "Well, if you don't mind . . ."

"I can hardly sit here drinking your coffee and have it any other way," he assured her solemnly. "Remember though, this informality stops as soon as you have any leaking pipes or heating problems."

Holly grinned, "At the first sign of trouble, he sneaks out the back door. Malone is the only handy one around here. Frankly I can't see what keeps those mines from collapsing if John has anything to do with building them."

"I don't build them."

Holly ignored his resigned protest and went on with her explanation to Maggie. "My brother is a mining engineer and spends most of his time wandering around the globe charging an exorbitant consultant's fee for dabbling in the dirt."

"Which shows how much my sister knows about mineral engineering," John said. "Isn't that coffee ready by now?"

Maggie blinked dazedly. "I guess it is."

"Good." He stood up and helped himself to cups and saucers from Agatha's cupboard. "Holly can't talk as much when she's eating."

"That's what you think," his sister threatened. "Right now, I want to know how Maggie found out about this apartment."

"There's nothing strange about that." Maggie told her. "I wanted to sublet an apartment for a month and checked with a real estate firm I found in the telephone directory. This was the best one they had." She unplugged the coffee pot and started to fill the cups on the table. "Miss Jarvis had been pretty definite about her requirements for a tenant. It had to be a single woman from out of town, with satisfactory references."

"A very paragon of virtue," John murmured, enjoying her flush of embarrassment as he took the cup she handed him. "Did they mention the free rent?"

"Certainly not," she told him stoutly. "As a matter of fact, the rent they quoted was staggering . . . more than I'd budgeted for. It was Miss Jarvis who insisted on waiving it. I couldn't believe her, at first."

"She must have wanted you here pretty badly."

"Why not?" Holly added sugar to her coffee and stirred it. "Anybody could see that Maggie would take good care of the place. She isn't the type to throw things around."

John's gaze strayed pointedly to his foot, and despite her resolve, Maggie blushed fiercely again. He watched her changing expression blandly for a few seconds before saying, "Agatha knew that I'd toss her out in a minute on a real sublet. I've just been trying to find a valid excuse of any kind."

"If you dislike Miss Jarvis so much, why did you let her rent an apartment in the first place?" Maggie asked.

Holly cut in, "He didn't have any choice. Agatha was already firmly ensconced when John bought the building. At first, she seemed a perfectly harmless old lady . . . a little eccentric, maybe," she smiled, "but that's not unusual for retired actresses."

"Sit down and drink your coffee before it gets cold," John reminded Maggie, pulling out another chair for her. "The saga of Agatha Jarvis goes on and on."

Maggie obediently carried her coffee over to the table and sat down. "What happened next?"

Holly continued. "Well, it wasn't bad enough that Agatha had a pet monkey who tore up the furniture . . ."

"That damned Yorick," John confirmed bitterly.

"Yorick!" Maggie exclaimed.

Holly nodded, "Shakespeare's own. Agatha liked *Hamlet* although she always complained that there wasn't a decent woman's part in the whole play."

"Of course. Yorick . . . the gravedigger," Maggie murmured aloud.

John sighed. "You needn't have any traumas about that miserable monkey. Yorick was very much alive when Agatha gave him to an Italian tenor friend of hers who lived in Berkeley."

"Why Berkeley?" Maggie asked.

John shrugged. "Because the veterinarian suggested a more favorable climate."

She was still confused. "You've lost me along the way. Why send a monkey across the Bay?"

"Because, poor Yorick, alas, had contracted bronchitis from Agatha's open windows. Obviously he needed a warmer atmosphere."

"And you know tenors," Holly added. "They *never* open a window—even if they live in Death Valley. Drafts come ahead of the bubonic plague on their disaster list."

Maggie stared suspiciously at them. "I think you're both putting me on. Nobody could be as eccentric as that."

"That's what you think." John's tone was laconic. "After Yorick was deported, Agatha really got down to business. She started communing with the spirit world in earnest, but all her social life took place after midnight when she held her séances. This place was like a tomb in the mornings—" he caught himself as he saw Maggie's stricken expression. "I mean," he went on carefully, "that the old lady received all her callers at night."

"And when John objected to the comings and goings, Agatha would become a doddering frail piece and explain that she held her 'gatherings'—not séances, mind you—just when the spirits were willing."

"Evidently her spirits only worked on the night shift," John concluded grimly. "Every time I got enough nerve to give her notice, I was sent away from home on another job."

"Actually, he was putty in Agatha's feeble but determined hands," Holly informed Maggie.

"Cut it out, or I'll toss *you* out on your ear," John instructed his sister. "You're worse than Agatha."

"You can't get rid of me," Holly announced in the tone of one on familiar ground. "I have a lease."

"Malone was a fool to sign it. If I hadn't been away, you'd never have gotten in here in the first place. I thought you were safely settled in Manhattan."

"Too bad," she said blithely and stood up with a graceful movement. "Thanks for the coffee, Maggie. Would you like to have lunch with me a little later? You'll be tired of unpacking by then."

"It sounds tempting." Maggie looked undecided. "Really, I should start working . . ."

"Take a sketchbook with you and salve your conscience that way," John suggested.

"Are you an artist?" Holly asked. Her glance swept

over Maggie's blue polka-dot silk and well-polished blue pumps. "Amazing! Much too neat."

"Artists look pretty much like other people." Maggie's tone was dry. "But wait until you catch me in jeans with clay up to my elbows. Then I live up to my reputation."

Holly grinned and said, "Let's go down to Ghirardelli Square or the Cannery for lunch. If you want to sketch, I'll see what's new in the boutiques."

"I can't resist that program," Maggie admitted. "Just give me an hour or so."

"Are you coming along, John?" Holly asked. "It wouldn't hurt you to be sociable for a change."

"Can't," he drawled. "Behave yourself and I might manage to ask you both out to dinner one of these days."

Holly put a finger to her chin and bobbed a mock curtsy. "La, master," she lisped, "you're so good to us." Then, turning to Maggie, she said in her normal tones, "I'll collect you in a little while. Will it be okay if I deliver Banjo's lettuce then? He seems healthy enough now."

Maggie nodded. "Later will be fine. He's like another bird entirely. I don't understand."

"I told you to stop fussing," John said with a measuring look. "Don't let Holly wear you out—her shopping excursions would exhaust a marathon runner." He got up and put his empty cup and saucer on the counter. Then he gave both women a casual nod. "See you later, I expect," and went out without a backward glance.

Maggie stared after him. On encountering Holly's amused gaze, she turned back to the stove in obvious confusion. "Will you have more coffee?" she asked, mentioning the first thing that came in her mind.

"No, thanks. I've had plenty and I must go." With disarming candor, Holly added, "Don't let my brother bother you. There's no percentage in it. After thirty-three years, I have yet to find one woman that has even dented that tough hide of his."

Maggie's eyebrows went up. "Is that a warning?"

"Heavens, no! That's the coach's pep talk before the kickoff." Holly's laughter bubbled. "Would you like a diagram of past plays?"

Maggie grinned despite herself. "What nonsense you talk."

"Well, we'll huddle on it over lunch," Holly insisted, moving into the hall.

"Honestly, there's no need to pursue it."

"I wouldn't be too sure of that. After all, you're the first woman to have a whole platoon of Agatha's friendly spirits on your team, so it might be quite a contest." Holly grimaced mockingly as she pulled open the door. "Frankly, I can hardly wait until the whistle blows."

Chapter
THREE

"I'm glad you didn't suggest driving," Maggie told Holly later when they had swung aboard the Hyde Street cable car on their way to lunch. The tiny wooden car was scooting down a hill so steep that it looked like part of a roller coaster. "What happens if the brakes don't work on these things?" She was clutching an upright support to keep from sliding down to the end of the bench.

"You pray. Don't worry . . . the law of averages is on your side. Just enjoy the scenery and we'll be down at the bottom in a minute."

Maggie peered down their route and shuddered visibly. "Anything less than five minutes would be sheer disaster. Oh, all right . . . I'll stop fussing," she said, catching a glimpse of Holly's amused expression, "but that sidewalk's so steep that I'd have to crawl down it on all fours."

"That's why you'll see steps cut in the cement on the next block. They're all over town in the steep places." Holly raised her head to sniff the air enthusiastically. "Beautiful day, isn't it? I'm glad you came, Maggie. I needed to get out of the apartment."

Maggie gave her a thoughtful glance. In her pale blue cashmere sweater and skirt with matching topcoat, Holly was the picture of casual sophistication; she didn't look as if she'd experienced a minute's urgency in her life. Maggie smoothed down her own red poplin raincoat ruefully. Beside Holly's "cover girl" appearance, she felt oddly unsure of herself. Good looks certainly ran in the Elliott family, she decided. Even in those rumpled coveralls, John Elliott had appeared disturbingly masculine and assured.

"Are you admiring the scenery or in a state of shock?" Holly asked. "You look as if you're miles away."

Maggie blinked, surprised at the other's astuteness. "Not any farther than Coit Tower," she said, mentioning the first landmark that came to mind. "I must spend a morning sketching it and Telegraph Hill." She turned back to face Holly again. "It's not very original, but there are so many gorgeous places for an artist . . . Washington Square with the church of St. Peter and St. Paul in the background . . . Nob Hill with Grace Cathedral . . ."

"Don't forget the Golden Gate. You can see the entire bridge today since the rain's stopped, so be sure to enjoy it. Think of the thousands of visitors who've only seen a patch of red paint in the fog." Holly clutched her purse more tightly as she stood up. "Here we are . . . end of the line. I told you we'd make it."

"I wasn't really worried." Maggie pulled the strap of her bag over her shoulder and swung down to the street. "Where's the Cannery that I've heard about?"

"Just ahead of us. That big brick building."

Maggie looked around happily. "What a wonderful location. Look at those sailboats on the Bay."

"There must be a regatta scheduled this afternoon."

"And such throngs of people!" Maggie moved carefully around a long-haired pair of flutists who were giving an impromptu concert on the edge of the sidewalk. A little farther along, a teen-aged guitarist was entertaining passersby in front of a sidewalk art exhibit. "This is like a fair. Is it a special occasion?"

"Happens every day of the week," Holly said, leading the way up some steps into the Square itself. "That's why it's such fun to live in San Francisco. Maybe I was silly to give up all my modeling bookings in Manhattan . . ." For a moment her lovely face sobered. "I'd worked hard to get to the top of the career heap."

"Have you stopped working entirely?"

"Oh, no," Holly paused by a fountain of reclining bronze mermaids and stared absently at their graceful figures. "I go back East when there's an especially good assignment."

"It must be nice to pick and choose." Maggie hardly knew what else to say. As they strolled on past a clump of eucalyptus trees, she added, "Besides, being happy living here is more important than earning lots of money."

Holly grimaced as she pulled open the restaurant door for Maggie. "Who said I was happy?"

"Aren't you?" Maggie waved an expressive hand at the interior of the restaurant which was decorated in French style with poster kiosks between the tables and gleaming brasses on the wall. "I thought that was the point of all this."

"I'll explain after we've ordered." Holly nodded at the hostess and nudged Maggie in her wake. "Looks as if we rate one of the umbrella tables. Typically San Francisco," she added. "It isn't warm enough to eat outside so people just bring the patio tables inside. You have to use your imagination," she added bitterly as they sat down in a pair of canvas-covered captain's chairs, "but an artist should be good at that."

Maggie's head turned in bewilderment. "I don't understand. It looks charming in here."

"Don't pay any attention to my grousing," Holly advised, passing her a menu. "They serve a grilled combination sandwich here that's awfully good. There's ham, turkey, and cheese in it." She saw Maggie's eyes widen at the printed price list. "This is my treat," she added casually.

The other shook her head definitely. "Nope. We'll go

Dutch. I'm beginning to get used to the prices in this city. At first, they're a terrible shock to a staid Midwestern mind."

Holly nodded with understanding. "That's why San Franciscans make such a big thing of the scenery—it's the only thing that's free."

After the gaily costumed waitress had taken their order and brought them coffee, Maggie unfolded her napkin in her lap and asked, "Now . . . what's all this about being unhappy? You're absolutely beautiful . . . healthy . . . plenty of money . . ." she paused until Holly gave a slight nod. "That only leaves one thing . . ."

"You sound like a doctor. The next question should be 'How's your love life?'" Holly was shrugging off her topcoat.

"That's right," Maggie smiled slightly. "Even Midwest doctors ask that one." She waited a minute and then probed gently. "Well, how is it?"

"Awful," Holly was staring determinedly through the view window to the left. "That's a corner of Fort Mason over there."

"Fascinating. What's wrong with it?"

"Not a thing. The main buildings are kept in good repair . . ."

"I mean your love life, duckie," Maggie reminded her. "It isn't fair to just drop hints."

"Sorry." Holly pulled her chair closer to the table and added sugar to her coffee. "His name is Tony. Anthony Parks."

"I know who you mean. He's the photographer in the apartment that Miss Jarvis was telling me about. She said he was obliging and . . ." Maggie's voice trailed off as Agatha's exact comment went through her mind.

"I can imagine what she said," Holly finished for her grimly. "And she's right. He's a marvelous photographer, and he's perfectly charming to everyone in sight. Every

[43]

model in Manhattan fought for his assignments. That's how I met him." She stirred her coffee absently.

"How does he happen to be living at your brother's apartment house?"

Holly shrugged. "That was my doing as well. I raved so much about San Francisco that Tony came out for a holiday."

"And?"

"He fell in love with the place. That apartment was vacant just then and he insisted on signing a long lease."

"Did your brother know about it?"

Holly shook her head. "John was away on his job. He retains a real estate firm to handle things like leases and maintenance in his absence." She leaned back in her chair so that the waitress could serve them with sandwiches and a heaping platter of fresh fruit. After the girl had gone, she pulled a grape from the arrangement and nibbled on it. "It wouldn't have mattered anyway. John likes Tony. *Everybody* likes Tony," she repeated, selecting another grape.

Maggie eyed her thick sandwich and then picked it up gingerly. She took a careful bite and swallowed before meeting Holly's inquiring glance. "It's delicious," she confirmed. "Better try yours. You can eat grapes any time." She watched Holly pick up her own sandwich before adding gently, "I suppose Tony found another girl?"

Holly's delicate eyebrows came together in a frown. "I don't know. Nobody noticed him with anyone special. He simply told me that he couldn't see me for a while. No other explanation. Nothing. The next thing I knew, he'd left town and returned to New York."

"Business, probably." Maggie speared a piece of fresh pineapple with some difficulty.

"Nope. I heard that he resigned his Manhattan partnership the very next week. Then I had a modeling job down in Jamaica and Barbados—you know, high-fashion

[44]

stuff—and when I finally got back to San Francisco, Tony had moved into his apartment here with all his belongings. He wouldn't explain where he'd been in the meantime."

"Maybe he just wanted time to think things over. How has he treated you since?"

"From a distance of about five feet." Holly sounded bitter. "He exhibited more warmth to Agatha than he did to me. Oh, he's pleasant enough, but it's the 'Go away, girl, and don't bother me' variety. I've never been treated that way in my life before."

Maggie surveyed her across the table and could well believe it. Even in a roomful of attractive women, Holly had commanded considerable masculine attention as they had walked in.

"It certainly sounds strange," she admitted finally. "Can't your brother help?"

"I don't want to ask him," Holly confessed, taking a sip of coffee. "John's had to play the stern disciplinarian ever since our parents died. Lately, I've made a point of taking care of myself. Just because John's eight years older than I am, doesn't mean he's omnipotent."

"You don't have to convince me." Maggie smiled. "Have you convinced him?"

"Not that you'd notice. Most of the time he still treats me as if I'm twelve years old."

"You can't have it both ways."

"Oh, I know." Holly managed a sheepish smile. "I'm sorry. What an introduction to San Francisco for you. You'll think that we're all crazy."

"My landlady is still at the top of that list," Maggie said with a spurt of laughter. "Frankly I'm delighted she left town. Now that Banjo is happily consuming your head lettuce, I think he'll be fine. When I get a chance to meet your Tony . . ."

"He's not my Tony any longer!"

"*Your* Tony," Maggie told her firmly, "maybe he'll tell

me something of his plans. I could ask his professional advice for a starter."

Holly's lips quirked. "So long as that's all you ask. You're too darned attractive for a neighbor. I felt much safer with Agatha."

Maggie pushed the fruit platter toward her. "Haven't you forgotten? I'm scheduled to be your brother's diversion."

"I wish I had more hopes in that direction. John's a worse case than Tony." Holly took a section of pear and started peeling it. "I don't know how many women he's wined and dined . . . plus heaven knows what else. Sisters are the *last* to find out," she informed Maggie gloomily. "Then just when the poor souls think they're making headway . . . poof!" She snapped her fingers. "He's off to Peru or Chile or someplace beyond suing distance."

"And when he comes back home, he starts all over again."

"Exactly." Holly dabbed at her lips with a napkin. "It's only fair to warn you, because when he isn't acting like a big brother, he's absolutely lethal with women. They go down like goldfish before a piranha."

There was a minute or two of silence while Maggie stared at her coffee cup as if the dregs fascinated her. Then she put her napkin back on the table and said resolutely, "Can you spare me an hour to make a sketch from the patio out there? I'd like to get part of the iron stairway with the fountain in the foreground."

Holly pursed her lips knowingly. "Of course . . . take your time. I have a couple of gifts I'd like to buy and then I want to see the manager of the boutique on the level above us. She expected to have some new evening skirts arrive this week. Why don't I meet you up there? She's an old pal of mine, so it won't matter if you're late."

Maggie reached for her sketch pad and purse. "Sounds marvelous. I'll settle with you later for lunch."

"I'll hold you to it." Holly was beckoning the waitress. "Scoot on now. See you later."

For Maggie, the next hour passed in a haze of contentment. Once she'd finished her rough sketch, she penciled in notes for color, visualizing her surroundings in terms of cobalt, raw sienna, and burnt umber. If she were lucky, she would be able to duplicate the scene in a watercolor later on.

She sighed happily and leaned back against the railing. At last she was able to spend her leisure doing the kind of creative work she'd yearned for. Now she'd have to wait and see if the results approached professional standards. She crossed her fingers for luck and closed her sketchbook before looking at her watch. Only five minutes late. Holly wouldn't complain about that.

She stood up and moved purposefully toward the iron staircase leading up to the upper level.

The boutique Holly had mentioned faced the gunmetal waters of San Francisco Bay and Alcatraz, the rugged prison "rock" that now waited in abandoned isolation for the city fathers to find a new use for it. Maggie paused for a minute to stare out at its craggy outlines before entering the dress shop.

Holly was sitting on a loveseat at the back of the boutique talking to a vivacious redhead. "Come on in and sit down, Maggie." She patted the cushion beside her. "This is Fran, who owns the place. Hang onto your purse though, or she'll talk you out of your last sou."

The redhead smiled good-naturedly and leaned against a kneehole desk. "Don't pay any attention to her, Maggie. A woman has to make a living somehow. Would you like a cup of coffee?"

"No, thank you . . . I'm still full from lunch." Maggie's trained sense of color responded automatically to the elegant shop displays around her. "You have some beautiful things. I like the way you combine your textures." Her compliment was spontaneous and sincere.

"Best place in town," Holly confirmed promptly. "I found just the thing for you while I was waiting."

Maggie started to shake her head. "I can't afford any clothes right now."

"Just wait until you see this dress. Fran, go get it and convince her."

The shopkeeper surveyed Maggie's trim figure speculatively. "I think Holly's right. You'd better take a look at it," she said, moving to a curtained recess and pulling out a dress of soft coral chiffon that made Maggie's eyes widen with pleasure.

"Gorgeous, isn't it?" Holly leaned forward. "And it's beautifully made, with scads of hand-finishing."

As if in a dream, Maggie fingered the material of the gently flared skirt. Her admiring gaze went over the sheer bodice with its high neckline outlined in delicate pearl and coral beading. The beading was repeated on the cuffs of the long chiffon sleeves as well. A strapless coral taffeta slip which lined the gown and a row of tiny buttons at the back of the bodice were the only other decoration. Maggie sighed, completely captivated by the understated elegance of the outfit.

"Coral should be a wonderful color for your hair and skin," Holly was saying. "At least try it on, Maggie."

"*That* doesn't cost a cent," Fran said, as she urged Maggie toward a dressing room. "Let me give you a hand, although it should fit perfectly."

It did. When Maggie came out of the fitting room and twirled before them, all three women knew that they had achieved a minor miracle.

"Simply gorgeous," Holly pronounced with authority. "Don't you dare wear it near Tony. That's an order."

Maggie's face was radiant as she looked in a long

mirror. "It's a good thing I don't have to worry about a rent check or I'd be scrounging Banjo's birdseed for the rest of the month." She turned to Fran. "I'll take it, thanks. It's the prettiest thing I've ever owned."

"You look lovely." The other's appraisal was professional. "If you ever want to get in the modeling trade, I could give you some introductions."

"No, thanks. I'm quite happy drawing catalogue illustrations most of the time," Maggie said firmly. She turned back to the dressing room. "I'd better change before I weaken any more. Otherwise I'll be out on the sidewalk having to sell some of my sketches."

Later that night, she took the dress out of Agatha's closet and admired its graceful lines once again. Pretty clothes *did* improve a woman's morale, she decided. Her purchase had buoyed her spirits long after she and Holly had returned to the apartment, even inspiring her to change into her jeans and start converting Agatha's dressing room into a studio. Her sculpture pieces were transferred to a sturdy table whose top had been carefully protected with a piece of canvas. Painting equipment was set up beneath the high windows, and after stopping for a quick cup of tea, she had started working on the watercolor she had sketched earlier. Banjo watched her comings and goings through the kitchen with interest but he remained stubbornly silent.

Maggie worked on until the daylight failed. Then she leaned back and stretched luxuriously as she surveyed her afternoon's project. Not bad. Not as good as she'd like, but really not bad.

She stood up and went in the kitchen to wash her palette and brushes, tired now that her hours of concentration were over. Achingly tired, she decided, flexing the muscles of her right forearm. And hungry, too. She looked on the cupboard shelves and then in the refrigerator. It was too late to make any elaborate mealtime preparations. She'd have to be satisfied with an omelette and green salad for dinner.

In the middle of whisking the eggs, she paused long enough to go into the living room and bring back her transistor radio. After finding a program of semiclassical music, she looked over at Banjo, who was honing his beak on a piece of cuttlebone. "This wouldn't be necessary if you'd furnish some melody," she told him. "I hope you're not one of those birds who's only turned on by rock operas or it's going to be pretty dull for both of us. I should have asked Miss Jarvis."

A half hour later, she was wishing that Agatha was still around to ask. Or any living soul . . . other than a silent canary. She wouldn't have believed that an apartment could be so quiet. Or so lonely.

It would have been nice if she had known Holly well enough to call up and say, "Come on down and keep me company for a while. I'm starting to talk to myself."

Maggie moved restlessly over to the window and stared down at the lights of the city below her. When she stayed alone in these rooms, all she could think of was Alfred and his miserable urn. So far, she'd managed to avoid spending any time in the bedroom with that open window. For tonight anyway, she'd make a bed on the davenport in the living room.

Her thoughts moved on inexorably. It was too bad that Holly's Tony hadn't stopped by. Or even John Elliott. After all, a landlord had an obligation to his tenants. He could have checked . . . checked what? The electricity, the plumbing, his tenant's pulse rate? Her lips curved in a reluctant smile. How ridiculous could she get! John Elliott wasn't the type of man who would invent a feeble excuse just to see a woman. According to Holly, he had names in his address book to cover every day in the week. Names of beautiful women who weren't jittery about ashes in urns and spirits coming through the windows.

Maggie ran an impatient hand through her hair and turned toward the hall closet. She'd get her jacket and walk to the all-night grocery. The fresh air would do her good and she *did* need cream for her cereal in the morning. If nothing else, the exercise would help her to get to sleep.

When she returned a half-hour later, she was glad for her attempt at self-discipline. The brisk, tangy air had dispelled most of her gloom, and the nighttime charm of San Francisco with its lighted hills and bridges would have improved the disposition of Scrooge himself. She remembered Will Rogers's famous quote as she'd walked along—"Cities are like gentlemen . . . they are born, not made. Size has nothing to do with it. I bet San Francisco was a city from the very first time it had a dozen settlers."

Maggie found herself agreeing with the humorist. San Francisco's zany warmth was infectious—there was no doubt about it.

She unlocked Agatha's front door while clutching her pint of cream with the other hand. After nudging the door closed behind her, she was still fumbling for the light switch when she suddenly realized that she wasn't alone in the apartment.

Her body stiffened with terror at the implication. Then, driven by desperation, she scrabbled for the switch like a drowning victim clutching for the only life raft in sight. It seemed an eternity before her tense fingers discovered the brass wall plate and she managed to snap on the overhead light. At the same time, a muffled sound erupted from the closet beside her.

Instantly her nightmare imaginings exploded into reality; her head was jerked back and she found herself clawing at a gloved hand which fastened like a band of steel around her throat. Another hand pinioned her against the door with a force that made her gasp in pain.

Frantically she tried to fight back but her resistance was hopeless against the other's superior strength. Her startled, painful whimper was sliced off ruthlessly when his fingers tightened their grip. Only her labored breathing rasped in the silence as she writhed in that suffocating grasp.

The agony was prolonged for an instant that seemed like a lifetime and her lungs were at the bursting point before darkness mercifully shuttered her senses.

She was totally unconscious by the time her attacker released his grip and callously dumped her limp body on the floor.

Chapter
FOUR

The next hands Maggie felt were considerably more gentle.

They moved quickly over her body while a concerned masculine voice said, "Miss Rome . . . Maggie . . . are you all right? Can you talk?"

She stirred weakly. When she attempted to speak, only a painful croak emerged. Her eyelids flickered apologetically, but it was too difficult to focus on the figure kneeling beside her.

"I'm going to move you to the couch," he was saying. "Then I'll call the doctor."

Even in her semiconscious state, she grasped his arm in an inarticulate protest.

"What's the matter? For God's sake, don't cry." She felt a handkerchief gently blot her cheeks and managed to open her eyes again. This time she recognized the outlines of John Elliott's concerned face.

"Don't . . ." the whisper came out laboriously.

"Don't what?" He caught her hand and brought it up to cup his cheek. "Tell me what happened, Maggie."

"Don't leave me. Please, don't leave me," she begged.

His frown deepened. Then he pulled her hand around and touched his lips to it lightly. "I'll be so close that you're tripping over me," he promised as he put his arm under her shoulders and lifted her. "Just relax—I won't let anyone hurt you."

Maggie found her nose resting against a broad shoulder and let her tired body relax in his arms. Her eyes fluttered open again when he deposited her gently on the living room couch. She watched him go across the room to the phone, and then the sound of dialing made her struggle to sit upright.

"You don't have to call a doctor." This time her whisper was urgent. "I'll be all right in the morning."

"Damned right you will." John kept the receiver to his ear. "I told you to relax. Never argue with your landlord."

Maggie's head dropped back against the arm of the couch as he switched attention to his call. Evidently the doctor was in and—wonder of wonders—the variety that still made house calls.

"He'll be over in ten minutes," John said after hanging up. "His instructions were to keep you quiet and warm. Just hold the fort and I'll get a blanket." He was back from the bedroom and tucking an eiderdown around her before Maggie realized he'd left the room. "Now," he perched on the edge of the cushion beside her, "if you feel up to it—can you tell me what happened?"

She nodded, huddling in the comforter for warmth. "There was a man . . . I must have surprised him when I came back from the store . . ." Slowly, painfully, she went on to explain what happened.

John listened without interruption, his face taut with concentration. As her voice finally trailed off, he squeezed her shoulder reassuringly. "Right. That's enough to report to the police." The door buzzer sounded abruptly and he got to his feet to answer it. "Don't look like that," he told Maggie. "It'll just be Dr. Lane. Right on time, too."

She heard him open the door and the subdued murmur of their voices in the hall. Then John came back into the room followed by a gray-haired man carrying a medical bag.

"Maggie, this is Dr. Lane. Let me know when you're finished, Jim. I'll be using the phone in the kitchen." John gave Maggie an encouraging grin and left them abruptly.

Dr. Lane moved over to the couch. "Now then, Miss Rome—I hear you've had a bad time. We're usually more considerate with our visitors."

Maggie relaxed visibly under his easy bedside manner. By the time he'd completed a brief but thorough physical examination, she was even reconciled to his prescription. "Two of these pills now." He disappeared into the kitchen and came back with a glass of water. "Tomorrow, I want you to stay in bed. At least resting and taking life easy." He noted her sudden frown and went on quietly, "You've had quite a shock, you know. The human body is a wonderful piece of machinery, but it needs time for its overhauls. Give yours a chance, Miss Rome."

Maggie swallowed his pills and handed the glass of water back to him. "I'm sure you're right, Doctor. It's just that I have so little time in San Francisco that I hate to waste any days."

"You're an artist, aren't you? John said something about it." His bushy eyebrows drew together thoughtfully. "No reason why you can't carry on with your work— provided you don't go gallivanting around the neighborhood." He watched her shift into a more comfortable position on the couch and leaned over to close his bag. "If you feel like it, of course. Why not wait and see how it goes tomorrow."

"I will. Thank you for coming, Doctor." Maggie had trouble getting the words out in proper order, and she rubbed her forehead irritably. "Those pills of yours must be awfully strong."

"At least they'll make you feel much better by morning. Good night, Miss Rome."

"But I want to pay . . ." Maggie's sense of order fought the waves of lethargy but she was being beaten on all fronts.

"That's all taken care of. Just ask John if you need anything. He's completely dependable." The doctor's reassuring words were the last thing Maggie remembered as she snuggled into the corner of the couch and closed her eyes in a drugged sleep.

The mournful sound of foghorns awakened her the next morning. She rubbed her eyes and glanced in bewilderment at the closed living room drapes. Then she turned abruptly to check the clock on the table beside her, wincing as her shoulder and back muscles protested. Eight thirty. It must be morning. A persistent buzzing nearby made her frown. If she didn't know better she could swear someone was using an electric shaver. She rubbed her forehead fretfully. Dr. Lane's pills were undoubtedly effective but she felt as if her brain were packed with goosedown. As she lowered her arm, her gaze zeroed in on the sleeve covering it. A blue cotton sleeve with the cuff carefully rolled up over her wrist.

Her thought processes shifted from low to high in two seconds flat as she shoved the covers back and sat bolt upright. Why in the dickens was she wearing a man's pajama coat? And whose pajama coat was it? She peered down at the pocket to see if there were a monogram.

"For God's sake, lie down. You'll dislocate your neck doing that." John spoke from the doorway where he was zipping an electric shaver back into its case. "The pajamas belong to me. I didn't want to plow through your stuff and you couldn't very well sleep in your clothes," he added blandly.

"Who . . ." Maggie colored as she stared down at the buttoned pajama coat and became aware that she was wearing only one part of the set. "Who . . . er . . . put me into it?"

He broke into her stammerings as he moved across to the kitchen doorway. "The doctor and I took care of things. There wasn't anybody else around. Holly was called down the peninsula to spend the night with an aunt of ours in Palo Alto. She'll be back today. Incidentally, you look a lot better this morning."

"I'm fine, thanks." Maggie's mind was working furiously backwards. The last she remembered, Dr. Lane was on his way out the door with his bag in his hand. Had he stayed around long enough to make sure his patient was properly attired for bed?

John observed the play of emotion over her delicate features. When her eyes suddenly narrowed with suspicion, he cut in hastily. "Don't worry about the disrobing process. All the proprieties were duly observed."

"Mmmm." She pulled the sheet back up to her chin.

"And it was damned difficult that way, too." He surveyed her morosely. "By the way, I put your jewelry in the drawer of the end table there. I hope the watch is still working—it was on the floor just inside the closet."

Maggie refused to be diverted. Instead she pointed to the shaver in his hand. "What are you doing here so early?" Then she shot an incredulous look toward the bedroom. "Don't tell me you spent the night in there?"

"Well, don't make it sound like a wife-swapping session," John said bitterly. "I had a hell of a time. That mattress of Agatha's is stuffed with corn husks and cabbage roots. When you add an open window blowing fog across the room and waking up to find that damned eye peering down from the ceiling—I'd done better stretched out in the bathtub."

Maggie was torn between maintaining her maidenly indignation or offering sympathy. The latter promptly won when she stared at his weary countenance. "I'm sorry. Really it was awfully nice of you to watch over me."

John merely yawned and then nodded. "Probably the police will round up that fellow in no time so you don't have to worry about him. If you want to brush your teeth or anything, I'll have breakfast ready in about ten minutes."

"Good heavens . . . you cook, too."

"Only when I can't get out of it. Can you manage to get vertical by yourself?"

"I'd better. Something tells me this pajama top doesn't cover much territory," she said with a severe look.

"Nuts! You're in a maxi by North Beach standards." His grin widened at her expression. "You've heard about San Francisco's famous ladies?"

"Who hasn't? The topless nightclubs take up a whole chapter in the guidebooks."

"Very little left to the imagination . . . so they tell me." He turned toward the kitchen. "Boiled eggs all right?"

"Fine, thanks." Maggie was pulling the eiderdown around her sarong-fashion as she got to her feet. A moment's dizziness made her pause. Then she took a deep breath and walked slowly into the bedroom to get dressed. Later, when she got around to unbuttoning the pajama top she was still wondering exactly what proprieties John had observed when he'd put it on. Certainly he hadn't wanted to discuss the subject at any length. Her lips tightened as she thought about it and then curved into an unwilling smile. She'd better forget about it too—if she knew what was good for her.

Her expression was properly serene when she finally appeared in the kitchen wearing gray slacks and a printed turtleneck top in gray and white. She had pulled her hair back from her face with a tortoise-shell barrette and had used lipstick sparingly.

"Anything I can do to help?" she asked calmly.

John turned from the stove and let his gaze wander over her. "You look about twelve years old with your hair like that," he commented idly.

"Is that all you can say?"

"That's all I can manage before breakfast." Privately he was deciding that the night's ordeal had given her clear skin a translucent look. The faint shadows under her eyes provided a frame for her thick lashes and, in the morning light, her mouth looked tremulous—her lips softly curved and inviting. Quite a different picture from the self-assured woman who had confronted him two days ago.

Maggie couldn't manage to stand quietly under his searching masculine appraisal. She moved deliberately over to the window. "It's strange how the fog hangs over the Golden Gate Bridge at the same time the sun is shining on the hills next to it."

The forced civility of her words made John grin. "*Isn't* it," he replied silkily. "Would you believe it happens about half the time? Some people claim that there isn't a suspension bridge there at all—it's just a fog bank with metal supports at either end."

She smiled reluctantly in response. "There was definitely a bridge there yesterday."

"Then I'll have to find another tourist to impress." He pulled out a chair for her. "Come on, sit down. Everything's ready and I'm starving."

"Ummm. So am I." She unfolded her napkin in her lap and observed, "Banjo looks as if he's enjoying his breakfast."

"Uh-huh. Apparently he's happy as long as the birdseed holds out. Put some bread in the toaster while you're drinking your juice, will you?" John was transferring boiled eggs into two cereal bowls as he spoke.

"All right." She filled the toaster and pushed the handle

down absently. "If he's happy, I wonder why he doesn't sing?"

"Who knows? I'll give him one of these eggshells when we're finished. Maybe the extra calcium will help." John sat down beside her and reached for his glass of orange juice. "I'm glad you felt well enough to get up for breakfast, but you'd better crawl back to the couch afterwards. You still look as if one good gust of wind would topple you."

Maggie took out the toast as it popped up and started to butter it. "Just wait until these calories take hold," she promised noncommitally. "I've been enough trouble to you without playing invalid all day."

"It's had its moments," he told her. "Pass the salt, will you?"

She delivered the salt with more force than was strictly necessary. "Well, I still don't intend to lounge around all day making you wait on me, Mr. Elliott."

He put down his spoon and leaned on one elbow as he surveyed her patiently. "My dear Miss Rome, in this town when a lady borrows a man's pajamas and shares an apartment overnight"—he waved a restraining hand as she would have interrupted—"she automatically gets the right to use his first name. Let's not have any more of that 'Mr. Elliott' guff."

Maggie started to answer but broke off to nibble on a piece of toast instead. There was no point in being silly. The man had a point—no matter how distastefully he'd phrased it.

The silence grew into an uneasy truce as they both concentrated on breakfast for the next few minutes. It was only after John had poured his second cup of coffee and pushed the pitcher of cream her way that she gathered her nerve to ask, "Why do you suppose that man chose to ransack *this* apartment? Did the police have any ideas when you reported it?"

"Just the usual statistics, I'm afraid." John used his napkin and then reached for his cigarettes. "Will this smoke bother you?"

She shook her head once and then shook it again as he offered her the package. "No, thanks . . . I don't usually." Pushing an ashtray over to him, she added, "Do you think he was searching for the usual valuables?"

"I guess so. The police did ask if you could furnish any positive identification. When you feel up to it, you'll have to file a formal report with them. I'll drive you down."

"More of a landlord's duties?" she asked wryly. He ignored that, so she went on, "You know, you still haven't told me how you happened to come to my rescue. Was it your arrival that frightened him off?"

"Could have been."

When he didn't elaborate, she went on doggedly. "Did you hear something strange or what?"

John looked mildly irritated. "Not really. I must have been coming to check the plumbing or the electricity or something. *Now* what's the matter? Did you choke on the coffee?" He leaned over to whack her on the back.

"I must have. How careless of me." She kept her eyes discreetly lowered so he wouldn't see the sudden gleam of laughter in them. His reluctant admittance did more to improve her morale than even Dr. Lane's prescription, but his stern profile made her decide not to pursue the subject of diligent landlords. She chose a safer ground, saying, "You'll be glad to see Agatha back if this keeps up."

His lips tightened. "You must be sicker than I thought. That old biddy is pure poison."

"All the same, I'd give a lot to see her walk through the door. The first thing I'd do would be hand Alfred's urn over to her . . ."

"And the second?"

"I'd give her back the key to this apartment. After last

night, I'll be scared to death to be here alone." Her eyebrows drew together warningly. "And don't make any noble offers about sleeping in the bathtub."

"I wasn't going to. There's a simple solution. You can go up and stay with Holly."

"But I can't leave this apartment untended. I *did* promise Miss Jarvis."

"Then Holly can come down and stay with you," John announced calmly. "She'll probably be crazy about that eyeball poster over the bed."

Maggie shuddered and took a sip of coffee. "The whole thing seems like a nightmare this morning. I can't even remember what happened . . . the struggle couldn't have lasted more than a minute or two—but it felt like forever." Unconsciously her fingers went up to the bruises on her throat.

John saw the gesture and frowned. "Can you identify the man? Honest-to-God police identification?"

"I'm afraid not." Her voice dropped to an apologetic murmur. "I saw his hand first. Then he whirled me around so my back was to him. I remember trying to get away—clawing at him—I must have scratched his face, at least." She looked down at her hands but her mind was obviously reliving the struggle in the hallway. "Then I couldn't get any breath at all and finally I couldn't see." She glanced toward the window. "It was just like that fog over the bridge. Dense, closing out all the light, suffocating . . ." Her knuckles were white on the handle of her coffee cup.

"Well, he's gone now." John made his tone carefully matter-of-fact. "Probably he'd heard about Agatha's possessions from one of her cronies. God knows, she's had enough visitors in here and most of them looked pretty seedy."

Maggie was frowning, "But this man didn't take any-

[62]

thing. Didn't you say he'd even left my watch on the floor?"

A bleak look passed over John's face. "That's right. It must have come off in the struggle. You were lucky that it wasn't damaged." He waited for her to respond and when she didn't, he leaned across the table and ground out his cigarette in the glass tray. "Your sudden appearance probably scared the hell out of him and after you'd lost consciousness, he obviously couldn't hang around the premises."

"Then he'll be back." There was quiet resignation in her tone.

"Why do you say that, for pete's sake?"

"Because I think he was looking for Alfred. I told you that urn's priceless."

"My God! Next you'll claim that the man came in through the window as a friendly spirit!"

She sat up straighter in her chair. "You don't have to take that attitude . . ."

"And you don't have to look down that delicate nose of yours," he warned her as he got up to shift his dishes to the counter. "The trouble with you this morning is that you have too much imagination and you're getting a re-action from Doc Lane's sedative. Incidentally, he'll be in to see you a little later."

"That isn't necessary."

"Oh, but it is." John was stacking dishes neatly. "Rule one of the landlord's protective association. You might decide to sue me later on. Injuries suffered on the premises . . . that sort of thing."

"Very funny." She watched him tucking part of an egg-shell in one of Banjo's feeding dishes. "Seriously, I wish I knew where to find Miss Jarvis. I can't renege on our arrangement without at least talking with her. If I could give her that darned urn, I'd at least sleep more soundly."

"You'd need more than a clear conscience to survive

on that damned bed of hers. I think she bought it on a month-end clearance after the Spanish Inquisition."

"Don't worry—I don't plan to leave the davenport in the living room. *That's* bad enough," she said, rubbing the back of her neck reflectively.

He walked over to rinse his hands at the sink and dried them on a paper towel. "Agatha didn't give you any idea of where she was spending her holiday?"

"Not really. She mentioned liking the beach . . . how restful the surf was and things like that. Nothing really definite."

John tossed the towel in the garbage and then leaned back against the counter. "There's a lot of shoreline in California alone."

She acknowledged that wearily. "I know. I just hoped she might have left an address with you or your manager when she vacationed before."

"To my knowledge, this is the first time she's been away overnight." His grin was without humor. "Probably thought I'd lock her out if I had a chance."

"Poor Agatha—with the hounds breathing on her neck."

"Some hound! Change that to a chihuahua and you'll be closer on target. Why do you think I took such long trips away from home?"

"Holly mentioned a couple of reasons." Her reply came out without thinking.

John's mouth settled into stern lines again. "Holly talks too much," he said bleakly. "Getting back to Agatha—*if* you don't mind—I can check with that real estate firm you contacted in hopes they might have an address."

"And there's always the post office." She followed his change of subject, wishing she hadn't alluded to Holly's discussion of his private life. It was hard enough keeping in the man's good graces as it was; he'd been irritable most of the time she'd known him. Probably wishing he'd never gotten involved with his temporary tenant. Certainly wishing he'd managed a decent night's sleep, she decided, as he tried to stifle a yawn.

"Post offices don't give out forwarding addresses," he told her finally. "They'll simply forward your mail."

"I could write to Agatha."

"Five'll get you ten we find out she hasn't even left a forwarding address. Her mailbox on the front steps has letters in it right now." He shook his head. "I'm afraid you might as well give up. Alfred can stay locked in my storage closet—" The peal of the doorbell punctuated his words, making Maggie jump a good six inches.

"Sorry," she murmured, seeing his worried gaze on her. "I guess I'm still jittery."

"Don't be—it's probably just the doctor." His strong hand clamped down on the fine bones of her shoulder and propelled her ahead of him to the living room. "I should have kept you in bed, after all."

But when he came back from the front hall a few seconds later followed by his sister and a strange young man, Maggie was relieved to be fully dressed rather than simply wearing an oversized pajama top.

Holly dropped down beside her on the davenport. "I hear you've been having an awful time." She broke off to wave a hand in introductions. "Maggie Rome . . . Tony Parks. He was practically on your doorstep so I brought him in to meet you."

"How do you do," Maggie managed to respond faintly even as she stared at the ragged scratch on the cheek of Holly's photographer when he shook hands with her.

"John told us what a rotten night you'd had," Tony said, bending over her.

John suddenly chuckled from his post at the end of the couch. "You can change your expression, Maggie. Tony's scratched cheek is completely honorable. He got it a couple of days ago in Malone's apartment when he was trying to help me fix the plumbing."

Maggie flushed at being caught in her suspicions. Other than the scratch, there was certainly nothing sinister in Tony Park's appearance. Just the opposite in fact. He was a studious-looking young man in his early thirties with very dark hair combed sleekly back from a narrow forehead. Dark-rimmed glasses framed a pair of intelligent eyes and there was a nice humorous quirk to his wide mouth. He wasn't particularly tall but his shoulders looked sturdy under a gray herringbone sports coat. Conservative gray flannel trousers completed his outfit.

Maggie smiled faintly. At first she would have expected the glamorous Holly to select a more outgoing type, but a second look at Tony's likable face made her realize that he was a very pleasant parcel of masculinity cloaked in a deliberately plain wrapper.

Her thoughts must have been obvious to the man in front of her, for he grinned engagingly. "Sorry, Maggie —the only woman I've been tempted to throttle lately is Holly. I never do it until I'm properly introduced."

Maggie's expression was suitably sheepish. "I'm an awful fool this morning, Tony. Please sit down, won't you." She looked uneasily across at John. "Did you ask Holly to come home early just for me?"

That young lady cut in. "It didn't take much persuasion, so don't fuss. I had no idea that Tony was in town, too." She glanced accusingly at her brother. "You didn't say he'd been helping you."

"Probably because I asked him not to." Tony pulled up one of Agatha's gilt chairs and settled in it gingerly. "I've been too busy for social life."

"You needn't have worried," Holly shot him a rebellious glance. "I wouldn't have wasted any of your precious time."

John interrupted decisively. "If there's anything Maggie doesn't need, it's a family fight right now."

"Sorry," Holly murmured, "I forgot about last night."

Maggie broke in with great tact, "Forget it. Actually you two came just in time. John"—why on earth did she have to stumble over his name each time she said it—"John and I were wondering how to locate Miss Jarvis. I want to settle some things with her if I'm going to stay in this apartment and she didn't leave a forwarding address."

Tony leaned forward, his sharp glance noting her tenseness. "Have you thought of checking the healing sanctuaries?"

Three pairs of eyes swung his way and three voices spoke simultaneously.

"You're not serious?" Maggie said.

"I don't think that's funny," Holly told him.

"What the devil's a healing sanctuary?" John wanted to know.

Tony put up his hands in surrender. "Hey . . . give me a chance. It was just a thought, and I still think it's a good one."

"Then clue me in," John persisted. "I know I'm out of things these days but I didn't think I was *that* far beyond the pale."

"You're not," Tony assured him. "You just weren't around dear Agatha as much as we were. Her conversation was full of terms like the psychometric theory of haunting and apparitions. Healing sanctuaries were nothing unusual."

"Tony's right," Holly confirmed. "Agatha made you feel that this apartment was bulging with visitors from the other world. She had visions all the time."

John groaned. "My God, I would inherit somebody like her." He shook his head. "Where do healing sanctuaries come into it?"

"They're places where Agatha's chums get together—sort of a convention thing for spiritualists." Tony glanced around. "Do you have today's paper? We could check the classified ads—they usually list them."

"Sorry, I haven't gotten around to subscribing to a paper yet," Maggie said.

"Never mind—there should be one up in my place." Tony got to his feet. "Why don't we continue this conference over lunch?"

"I just finished breakfast but that sounds very nice," she began hesitantly, only to have John interrupt before she could finish the sentence.

"Better wait and see what Dr. Lane says," he instructed brusquely.

Tony was reassuring. "I'm betting he proclaims the 'all clear.' Give me a call when you know—I'll be upstairs." He turned to Holly. "How about you, beautiful? Want to spend an afternoon lotus-eating?"

"I can't. I'm modeling at a charity tea on Nob Hill this afternoon. Let me take a rain check"—her voice sharpened—"*if* you're going to be around town so I can collect."

If Holly hoped to disconcert Tony by her refusal, it wasn't apparent in his reactions. He merely rubbed his jaw and shrugged. "We'll play it as it comes."

Maggie watched the byplay with a frown, and even John was listening from his perch at the end of the couch.

Tony paused by him on his way to the hall. "Can you think of any reason why I should ask *you* to lunch today?"

A reluctant smile flickered over the other's stern features. "Not a single one. Besides I have a business appointment that'll keep me occupied until the middle of the afternoon." He got to his feet. "If Doc Lane lets Miss

Rome out of quarantine, don't urge her to climb Coit Tower. She's frailer than she looks."

Maggie sat up straighter and gave him a withering glance. "I'm still here, you know, and I *don't* need a permission slip to leave the building."

"Atta girl, Maggie," Tony encouraged. "I'll go check the paper now and we'll try to leave at twelve thirty. Does that give you long enough to get ready after you've seen the doctor?"

"I think so." Maggie glanced toward her wrist to check the time and grimaced with disgust. "Darn! I forgot to put my watch on."

"I was wondering when you'd get around to it," John said sarcastically as he strode over to the end table and pulled out the drawer. "You'd better take care of this stuff. It's too valuable to leave lying around." He leaned across the davenport to give it to her.

"Well, it's a nice watch, but it's not *that* valuable," Maggie protested as she held out her hand. She started to fumble with the bracelet catch on the dainty round timepiece, but, as she did so, a ring slipped through her fingers and into her lap.

"Look out, you'll drop it!" John protested, making a dive for it. "My lord, you're certainly casual with that ring. I hope your fiancé insured it."

Maggie stared up at him, completely bewildered. "Am I going crazy—*what* ring?"

John turned her palm upright and dropped a magnificent marquise diamond ring into it. "*This* ring. Not many women would overlook a rock like that—it must be over two carats. Evidently it came off in the struggle, along with your watch. That thief must be kicking himself over half of northern California by now for leaving it behind."

Maggie was still staring at the ring with Holly and Tony peering over her shoulder. Finally she managed to tear her glance away to meet John's angry one. "You think this belongs to me?" she began. "From some obliging fiancé?"

He nodded stiffly. "That's what I thought."

"Well, you know what I think?" Her voice rose as she reached out and slapped the ring into his hand like a surgery nurse delivering a scalpel. "I think you're as crazy as your balmy tenants."

"Take it easy, Maggie," Tony soothed. "You can't blame John."

"The dickens I can't," she said, struggling to her feet. "In my part of the country, people who have diamonds like that aren't baby-sitting canaries and cadging free rent from little old ladies." She directed a scornful look at her landlord. "And if they have fiancés, they're wearing their rings—not playing charades with the first man who comes on the scene."

"We get the picture," he broke in, "so go back and sit down."

"Stop ordering me around."

His voice took on authority. "Sit down, Maggie, or I'll give you a relapse myself." He waited for her to subside with a flounce in a rickety chair and then walked over to hold the ring in front of her nose. "Now—without dramatics—you've never seen this before?"

Her eyes flashed fire but she merely shook her head.

"And you, Holly?"

"It's new to me." His sister reached out to tap the ring gently with a slim finger. "And that's the kind of jewelry a woman remembers. I wonder if it could have belonged to Agatha? What do you think, Tony?"

The latter took the ring from John's grasp to study it more carefully. "If it's Agatha's, the séance business is better than I thought. The bill for this beauty would run well into five figures. Properly cut marquise diamonds are scarce *and* expensive."

"But Miss Jarvis was wearing costume stuff when I saw her," Maggie protested. "There were layers of it—but nothing that looked valuable."

"That's what I remember, too," Holly confirmed. "Agatha went in strictly for quantity—not quality. As if she bought it by the pound."

"So where are we?" Tony dropped the ring back into John's hand. "Maybe you'd better put it back where you found it."

"On the floor in the hall." John snorted with derision. "Hardly." He turned back to Maggie. "I take it that the watch does belong to you?"

"Yes, of course." She flushed under the gentle sarcasm, wishing she hadn't lost her temper earlier. It had been the injustice of hearing his suspicions—thinking she was the kind of woman to be engaged to one man while casually spending the night and breakfasting with another. Although it was obvious from his diffident manner that he hadn't particularly cared. Perhaps he'd been relieved that his new tenant wouldn't provide any lasting complications.

"I don't know why you keep growling at Maggie," Holly told him mildly. "She didn't find the ring—*you* did. It looks as if you'll just have to tuck it away until you find Agatha. Then you can ask if it belongs to her."

"What if it doesn't?" Maggie countered. "What if it belongs to the man who came last night and he wants it back?"

"Then you post a sign on your door that says 'Lost and Found Department in Apartment A,'" John said dryly, putting the ring in his pocket.

"There you go again," Holly said helplessly. "Don't worry, Maggie—John's just teasing you. We'll work it out somehow."

Maggie still surveyed her landlord uneasily until he shoved his hands in his pockets and said, "I wish you'd cut it out. Anybody'd think you were the next reluctant candidate for a Black Mass. I promise you, you won't be left alone until we have this mess straightened out." He turned briskly to Tony. "Start looking through the paper for those ads for healing sanctuaries and if there are any likely looking candidates, I'll drive down to search for Agatha tomorrow."

"I can drive down myself," Maggie said sturdily, not wanting to accept any more favors.

"I want to go, too," Holly insisted. "You can't leave me at home after all this."

Tony stopped at the door and grinned over his shoulder at them. "Maggie and I will do extensive research on the project at lunch and give you our decision later. Right, Miss Rome?"

She managed to smile. "Absolutely." Her defiant gaze confronted John. "A healing sanctuary sounds great after everything that's happened. If I find any of them advertised in Alaska or the Yukon, I think I'll write for reservations."

"Hop to it," he told her austerely.

Her spirits hit bottom at that cold comment. He was so anxious to get rid of her he wouldn't even rise to her bait.

"John!" Holly was shocked at his callousness. "You're being terribly rude."

"Not at all." There was a glint of humor under his denial. "My next inspection job is scheduled out of Anchorage in a couple of weeks. A healing sanctuary sounds great to me, too." His masculine gaze raked Maggie's slim figure deliberately. "Reserve a nice friendly spirit, too, Miss Rome, and we'll leave our windows open."

Chapter
FIVE

"Exactly what does a lotus-eater look like?" Maggie found herself asking Tony later that afternoon. "I'm beginning to think I'm qualified for the job."

He looked amused as he half-turned to face her from his perch on the low concrete retaining wall at the top of Telegraph Hill. "According to Homeric legend," he quoted, "they were people who ate of the lotus tree . . ."

She picked it up, "And having done so, never desired to return to their homes again. All they wanted was to live in idleness in Lotus-land." Her finger traced an abstract design on the concrete as she murmured, "The original happy faces. That's the way I've felt ever since I got to San Francisco. I eat the fabulous food, gape at the scenery, ride the cable cars, daydream in the sunshine . . . like now." She tilted back her face to enjoy the warmth. "When I think of the projects I planned— and so far I've accomplished practically nothing." She shook her head ruefully. "And you're no help at all. Tempting me with that French pastry after a huge lunch."

"Orders are orders. Dr. Lane told you to have a quiet day, and John said you needed fattening up."

"I'm surprised he didn't put a clean handkerchief in my purse and pin a pair of mittens on my cuffs," Maggie flared. "Why does he insist on treating me as if I were three years old?"

"Dr. Lane?"

She bestowed a withering glance. "Don't *you* start."

"Okay, I'll stop teasing." Tony patted her hand comfortingly and stood up, slinging the strap for his Nikkon around his neck. "Enjoy the sunshine for a few minutes. I want to see what I can find for background shots. There's a fashion layout scheduled here next week."

"Take your time. I'm getting good at this lotus-eating by now."

"That's my girl. If you want to sniff the blossoms"—he gestured toward the flowerbed in front of her—"go right ahead. The natives are used to it." With a casual wave, he disappeared on the path which curved around behind the imposing bulk of Coit Tower.

Maggie watched him go. Then her gaze wandered bemusedly to the tall monument; San Francisco's legacy from an unusual lady who liked fire departments so much that she left a fortune for construction of a fire hose lookout tower in white stone. Forty years later, her memorial was an integral part of the San Francisco skyline . . . a colorful wedding cake decoration for the top of Telegraph Hill.

Maggie turned on her perch to face the water again, noting that the gray cast of the Bay was bluer than usual under the clear spring sky. All the early morning drizzle and fog had disappeared by noon and the city was flaunting itself in rare sunshine like an eccentric lady whose temperamental vagaries are overlooked because of her sheer personal charm.

Down to the right, new apartment buildings were lining the Embarcadero, but their bulk was tiny compared to the skyscrapers towering over them. Their styles of architecture ran the gamut—from needle-nosed office buildings to rectangular boxes which would have had Frank Lloyd Wright shaking his head in horror. The skyline was changing, but in this case as well, the city's rugged past helped it assimilate the controversial additions and thrive on them.

Maggie opened her sketch pad and then closed it again. For the moment it was enough to sit, to savor, and to enjoy.

Tony was back before she could get restless. "Sit still a minute," he instructed when she would have moved. "I like your pose." His fingers were busy adjusting the focus as he directed the view finder toward her.

She remained motionless as he asked, but after he'd snapped the shutter she said, "You have the wrong girl for pictures. Holly's the one you need." When she saw a bleak look come over his face, she added impulsively, "I'm sorry. You've already figured that out, haven't you?"

He sat down beside her, zipping his camera case closed and removing the strap from his neck. "I didn't know I was so transparent. It must be that artist's eye of yours, or do you tell fortunes on the side?"

She shook her head. "Hardly. It doesn't take extra-sensory perception. Why on earth did you ask *me* out to lunch? You're entertaining the wrong woman."

"That's where you're wrong." Tony was a picture of dejection as he rested his elbows on his knees and stared straight ahead of him. "Can you imagine how a man feels when he falls in love with a successful career woman who has so much money that she'd never have to work if she didn't want to?" He turned his head slightly to peer through his glasses at Maggie. "I'll tell you how it feels —it scares him to death. He wonders if he can make enough money to support her, he wonders if she'd be bored as a housewife, and he wonders if she'd ever stop modeling long enough to ruin her waistline and have a baby. Most of all, he wonders if someday she'd wake up realizing she could have done a lot better in the marriage stakes. It's like a lousy cart horse coming up against Seabiscuit in his first race."

Maggie took a deep breath and then prodded his arm gently.

"Tony—listen to me . . . you've let things get out of focus, which is downright stupid for a photographer. Don't shake your head." Her voice became impatient. "Oh, you men are all alike; you only see things from your own point of view. You talk about competing with champions. Well, if you'd think things over, you'd realize that Seabiscuit had his moments, too."

"In what way?" He kept his voice casual but Maggie thought she heard a hopeful note underneath.

She spread her hands. "Just think—if you're at the top of the heap, it must be wonderful to know somebody still likes you when you have a cold in the nose or you've suddenly gained three pounds over the weekend." Her eyes took on a dreamy expression. "I've always thought those European men who liked plump women sounded positively divine."

Tony burst out laughing. "Maggie—you're a fraud! Holly can eat spaghetti by the bucket and never gain an ounce."

"But it would be wonderful if she knew you'd love her just as much if she did. I'll bet she'd adore a nice husband who'd be so busy caring for her that he'd forget all about her bank balance. Besides—" she tried to look stern—"from what my married friends say, you should be finding out more important things now. Anyone can live with bearer bonds but imagine discovering that you've married a fresh-air fiend when you like the thermostat at seventy all the time."

Tony chuckled, "Maggie, I love you. If you weren't already spoken for, I'd put in a claim."

"Now that's plain silly. You're going to marry Holly." There was an instant's pause. "Aren't you?" she probed.

His expression sobered although his eyes still gleamed with laughter. "Yes, I think I am." He stood up on the sidewalk and pulled her to her feet beside him. "At least, after your pep talk, I'll give it a try."

"You're serious?"

This time his glance was solemn. "Word of honor, Maggie. But you'll have to promise to stick around and console me if Holly pushes me off her doorstep. Now, come on—I promised I'd phone John about this time. There's a coffee shop at the bottom of the hill—they'll have a telephone in there."

She waited until they were both back in the car before asking, "What did you mean about my being spoken for? You didn't take John's remark about a fiancé seriously, did you?"

"When he was seething over that diamond ring?" Tony looked amused at the memory. "No, that wasn't what I meant. I'm glad we came up here fairly early. This good weather will bring out all the sightseers later in the day."

Maggie didn't follow his red herring. "Why are you calling John at all?" she persisted. "He gave us a complete brush-off with his talk about a business appointment."

"Now you sound like Holly when she has her dander up. The poor guy just meant that he had to report in at his office for a while." Tony was carefully threading through parked cars and tourist groups at the base of the tower before turning down the narrow, winding road leading to the bottom of Telegraph Hill. "Incidentally, he wasn't completely satisfied when I said I couldn't find anything in the classified listings that might have pertained to Agatha."

"But there wasn't anything in the whole column except mediums offering appointments and promising 'absent healing,' was there?"

"Not that I could see."

"Did you bring the paper with you?"

"I think so." He took his attention from the road for a minute. "It must be around here someplace."

"Never mind, I'll find it." She was burrowing on the floor beside the seat. "It probably slipped under here . . . yes, here it is."

Tony made a grimace of satisfaction as he turned and drove past Washington Square with its quota of elderly gentlemen sitting on sunny benches. "Our coffee shop is over there at the corner," he said pulling into a convenient parking place. "Are you ready for a 'cuppa'?"

"You know I am." She reached for the door handle, shaking her head. "Why am I so weak? If I keep on eating this way, I'll be positively obese by the time my vacation's over."

He came around and closed the car door behind her. "Never mind, honey. You have pounds to go before you have to worry."

"Famous last words if ever I heard them." She was still clutching the newspaper as they entered the coffee shop. "I'll look through the classifieds again while you're phoning," she told him as he ushered her into a booth.

"Fair enough. Order me coffee and a doughnut, will you?" Tony selected a dime from the change in his pocket and moved toward a partially screened telephone at the back of the room.

Maggie obediently gave their order to a waitress, taking care to only order a cup of tea for herself despite Tony's blithe comment about calories. Then she opened the newspaper on the table in front of her and carefully perused the "Personal" column again. She was shaking her head over an advertisement for a salve which claimed to heal everything from falling hair to fallen arches when Tony slid into the booth across from her, a wide grin on his thin face.

"Bullseye! We're back in business again!"

She stopped refolding the newspaper long enough to stare at him. "What does that mean?"

"Just what I said—John thinks he's found Agatha's hideaway."

"But how . . ."

"When we drew a blank on the 'Personal' column, he started checking the local real estate firms and their publications."

"I thought he had a business appointment," she persisted.

Tony made an impatient gesture. "Maybe he had his secretary do it or somebody in the office. What difference does it make *how?* The important thing is that he's dug up a healing sanctuary in Carmel."

She frowned and tried to remember. "Carmel is south of here on the Monterey Peninsula, isn't it?"

He nodded. "Very rarefied atmosphere. These days it's big for the arty-crafty people. Sounds as if Agatha would like it fine, and the sanctuary's having a special service this weekend. Some big bash to welcome a visiting spiritualist." Tony took a hurried sip of his coffee. "There's one more thing; John wants you to check in with the police later this afternoon. Probably you'll have to go through the book of mug shots and try to identify your friend from last night." As he saw her give a tiny shudder, he added reassuringly, "It shouldn't be bad."

"But I didn't really see him . . . at least not enough to identify him for sure."

"Then just tell them that." He reached across the table to grasp her hand. "I'll go with you for moral support if you'd like."

"Thanks, Tony." She wrinkled her nose slightly. "Don't worry, I'll do the best I can."

"Fine!" He gave her fingers a reassuring pat and then

picked up his coffee cup again. "After the police visit, you're to go straight back to the apartment and rest. Holly will help you pack your things and spend the night with you."

Maggie choked on her swallow of tea. "Pack my things? Why?" She paused to get her breath. "Where am I going?"

"To Carmel, natch. John's making the reservations now." Tony grinned, his eyes alight with the spirit of the chase. "We'll all go, probably."

Maggie's tea cup was slammed down in the saucer. "Doesn't that man ever ask anybody anything? It's been 'do this' and 'do that' ever since I walked in his building."

"You can complain to your congressman as soon as you get back home. Right now, just be a good girl and do as the man says."

"I swear he's got all of you under his spell," she protested.

"Nope. Wrong cart for the wrong horse," Tony told her cheerfully. "Agatha's the one for weaving spells at Spirit Lane. The rest of us just stand around and watch."

Nevertheless, by the next morning, Maggie was not surprised to find herself doing exactly as John had ordered. From her seat beside him, she watched as he drove his sleek, late-model car expertly along the crowded lanes of the Bayshore freeway. He drove just the way he did everything else, she reflected, efficiently and with an air of assurance that she secretly envied. There wasn't a waste motion as he steered through the heavy traffic, keeping his speed fast but not excessively so. She speculated on his taut profile, wondering how he felt about this impromptu plan for the weekend. Probably he was covertly wishing that he could relax at home rather than trying to find an eccentric spiritualist after a mad chase down the coastline.

She cleared her throat inadvertently and John flicked

a sardonic glance her way before concentrating on the traffic again.

"Actually," she said finally, out of sheer desperation, "you didn't have to make this trip at all. I could have driven down to Carmel and found Miss Jarvis by myself."

There was an audible sigh from his side of the car. "I thought we'd been over all that."

"If I remember correctly, there wasn't any discussion," she pointed out. "I was merely told to follow orders. Besides when I agreed to come, I thought Holly and Tony were driving down with us."

"My car's more comfortable for two people than four." John didn't even bother to glance at her this time. "Holly's driving down with Tony a little later. You're certainly not worried about the proprieties over the weekend?" His amused tone dared her to admit it.

"Of course not. I'm delighted to share a room with your sister," Maggie replied indignantly. "She was marvelous to come down and stay in Agatha's apartment with me last night."

"I'm glad she made herself useful." His hands shifted on the wheel as he maneuvered around a truck and pulled into the fast lane. "From the way you're yawning, I suspect that Holly kept you up half the night talking."

Maggie resisted an urge to check her appearance in the mirror on the sun visor. She certainly wasn't going to admit that it had been close to two in the morning by the time she and Holly had finished packing and finally settled to sleep.

"Don't bother to deny it," John was going on calmly. "I know Holly—she's part night-owl. If Tony's smart, he'll make up a new schedule for her when they're married."

"Then you know about"—Maggie had trouble finding the right words—"you know that Tony's serious?"

"He has been all along, but I gather that he's finally planning to put it to the test. Up until now he's pointedly avoided the subject of matrimony." John's voice was dry. "I'm wondering if you had anything to do with his change in attitude."

"Of course not. I just had lunch with Tony and it wasn't a case of love over the noodles, for heaven's sake."

"That wasn't what I had in mind," he complained mildly. "I'm just curious about your coaching from the sidelines."

"Well, I'll wait until I see the results before I start signing testimonials," she admitted, "but keep your fingers crossed."

He looked amused in turn. "So you're not taking bows yet? In that case, I might as well change the subject. It's a long way to Monterey and I'd prefer some answers."

"You could always turn on the radio if the silence gets overwhelming," she suggested solemnly.

"I'm getting enough static without it. How did your visit to the police station go?"

"It was short and sweet. They hauled out a book of mug shots, but I wasn't able to give them any positive identifications. Once I'd explained the situation, they were very nice about it. Talking to the authorities did resolve one thing though," she admitted.

"What's that?"

She brushed her hair back impatiently with one hand. "Remember how I had that feeling that I'd scratched the man?" She saw his slight nod and went on. "When I thought it over, it came to me the scratch was on the man's wrist and lower arm."

"Scratch or scar?"

"I'll be darned." She stared at his stern profile. "You're more clairvoyant than Agatha. That's just what the detective asked."

"And?" The word came out impatiently.

"I had to tell him I didn't know. But now I think it must have been a scar. I was almost helpless by then—I didn't have enough strength to hurt him."

He drove on in silence while he digested her remark. "Did you tell them you were going out of town for the weekend?" he asked finally.

"Uh-huh. They said something about getting in touch with me when I got back. I also wrote to my folks. But I didn't say anything about delivering an urn of funeral ashes to my landlady."

John chuckled. "It might have strained the line of communication."

"I can hardly believe it myself," Maggie told him gloomily. "You *did* remember to bring Alfred's . . . er . . ."

"No need to be diplomatic—I know what you mean." John hit the horn as a Volkswagen changed lanes precariously in front of him. "The urn is in the trunk and I'd drive farther than Monterey to get rid of the damned thing."

"What about the diamond?" she wanted to know. "Did you bring it along, too?"

"No," he was checking in the rear mirror as he pulled away from the smaller car. "That's still safely tucked away in San Francisco."

"But it must belong to Agatha."

"Why? It could just as easily belong to your friend from the other night."

"Did you tell the police about it?" she asked.

He shot her an amused look. "What's the matter? Afraid I plan to run away with the loot?" He pretended to consider. "I could always head south with the proceeds."

"Practically to the Antarctic from the way you talked."

"Are you offering to come along?"

"Sorry," she shook her head in mock chagrin. "I hate cold weather."

"Ah, well, that's the way it goes. We'll just have to settle for a weekend in Carmel and abandon the criminal life." He glanced at his watch. "I'll be ready for a cup of coffee at San Jose. How about you?"

She sat up straighter and glanced out the car window, noting that the sunshine had brightened and tall palm trees were now edging the side of the road. "That sounds good. Have we passed Stanford already?"

"About five miles back on the right," he confirmed. "I didn't know you were interested."

She shrugged with resignation. "That's the trouble with freeways. Just miss one exit and pouf! you're in the next county." Settling back on the seat, she added, "It doesn't really matter. I wanted to see the Inner Quad and the Chapel, but I'll take the train down one day and bring a sketchbook."

"The campus is well worth it," he surprised her by saying. "We'll detour by on the way home so you can find your bearings."

Maggie nodded automatically, but her thoughts were racing. John had spoken of going home so normally that for the moment they might have been an old married couple. Her fingers tightened on the guidebook in her lap and she looked blindly down at its cover. Take it easy, she told herself. Now was the time to remember Holly's warnings about her brother's success with women. Certainly Maggie had never met a man with such a mesmerizing effect on her senses; a man so ruggedly masculine that she felt decked out in ruffles every time she was with him. Even now, the thought of just touching his hand made her pulse rate keep pace with the speedometer dial. She drew in her breath suddenly, afraid of the way her thoughts were leading.

"What's the matter?" John's voice barely penetrated.

She glanced across to find him frowning at her. "What do you mean?"

"I thought you'd gone into a trance like Agatha. You looked like it, too," he persisted stubbornly. "If I had to describe you right now, a 'washed-out' look would come closer than 'well scrubbed.'"

Maggie winced inwardly, acknowledging the truth of his statement but chagrined that she hadn't been able to mask her feelings more effectively.

"Honestly, I don't mean to be brutal," John was going on, "but you should have made Holly let you get some sleep."

She nodded noncommittally, perfectly willing to have him diagnose her pallor as the result of a sleepless night.

All she needed to do was stiffen her backbone and pretend that he was like an allergy or something. If strawberries made a woman break out in spots, she dispensed with the strawberries and all the symptoms went away.

Maggie frowned thoughtfully, wondering if her symptoms would disappear as easily. It would certainly be better if they *did* go away—the quicker the better.

She felt a prodding forefinger against her shoulder and looked up to find John studying her clinically.

"Did you say something?" she managed.

"About five minutes ago," he confirmed. "It wasn't important. Tell me, do you make a habit of going into trances?"

"Not as a rule," she snapped. "I was thinking of something."

"I'm glad it wasn't someone. You looked ready to wield a meatcleaver. Anything I can do to help?"

Her eyes widened at the irony of his offer. Aloud she merely said, "Hardly. It's personal."

She could feel his withdrawal even before he said stiffly, "Sorry, I didn't mean to intrude."

"No, *I'm* the one to apologize," she confessed, resting her fingers on his arm impulsively. "Honestly I don't act like this all the time, but I'm getting confused. First, there was Alfred and that darned urn—then finding the man in the apartment. Now, I even feel guilty about going and leaving Banjo. Are you sure he's all right?"

"I *told* you," he took his hand from the steering wheel and captured hers. "The lady who cleans for me will check on him twice a day. Besides, there's nothing wrong with the darned bird. He's eating his head off—you said so yourself."

"He still doesn't sing." She was trying to ignore John's touch but not succeeding. "Canaries are supposed to sing. Parakeets twitter, mynahs whistle, canaries sing. It says so in all the books."

"Maybe he's not in the mood."

"But why not?"

"Who knows? Could be he's unhappy in his love life. We can ask Agatha when we track her down." John absently put his hand back on the wheel. "Women worry about the damndest things."

Maggie was wishing that brief physical contact hadn't left her even more aware of his masculine presence than before. As a consequence, her tone was sharp. "That's the way the feminine sex is made. It's a little late to complain about our basic design."

He chuckled. "Now you're putting words in my mouth. I wouldn't think of tampering with the standard equipment."

"How reassuring," she said dryly and started searching through the pile of maps and pamphlets between the seats.

"What are you looking for?"

"That brochure on Carmel and the Seventeen-Mile Drive . . . oh, here it is." She leafed through the brightly colored pamphlet. "Don't forget—I'm a stranger in these parts. I don't want to miss a thing."

"You won't have to," he said. "There's no reason for

you to get involved personally during the hunt for Agatha. You and Holly had better spend your time driving around the Peninsula."

"Umm . . ."

"What's *that* supposed to mean?" he grated out.

"The visitor finds the Seventeen-Mile Drive from Pacific Grove to Carmel a scenic delight," Maggie read aloud from the booklet in her lap. "Golf devotees will find Pebble Beach, Spyglass Hill, and the Monterey Peninsula course truly outstanding. Public golf courses in the area are dotted with the famed Monterey cypress trees."

"There are other points of interest," John persisted doggedly.

Maggie flipped the page. "The visitor shouldn't miss Seal Rock and Cypress Point—highlights of any visit to this coastal region."

"Or if you just like shopping, you and Holly can spend hours in Carmel." John was trying hard not to lose his temper.

"Carmel's compact business center contains many unusual shops and the works of local artists are displayed." She read on obligingly. "At the foot of Carmel lies a broad expanse of white sand beach bordered by the picturesque Monterey cypress trees."

"I'd forgotten that," he admitted. "You could even spend the day lounging around on the beach if you wanted to." When she didn't reply, he glanced over inquiringly. "Well, what's it to be?"

"What do you mean?"

He curbed his impatience visibly. "I mean—how *are* you going to spend your time over the weekend?"

She smiled mischievously. "Looking for Agatha, of course."

His jaw clamped down. "Did anyone ever tell you that you were a stubborn . . . unswerving . . ."

"I prefer 'determined and firm.' "

"Unreasoning female," he finished triumphantly.

Her smile deepened but she kept discreetly silent.

He let a produce truck maneuver into the lane ahead of them before he spoke again. This time his voice was sober. "You realize that we could be walking into trouble down here. From what I learned, this convention is by invitation only."

"Who do they invite?"

"Believers," he said tersely. "People who have attended spiritualist gatherings or séances before and have backed their interest with cash."

"But why do we have to attend the meetings? Can't we just go up to the door and ask if Agatha Jarvis is around?"

"We could," John admitted. "But I suspect that all we'd get is a flat 'no' in reply. If Agatha had wanted you to know where she was, she would have left a telephone number or forwarding address."

Maggie chewed on her thumbnail while pondering his words. "I suppose you're right," she admitted. "What do you think we should do?"

"Walk in and try to look like a couple of believers. Once we get through the front door, we can see if Agatha's anywhere on the premises."

"All right." She looked embarrassed. "I hope they don't ask me any questions because I don't know a darned thing about spiritualism—not even enough to be a 'believer' or a 'nonbeliever.' What about you?"

"I'm in the same fix. Until you handed over Alfred and his urn, I'd never given it a thought. Actually we might have a better chance of getting in their sanctuary if we took Alfred with us."

Maggie shuddered visibly. "You can't haul him around like a sack of potatoes. Besides, spiritualists aren't interested in ashes—just apparitions."

"Did you ever see any of those?"

She looked at him solemnly. "Nary a one, but then I only attended one séance. And that was years ago."

"I doubt if the technique has changed." He sounded sheepish. "I'd better admit that I spent last night reading a book on psychic phenomena."

"Ah-hah! *Now* it comes out. How did you feel when you were finished?" she asked with real interest.

"Confused." He settled into a more relaxed position and let up on the accelerator. "Definitely skeptical but a little like Napoleon, too."

"Where does he come into it?"

"He's supposed to have said that 'Impossible is the adjective of fools.'" John kept his eyes on the road. "Or maybe it's just that each of us—every human being— really wants to believe. Do you know that one out of every four people in the United States claims to have been in contact with some phenomena from the spirit world? That makes people who go around publicly disproving it pretty unpopular. Even Houdini had trouble when he revealed the fraudulent tricks of the trade. His audiences didn't want to hear his exposés of how humbugs operated; they just wanted more séances."

There was a moment of silence between them. Then Maggie asked, "Aren't there cases of 'genuine' mediums or 'sensitives'?"

"According to the book I read, quite a few. There was some Dutch citizen called Gerard Croiset, for example, who never charged for his information, nor accepted any money in connection with his services. Apparently he was thoroughly tested by a parapsychology commission there and used more than once by the Dutch police in connection with their criminal cases. After a brutal slaying with a hammer as the murder weapon, Croiset is reported to have given police a description of the murderer and where he could be found. That was after merely looking at the hammer used in the crime."

"And they found the man?" Maggie sounded incredulous.

He nodded. "So the story goes. Every time I was convinced that the whole psychic thing was hogwash, I'd run up against something that made me read a little further." His voice deepened with conviction, "I still think Agatha's stuff is mumbo-jumbo, though. All I want is for her to get out of my building and take Alfred, her jewelry, and assorted apparitions with her." His expression softened. "Sorry, I didn't mean to explode again."

"That's all right. Actually I feel the same way," Maggie admitted. "The only thing I got out of the one séance I attended was a splitting headache."

"Not very convincing, eh?"

"It was terrible. At one point, I was hit on the head by a trumpet that was flying through the air."

"No wonder you got a headache."

"It was a toy trumpet," she informed him smiling. "The only music took place when my nurse messenger sent word from the spirit world. It sounded just like wind chimes. You know, the glass ones people hang on patios."

"At least that added a note of authenticity."

Maggie shook her head sadly. "Not really. When the séance was over and they turned the lights on again, I saw a glass wind chime on a hook over the medium's head."

"So there went all your faith."

"Well, it didn't keep me awake nights," she admitted. "All this happened when I was in college and the next weekend, we simply went to another woman and had our fortunes told in tea leaves."

John chuckled. "A real scientific approach."

"Absolutely. She said I'd meet someone interesting in the water, so I started hanging around the swimming pool on campus."

"Nothing?" he prompted.

"Nothing. Since I was in the girls' gym swimming pool, it wasn't surprising, but I didn't figure that out for several weeks. In the meantime, I had to put up my soaking hair every night." She shook her head, remembering. "It was awful."

His chuckle turned to a roar of laughter. "Honestly, Maggie, you're the most confusing woman I've ever met. One minute, you put up a barrier of cold sophistication that would stun a jet-setter, and the next, you're confessing things that sound like Holly in her zanier moments."

"I did most of those silly things when I was a lot younger," she pointed out.

"You're not *that* old now," he observed shrewdly. "I imagine I can give you six or seven years and I still do foolish things occasionally."

"Not often, according to Holly," she murmured. She could have told him exactly how much older he was—the figures were also courtesy of Holly—but she didn't think he'd be pleased to learn how extensively the two of them had discussed him the night before.

She was right about that. John was irritated even at her tactful reply. He shot a suspicious look at her, noting absently that her face was still too pale. He turned his attention ostensibly back to the highway, but his glance was troubled as he thought of the weekend ahead. Somehow, he'd have to find a way to track down Agatha Jarvis by himself! There was no point in arguing further with Maggie about it; she was just as stubborn as he was when it came to getting her own way. His expression lightened as he thought about that. How she'd resent that word "stubborn." Those beautiful eyes of hers would flash and the delicate lips would clamp down firmly . . . not that she'd become any less attractive. If anything, anger made her more provocative than ever. He became aware of the way his thoughts were leading and abruptly brought his mind to heel. This wasn't the time or the place for that kind of thinking, he told himself sternly.

Maggie was watching his change of expression from the corner of her eye and she sighed as he frowned. So it was back to the Cold War again! She could only hope things would be better when they got to the Monterey Peninsula.

Chapter
SIX

Unfortunately, the weatherman didn't cooperate.

The sun that had smiled so benignly in San Jose had completely disappeared when John turned the car into the famous Seventeen-Mile Drive that meandered along the coastline to Carmel.

"Damn!" he said, peering through the windshield, "I hope it isn't going to be overcast all weekend."

"Maybe it's just temporary," Maggie told him as she sat up and tried to push her hair into a semblance of order. She'd wakened from a nap as they entered Monterey to find her head securely lodged against John's shoulder, and now she was wondering if she'd looked awful, drooped against him all that time. "Why on earth didn't you wake me? Your shoulder must be terribly stiff."

"Why should I wake you? You looked very peaceful." A slight smile flickered and was gone as he added, "Besides, you obviously needed it."

"I didn't want to miss anything," she said stubbornly.

"You didn't. A few acres of artichokes aren't that great. Besides, you can look at them on the way back." He indicated the scenery on either side of them. "This is the famous landscape—something to tell the folks back home."

Maggie nodded meekly, wishing he hadn't mentioned going back home. The desire to see her family and friends again and the challenges of her job had faded inexplicably in the last few days.

"It's spectacular, isn't it?" John was saying. "Those bent cypress trees silhouetted against the rocks and ocean." He gestured to his left. "A lot of the homes in this section are real showplaces. Look at those up there."

Maggie's eyes were round as she stared at the cluster of magnificent dwellings perched on the rocky crags and tucked in crevices next to the beach itself. "They're perfectly gorgeous," she said in awed tones. "Are they private homes? They look big enough to be hospitals or schools or something."

"Not here," John assured her. "All very private . . . very posh. Carmel itself is a little different these days. It has more avant-garde designers and 'creative' people per block than any place I know." His tone became dry. "That's probably why they're holding this blowout at the healing sanctuary there. It's a fertile field."

Maggie was still staring at the magnificent coastline stretched ahead of them. "The grass is so green—the color is wonderful against the surf," she was murmuring. "And look how those trees are bent—simply crouching over the ground. No wonder every artist is dying to come here!"

"I needn't have wondered how you were going to spend your time," John said dryly. "Too bad Holly won't take up art. Her weekends down here wouldn't have cost half so much."

Maggie wasn't paying attention. "I hope we're staying where I can see the ocean," she said absently. "That cloud effect over the water is particularly good."

"Looks like plain overcast to me," he said with amusement. "I think you'll approve of where we're staying. Most people do."

"Now you're making fun of me, again."

He hastened to reassure her. "Simmer down. Just enjoy the scenery and take things as they come."

When he finally turned into the huge inn where they were to stay, Maggie decided that her fairy godmother was working overtime on her behalf.

"All this?" she murmured, gazing wide-eyed at the sprawling complex of buildings which surrounded two famous golf courses and the hotel itself.

"You deserve something special after all you've endured at the apartment," he said, pulling into a parking space close by the entrance to the inn. "You should be comfortable here."

"That's an understatement if I ever heard one." She stared at the buildings around her as she waited for him to come around and open the car door. The inn itself was a sprawling, two-storied structure of whitewashed brick with separate guest establishments on either side overlooking the lush greenery of the golf course and ocean frontage.

As Maggie followed John in to register, she saw that long glass windows provided guests in the lobby and dining room with a chance to watch either marine traffic or golfers completing the eighteenth green which was located squarely in front of the building.

After John finished registering, he found her viewing a hapless foursome who were three-putting the last green.

"I wondered where you'd gotten to," he said, strolling over beside her at the window. "Aren't you even curious about our accommodations?"

She shook her head and sighed happily. "I don't think that I even want to stir from here. Why didn't somebody tell me that Pebble Beach was like this?"

John's answering smile was without its usual reserve, making him look much younger. In his casual outfit of white turtleneck with beige slacks and matching golf sweater, his rugged good looks were especially apparent at that moment.

Maggie took a deep breath and tried to keep her head.

"Don't we have to get our bags or something?" she asked.

"It's all arranged." He put a hand under her elbow and steered her back toward the entrance. "We'll drive down to our rooms so you can give them the once-over before we come back here and have something to eat."

Maggie blinked as they went back outside and retraced their steps to the car. "You're going about this very professionally. I take it you've been here before." To her chagrin, she heard the chiding note of sarcasm in her voice.

Evidently John did, too. His pleasant look became more guarded. "Occasionally," he admitted. "If you want to know whether I make a habit of inviting young ladies down for the weekend, the answer is no."

"That wasn't what I meant."

"No?" Plainly he wasn't convinced.

She decided to change the subject. "We must be in the very last unit." As he parked in front of a two-story building, she added, "This is the nicest view of all . . . the golf course in front and uncluttered beach beside us." Her attention was suddenly captured by an elderly man with a German shepherd on a leash who was coming up the path from the beach. "What a gorgeous dog!" she murmured as she watched them move toward the end unit of the building.

"The desk clerk told me some guests had a dog in the room next to yours and Holly's," John said as he went around to unlock the trunk of the car. "He shouldn't disturb anything. Apparently he's very well-mannered."

"He looked it," Maggie said, "But I'd hate to tangle with him."

"That possibility is highly unlikely." John was depositing her overnight bag on the path. "We may tangle with a few of the unfriendlier spirits this weekend but that's all. Anything else you want in the room?" He gestured toward the open trunk.

Maggie frowned as she surveyed the corrugated carton by the spare tire. "What about Alfred?"

"My God, surely you don't want him as a roommate?" John was incredulous. "Besides, your room's just a double —not a triple."

"Stop being funny," she told him crossly. "Is it safe leaving him in the trunk?"

"Well, I can't very well ask the desk clerk to put him in their safe deposit vault."

Maggie sighed and bent over to pick up her tote bag. "I suppose not," she admitted. "But the whole thing seems indecent somehow."

"I'm not keen on the arrangement myself." John slammed the trunk lid down and picked up the rest of their bags. "With any luck, we can get rid of him to-morrow. Once we find Agatha, the problem will be solved." He glanced toward the doors at the south end of the unit. "Sixty-four and sixty-five . . . those are ours. You and Holly are in the farthest one—the view is a little more spectacular."

Maggie watched him put down the bags and haul out two room keys from his pocket.

He unlocked the end unit first and handed her the key. "Go on in and see if you like it."

She smiled faintly as she paused in the doorway. "My only worry is that I'll like it *too* much and not want to go home again."

"Well, don't get carried away with the scenery right now—I'm starving to death. How about allowing fifteen minutes to comb your hair and wash off the dust before we go and eat?"

"It sounds good." She glanced at her watch and then down at her green knit pants suit with its striped jacket. "Should I change?"

He appraised her judicially. "You look okay to me. I think your nap helped."

"I meant my clothes." Her voice was flustered.

That brief but comprehensive glance of his slid over her again. Maggie felt he let it linger deliberately.

"What about them?" he asked blandly.

"You know what I mean. Stop being obtuse."

"Okay," he tossed his key in the air and caught it. "That outfit's fine for a late lunch in the bar and a slow tour of Carmel later on."

"Is that the schedule?"

"Unless you have any strong objections."

She shook her head as he put her bag in the hallway. "Not a one!"

"Fine. Fifteen minutes then. Pound on the wall when you're ready. Make sure it's the proper wall though. That German shepherd on the other side might not be amused." He pulled the door gently closed between them.

Maggie was still smiling as she went in the hallway and stared entranced at the luxurious twin bedroom in front of her. Its color scheme made it look as if the outdoors had simply been brought inside. There was a deep-piled carpet of moss green and draperies of the same background shade patterned in a stylized white and yellow design. The yellow tone was repeated in the damask bedspreads and on the upholstered chairs near the long sliding windows which looked out onto the sun deck. She opened a glass panel and went outside, absently testing the springs on one of the two lounges by the railing. It would be fun to stretch out on it with a sketch pad and take her choice of subjects: the coastline with its wonderful rock formations, that picturesque knoll with the bent cypress trees, or the cloud effects behind the hills in the distance.

A muffled bark from the next unit made her look up, startled. The low railing separating the individual sundecks wouldn't be any barrier if ninety pounds of German shepherd decided to come calling. Fortunately the long windows of the next unit remained firmly closed. Her gaze moved to survey the windows on the other side. Evidently John didn't intend to come out and inspect his view. She consulted her wristwatch and frowned suddenly. No wonder! She'd better get inside and get cleaned up or she'd never make his fifteen-minute deadline.

When she was ready, she made sure that her room key was safely tucked in her purse before closing the door behind her. She went down the outside hallway a few feet and tapped quietly on John's door.

It was opened almost immediately, but his eyebrows went up in surprise to find her standing there. "I thought you were going to pound on the wall."

She smiled. "I was taught never to honk my horn nor pound on the wall when calling on strange gentlemen."

"I stand corrected." He patted his pockets as he replied, obviously taking inventory. "I don't have my key. Wait a minute, will you." He was back almost immediately and found her leaning against the door jamb. "Sorry," he sounded slightly flustered. "I didn't think you'd be ready on time."

She pretended to take offense. "How do you prefer to carry your head, Mr. Elliott? Under your arm or in a paper bag?"

"I prefer to apologize for such a misguided remark. Next time I'll know better." He took her elbow and closed the door behind them. "I could use some exercise. Shall we walk to the main building?"

"Of course." Maggie took a deep breath of the sweet-smelling air as they strolled up the deserted path. "It's a wonder I *was* on time. Once I went out on the sundeck, I almost forgot everything."

"Maybe you'd rather stick around here than go into Carmel this afternoon?"

She nibbled her lip thoughtfully. "I'd hate to miss anything new. Are you going to stop by the sanctuary today?"

"Absolutely not. Now, don't start getting that stubborn look again. The conference doesn't officially start until tomorrow, so why beat on locked doors today."

"Unless the caretaker could tell us if Agatha was around."

John had no intention of asking questions until he was alone. Once Holly arrived, she would be instructed to keep Maggie safely out of harm's way for the rest of the weekend. He frowned slightly as he looked at his watch. The trouble was, just *when* was Holly going to arrive?

"What's wrong?" Maggie asked.

He checked his stride and glanced down at her puzzled face. "Nothing's the matter. Why?"

"Well, you didn't answer when I suggested checking with the building caretaker about Agatha."

"I was thinking of something else." When she still stared suspiciously, he added hastily, "Just wondering when Holly and Tony were going to get here."

Her smile flickered. "Don't count on it's being early. Tony had a business appointment this morning and Holly's determined to find out why he's being so secretive."

"He'll explain everything in good time."

Maggie stopped in the middle of the path. "Then you know what his plans are?"

"Some of them." John urged her forward. "Come on, I'm hungry."

She gave him an exasperated look but allowed herself to be marched along. "There *are* more important things than eating."

"Name one."

"Your sister's love life."

He pretended to consider and then shook his head. "That's not on my list. Besides, you know almost as much about Tony's plans as I do, and after this weekend maybe we'll both know the whole story." His hand slid down her arm to grasp her fingers companionably. "In the meantime, I'll be surprised if they appear in time for dinner."

"You're probably right."

"So I'll make a reservation for just the two of us. We can always change it later." He stepped ahead of her to pull open the wide door to the main building, releasing her hand at the same time. By the time they passed through into the lobby, Maggie was careful to keep a discreet eighteen inches between them.

A smiling waiter bowed them into a pleasant lounge decorated with athletic trophies where a few couples still lingered over lunch. He led them to a table in the corner and offered menus. "Would you like something to drink?" he asked politely.

John glanced across at Maggie and raised his eyebrows.

"No, thank you," she told him.

He turned to the waiter. "Just food, then. Give us a couple of minutes to make up our minds."

"Certainly, sir. Coffee now?"

"I'll wait . . . Maggie?"

"With my sandwich," she requested. After the waiter left, she smiled impishly. "Getting coffee later is as difficult as trying to get a sandwich without lettuce."

John's eyes crinkled with amusement. "Who knows, maybe it's a good omen for the weekend. Impossible things accomplished while you wait."

Maggie crossed her fingers on top of the table. "If that means getting rid of Alfred on our first try, I'm all for it."

It was as if they both were following an unspoken command to avoid unpleasant topics for the rest of the afternoon. Once they had pleasantly dawdled through a delicious lunch and sat long over second cups of coffee, they got back in the car and drove the remaining part of the Seventeen-Mile Drive into the picturesque village of Carmel.

At her first sight of the town's narrow, winding streets

which were lined with unusual shops, Maggie's enthusiasm started to bubble. She was kept busy glancing from one side to another as John drove slowly past. "This is marvelous!" she exclaimed. "Did you see the fountain in that last display window? They'd combined wood and brass wonderfully."

"Uh-huh." John was noncommittal but secretly amused. "I'll take you back for another look if we can ever get rid of the car. Be a good girl, and use that energy of yours to find a parking space."

"Oh, of course." She looked sheepish. "I guess I got carried away."

"Stop apologizing. We can rubber-neck all you like in a few minutes. Hey!" He nodded toward a car pulling out ahead of them. "We're in luck. Practically on the main street, too."

"I had no idea there'd be so many people," Maggie murmured as he drew alongside the empty space and started to back into it. "The sidewalks are jammed."

"I know"—he was concentrating on parking and answered her absently—"it's this way every weekend and twice as crowded during their summer festivals. Are we close enough to the curb?"

"Just right!" she exclaimed, after leaning out and peering at the sidewalk. "I can never do it that well on the first try."

"Women have to leave us a few things to brag about."

Her eyebrows went up. "You're just lucky."

"Don't I know it," he replied enigmatically. "What do you want to do first?"

She smiled and clutched her purse as she got out of the car. "Window-shop, I guess. Or did you have something else in mind?" She didn't have nerve enough to ask if they could at least scout the location of the sanctuary while they were in town. Of course if they separated, there was no reason why she couldn't go there on her own.

John refused to cooperate. "I'll tag along with you," he said easily as he locked the car and stood on the sidewalk beside her. "There are a couple of art galleries nearby that have some interesting stuff. Shall we start there?"

It was impossible for Maggie to feel more than a fleeting twinge of regret at his answer. A visit to an art gallery in his company sounded infinitely more appealing than haring off by herself to a spiritualist sanctuary.

They joined the other strollers and moved past small shops that were fitted in, shoe-horn fashion, at the edge of the sidewalk. Maggie shook her head wonderingly as they passed a teen-aged twosome where the coloring of the girl's tie-dyed jeans resembled the many-shaded bleach job in her hair. Her escort had his shoulder-length hair pulled back in a ponytail as he strode along in a garment that looked like a Moroccan caftan except for the Wild West fringe on the bottom.

"If I didn't know better, I'd swear this was a 'Come as you are' party," Maggie murmured to John.

"You sound like some of the older residents." He pulled her to a stop in front of a store which featured everything from surrealist oil paintings to welded pieces of statuary. "Now you can take a busman's holiday and explain some of this stuff to me."

She stared at the interior dubiously. "What makes you think that I understand it?"

"That's the nicest thing you've said all day. Shall we try another place where a few of the paintings are recognizable?"

"If you don't mind. I'll defend modern art another day." As she spoke, she was admiring the colorful flower boxes in the windows of the various shops and in the tiny park on the opposite side of the road. Then the figure of an elderly woman turning the corner and going up the next block made her freeze in sheer astonishment.

John had walked on a few steps before he looked around, frowning. "Now what?"

"That woman . . ." Maggie started to point, then dropped her hand with a frustrated gesture. "There *was* a woman," she amended, "only she's gone now. She disappeared behind the building over there."

"What about her?"

"I could have sworn it was Agatha. She moved the same way and she wore the same kind of fluttery clothes," she said, noting the skeptical look on his face.

John merely nodded toward two matrons coming toward them who were wearing fussy afternoon dresses and enough costume jewelry to make Christian Dior blanch with horror.

Maggie sighed. "I suppose you're right. But there *was* something . . ."

John pulled her alongside him. "The trouble with you is that you're hungry."

"You're crazy. We just finished lunch."

He shook his head sadly. "Delusions are the first sign of malnutrition. Maybe a cup of coffee would help. There's an outdoor restaurant down here that overlooks the beach."

She began to catch on. "Besides, if we're eating, you don't have to go shopping in the boutiques with me."

He grinned but didn't pause in his purposeful stride as he turned into a side street. "Something like that. I wouldn't mind if there was an honest-to-God hardware store or something like that. But a couple of blocks of gift-shop gimcracks and I've had it."

The rest of the afternoon passed in a pleasant haze with a judicious mixture of strolling on the beach and window-shopping, although Maggie was careful to keep the latter limited. At dusk, she was relieved to be on the way back to Pebble Beach with the prospect of a leisurely dinner still in store.

John saw a piece of paper partially tucked under his door as they walked down the hallway to their rooms. "Oh, oh, I guess Holly and Tony aren't going to make it by dinnertime. Let's see what their note says."

The message was brief but explicit. *"Arrive about midnight. Sorry for the delay. Tony."*

John flicked the note idly with his finger when they'd finished reading it. "It's a good thing we didn't count on them. I must say that knowing Holly, I'm not surprised."

Maggie regarded him curiously, trying to judge his mood. If his sister's late arrival disconcerted him, it wasn't apparent.

John confirmed this by his next comment. "Actually it couldn't have worked out better if I'd planned it this way. All the proprieties are satisfied, but we can still . . ." His voice trailed off as if he suddenly had second thoughts.

"Still what?" she wanted to know.

"Er . . . nothing."

"I wish you'd stop being mysterious."

"You're imagining things again. Is an hour long enough for you to get ready? If it isn't, I can switch our dinner reservation around."

"I'll be ready," she promised and moved down the hall fumbling for her room key. Her forehead creased as a disconcerting thought struck her. How in the world was she going to fasten the back of her dress if Holly wasn't around?

"Is something wrong?"

She glanced over her shoulder to find John still watching her from his partially opened door. "Not a thing," she said, managing to smile. "See you in an hour." Certainly she wasn't about to confess that she couldn't get dressed without his help. If worst came to worst, she could always call the housekeeping department for an obliging maid.

Once inside her room, she went over to the closet and surveyed the coral chiffon dress she had hung there. She'd have to wear it, as it was the only dressy thing she'd packed. And to be honest, she'd been waiting for a chance to wear it ever since she'd bought it. Her eyes surveyed the long row of tiny covered buttons at the back of the dress, and she shook her head ruefully. They definitely called for a husband or a roommate. Well, in a real emergency, she could always ask John's help. Better that than appearing in a knit suit for dinner-dancing. Growing up with a sister, he'd probably helped with plenty of awkward zippers and buttons in his time.

As she went in to run her bath water, it occurred to her that John might have garnered experience from other feminine quarters as well. This particular thought was so disconcerting that she'd filled the tub more than half-full of steaming water before she came to her senses and hurriedly turned on the cold tap.

Fortunately the elderly maid who came to turn back her bed a half-hour later was able to solve the problem. She was delighted to put down her armful of linens and do up Maggie's buttons.

"It's a lovely dress, miss," she said when she'd finished and stepped back to admire the result. "That coral is just right with your coloring . . . brings out the lights in your hair, too. I wish I could convince my daughter to wear things like that. She won't believe that her boyfriend wants to see her in anything but a pair of jeans. Says intellectual communication is all that matters." The older woman uttered a clucking sound. "Won't listen to me when I tell her that men don't want to see a woman looking like she's going out to weed the garden even if she's spouting the history of the Roman Empire. I reckon Cleopatra had enough sense to wear a nice-looking outfit now and then. Otherwise Mark Antony wouldn't have taken a second look. That girl of mine will learn though." The maid nodded sagely. "One of these days she'll be stuck with Julius Caesar, after her boyfriend wanders off with a dim blonde in a miniskirt."

"Oh, I hope not," Maggie commiserated.

"Well, at least you won't have that trouble, miss. Any man'd go for that dress. Chiffon gets 'em every time. It's physical—not mental," she added knowingly.

When John came to the door fifteen minutes later, Maggie noted happily that the older woman's prophecy was still true. John's glance swept over her and he whistled softly in admiration.

"Do you like it?" Maggie murmured shyly, smoothing the skirt.

"Anybody who didn't would be crazy. Turn around . . . let me see the whole effect." He waited while she pirouetted before adding, "I'm glad I don't know anybody who's down here for the weekend. Something tells me I'd have a hell of a time keeping away poachers."

"It's just a dress," she remonstrated.

"That's like saying Aphrodite was just another goddess." He watched her collect a gauzy stole. "Are you going to be warm enough with that?"

"Probably not," she acknowledged, "but this isn't the kind of dress where you drape a sweater over your shoulders, and I left all my sable coats at home."

"Then we'll have to walk fast, eat a great deal, and dance in double-time."

She looked puzzled.

"To keep your circulation stirring," he explained.

"Oh, I see." She pretended to consider it. Then, "It sounds awfully good to me."

He tucked her hand into the crook of his arm. "It does to me, too. Let's go. I don't want to waste any more time."

Once in the dining room at a table by the window, the dinner that was served to them would have delighted anyone. By the time they'd finished their entree of prime ribs, Maggie could only wave the dessert menu away weakly. "No more," she said. "I'm not sure that I can even move now."

"Nonsense," John watched the waiter fill their coffee cups. "Dancing will help—three times around the floor and you'll be ready for Cherries Jubilee." He stood up and reached for her hand. "That's a fox trot they're playing at the moment. Come on—before they change to something more exotic."

On the dance floor, Maggie discovered that their steps blended effortlessly and she was able to relax in his arms. John unobtrusively tightened his hold so that her hand moved naturally from its resting place on his shoulder to curve around his neck.

After the fox trot, the musicians went into a medley of romantic show tunes which brought still more dancers to the floor and restricted the movements of the ones who were already there. Maggie heard the click of a switch, and the overhead lights dimmed, leaving only the flickering candlelight on the tables for illumination. Hemmed in by the other couples, John danced almost in place and Maggie was extremely conscious of his lean length next to her as they slowly swayed and moved to the throbbing melody. As the music went into another chorus, she took a deep breath and tried to steady her bounding heartbeat which must have been only too apparent through its thin chiffon covering. When the music ended a few minutes later, she pulled hastily out of his firm embrace.

John caught up with her at the edge of the dance floor. "Where in the devil are you going?"

"Just back to our table. Why?"

"When a lady dashes off the floor, it's hardly complimentary." He watched her sit down in her chair without meeting his glance. "S'matter of fact, I was enjoying the dancing," he went on as he settled opposite her. "Thoroughly."

Maggie reached over and picked up the dessert menu with an air of concentration. "You were right about exercise being all I needed to make me hungry again," she said aloud while thinking she'd be lucky if she could manage a swallow of anything. "I can't make up my mind."

He raised an eyebrow before summoning their hovering waiter. "I'd noticed that. How about Cherries Jubilee? French pastry?"

"Oh, no!" The words came out faintly before she could qualify them. "Perhaps a small dish of sherbet . . ."

"Nonsense! They have a special chocolate cake here . . . four layers with a whipped cream topping . . ."

Even a vision of it made Maggie's stomach tighten. "Just some raspberry sherbet, please," she said faintly.

If she'd looked up then, she would have seen John's usually firm lips curve with laughter as he told the waiter, "One sherbet and more coffee, please." He watched him disappear and glanced across the table to find Maggie had replaced the menu. She was staring unhappily out into the darkness beyond the window. Deliberately he let the silence between them lengthen.

By the time the waiter had arrived with her dessert and refilled their coffee cups, Maggie was able to meet John's eyes once again.

"I was wondering if you were ever going to come back to the party," he chided her gently. Before she could do more than color slightly, he'd taken a sip of coffee and said, "Actually, we should make an early night of it."

"Of course. It won't take me long to eat this." Maggie took a bite of sherbet, wishing they hadn't given her such a large serving. She'd have to eat at least half of it or John would be suspicious. "I have a lot of things planned for tomorrow," she said brightly.

"In that case, I'll get the check now."

Maggie darted a hurt look across at him when he was signaling the waiter. Evidently her flight from the dance floor had amused him more than anything else. So much for her attempt to maintain a platonic friendship. She sighed softly to herself and then tried to take another half-dozen bites of sherbet without choking in the process.

John appeared willing to observe her strict formality on the walk back to their rooms; he discussed the weekend weather with solemnity and even explained why pockets of fog hung over Carmel in the early summer. When he finished this discourse, he caught her in the middle of a yawn which she was unable to hide.

"Sorry, I didn't mean to bore you," he observed calmly.

"You didn't . . . it was just that . . ." Her words trailed off under his amused look. "I guess I'm tired."

"That must be it. Do you have your key?" he asked as they went up the steps to their building.

"Yes, thanks. Right here." She was fumbling in her purse.

"Then I'll leave you to it." He paused by his door after unlocking it. "I wouldn't wait up for Holly if I were you—she'll be along in good time. Good night, Maggie." He sketched a brief salute and ducked inside.

Maggie's mouth dropped open as she watched his disappearing back. Never . . . *never* . . . had a man treated her so casually after a date. She glanced down at the key in her hand as if discovering an unwelcome appendage. Then, irritably, she flounced to her door and unlocked it. It was slammed behind her before she remembered the people in the next unit with a guilty start.

More quietly, she went into her bedroom, her mind still churning with John's casual leave-taking. He hadn't even given her a chance to thank him for dinner, or the dancing. She winced suddenly as she thought of that.

Maybe it was just as well she hadn't mentioned the dancing.

But even if she hadn't intended to let him kiss her good night, he could at least have hovered for a minute or two and looked as if it had crossed his mind. There was no need for him to flee as if she were Typhoid Mary. Surely the other women he'd taken out hadn't been dropped in the middle of the hallway with a casual wave of the hand. She slammed her purse on the dressing table. Damn the man! Damn, damn, *damn!*

She kicked off her pumps and slipped into a pair of satin-trimmed scuffs. Then she looked in the mirror and an expression of blank dismay settled over her features.

How was she supposed to get out of her dress? Earlier, she'd imagined that Holly would have come by this time. Now, it appeared she'd have to sit in a chair for another two hours until she arrived. Which, if she faced it, didn't appeal to her at all!

There was only one thing left to do. She'd have to sink her pride and ask John's help with those miserable buttons. It was certainly too late to phone the housekeeping department—even obliging maids quit work earlier in the evening.

Slowly Maggie went to her door. Before she could have second thoughts, she opened it and scurried down the outer passage to knock softly at John's room.

His response came immediately. "Who is it?"

"It's me . . . I mean it's I . . . Maggie," wishing she didn't have to announce it to the world.

There was an instant of astounded silence, then, "Just a second—I'll be right there."

When he opened the door a few minutes later, he was still smoothing the collar on a maroon silk robe which he'd apparently just thrown on over his pajamas.

Maggie was so anxious to get out of the open hallway that she brushed past him into the foyer without giving him a chance to speak. Since she wasn't anxious to meet his glance, she missed seeing his perplexed expression change to one that was harder to interpret.

He closed the door then and leaned back against it. "Come in, won't you." There was a thread of humor in his voice.

"Oh, I'm sorry." She glanced around, more flustered than ever. "It's just that I didn't want to stand out there where everybody could see me." She took a deep breath and got a firmer grip on her words. "Actually, I wondered if I could ask you a favor?"

"What did you have in mind?" He stayed in his place by the door.

"It's my dress. I should have remembered when I put it on." She thought of explaining how she'd enlisted the maid's help and then dismissed the idea.

His glance went over her coolly. "What's the problem?"

"These buttons," her hand fluttered ineffectually toward her neckline. "They're hard to undo. If you'll come in where it's brighter, you'll see what I mean." She nodded toward his bedroom.

Obligingly he trailed behind her until they were standing by the edge of the bed. "You mean," he said carefully, in the tone of a man who wasn't making any mistakes, "that you want me to unbutton the dress?" His glance wandered over the fragile chiffon covering on her back and shoulders. Other than the attached taffeta slip next to her creamy skin, apparently she wasn't wearing anything else at all.

"Well, yes," Maggie murmured in some confusion. She waited until she felt the warmth of his fingers against the sheer material before saying, "If you don't mind."

"Not at all." He went methodically down the row because she could feel the seam open although she put her hand at the back of her neck to hold the frock as securely in place as possible.

John didn't speak again until he had apparently reached the waistline fastening. Then he straightened and turned her around deliberately. "There you are, Maggie, as ordered. No extra charge for special services."

"Thanks very much." She darted a quick glance up at his face and was surprised to find it remote, almost austere. As she watched, he smiled slowly, but the amused look didn't reach his eyes.

"I must be going," she said automatically.

"Sure," his hand remained firmly on her elbow, "but there's no hurry, is there? Holly won't be along for another hour or so."

She frowned. "I don't see what that has to do with it."

His voice roughened. "Come off your high horse, Maggie. Let's not play any more games." He pulled her close against him suddenly, and she felt his strong fingers on the bare skin at her back. At the same time his head bent to nuzzle the soft hollow of her shoulder. "You had me fooled," he was murmuring against her satiny skin, "I was playing on a different set of rules. I didn't think you were the type."

Spoken as softly as they were, his words penetrated Maggie with hurricane force. Her eyes widened with shock. Dear God, he'd thought she'd been angling for something like this ever since she'd knocked on his door. It was merely an excuse to fall into his arms.

Maggie shoved back from his embrace with a strength she wouldn't have believed possible. John was so startled that his arms dropped automatically and he found himself staring down at a furious pocket-sized virago who was still clutching a handful of chiffon on her shoulders.

"Why, you egotistical . . . insufferable . . . Casanova!" she sputtered, pulling away from him fastidiously. "Thinking that you're so damned irresistible that a woman would come and throw herself at your feet," her voice crumpled with fury. "Oh, how could you!"

~ John had partially recovered from his surprise by then, and his jaw hardened. "Drop it, honey," he drawled silkily, "outraged feminine virtue went out of style years ago. What in the hell do you expect when you knock on a man's door practically asking him to——"

"Don't say it!" she interrupted. "I came here because I couldn't get out of this dress without help . . . not for any other reason."

"How did you get into it?" His question shot out.

"With the assistance of the maid," she flared back and had the satisfaction of seeing him frown. "If I'd known you were going to act like a Keeper of the Harem, I'd have slept in it before I asked for your help." She stumbled toward the door and yanked it open with one hand while carefully keeping her dress around her shoulders with the other.

She was halfway out into the lighted passageway when she heard a car ignition being shut off. Holly's voice cut through the clear air.

"It's your fault we're so late," she was telling Tony with amusement. "You and your shortcuts. Whoever heard of anyone getting lost on the Seventeen-Mile Drive? John will be ready to shoot us."

"Well, I hope he waits till morning. I'm bushed." There was the creak of a car door being opened.

Instinctively, Maggie stepped back into John's hallway. She closed the door softly and turned to see him frowning from the bedroom doorway.

"*Now* what?" he asked finally.

She swallowed. "I need your help."

"And get my head taken off again?" He shook the feature in question emphatically. "No, thanks. I'm not sure it's safe to even be in the same room with you."

"Stop being silly," she hissed. "Holly and Tony have just arrived. I can't go down that lighted passage to my room. They'd see me."

"So what? I'll button you up again." He moved toward her as he spoke. "Everything will be . . ."

". . . an unholy mess!" she finished in an urgent undertone. "What excuse do I have for coming out of your room at this time of night—with you dressed like that." Her hand indicated his pajama'd attire.

"There are worse things than being caught in a man's room."

"Name one."

"Well, there's . . ." he frowned in concentration. "Oh, for lord's sake."

"Exactly." Her fingers yanked the slithering chiffon back into place. "It's the classic seduction scene. Even *you* can't think of a decent explanation."

"You make me sound like a first cousin to the Marquis de Sade," he snapped.

"Don't quibble." She kept her eyes resolutely on the top button of his pajama coat so she wouldn't have to meet his angry glance. "Just help me get out of here. They'll be along any minute."

"How about the sliding door on your sundeck?"

"It's locked."

"You could go out by my deck and circle 'round the building . . . tell Holly that you were taking a walk."

She stuck out her foot. "In these?" They both stared at the flimsy satin scuffs.

John sighed and tightened the belt on his robe. "Never mind then, I'll draw them off somehow." He went over to the door and opened it, saying over his shoulder, "Beat it down to your room when I've pulled them away. But for God's sake, make it fast!"

"You don't have to remind me," she said, her cheeks flaming.

He started to answer and then shook his head helplessly before striding across the lighted passage and down the steps.

Maggie heard him greet his sister and Tony as she huddled behind the half-open door. He must have raised his voice purposefully when she heard him say, "I'm not very happy about the left front tire on my car. I think I've picked up a slow leak."

"Let's take a look," Tony offered.

Maggie's heart sank as Holly said casually, "You don't need me. I'll go on in."

"What's the hurry?" John wanted to know. "I imagine Maggie's asleep by now. Come in our room and give me the latest news first."

"Well, if you say so." Holly was hesitant. "You don't have to carry my things. What's wrong with you, John? I've never known you to be so obliging before."

"Merely setting Tony a good example. Now what do you think about that tire of mine? It looks soft to me . . ."

Maggie stuck her head around the door and saw the three of them strolling away from the building toward John's parked car. Leaving the door ajar behind her, she made a dash for the other end of the unit and thankfully slipped inside her door. She scarcely paused by the closet long enough to drape her dress on the nearest hanger before racing to her suitcase and donning her pajamas. Once that was accomplished, she detoured past the bathroom in a fast sweep and set a new record for washing her face and brushing her teeth. She had just flipped off the light and slid into bed when she heard Holly's heels on the passageway and then the cautious noise of her key in the lock.

Maggie buried her face in the pillow and closed her eyes. After all that had happened, she couldn't manage a casual conversation. The memory of John's scorn was just now flooding back . . . she had to have time to think.

The outer door opened carefully and Holly tiptoed into the bedroom hallway. She stood there for a moment before her footsteps receded. Then her whisper came from the outer doorway. "You're right, she *is* asleep."

"I told you she would be." It was John's voice. "Might as well come in and talk to us for a while unless you're too tired."

Holly laughed softly. "No such luck, I'm wide awake *and* hungry. Let's call room service." The door closed behind her, and their footsteps faded as they moved down the passageway.

Slowly, Maggie sat up in the deserted bedroom and punched her pillow into position behind her. She leaned back against the headboard and stared into the darkness. Now she had plenty of time. Time to painfully acknowledge what she had known all along.

She was in love with John Elliott—completely, thoroughly in love with the man, and she just finished making a complete fool of herself in front of him.

Chapter
SEVEN

"I don't see why you have to be so darned stubborn," Holly said to her the next morning at breakfast. "Why do you want to disappear for the entire day trying to find Agatha Jarvis? Even if you *do* find her, she'll cling like a leech for the rest of the weekend."

"Not after she hears what I have to say to her," Maggie said. Her glance moved restlessly to the long dining room windows which were curtained in citron silk shantung for protection against the bright morning sun. As her gaze switched to the empty dance floor and the memory of last night's debacle flooded over her, her lips tightened. It was bad enough to lie awake thinking about it . . . now she had to face it all over again even before breakfast. She reached out for her glass of juice and tried to concentrate on what Holly was saying.

"You can't dent Agatha's feelings with a bulldozer, so the announcement that you're moving upstairs with me for the rest of your vacation won't faze her. She'll just tell you to move Banjo and his bird cage one flight up as well."

Maggie replaced her juice carefully in its saucer. "I meant to talk to you about that," she began, "only there hasn't been any chance."

Holly nodded. "I know. It's my fault for being so late in getting here last night. I didn't dream you'd already be asleep." She leaned forward and put her elbows on the table. "I was going to wait until we were all together at breakfast for our big discussion, but I didn't know then that you got up with the larks. Never mind, Tony and John should appear any time now."

"But Holly, I can't wait. Actually I want to try and track down Agatha at the sanctuary early this morning. Then"—she swallowed and went on with difficulty—"I have to go back to town."

"To San Francisco?" Holly was incredulous. "For heaven's sake—why?"

"Something's come up, that's all." Maggie didn't intend to explain that the obstacle in question was a six-foot male—well known to both of them. "There must be a bus around noon. I'll ask when I get into Carmel."

"You can't be serious," Holly wailed. "What about our lovely weekend?"

"I'm sorry." Maggie kept her glance lowered so that Holly wouldn't notice the tears that were stinging her eyes. "There's no reason for any of the rest of you to change your plans."

"I can't see John spending the rest of the weekend with his sister as the only woman around. Does he know about this?"

Maggie didn't answer, she merely shook her head.

"I didn't think so," Holly's tone was triumphant. "He won't let you do it."

"He won't have a darned thing to say about it! He's said enough already!" The impulsive words were out before Maggie realized.

"I *knew* it! Something's happened." Holly pounced. "Come on, Maggie . . . give!"

Maggie sighed, wishing she had managed to keep quiet. Now she couldn't admit that she also planned to move out of the apartment building once she got back to San Francisco.

"Stop dreaming up a good story, Maggie," the other

commanded. "What did my brother do to send you back to the city two days early?" She looked thoughtful suddenly. "Or maybe he didn't do anything. Is that the trouble?"

"Hardly. You must take me for an amiable lunatic if I'd act like that."

Holly waited until a busboy refilled their coffee cups before saying, "Don't think I can't recognize evasive tactics, my girl. I've been using them for years. Honestly, getting any news out of you is as hard as taking a turtle's temperature."

"On behalf of the turtles and me, thanks very much." Maggie tried to sound severe. "Holly, be serious. Would Tony let me borrow his car to go into town this morning?"

She had no sooner mentioned the request than she felt a masculine hand on her shoulder and heard Tony's voice saying, "Never ask favors of the small fry. Go right to the top." He bent over and kissed her cheek before performing the same service for Holly. Pulling out a chair to sit down between them, he said, "I promise to think about it. But first things first . . . what is there for breakfast?"

Holly stared at his preoccupied profile, admiring the casual figure he presented in a blue-checked sport shirt and a white golf sweater. His dark hair was brushed smoothly back and still damp from the shower.

"I thought you were going to sleep all day," she commented finally.

"Just half of it. How are the waffles?"

"Fattening." Her eyes half-closed in amusement. "It must be nice to be a man and ignore things like that. Where's John?"

"John?"

"My brother. He's tall . . . in his early thirties . . . you're sharing a room with him."

"Oh, *him*. He stopped off in the lobby to talk to a

friend of his . . . a good-looking blonde," he added judiciously. "After that, he plans to play golf."

"But he can't." Maggie sounded stricken. "Not today. You must be mistaken."

"Not about the golf game. I might be wrong about the blonde . . . maybe she isn't an old friend."

"Yes, she is," Holly confirmed. "Her name's Minda Carlisle, a divorcee who's spending the weekend here with her father. We've known them for quite a while."

Maggie pressed her hands to her temples. "Could we start over again? I don't care about John's blonde divorcees . . ."

"She's *not* John's divorcee," Holly put in. "Although the idea does seem to appeal to her."

Maggie kept her voice level with an effort. "I just meant that he said he was going to the sanctuary today. This is the first I've heard of a golf game."

"Probably because he knew you wouldn't be interested," Tony retorted before ordering his breakfast. When the waiter had departed for the kitchen, he added, "Besides, he's already been down to that place where they're holding the séances . . . or the enlightenment meetings or whatever they're called, and it was locked tight. Apparently the service has been postponed until five o'clock this afternoon. You can come along with Holly and me to Monterey for lunch or if you'd rather be on your own, John left his car keys at the desk for you. He said you might enjoy sketching the Mission in Carmel if this weather holds."

Maggie leaned back and stared unhappily across the table. She suddenly realized that there was only one thing worse than having to face John at breakfast—and that was having to look at his empty chair instead. It wouldn't have been so bad if she knew he was hovering in his room, full of repentance after his outrageous behavior the night before. But a man who was at that very moment chatting with a blonde divorcee in the lobby before ambling on to the golf course obviously wasn't suffering any tortures of the damned.

Maggie glared so hard at the silver pitcher in the middle of the table that Holly, who was watching with amusement, half-expected to find the cream curdled when she poured it into her coffee cup.

"Why don't you come along to lunch with Tony and me?" she suggested gently. "They have some interesting Spanish Colonial architecture you could sketch in Monterey."

Maggie shook her head. "No, thank you. I'll just go in to Carmel again. Maybe I'll run into Agatha somewhere in town."

"If you're being tactful, it isn't necessary." Tony finished his grapefruit and then reached over to pat Holly's hand on the table. "We'd be pleased to have a good listener along."

Maggie's eyes widened. "I *am* behind the times, aren't I? Why didn't you tell me?" she asked Holly.

The other's lovely smile flashed. "You didn't give me a chance. It was all I could do to keep you from dashing back to San Francisco before your omelet arrived."

"I'm sorry to have been so thick." Maggie's cheeks were flushed. "Tell me all about it."

"No, you don't," Tony interrupted, "or we'd never get away from the table. Just the bare essentials," he commanded his fiancée.

She ticked them off on her fingers obligingly. "First, he's going to make an honest woman of me. Second, as soon as I can drag him to church . . ."

Tony reached over and folded her finger down. "We'll set the date. We have an appointment with the minister for next week."

Holly rubbed her cheek against his hand fondly. "Such a chase you've led me. I don't think you're worth it."

"Wait and see, woman." He turned to grin at Maggie.

"All because I wanted to make sure I could earn a living in San Francisco."

"As if I had any doubts!" Holly said scornfully. "I wouldn't have cared where we lived."

"Well, I did. Anyhow," Tony added for Maggie's benefit, "to keep the story short, I found that I can work out of the West Coast just as well as Manhattan. Now the only thing we have left to fight about is whether I move into Holly's apartment or she moves into mine."

"After this weekend, maybe we'll be able to include Agatha's place in the selection," Holly said. "Friendly spirits and all."

"Why do you say that?" Maggie asked.

"John's putting his foot down. This time he's ready to see his lawyers if necessary." She smiled across at Maggie. "You've probably discovered that my brother can be as stubborn as any man. Once he's made up his mind about someone, there's no changing it."

Maggie winced inwardly. Holly's words merely confirmed what she already feared. After the contretemps with John last night, it was no wonder that he was staying as far away as possible. Since he thought that she was throwing herself at his head, he was exhibiting characteristic male caution and prudently making himself scarce.

"I almost forgot!" Tony exclaimed, reaching in his sweater pocket for a slip of paper. "Here's the address of the sanctuary. John said it's on the south side of town. You're to park a half block away about ten minutes to five. He'll meet you at the car."

Maggie's heart gave a bound as she heard that, but she was careful not to let it show. She took the paper and said rebelliously, "He's taking a lot for granted. What about his darned golf game?"

Tony looked amused. "It's only one game . . . not a life's work. He'll be there by five o'clock."

"*I* might not be."

Her threat didn't seem to bother Tony in the least. "I don't see why you're so upset. After all, he's not inviting you to hop on the next tumbrel or anything. All you have to do is wait in his car until he comes along to meet you. Incidentally, he said to remind you to take good care of Alfred. Something about his being your responsibility after all. I hope you know what he's talking about because I don't."

Maggie's defiance melted. She'd forgotten about Alfred in the trunk of the car.

"What's the matter? All of a sudden you're pale as a corpse." Holly leaned forward, concerned.

"I wish you wouldn't use that expression," Maggie told her absently.

"You're as bad as John. The other day I happened to quote that saying, 'Ashes to ashes, dust to dust,' and he turned positively gray."

"Could we please climb up out of the tomb," Tony complained mildly. "You're ruining my appetite."

Holly eyed the waffles and sausage that he was attacking. "All right, but I'd hate to see you when you're really hungry—you'd be a real drain on the grocery budget. Maybe it's a good thing you have a job after all."

"That reminds me," Tony paused with his fork halfway to his mouth. "I forgot to ask if you can cook."

Holly drew back, horrified. "You mean *you* can't. Heavens, we'll have to start negotiations all over again."

Maggie watched their raillery with a faint smile, envying them their confidence and obvious affection. At the same time, their lighthearted banter made her feel more of an outsider than ever. She took a final sip of coffee, patted her lips with her napkin, and pushed back her chair. "I'll leave you to fight it out," she told them. "If worst comes to worst, you can always eat in restaurants for the first month."

"Or live on nuts and berries," Tony agreed helpfully.

Holly shuddered. "Over my dead body . . . oh help, there I go again."

"Back in the crypt," Maggie said. "This is where I came in," feeling that indeed it was. She wondered what their reaction would be if she asked Holly to watch over Alfred for the day, and then clamped down on such flippant thoughts.

"Don't forget that we're celebrating with an engagement dinner tonight," Holly said, pointing a shapely finger for emphasis. "We won't accept any excuses. John has already agreed to it. All we have to do is set a definite time."

"Does he know that you're asking me? After all, he might be making other plans." Like asking a blonde, she thought, the old "friend of the family" in the lobby.

Even Tony could apparently read her thoughts because he looked up from his food long enough to grin and say, "He knew. Definitely, you're it. As Holly says, we won't accept excuses."

Maggie's face turned rosy with pleasure. "Then, thank you. I'd love to come."

It was true. Somehow she and John would have to declare a temporary truce for the evening's festivities. They both owed the engaged couple that much.

Maggie was still keeping her resolution firmly in mind as she parked on a side street in Carmel at a quarter to five that afternoon. Before she turned off the ignition, she checked the address John had noted once again and frowned as she surveyed the ramshackle structure on the other side of the street.

Obviously constructed during Depression years, the sanctuary, with its sagging roof beams and leaning porch supports, provided an incongruous note between the tidy buildings on either side. A ragged patch of grass surrounding the old structure insured a partial buffer state against inquisitive neighbors, and only a small wooden sign next to the sidewalk identified the place as the Carmel Sanctuary for Salvation. The title promised a multitude of services, Maggie thought irreverently as she turned off the ignition key, but from the looks of the place none of them were very profitable.

Just then, the worn front door opened and an elderly, overweight lady wearing a purple pants suit removed the written notice from the middle of it. She went back inside, leaving the door hospitably ajar behind her.

Automatically, Maggie stared up and down the sidewalk beside her, but its empty state showed that throngs of people weren't waiting for the sanctuary's doors to open.

She saw a car pull up at the intersection behind her and then she caught her breath as John's tall figure emerged from it. He bent down for a minute to speak to the driver before straightening and watching the car pull away toward town. Maggie tried to identify the figure in the car but it moved too rapidly out of sight.

She was so intent on her scrutiny that John was alongside before she realized it. He pulled open the passenger door and climbed in while she was still trying to decide whether she should move from behind the wheel.

"Do you want to drive?" she asked in some confusion as she fumbled for her purse where it had slid beneath the seat.

"No, we're not going anyplace right now." If he was amused by her lack of greeting, he didn't let on. Maggie realized that he looked tired and sounded unusually reserved. Her heart sank. Any hope she might have had about his forgetting the previous night's escapade disappeared in a second. Even the way he was dressed—in a conservative dark blue blazer, white shirt, and subdued striped tie—contributed to that impression of austere formality.

She was glad that she'd worn an undeniably becoming

silk dress in orange and green which did flattering things for her hair and figure. It was easier to maintain her own semblance of dignity when she was looking her best. "Did you enjoy your golf game?" she asked, adopting her nicest drawing-room manners.

"It was all right." He half-turned to face her in the seat. The provocative fragrance of her perfume reached him and made him more aware of her soft femininity than ever. He cleared his throat and started again. "Maggie . . . about last night . . ." He heard her quick intake of breath and plunged on before she could interrupt. "There was no excuse for what I said and did. Actually, I wanted to come and apologize ten minutes later"—he paused and looked embarrassed—"but there wasn't any way with Holly hanging around."

Sheer relief made Maggie want to fling her arms around his neck, but pride and something else held her back. Just because he was sorry, she told herself hastily, didn't mean that she was any more than a convenient date for the weekend. If she had any sense, she'd remember the blonde, the "old friend of the family" who probably had dropped him off.

John noticed her lowered gaze and rubbed the back of his neck wearily. Evidently he wasn't out of the woods, not by a long shot. He sighed and went on, his next words stiffly conventional. "I hope you had a nice day. Did you enjoy seeing the Mission?"

Maggie was happy to assert a small measure of independence. "Actually I didn't get around to it. I spent most of my afternoon sketching the beach and a clump of cypress trees. The rest of the time I just wandered around town."

"No luck with Agatha, I suppose?" He tossed it in.

"Not a bit," she said, before remembering that she wasn't going to admit why she'd combed the shops.

He sighed again. "Well, that leaves the Sanctuary for

Salvation. I see that they've finally unlocked the door."

"About five minutes ago. There wasn't exactly a stampede to get in. Are you sure the convention is this weekend?"

John nodded. "Actually it goes on for several days, so maybe the faithful pick and choose their events. We might as well wander across." He was glancing at his watch.

Maggie shifted slightly in the seat to check her appearance in the rear-vision mirror. "If we can get inside for a few minutes, somebody could surely tell us if Agatha's around."

"I'd settle for a forwarding address. That way, I could send her an eviction notice by special messenger."

"And air-mail, special-delivery Alfred to her at the same time."

"That's for sure." He got out of the car and smiled ruefully. "I almost got in trouble with that leaky tire story last night; Tony wanted me to drive to a service station and change to the spare in the trunk. I couldn't think of a single logical reason why I couldn't without explaining about Alfred."

"What happened?"

"Fortunately Holly complained that she didn't want to spend the rest of the night looking for an all-night service station." He shook his head reminiscently. "Tony still thinks I'm out of my mind."

"No, he doesn't." She waited beside the car while he locked it. "He was covering for you at breakfast very nicely. Even to explaining about the golf game and your blonde friend in the lobby."

John's head jerked up at that. "The devil he did!" Seeing her expression, he thoughtfully scraped his car key along his jawbone. "So I'm in deeper than I thought. Well, I guess I'll have to explain later."

"There's no need. I understood perfectly."

He caught her elbow a little roughly. "Uh-huh—and pigs can swim. Damned if I know what it is about you," he added in a conversational tone as they cut across the street in the middle of the block. "I've done more explaining—and apologizing—in one weekend than I have for the last ten years."

"It's probably been good for you. Think what a clear conscience you have now." She was hurrying slightly to keep up with his strides, but for an inexplicable reason her heartbeat was racing so fast that it made her breathless.

He merely snorted and then slowed his pace as they approached the aging building which was set back from the sidewalk. Glancing over its peeling facade, he said, "I wonder why they don't bother to paint it once in a while?"

"Where would they start?" Maggie indicated the rotting porch supports and sagging siding. "It needs a complete face-lifting."

John hesitated before turning up the path from the sidewalk. "The easiest thing would be to hire a bulldozer and start all over again. I've seen condemned places that looked better than this."

"Maybe they can't afford it."

"Well, I hope the next earthquake holds off until after this weekend," he commented grimly, helping her mount the worn porch steps. "Watch your heels on that splintered plank."

"I am." She stopped beside him to read a notice board by the side of the door and looked around nervously. "It wouldn't take an earthquake. Just a few people huffing and puffing should do it."

John peered around the open door. "The only ones I can see wouldn't have the strength for it." He glanced back at her. "Ready for the plunge?"

"Ummm . . . I guess so . . . I'll try to appear eager."

"I'd settle for relaxed," he murmured as he pulled her forward. "You look like a ghost yourself. Don't worry, they won't eat you." He turned around as they paused in the doorway. "Nobody's paying that much attention."

Maggie had to admit he was right. The only people in evidence were two women sorting papers on the counter of a gift shop to their right. One of them was the gray-haired lady in the purple pants suit whom Maggie had noticed earlier at the door. Her companion's appearance fitted more easily into the unorthodox surroundings of the sanctuary. She had jet-black hair which was pulled severely back from her face in a center part, and her stringbean figure was covered with a crimson flowing robe which reached her ankles. Maggie's fascinated gaze remained riveted on the woman's elaborate makeup which featured a sizable green jewel glued squarely in the middle of her forehead. Dark eyebrow pencil brought her brows up almost vertically, giving her face a "Dragon Lady" appearance—further enhanced by the thick gummy coating of green shadow on her eyelids.

"My God," John breathed in Maggie's ear. "Is it real?"

Since the apparition at that minute unwrapped a stick of gum and stuck it in her mouth, Maggie whispered back, "I guess so. Maybe she's one of Agatha's spirit friends."

"Can't be. She's either one of the Salem witches or something left over from Hallowe'en." His tone deepened. "Lord, this whole place is unbelievable. Look at the people in those paintings. I wonder what they represent—heaven or hell."

"I don't know. I suppose it's some symbolism." Maggie tried to appear impressed as they strolled over to stare at a large oil painting. "Do you see all those flames behind the man's head?"

"I can't get past the rhinestone sequins sprinkled on his eyeballs."

"You'd better take that frown off your face," she cautioned, "there are some other people coming in now." She watched six young men dressed mainly in beards and jeans head straight for a larger room which was separated from the gift annex by a limp purple curtain. "Let's go see what's happening in there."

John glanced back at the two women who were still busy sorting tracts and mimeographed papers on the counter. "Okay . . . we might as well. There's nothing going on here."

The first thing they saw when they passed into the auditorium was a three-foot-deep banner stretched from wall to wall, proclaiming, "Love Never Faileth."

"Very commendable," John murmured, ducking to get under it. "They must have a congregation of midgets."

"Shh . . . they'll hear you," Maggie warned.

"Who, for pete's sake? The place isn't swarming with people." He gestured graphically. The young men were subsiding in theater chairs at the side of the room and talking loudly among themselves. Down at the left-hand corner of the stage, a gray-haired woman whose wig was badly askew was practicing finger exercises on a small electric organ. Beyond her, a tall oak lectern took up the center of the stage. Purple satin covered the base of the lectern, which was hung with one of the most garish posters Maggie had ever seen. It featured a bizarre montage of flames, pyramids, and tortuous rope knots in surrealist confusion. On the wall behind it, a blank film screen was sandwiched between another row of Indian paintings—ranging this time from early Cherokee to contemporary Guru. What was obviously a spiritualist's cabinet partitioned off the remainder of the stage.

Suddenly the organist used both hands on the keyboard, and finger exercises became Bach. Poorly played

Bach, Maggie decided, but Bach all the same. Her eyes widened when a loose piece of plaster over the organist's head vibrated alarmingly as the woman hit a diminished seventh chord. The Sanctuary for Salvation might not last through the "Fugue in D Minor," let alone a minor earthquake.

At that moment, the sudden whir of an electric motor distracted her attention and she peered around John's shoulder to see a man wearing a yellow satin shirt and turban bent over a film projector on a metal stand at the far side of the room. Evidently he was having trouble making it work properly, because all that appeared on the screen were magnified particles of dust which became Mod-shaped Mexican jumping beans when the film snapped out of sprocket.

"Do you suppose he's the fellow in charge?" John mused. "If he is, we might as well go over and ask if he knows Agatha."

"What if we get thrown out?" Maggie started counting the congregation, who were now straggling in by twos and threes. "I thought there'd be a lot more people than this —it's hard to melt into a crowd of fourteen bodies."

"Forget it. Here comes that purple-pants lady from the gift counter."

Before he had finished speaking, the gray-haired woman was beside them, clutching a typewritten list in her hands.

"Excuse me," she began in a thin voice which matched her parchment-like face, "but I wonder if you're on our lists. The sanctuary is open by special invitation only this weekend, unless you made arrangements with some- one . . ." She peered hopefully at them.

"Actually, we're friends of Agatha Jarvis," John told her confidentially with a smile that made the elderly woman put up a hand and start fussing with her hair. "We just stopped by to say hello to her. Do you know if she's around this weekend?"

"Why, I think so. I saw her the day before yesterday." She simpered under his encouraging gaze. "Of course, if you're friends of Agatha's, it would be all right for you to stay during our service." Her eyes darted nervously toward the man who was now rethreading the projector. "Perhaps I'd better check with Dr. Vincent to make sure." She extracted a pencil from her tunic pocket after sorting through a miscellaneous collection that included a paper handkerchief, a bracelet of purple beads, and two lemon drops stuck together. "Could you give me your names?"

"I'm John Elliott. This is Miss Rome."

The woman scribbled the names and then managed a singularly sweet smile. "I'll ask the Doctor," she confided, before trotting off.

"Doctor of what, do you suppose?" Maggie asked, looking after her.

"I could make an educated guess."

"You're a cynic."

"Uh-huh," he muttered absently. "But how many doctors have you seen lately running around in satin turbans?"

"Not many, but we're old-fashioned at home." She was peering around his shoulder trying to watch the conversation by the side of the projector without being too obvious. "Oh, oh. I don't think we've impressed this one. He just gave us one quick look and has been shaking his head ever since."

"Damn!" John took her elbow. "Come on, let's eliminate the middle man and talk to the Doctor ourselves." He marched her purposefully across the aisle.

They were only a few feet away from the projector when Dr. Vincent saw them coming. He put up a hand to push his turban down more firmly on his head and strode off abruptly through a side exit.

"Hey . . . just a minute," John called, trying to catch up with him.

"Mr. Elliott, you can't go through there!" The gray-haired lady thrust herself in front of the door before John could reach the knob. "Absolutely no visitors are allowed in this part of the sanctuary." She was firmly edging them back up the aisle. Without causing a commotion they could only let themselves be herded toward the auditorium entrance.

"But what did Vincent say?" John asked in exasperation.

Any previous friendliness in the woman had completely disappeared. *"Dr.* Vincent," she stressed the formal title, "will only allow persons with invitations at this service. You'll have to go."

"Now just a minute." John wasn't capitulating without a struggle. "What about Miss Jarvis?"

"Miss Jarvis has left Carmel." The woman was marching them to the front door as she spoke. "She won't be attending any services at the sanctuary this weekend. If you want to get in touch with her, Dr. Vincent suggests you write a letter to her address in San Francisco."

"That's not good enough," John said angrily. "We want to contact her this weekend. Where can I find Vincent? I'll talk to him myself."

"The Doctor has gone into meditation and cannot see anyone . . ." the woman began huffily.

Maggie didn't let her finish. "In that case, we'd better go," she was tugging at John's arm as she spoke. "Right now."

"But Maggie . . ."

"After all, we don't want to bother anybody," Maggie told him insistently when he would have pulled loose.

He frowned down at her, "Haven't you forgotten the package in the trunk?"

She ignored that and turned to the elderly lady who

looked like a ruffled bantam hen guarding the doorway. "Thank you so much for your kindness," she told her. "We'll come back some weekend for a public service. Actually we're both *terribly* interested in learning about universal self-realization. Aren't we, John?"

"About what?" Then, as he felt a poke under his ribs, "Oh . . . sure. It's the only way to . . ." his voice trailed off when both women frowned. "Sounds very interesting," he managed finally.

"So, thank you again," Maggie said over her shoulder as she pulled him down the steps. "And we'll keep studying in the meantime."

"You don't have to act like a Seeing-Eye dog," John told her bitterly as they turned onto the sidewalk. "I can manage to find the car on my own. What the devil's gotten into you?" he added angrily as she started to cross the road. "Why wouldn't you let me chase that jerk Vincent? Obviously he knows where Agatha is. But, no, you have to let that pouter pigeon toss us out as if it didn't even matter."

"Just get in the car," Maggie said between her teeth. "I'd rather they didn't see us fighting it out in the street."

"Look here, Maggie . . ."

"No, *you* look, Mr. Elliott. I'm not fooling—I want to get in the car and go away from here."

"Okay, I give up." He shoved the key in the car door and unlocked it for her, but frowned as he started to help her in. "What's the matter? You look terrible suddenly."

"I'll be all right in a minute." She leaned her head back against the car seat and closed her eyes with relief.

"Maybe you should put your head down." He was opening the window beside her as he spoke.

"I'm not going to faint, but for a minute there, I thought that I was going to be sick," she confessed. "Thank heavens, that awful feeling's going away."

He nodded and then went around to the driver's side

and slid in beside her. "Probably the incense in that place —it was strong enough to choke a horse." He paused with his hand on the ignition. "Want me to wait a while?"

Maggie took a deep breath. "No, let's go." She watched him pull away from the curb and turn right on the next block before she said, "It wasn't the incense. I just got an almighty shock. Remember how Dr. Vincent put up his hand as if he wanted to shield his face when we got close to him?"

John glanced across at her and waited.

"There was a scar running along the underside of his arm," she went on. "It looked just like that one on the man in Agatha's apartment."

"I'll be damned!" He pulled over to the curb where he braked and turned to face her. "Are you sure?"

She frowned and rubbed her forehead fretfully. "In my own mind, I am. If you mean could I swear on a witness stand . . . no." Her glance met his. "But even the possibility that I'm right made my stomach turn over."

"I'd never have guessed it." He put the car back in gear and pulled out on the road again. "You were being so damned charming to Purple Pants Suit that I could have throttled you."

"I didn't want her to report anything that would make Vincent suspicious. Do you suppose he disappeared because he recognized me?"

"It's a possibility. Either that or he didn't want to be connected with Agatha Jarvis. I wonder why?" he mused. "From what our watchdog said, Agatha's well known at the sanctuary."

"That's hearsay," Maggie said wearily. "We're fresh out of any nitty-gritty evidence that the police would accept."

"But there's enough that the San Francisco police will be interested in hearing the story. I'll call them when we get back to the inn. They might want to make their own inquiries with the Carmel police department. Dr. Vincent was colorful enough to have attracted their attention before this."

"You mean his costume?"

"Nope, his occupation. You'd be surprised how much money people like Vincent can collect, despite the run-down appearance of the place. While you were noticing the scar on his arm, I was looking at the rings on his fingers. They might have been awfully good paste, but I'll bet they were worth plenty of money."

"That marquise stone in Agatha's apartment wasn't paste either," Maggie cut in thoughtfully, "and he could have dropped it. There's no use guessing though. He probably has an alibi for every night last week."

John pulled up to show his gate pass to the guard at the entrance of the Seventeen-Mile Drive and then increased his speed. "That's for the police to find out. They don't need any gifted amateurs like us. Besides, I promised Holly that nothing would spoil her engagement dinner tonight. You *do* feel better now, don't you?"

"I'm fine, thanks." She turned to partially close the window beside her. "All I needed was some space between Dr. Vincent and me. Actually, I'm glad we didn't have to wait for Miss Jarvis. I think that service of theirs would have lasted for hours."

"Well, they weren't in any hurry to get started," John agreed. "As far as Agatha's concerned, leave a note on her door and move up with Holly."

Maggie decided not to mention her own change of plans just then. "What about Banjo?" she asked feebly. "And Alfred?"

"Banjo can roost in my kitchen, and Alfred"—his voice took on grimmer tones—"Alfred can return to the front closet. Once Agatha makes an appearance, I'll have my attorney talk to her."

"Well, we'll see," she temporized.

He slowed for a sharp corner where the road wound through a grove of pine trees clustered by a rocky shelf overhanging the ocean. "I've heard evasive answers like that before. My sister has been using them all her life. Don't get any brainstorms, Miss Rome."

"In my weakened state I wouldn't dream of it," she countered. Then, deciding it was safer to change the subject, "What did you think about Holly's engagement?"

"We started celebrating last night after you'd gone to bed. Too bad you missed the champagne. Holly wanted to wake you up but . . ." from the way his voice trailed off, he was wishing he could change the subject, too.

"I'm glad you didn't. I went right to sleep," she lied glibly. "Anyway, I'm glad they finally made it. There wasn't any doubt of Tony's affection; the only thing that held him up was his decision to move his business."

"There's nothing strange about that. Since he was taking on a wife, he had to find the best way to support her. Not many of us believe that old proverb about 'In buying a horse or taking a wife, shut your eyes and throw yourself on the mercy of God.' "

"That doesn't say much for modern women," she protested. "Holly could have helped with their finances."

"Somebody has to make the final decision in a marriage," he said flatly. "In their case, I'd pick Tony. He was concerned about paying the grocery bills for the next forty years or so, and I respect him for it."

She flushed. "I'm surprised you didn't quote another proverb—'It's a silly flock where the ewe wears the bell.' "

"That makes more sense than you'll admit," he said calmly. "The original definition of 'husband' meant 'to manage or care for.' Most men still have that in mind when they choose a wife."

"I like your second word choice better than the first," she admitted. " 'Care for' has some warmth and affection at least."

"So you still approve of falling in love then? I'm glad." A smile played around his mouth. "For a minute, I thought the pillars of matrimony had crumbled."

She could only shake her head without answering. If he thought she was taking his talk about marriage seriously, he really *would* be amused, Maggie decided. The sooner she moved away from the building on Spirit Lane, the better it would be.

John turned into the entrance at Pebble Beach and let his glance rest fleetingly on her still profile. Her pale features made him frown and wish again that he'd never suggested coming to Carmel. Running into Vincent had been the crowning touch! Things had been bad enough before. He remembered his sudden, unreasoning flare of anger when Maggie had appeared at his bedroom door the previous night. In an instant she had become a carbon copy of all the other women he had known—charming, superficial, and conveniently available.

By the time he'd realized his mistake, his harsh words had shattered everything between them. Her bleak expression now only confirmed what he'd feared all day. Despite her polite facade, Maggie Rome wasn't letting him get near her again. She'd agreed to continue as the weekend guest for Holly's sake and Tony's—nothing more.

He edged toward the center of the road to avoid a pair of cyclists on the shoulder, but his mind was pursuing a straighter course. He'd simply have to take it easy for the rest of the weekend; avoid any more emotional disturbances. Try to shield Maggie from unpleasantness of *any* kind. Perhaps then she'd look the way she had the first day he'd seen her—bright, sparkling, lovely—as if Spring herself had come through the front door.

Even *that* day he hadn't been particularly charitable, he reminded himself—growling at her two minutes after they'd met. Not that he hadn't had good reason. How many men would be the life of the party after a plumber's wrench was dropped on their foot? His lips twitched at the memory, and Maggie, who had been disturbed by his long silence, wondered what the joke was.

John drove on past the crowded street near the pro shop and the putting green before turning left into the short cul-de-sac that led to their cottage. Once he'd parked in front of the unit, he helped Maggie get out and walked her to the front door.

"I'm going to do some phoning about Vincent," he said as she was still searching for her key. "You'd better rest until dinner. Want me to order some tea or something?"

"No, thanks." She was wishing devoutly that she had never mentioned feeling ill. Probably his blonde companion was the picture of glowing health.

Maggie shoved the key at the lock irritably, only to have John take it away from her and put it in right side up. "Thank you very much," she said, not meaning anything of the kind. "Will it be all right if I wear this dress to dinner? I didn't bring anything else that's suitable."

"There's always the one you wore last night," he pointed out gently. "I thought it was very nice."

She swallowed a desire to tell him in fifty words or less just why she'd never wear that dress again.

He must have caught at least part of her wavelength because he added hastily, "Actually, the one you're wearing will do very well. The best I can manage is a clean shirt." He stepped back. "I'll give you a ring if the police seem impressed by our report."

Evidently the police preferred to get their own evidence because the phone didn't ring again until it was time for dinner. By then, Holly had gotten back from her outing in Monterey and was changing into a white Thai silk frock which highlighted her dark beauty. The elegant lines of the dress together with the inner radiance brought about by her engagement to Tony made her positively breathtaking these days, Maggie decided with a twinge of envy. She smoothed the skirt of her own neat print and wavered for a moment when she saw the more flattering chiffon creation hanging in the closet. Then her jaw firmed with decision. She'd wear the print and forget about vanity. If she could only slam the door on her memory as easily, she would have been happier.

Despite her fears, the evening went along smoothly. Aided by champagne and a fabulous dinner of broiled lobster, conversation at their round table by the window flowed easily. Tony and Holly were living in a rarefied haze of happiness, and John was a genial, easygoing host. When it was time for dancing, they traded partners casually, and Maggie was careful to keep a discreet six inches away as John's arms went around her. If this bothered him, he certainly didn't let on—describing in exhaustive detail what she'd missed at the Carmel Mission that afternoon. He was still telling how the Mission was moved from Monterey to Carmel when Minda Carlisle and her father stopped by the table on their way to dinner. The tall blonde looked ravishing in aqua chiffon, and she hung on John's arm with flattering attention when he introduced Maggie. The Carlisles stood chatting for a few minutes while Maggie held her breath to see if they would be invited to join the party. When no invitation was forthcoming, they moved on—but not before Minda had dismissed Maggie in one comprehensive, icy glance.

"You don't seem to be in favor," Holly whispered as the music started up again. "I'm not surprised. Minda doesn't like competition."

"She doesn't have any," Maggie murmured in response. "Did you see those diamonds of hers? I felt like a poor match-seller in an Italian opera by comparison."

Holly chortled with laughter. "Don't you believe it! Minda would have you served up like a shish-kabob if she could get away with it. She's probably heard all about you from her father anyway. I know that he was asking questions during the golf game this morning and later when he took John into town."

"So *he* was the one in the car . . ."

"Of course." Holly was still amused. "Actually he's very nice."

"There doesn't seem to be any lack of money in the family," Maggie observed.

"Nope. Just common sense. Minda was behind the door when that was dealt out."

"What are you two grizzling about?" Tony wanted to know as he pulled his chair closer and leaned over Holly's shoulder.

Her eyebrows went up. "You don't honestly think we'd tell you?"

John overheard that. "Give up," he told Tony. "Holly was claiming the Fifth Amendment before most people even knew it existed. Besides"—he shoved back his chair and stood up—"from the look on her face, she's just finished shredding someone's reputation. I really can't understand why you want to marry her," he added with brotherly candor before turning to Maggie. "Come on, let's dance. We'll let Tony apply the thumbscrews on his own."

Holly was reaching for her purse. "In that case, we'll pick some place that's a little more private."

Tony obediently got to his feet. "I feel like a walk along the shore myself." He grinned at John and Maggie. "You'll excuse us? We'll see you back at the rooms eventually."

"Make sure you don't stage any elaborate farewells on the threshold," John warned them. "If you wake me up, I'll throw a shoe at you."

Holly assumed a martyred look. "You see what I've had to put up with all these years," she told her intended.

"Is it any wonder that I leaped at a chance for marriage? I would have accepted any reasonable offer, believe me."

Tony's dark glance lingered intimately on her. "We'll go into that a little later. Thumbscrews may be too good for you after all."

"I could have told you that," John told him. "We'll see you in the morning, if not before. Damn! We've missed the fox trot," he added for Maggie's benefit, leading her to the floor. "I hope you don't expect great things in a tango."

"Ever since I saw Rudolph Valentino do it in an old-time movie, every other man has been a disappointment," she said solemnly.

He pulled her into his arms, ignoring her six-inch buffer zone. "You can't expect me to get worked up like that. Probably Valentino's partner had a rose in her teeth. That makes a difference." He felt her shoulders shake with laughter before pulling her closer so that she had to let her body mold itself against the hard length of his. They danced for a few moments in silence, neither wanting to break the spell. When the orchestra finished, Maggie kept her eyes on the floor, still unable to meet his gaze.

"I take back everything I said." He addressed the top of her bent head. "All these years, I've been doing the tango an injustice."

The pianist rippled a closing chord on the keyboard signifying an intermission for the musicians. Thank heavens, Maggie thought. She shook her head slightly to clear it.

John touched her shoulder and turned her back toward the table like an automaton. "If we stand here much longer, they'll think we're part of the floor show." His voice was whimsical.

Maggie pulled up at the edge of the floor. "Actually, I'm rather tired," she began.

"But it's still early. You'll have a nightcap, at least?"

"No, thanks." She did manage to meet his glance then. "There's no reason for you to cut the evening short. I'm sure that you can find a dancing partner by the time the musicians get back." She debated suggesting Minda Carlisle, but another glance at John's remote expression made her think again. "Of course, that's up to you," she added hurriedly.

"So it is." He moved to their table and signed the check. "Got everything?" Evidently it was a rhetorical question because he was guiding her out of the room before she could nod her head.

They walked through the lobby and out the broad front door. Maggie tried to sound reasonably calm as she asked, "What happened when you called the police this afternoon? I was going to mention it earlier, but . . ."

". . . you saved it for a safe topic of conversation on the way home," he drawled as they turned down the deserted path to their rooms. "The feminine sex has a strange sense of timing."

She flushed in the darkness, wishing that she hadn't been so obvious. "I don't know what you mean by that. It was a perfectly normal thing to ask." She kept her pace brisk as they moved past the dense shrubbery. "What did they say about Dr. Vincent?"

"The San Francisco detective I wanted wasn't in, so I had to leave a message. I'd liked to have called the Carmel police and asked about Vincent."

"You could hardly complain about the looks of his scar or the fact that he wears a yellow turban."

"I know. That's why I didn't. At least I can call the fellow in San Francisco again tomorrow if we haven't heard by then." He made his voice more cheerful. "Holly and Tony are apt to be a while. Are you sure you won't change your mind about that nightcap?"

"Honestly, I don't need one—not after the champagne

at dinner." She fumbled for her key as they turned up the lighted path to their building. "I expect I'll go right to sleep after all the excitement," she added brightly so that he wouldn't feel obligated to stay in the building.

"I hope you do." He leaned against the passage wall and watched as she unlocked her door.

Maggie kept her smile glued on as she stood in the open doorway. "Well . . . thank you for a lovely evening . . ."

"Sure there's nothing else I can do?" He sounded slightly amused as his glance swept over her dress.

"Not a thing," she flared, and then bit down on her lip. "Are we leaving early in the morning?"

"Not early enough to set an alarm, so don't worry about it." He pushed himself upright in a lazy movement. " 'Night, Maggie—sleep well," he drawled and moved down the hall.

It was at least forty-five minutes later before Maggie heard a noise of someone moving on her patio deck. By then, she had changed to pajamas and been in her bed for some time. Despite her declared intention of going right to sleep, she was apparently destined for another night of insomnia. She had just decided that John Elliott should be proclaimed a menace to women's health, like the warning on cigarette packages, when she became aware of a rustling presence outside the sliding glass doors.

Her body stiffened as she heard the intermittent shuffle of someone on the gritty concrete. She had noted the thin coating of sand on the deck earlier in the day and decided it probably was blown there from the nearby sand bunkers which rimmed the eighteenth hole of the golf course. Now the rasping surface made the intruder sound as if he were shuffling along in a soft-shoe routine.

Maggie's hand reached out for the switch on her bedside lamp, but she hesitated before flipping it on. Obviously the person on the other side of the glass would beat a hasty retreat at the first sign of light. It would be better if she could get across the room to the telephone and call for a security guard.

There was another muffled sound on the other side of the window which came through the small ventilation pane beside the sliding panel. Then she heard the barest chink of metal as if something heavy had been deposited on the concrete.

Maggie's expression glistened with fright as she tried to visualize who was behind the curtained glass. Was it an ordinary sneak-thief planning to break into a darkened room or someone whose twisted mind was bent on more unspeakable crimes?

She couldn't just lie there passively until he smashed the lock on the sliding door and was in the room with her. Unbidden, her hand went up to her throat where the skin was still bruised.

That memory was enough to make her swing her feet over the side of the bed onto the floor. She blessed the thick shag rug which muffled any squeaky boards as she stood beside the bed, trembling with emotion.

Her strongest impulse was to race to the hall door and escape down the passage to John's room. She shivered, as much from the cool air penetrating her thin nylon pajamas as from pure nervousness. It was a pity she couldn't rummage for her robe in the closet, she thought and then shook her head despairingly. Why worry about modesty at a time like this!

She crept across to the telephone which rested on the dressing table partway to the windows. She lifted the receiver and crouched over it. Now! If she could only muffle the dialing so that it couldn't be heard.

Her finger was just fumbling for the "O" on the dial when suddenly there was a sharp clang of metal from the deck and a muffled curse of pain.

Almost simultaneously, the deep-throated barking of the German shepherd in the next unit split the still night air, and Maggie saw the reflection of lights going on in his quarters. The shepherd was in a frenzy of barking by that time, and his paws could be heard scratching frantically at the wall. Outside the window, there was a violent but muffled epithet, a sudden rustle on the sandy floor, and then nothing.

Maggie sank onto the rug in relief, the telephone still clutched to her chest as she heard the shepherd's owners issuing sharp commands to calm the dog. All Maggie could do was crouch by the end of the dressing table and rest her head against the cool wood as reaction set in.

It wasn't more than thirty seconds later before John was pounding on the hall door, shouting, "Maggie! Are you all right? For God's sake, let me in there!"

Still dazed, Maggie left the telephone in the middle of the rug and stumbled to unlock the door which was vibrating under his frantic pounding.

John almost fell inside as she twisted the knob. Then she was being clutched tightly, thankfully, in his arms.

"Maggie, darling—are you all right?" he asked roughly as he bent over her.

"Uh-huh," she responded automatically, but her nose was pressed so tightly against his chest that he could hardly hear her. Gently he tugged on her hair, "Let me look at you and see for myself." He glanced around in some confusion. "I'll turn on the light—it's like a tomb in here."

"Don't go away!" She burrowed into his open shirt front like a wounded animal.

"But what happened?"

"There was somebody outside the window trying to get in. I was absolutely terrified."

John muttered something profane and pushed her down on the end of the bed as he moved toward the glass sliding panel. "Stay there, while I take a look around," he commanded.

She heard him unlock the glass door and slide it aside before he disappeared out on the deck. As soon as his footsteps sounded on the concrete, the shepherd burst out in another volley of barking. Then Maggie heard the low rumble of voices—evidently John was talking to the couple in the next unit.

She shivered again and frowned as she glanced down at her thin lilac pajamas. Almost absently she stood up and went over to the closet to pull her matching robe from a hook on the back of the door. She was still buttoning it when John came back into the room and slid the glass panel closed behind him. His glance encompassed her shaking fingers and he moved over to gently finish the job for her.

"Sure that's warm enough?" He indicated the knee-length nylon robe.

She nodded and subsided once again on the end of the bed, strangely shy now that life was returning to normal. "Maybe you could turn up the heat, though." She watched him go over to the thermostat, noting that he was still dressed in the same clothes he'd worn earlier, although he'd shed his coat and tie and had loosened his shirt at the throat. "I take it you didn't find anything outside," she said, keeping her voice level.

John leaned against the wall by the heat control. "That's right. There's nothing like a hefty German shepherd for discouraging callers. His owners are calling the desk to report it."

Maggie shuddered. "Thank heavens for that. I don't know whether I made too much noise when I started to telephone or not—but that's when the man dropped something and started the dog barking."

"Who were you calling, Maggie?"

She looked up and then dropped her eyes to the bedspread again. "The desk clerk, I guess. I really hadn't figured it out. Actually I wanted to tear out of the room and beat on your door."

"Why didn't you, for God's sake? How do you think I feel . . . coming in at the end of it?"

"I couldn't." Her clear gaze held his then. "I remembered last night . . . and I . . . just couldn't."

In a second, he'd reached down to pluck her from the end of the bed. "Since when have you cared what I thought?" he asked roughly, his arms like a vise around her.

Maggie tried to push away. She tried for a good three or four seconds, then she simply decided it was too much trouble and relaxed against his broad chest where she'd wanted to be from the beginning.

"I asked you a question." His hands were gentle on her shoulders. "How long have you cared what I thought about you?"

"Too long." She raised her head defiantly, but her eyes softened when she saw the look on his face.

"Not as long as I have," he confessed.

"When?" She barely breathed the word.

"About the time I carried your things into Agatha's apartment. I think you worked a spell on me." Then he abandoned conversation as his mouth came down over her parted lips. The kiss started in light, exploratory fashion but changed abruptly to a hard, possessive embrace that left both of them breathless when they drew apart.

John could only stare down at her glowing face like a man mesmerized by a miracle. "I always thought we'd get there," he managed finally, "but you've certainly led me a hell of a chase. It'll take me years to recover."

"I've had a few qualms myself," she admitted. "You didn't have to cope with blondes who wait in hotel lobbies."

"Well, since it's been such a thrash, we'll take a few minutes to enjoy what we could have been enjoying days ago if you hadn't been so stubborn." He pulled her back into his embrace and nodded approvingly as her arms crept up around his neck. "You know," he added conversationally, "one of these days, I'm going to kiss you when you have all your clothes on."

"That's a terrible thing to say."

He chuckled as her body stiffened and shook her gently. "Stop being such a puritan, my darling idiot. Don't you know when a man's in love with you?"

Her resolutions melted at that declaration. "Are you— *really?*"

"You take a lot of convincing." Then his voice deepened. "We'll discuss my honorable intentions later."

"What do you have in mind for right now?" she managed to whisper.

"Now?" His hands slipped down her back caressingly and Maggie abandoned every thought of resistance. His lips were close to her ear as he murmured, "Now behave yourself, Maggie darling—and let me kiss you properly."

Chapter
EIGHT

"I wish you wouldn't look at me like that," Maggie told John the next afternoon as they waited in the car for a traffic light at a busy intersection.

"Like what?" he countered.

"You know what I mean," she said in confusion.

"And all the time I thought I was doing so well." He eased the car forward and turned onto the freeway entrance at Carmel's city limits. "What bothers you especially?"

She laughed despite herself. "If you think I'm going to give you a detailed list of the effect you have on my physical condition, Mr. Elliott—you're crazy. Besides, you heard enough last night to send your ego soaring."

"So why is there at least twelve inches on the seat between us this afternoon?"

"Because it's safer that way," she admitted. "I can't even think straight if you're much closer."

He grinned but kept his attention straight ahead. "That makes two of us. And since we're on a freeway, I'd *better* behave."

She sighed audibly.

"Is that relief or disappointment?" he wanted to know.

"I'm not sure," she admitted honestly. "You should have had Holly waken me earlier—I feel as if I'm still dreaming."

"You needed the rest," he was serious then. "It was

close to three by the time the hotel detective and the police stopped asking questions and combing the bushes outside."

"I know. It's a wonder that poor German shepherd didn't have a stroke. He was ready to eat everybody in sight by then. Holly told me that his owners finally shut him in their car to quiet him."

John nodded absently. "It was quite a night for everybody. Reach in the glove compartment and get my sun glasses, will you? I think this good weather's going to last."

Maggie rooted around until she found the leather case and then polished the lenses carefully before handing them to him. He smiled his thanks as he took them but kept his attention on the highway ahead. Maggie stared at his profile fondly, thinking what a relief it was not to have to hide her love any longer. She would always remember the enchanted quarter-hour they'd spent before Holly had returned from her stroll and the police started arriving.

"You promised you'd tell me what I missed this forenoon," she reminded him. "Did you finally get in touch with the detective in San Francisco?"

"I talked to him a couple of times. He ran a search on Dr. Vincent and then called me back. There's a man who uses that alias—actually the record shows that he's a confidence man and jewel thief. Right now they need a positive identification. I'm supposed to check in as soon as we get back to the city."

Maggie bit her lip thoughtfully. "A jewel thief," she repeated. "Maybe there's a connection with that diamond in Agatha's apartment."

"Go to the head of the class, my love. Actually, I showed that diamond to a friend of mine. He's assistant manager for the San Francisco branch of one of the best-known jewelry firms in the United States." Maggie looked impressed as he named a shop whose name was an international byword for fine gems. "Even in a store like that," John went on, "they just have a handful of expensive marquise diamond rings on display. Because of their rareness, a stolen marquise diamond is hard to fence. They're just too damned distinctive. Anyhow, when my friend examined the stone from Agatha's apartment, he was able to give me a complete technical description."

"Wait a minute," she protested. "You're going too fast. How can you describe a diamond other than by saying it's beautiful?"

"By weight, color, type, the number of imperfections . . . things like that. And listen to this." John's voice was laced with excitement. "The people in the shop were pretty sure they remembered who had purchased that ring about five or six years ago. My friend promised to check the store records and the most likely insurance companies in town."

"Have you spoken to him since?"

"You bet. Right after I talked with the police this morning and heard that Dr. Vincent had a history of jewel thefts."

Maggie's eyes were sparkling. "What did they say?"

"That we're pretty good amateur detectives. An insurance company confirmed that particular marquise diamond or its identical twin was stolen eighteen months ago from a Mrs. Robert Lincoln who has homes in San Francisco and Carmel. According to their records, the thieves made quite a haul. None of the jewelry has been recovered."

"I'll be darned," Maggie breathed. "Carmel! That makes an awful lot of coincidences, doesn't it?"

"Too many. That's why I suggested the insurance company get in touch with the police department now that the marquise has reappeared." He frowned. "It would be interesting to know exactly what else Mrs. Lincoln lost that night."

Maggie was inclined to agree with him. "What I can't understand," she persisted, "is where Agatha Jarvis comes into all this. Or even *if* she does."

"There isn't any proof of criminal implication. Maybe Vincent simply knew that Agatha was away. They apparently moved in the same spiritual circles. And if it *was* Vincent in the apartment that night, what better time to see what he could pick up . . . literally. Of course, he didn't know that you were occupying the apartment." John waited until they had safely passed a heavily loaded oil tanker before he glanced over to her thoughtful profile for confirmation.

"In that case, where did the diamond come from?" she wanted to know.

"That's a good question. What do you want to bet that the police will ask the same thing. Especially when they catch up with Dr. Vincent."

"Isn't he at the sanctuary any longer?"

"At the latest count, the sanctuary boasted one caretaker, one lady in a purple pants suit, and some witch with an emerald plastered on her forehead." John grinned reminiscently. "That's an actual quote from the security guard back at the inn. He'd talked to the Carmel police this morning."

A look of satisfaction surged over Maggie's face. "Then they *were* interested in our story last night . . . about visiting the sanctuary and seeing Dr. Vincent, I mean."

"They're more interested in finding who was prowling around the inn last night. They weren't overlooking the possibility of Vincent being connected with that attempted break-in since you were convinced he'd done it before. At any rate, they went down to check his alibi this morning. Unfortunately, he'd left, for a period of meditation—the lady with the emerald told them." As

Maggie caught her breath, he added hastily, "Don't get any ideas about her emerald. It's pure paste. Vincent wasn't scattering his favors around the high priestess or whoever she was."

"What a pity. She certainly tried hard."

"Well, she didn't appeal to me either, but you might try gluing a rhinestone on your forehead some evening and see what happens."

"I'll do that," she promised just as solemnly, "the very day my harem costume arrives."

"It sounds better all the time," he said.

"At least I wouldn't have to worry about your scheduling a golf game and not showing up for the floor show."

"Ouch." He winced visibly. "I knew that would come back to haunt me."

"You're darned right! What was I supposed to think?"

"You already had me in the doghouse from the night before," he explained. "All I could do was keep away from you and hope that you wouldn't do anything drastic —like leaving town. That's why I asked Tony to remind you of Alfred in the trunk. By the time I met you at the sanctuary, I hoped you would have cooled off." He laughed ruefully. "You were cool all right. I could feel the frost ten feet away from the car."

She made her voice stern. "It served you right. I'd had a terrible day. As a matter of fact, the night before wasn't so great either."

His fingers moved from the steering wheel to rest for just a moment on her thigh. Then he shot her an amused glance and replaced his hand on the wheel. "Thank the lord, that's in the past. Personally, I prefer the present, and the future looks great." He kept his tone businesslike with an effort. "If you don't have anything planned tomorrow, we might go downtown and visit my jeweler friend."

"To discuss the marquise diamond?"

"That and other things. How would you like to choose an engagement ring?"

"Oh," her lips curved in delight. "I hadn't even thought about that."

"Well, *I* have. You can choose whichever style you like best."

"Anything *but* a marquise."

"It all depends on how you look at things," he said judiciously. "Frankly, if it hadn't been for Agatha, and the apartment, and her canary, you never would have come to Spirit Lane to drop a wrench on my foot."

"I hoped you were going to forget that."

"Never. Remind me to show you my scar sometime."

She glanced at him unbelievingly and then started to laugh. "You would, too."

"Damned right. I could have been wounded for life," he said in a righteous tone.

"Next time I drop a wrench on you, I'll be careful to hit the other foot," she promised.

"What am I letting myself in for? Maybe we'd better make this a long engagement," he threatened.

Maggie bit her lip. "Actually I think we'd better," she said quietly.

"You can't be serious." John's expression sobered and he shot a quick glance at her. "Why, Maggie? Surely you don't have any doubts?"

The quiet logic of his tone made her stare miserably out the car window. "It's not that," she confessed, "but everything's happened so fast. We hardly know each other."

"In one sense that's true. But look at it another way . . . we've crowded a lot of living into the last few days. Right now, I feel as if I'd known you half my life."

She nodded but was still on the defensive. "That's the way it seems to me, too. But if we're going to be married . . ."

"Look here, angel, the word is *when* . . . not if."

Her tone softened at that. "All right. When we're married—I don't want it to be one of these 'Let's fly to Las Vegas' things. I want the minister I've known all my life . . . and my family . . . even the cousins who aren't speaking to each other." She glanced appealingly at him. "Is that being silly and demanding?"

"Of course not," he assured her. "Darling, you don't have to defend your choice of wedding. I'm pretty demanding myself—making damn sure that you're the bride."

"You're being so nice about it. I might have known."

"Would you rather I snarled and threatened you with the back of my hand?" His features lightened. "Don't worry, you can take your time and get used to being engaged. When I get back from this Alaskan project, I'll expect to hear all about the wedding plans."

"When will that be?"

"If things go as planned . . . about a month." He rubbed the back of his neck reflectively. "But cross your fingers that we don't hit a snag. That Alaskan weather can be temperamental and throw our work schedules off." He saw her frown and added soothingly, "Anyhow, we'll shop for the ring tomorrow, if that's okay."

"I'd like to very much," she confessed shyly. "That will give me time to come back to earth gradually. I'm still in heaven after last night."

"Damn it, Maggie. You would say a thing like that when I'm driving on the freeway and can't do a thing about it. And don't laugh—just wait until tonight. In the meantime," he reached over and pinched her arm smartly.

"Ouch!" She pulled away, rubbing the offended member. "What's that for?"

"To let you know I'm real. There's nothing ethereal

about our engagement, either. Remember that, Miss Rome."

Maggie blinked. She looked like a woman who had expected to find a mouse in the corner but found a tiger licking his chops instead. "Remind me to dig out that wrench when we get back to the apartment," she told him. "I'm coming back down to earth fast."

"Good," his grin taunted her. "I hoped you would."

It was late afternoon when they turned off the Bay-shore freeway and made their way through crowded San Francisco streets toward Russian Hill.

John frowned as he checked his watch. "Hell's bells! It's later than I thought. Do you mind if I drive straight to the police station? Then I can still see that detective before he goes off shift."

"Of course not," she assured him. "I'll wait in the car for you."

"There's no need for that. You take the car and drive on home. You'll want to change for dinner, and I told Holly and Tony we'd join them about six thirty at that new place on Nob Hill."

"But how will you get home?"

He shrugged negligently. "There are plenty of cabs at this time of night. That won't be any problem."

"Well, if you're sure . . ."

John turned left on an arterial and increased his speed slightly. "I am. Don't worry, I'll be as quick as I can. It shouldn't take long to look at a mug shot. Either it *is* Vincent or it isn't." He gave her a sidelong glance. "Do me a favor and wear that chiffon dress again tonight, will you? You know the one I mean . . ."

"You're darned right I do. How could I forget it?" She started to smile. "I'm afraid it might be tempting fate."

"What are you worried about?" he countered. "Holly will be around to take care of the buttons tonight."

"I wouldn't even consider it if she weren't," Maggie

told him tartly. "It isn't that—I guess I'm superstitious. The dress didn't bring good luck the other night."

"Then we'll exorcise the spell tonight and change our luck. Do it for me, Maggie. You looked positively beautiful in that creation."

She smiled across at him as he braked in front of a brick building housing the precinct police station. "In that case, I'd love to."

"Fine." John got out of the car and hesitated before closing the door. "Want to come around or slide across?"

"It's easier to slide across in all this traffic," she was suiting her action to the words. "I hope I don't damage your beautiful car. The streets in this city are too darned narrow."

"Just don't try to pass anything bigger than you are," he said as he slammed the door and stepped back. "Don't worry about the luggage. I'll unload the trunk when I get home. See you later."

Maggie smiled and waggled her fingers at him before driving off. She soon found that handling a strange car in the afternoon traffic took all her concentration, and when she finally arrived at 727 Spirit Lane, she could only sigh with relief that all four fenders were still unscathed.

The old brick apartment building looked peaceful and welcoming in the late afternoon sunlight. On the parking strip, the neat shade trees made a restful picture as their branches cast lengthening shadows over the deserted sidewalk.

Maggie turned off the ignition, put the gear shift in "park" position, and carefully set the emergency brake before getting out of the car. The street was empty of traffic, so she could indulge in a satisfying stretch beside the open car door. It was amazing how stiff a person could get after only a few hours driving. She bent down and looked in the side mirror, automatically pushing her hair into place. Too bad there wasn't time for a visit to the beauty shop before the night's festivities. Like John, she glanced at her watch then and hurriedly slammed the door. She certainly didn't have enough time to be standing in the middle of the street dreaming!

Despite his promise about the luggage, she marched purposefully back to the trunk of the car and unlocked it. One of the first things on her evening's priority list was pressing the dress packed in her overnight case. She reached in the trunk for her bag and then let her hand rest on the handle without picking it up, her glance still riveted on the cardboard carton containing poor Alfred's ashes. It sat stolidly in place next to the spare tire as it had all weekend.

Maggie straightened, staring with displeasure into the open trunk. It just didn't seem right to leave the urn there while she callously went about preparing for a gala evening. Call it sacrilegious or whatever . . . Alfred should be moved out of the trunk into the safety and respectability of a hall closet before other things were enjoyed.

She bent over the trunk again and pulled the carton closer so that she could get a firm grip on it. If she left the urn in Agatha's apartment hallway, John could transfer it to his closet later. Maggie hoisted it in her arms carefully and used her elbow to push the trunk lid closed before she went into the building.

As she walked through the entrance foyer, her mind was busy making a schedule of "things to do." First, she would tuck Alfred safely out of the way in her apartment, then she'd go back to the car and get her overnight bag out of the trunk. Once she'd pressed her dress and hung it up, she'd try and make running repairs to her hairdo.

The sight of John's apartment door made her wish that she'd asked for his latchkey so that she could go in and move Banjo back to his familiar surroundings. She stopped walking for a minute and put her ear against the door frame. Still no canary trills from inside the apartment. Maggie smiled wryly. Banjo was consistent; he wasn't singing anywhere.

She moved on down the hall to Agatha's apartment and put the cardboard carton carefully down on the floor while she unearthed her front-door key from the bottom of her purse. Why was it that keys always hid themselves when they were needed? Finally she liberated this one from under her checkbook and coin purse and inserted it in the lock.

Once the door swung open, she bent down to lift the carton again and nudged the heavy door shut behind her with a sideways motion of her hip. She was so preoccupied with Alfred's remains that she didn't bother to glance up until an inner sense told her that she wasn't alone in the apartment.

Her worst fears were confirmed when Agatha Jarvis appeared suddenly in the kitchen doorway and beamed at her. Maggie could only stand gaping, scarcely able to believe her eyes.

"Ah, there you are, my dear." Agatha blinked like a mole emerging into sudden sunlight. "My voices told me that you'd be coming and you're right on time." Her glance flicked over the carton in Maggie's arms. "Something tells me that you have dear Alfred with you, too. How thoughtful of you to take such good care of him."

"I wasn't given much choice," Maggie said dryly. "Seeing you is an unexpected surprise, too."

"Well, don't look so stricken." Agatha's manner was offhand. "I won't be staying. I just stopped by to get some things I'd left behind."

Maggie managed to pull herself together. "Actually I've been looking for you all weekend."

"Have you, dear? How very nice. I suppose I should have given you an address, but I had to leave so suddenly." Her landlady adjusted a maroon scarf which was tucked inside the collar of her gray squirrel coat. The molting coat, like Agatha, had seen far better days. "Where is dear little Banjo? I looked in the kitchen but I couldn't find him."

"John . . . er . . . Mr. Elliott's keeping him." Agatha's unblinking stare put Maggie on the defensive, and she found herself babbling. "You forgot to leave a diet for him. He's not singing at all, and we've been terribly worried."

"Never mind." Agatha closed the distance between them. "Banjo will sing when the cosmic forces are right. Animals know these things. Now—if you'll just give me poor Alfred and my urn . . ."

Maggie started to hand over the box when a sudden noise from the bedroom made her pull it back instinctively. "Who's in there? I thought you were alone," she accused Agatha.

"A friend insisted on accompanying me." The other's voice went up in pitch as she called casually. "You might as well come out now, Doctor. Margaret knows you're here."

"My lord," Maggie breathed as she saw the man stride in from the bedroom. "Dr. Vincent! And you *are* the same one," she added impulsively. "You were here in the apartment that night."

Vincent's deep-set features were in a surly mold and his stocky frame seemed to hold a leashed power. He had shed his yellow turban and tunic for an uninspiring tweed topcoat, but there was nothing nondescript about the scathing glance he shot her way. Then, deliberately, he turned to Agatha. "I *told* you it was a mistake to come here today. You should have let me handle it by myself later on."

"I don't think so, Vincent." Agatha's fluttery manner dropped away and she was the most relaxed of all of them as she stood there. "You're too heavy-handed, dear

Doctor. Look what happened the last time." From her analytical tone, she might have been discussing the weather.

Maggie glanced from one to the other. "The marquise diamond . . ." she murmured with dawning comprehension. "That's why you've come back, isn't it?"

"How clever of you, Margaret. I was sure you'd found it," Agatha said in a pleased tone. "It's such a pretty thing, and Vincent's very fond of it. He insisted on recovering his property—that's why he came along today."

"If you hadn't been such a damned fool to leave it here in the first place, none of this would have happened," Vincent spat out viciously.

"That's quite enough!" Agatha cut into his tirade. "All we have to do is pick it up and be on our way. Of course, this time I'll take Alfred, as well." She reached out again for the cardboard box.

Maggie clutched it instinctively as she took a step backward. "I can't give it to you. I don't have it."

Agatha's lips thinned. "Don't be ridiculous, girl. It's right there in front of our very eyes. Don't try stalling for time in such a silly way."

"I've heard enough." Vincent brushed past Agatha and reached over roughly to jerk the box from Maggie's grasp. "This is taking too long. Now—let's have the diamond."

"I don't have the diamond." Maggie shrank back from him against the wall. "That's what I was trying to tell you."

Vincent grabbed her wrist with his free hand and twisted it cruelly, ignoring her whimper of pain. "Don't give me that! Where is it? Where've you put it? Tell me, or I'll . . ."

"Vincent, be careful of that box! I don't want that urn broken," Agatha warned him sharply.

"Is that all that bothers you?" Maggie asked aghast.

"At the moment. You'd better tell him where the diamond is, Margaret." The older woman smoothed the fur of her coat collar. "Vincent's temper is hard to control. It gets him in trouble all the time." She smiled strangely. "Don't you remember?"

"I remember very well," Maggie started to say and then gritted her teeth as Vincent's strong fingers bit into her wrist. "The diamond is gone, I tell you. Mr. Elliott took it to a jeweler last week. By now, it has been turned over to the insurance company or the police." She was unprepared for the effect of her words on the man beside her, and his savage pressure on her wrist made her light-headed with pain.

"DAMN . . . there's fifteen thousand dollars down the drain!" he snarled. Turning, he shot a baleful glance at Agatha. "You and your bright ideas about leaving the stuff here in the apartment. Why in hell didn't you bring it to Carmel? Now we'll have to go to the trouble of taking dear Margaret along with us." He drawled the name out hatefully.

"Why?" Agatha snapped, as the color drained out of Maggie's cheeks. "What do we want with her?"

"She can call Elliott for us and arrange the return of the diamond. It's a fair trade—we get the diamond and he gets his girl friend back in good condition."

"But what if he can't?" Maggie whispered.

Vincent's dark eyes were almost opaque. "Then he still gets you—but not in very good condition. Understand?" His grasp tightened suggestively.

Maggie moistened her lips with the tip of her tongue and glanced shakily at Agatha. "You'd let him do that?"

There was a moment of silence before Agatha shrugged, "Why not? It might work. Vincent's so practical."

"But what about the sanctuary?" Maggie appealed. "You'd never be able to go back to it. The police would be waiting . . ."

He broke in roughly. "The psychic gag's been drained dry in that neighborhood. We were cutting out of town anyhow. Agatha forgot to tell you."

"That's enough talk." His explanations stirred the older woman when nothing else seemed to. "Bring her along, Vincent. We'll try it your way. Get her out to the car before that damned landlord of mine comes pounding on the door." She picked up an attaché case from the end of the davenport and gave a final look around. "I'll carry the box. You'll have your hands full with her."

"I'm not going," Maggie announced loudly. "Let go of my hand or I'll scream this place down."

"Just try it, sister. You won't have a voice left to make that telephone call," Vincent threatened. "And hold still, or I'll take care of you right now." He shoved the box toward Agatha as Maggie yanked and struggled in his grasp.

"Look out, you fool, don't drop it!" Agatha shouted as Vincent's fist swung toward Maggie before she could clutch the slipping box.

Maggie saw the blow coming and pulled backward with a terrified scream at the same instant the box hit the floor between their feet.

The corrugated top flew open and Alfred's ashes cascaded across the rug. Winking like pieces of flame in the middle of them was the most beautiful diamond necklace Maggie had ever seen.

"My diamonds," shouted Vincent, making a grab for them.

"My urn," moaned Agatha, scrabbling on the rug for the antique porcelain lying on its side half out of the carton.

"My ribs," moaned Maggie, painfully rubbing her side which had suffered when she fell against the end table.

"I'll be damned! We couldn't have timed it better if we'd carried a stopwatch," a gray-haired man in the doorway said to the man behind him. Then, to the figures on the floor, he added, "Freeze, right there, you two. You're under arrest."

Maggie dazedly watched him level the .38 revolver in his hand with calm authority. She turned her head with an effort and saw John start to thread his way across the room toward her.

As he stepped over Vincent's legs and the gleaming Capo di Monte urn, Maggie felt her own knees give way. Then, looking strangely like a slow-motion sequence in a film strip, she slithered gently to the floor—simply because she didn't have the strength to stand up any longer.

Chapter
NINE

Later that night, the waiter diligently serving a party of four people at a rooftop table wouldn't have suspected such goings-on.

All he noticed was that both women were exceptionally good-looking—even in a city where he'd gotten used to beautiful women. The brunette in a black-and-white print was the one he'd noticed first, but the brown-haired young woman in coral chiffon was the one who held his interest. Not that she paid any attention to him; her glance seldom wandered from the face of the man sitting next to her.

None of the party had left the table for dancing even as the lengthy dinner progressed. They hadn't bothered to look at the scenery either, so it was obvious they weren't tourists.

The waiter lingered a minute by his station to stare out at the fairyland of city lights stretching in all directions around Nob Hill. The prosaic Bay Bridge became a thing of beauty at nighttime when its utilitarian gray supports were cloaked with darkness and the steady stream of automobiles became a serpentine of white headlights. Skyscrapers were changed to oddly shaped geometric forms—the Transamerica Building with its pointed top looking the most bizarre of all. Unique Chinatown buildings were spotlights of color and added a vibrant, flamboyant touch to their black-and-white counterparts.

The restaurant waiter took a deep breath and then glanced again at the foursome in the corner. They might not be scrutinizing the scenery but he'd never seen a party look happier. It must be a celebration of some kind, he decided, picking up the coffee pot and advancing on their table. As he refilled their cups, his impersonal manner thawed. Celebrations meant better tips than usual. And unless his intuition was wrong, this tip would be one to remember!

Maggie wasn't aware of the coffee being poured until her cup was full again. Then she said, "Oh, heavens, I shouldn't have any more. I've had so much caffeine now that I'll be awake until daybreak."

Tony accepted his refill more philosophically. "I might as well have an excuse for not sleeping. I never close an eye on an airplane anyhow." He pushed back his shirt cuff and looked at his watch. "We'd better be leaving pretty soon."

"You'll be exhausted when you finally get to New York," Holly said with some concern. "I wish you could have put the trip off for another day or so."

"The sooner I go back and sort through the negatives and equipment I want moved, the sooner I can get back here to set up shop," he reminded her. "Besides, you'll be so busy shopping for a trousseau that you won't have time to miss me."

"Want to bet?" John was watching them as he stirred his coffee absently to cool it. "She'll lead us an awful dance. I'll do my best with her, but she's your responsibility."

Tony watched the waiter move to another table before saying, "Especially since you've taken on a new responsibility of your own."

"Something like that." John sounded amused, but his glance sobered as it flicked over Maggie. "Sure you're okay?"

"Yes, thanks. I still feel like a fool for collapsing at the crucial moment." She straightened her shoulders. "It was just reaction after all the excitement."

"Well, it sets a terrible precedent," Holly told her soberly. "Now that my brother is accustomed to having you collapse at his feet, there'll be no living with him."

John's lips twitched. "Don't you believe it. Once she gets her strength back, I'll be restored to my proper place. Isn't that right, darling?"

"Don't answer that, Maggie," Tony advised. "Tonight I feel too happy for any arguments—even in fun." He pushed his glasses up on his thin nose and added, "You look beautiful in that dress but imagine the sensation you would have caused if you'd worn that diamond necklace. Too bad you couldn't borrow it from the police for the occasion."

Maggie managed to smile. "I thought Vincent was going to break down and cry when they impounded it. It was unbelievable."

"You were probably so foggy that you didn't hear Agatha tearing strips off Vincent about that time," John told her. "Deliver me from sweet little old ladies, after this. She made Jack the Ripper seem tame."

Maggie nodded, remembering. "She heads my list of 'Four-Star Horrors'! With all that honeyed talk about caring for Alfred and Banjo, too."

"I know Banjo's been moved back to his own kitchen," Holly cut in, "but what happened to Alfred?"

"Alfred went down to the police station along with the urn and the diamonds to be impounded for evidence," John told her. "Only I found out this afternoon that appearances were deceiving. Alfred wasn't Alfred at all."

Holly's eyebrows drew together. "You've garbled that transmission. What do you mean—Alfred isn't Alfred?"

"Simply that I took a sample of his ashes down to the

police to have them tested the day before we went to Carmel. They had the lab report today. Alfred's previous appearance on earth wasn't as a mortal; he came out of a fireplace all right, but before that he was part of a Japanese cherry tree."

Maggie uttered a stifled moan. "Oh, no! To think how carefully we trundled those darned ashes around all weekend. Why, I felt like a grave robber every time I passed the trunk of the car."

Tony threw back his head and laughed uninhibitedly. "I'll bet that was Agatha's plan all along. She knew that decent people would take the greatest care of memorial ashes and she chose a priceless piece of porcelain for the urn so that you treated the whole package like the 'Mona Lisa'." He started to chuckle again. "It was better than a safe deposit vault for her stolen goods. I tell you that woman has a head on her shoulders. Not a nice head, I grant you—but it's no wonder that she's been so successful as a fence for stolen jewelry."

"Is that what she was?" Holly asked.

John nodded. "The police think she fits in with the recent rash of jewel robberies they've had in this area. Especially since she rated a suspended sentence for the same charge in St. Louis five years ago. At the moment though, she isn't talking—except through her lawyer. Vincent is our great white hope; he isn't about to shoulder the blame for those diamonds alone. After all, it was Agatha's urn where the necklace was hidden, and now he claims that he retrieved the marquise ring in her apartment before Maggie interrupted him."

"If he'd just told me," Maggie said, "he could have had all the loot. Agatha could even have sent a note requesting that I give him the urn."

"Chances are, Agatha didn't want anything of the kind," John pointed out. "She preferred having the jewelry neatly tucked away in the apartment. If the police came asking questions, they would just have found an innocent young artist."

"As gullible as they come," Maggie finished in some disgust. "No wonder she wouldn't take any rent! She should have paid *me*."

John tried to keep his expression suitably solemn but he didn't succeed very well. "At least she didn't persuade you to buy the Golden Gate Bridge." He patted her hand reassuringly on the table top. "Never mind, darling. If Agatha's been running the authorities ragged, how could you hope to compete?" He glanced across at Holly and then turned to Tony before she could say anything. "Watch out when you see that glint in my sister's eye. The last time I saw it was when I was in Montana at Eastertime. She sent me two rabbits for a present."

"I like rabbits myself," Tony said. "What was wrong with that?"

"Well, for one thing, it was damned crowded when we all tried to squeeze in my fifteen-foot travel trailer."

Tony's eyes gleamed with amusement. "Now I understand. I'll pay proper attention in the future."

"If you can drag yourselves back to the present," Holly said in a patient voice, "I have a perfectly logical question. What did Agatha's spiritual stuff have to do with all this? Was she a 'clairvoyant' first, with jewelry as a sideline, or the other way around?"

"I wondered about that, too," Maggie said.

"Since she isn't talking, it's hard to know for sure," John acknowledged. "The police suspect that she used the spiritualism as a front for her extracurricular sources of income. That way, she could have people in and out of the apartment at all times of the day and night without raising any suspicion. Since there aren't any business hours for séances, no one thought much about it."

"Except her irate landlord," Holly put in.

His lips compressed at that. "Exactly. But even then, I

[*171*]

wasn't suspicious. Just annoyed. She could have had the British crown jewels delivered by special messenger and I probably would have signed for them."

"Come join the party," Maggie told him with a lilt in her voice. "But think what a shock it must have been when she heard Vincent had broken into the apartment and dropped the diamond ring. Then she *really* must have been alarmed when she heard we were looking for her in Carmel."

John deliberately kept his eyes on his coffee cup in front of him. "It shook Vincent up at least. He's admitted that he was the prowler outside your room at the inn."

"But why?"

"He wanted another chance to recover the marquise ring. At least that's what he claims. He probably knew you'd recognized him in the sanctuary. If he could have put you . . . out of commission for a day or so"— John chose his words carefully—"then he could have left town ahead of the police."

Maggie felt a cold chill go through her at his pronouncement. "Thank heaven for that German shepherd next door. It's too bad he couldn't sink a tooth in him."

"That's the way I feel myself," John told her. "Never mind, darling. Now that Vincent's in jail charged with two counts of grand theft he'll have plenty of time for meditation." He grinned suddenly. "I wonder if he can go into a trance without his yellow turban."

"How about Agatha?" Holly asked.

"She's being held as a suspect before a formal charge is lodged, so she'll need every friendly spirit she can get," John said tersely. "I sent word that her belongings would be put in storage. If she ever shows up at the apartment again, I'll call the police."

Holly sighed happily at his ultimatum. "Then there's just one more thing . . . I meant to ask how you and that police lieutenant got into the apartment at the crucial time?"

John glanced at Maggie and started to chuckle.

She shook her head ruefully before telling Holly, "My reputation's in shreds already—one more confession won't hurt. The detective brought along Vincent's mug shot for a second positive identification. When he and John arrived, they found that I had left my keys in Agatha's door. I was so darned busy juggling that box with the urn and those miserable ashes—" She broke off as all three of them dissolved into laughter.

"Never mind, Maggie darling," Holly said finally when she was able. "At least you got a pretty canary out of the experience."

"Banjo?" John's eyes were still alight with laughter. "I plan to give him to Maggie as my wedding present."

"I *was* going to say that Maggie got a pretty canary and a husband out of the experience," Holly told him. "I'm sure that Banjo is the better part of the bargain."

"No doubt about it. But we're a matched pair and can't be broken up," John agreed solemnly. "Like a double-feature at the movies . . . one pipperoo and one stinkeroo."

Holly shook her head. "Maggie darlin'—there's only one thing to do. Marry him fast and start training him properly. I'm available as a perfectly dandy maid of honor for the next week or so." She paused. "When *is* the date of the big event, or have you chosen it yet?"

There was a moment of silence while Maggie bit her bottom lip and looked stricken. John took pity on her when it became obvious that she didn't know what to say.

"Maggie's being sensible about things." He kept his tone easy. "Since she has to work out her notice on her job and make all the arrangements for the ceremony, we've decided to wait until I get back from my Alaska project."

Holly stared at him, obviously puzzled. "But John, you know how those jobs drag on sometimes. It could take months." She broke off as she noticed Maggie's suddenly tremulous expression. "Forgive me. You should tell me to mind my own business."

"Just what I had in mind, angel," Tony leaned forward to capture her hand. "If we don't leave for the airport pronto, I'll miss the plane and then *our* wedding will be off schedule." His glance softened. "Besides, I have a profound faith that my sister-in-law-to-be has things well under control. If Maggie can cope with a hoarse canary, a jewel thief, and Agatha Jarvis, she can certainly handle her own wedding."

"My thoughts exactly," John said easily. "Have a good trip, Tony. We'll see you in a few days."

"Just as soon as I can wind up some details back there." Tony stood up and moved aside so that Holly could get past him.

"I'll see you back home eventually," she promised her brother. "It may take a while. The traffic's terrible on the freeway and around the airport. Besides, I want to wait until the plane takes off." She looked down at Maggie. "Are you sure you're happy staying alone at Agatha's? You know that you're welcome to my guest room for as long as you like."

"I'll be fine down there now." Maggie's voice faltered as she added, "Besides, if I'm going back home soon, it seems silly to inconvenience everybody."

"Well, whatever you think."

"Come on, Holly, we have to go." Tony shook hands with John and bent down to hug Maggie and drop a kiss on her cheek. "See you soon."

"Take care, Tony." She returned his hug fiercely and watched the two of them thread their way through the dinner patrons to the outdoor elevator on the other side of the room.

John's eyebrows went up in surprise as he saw her dabbing at her lashes with her knuckles. "What is it, honey? There's nothing to be unhappy about, is there?"

"Of course not," she decided to search in her purse for a handkerchief. "I just hated to see them go."

"Tony will only be away for about a week and Holly will be pestering you bright and early tomorrow morning."

"I know that. Don't be so darned logical." She blew her nose and stuffed the handkerchief back in her bag. "Men are always talking about a rational approach to things and it's terribly irritating."

"Sorry, darling. Pay no attention." John signaled the waiter's attention for the check. "It's been a long day for all of us."

She waited while he put some bills on the salver and waved his change away. Then without saying anything more, she picked up her wrap and let him drape it carefully around her shoulders.

"Shall we go?" he asked politely.

She nodded, keeping her glance carefully on the tops of his black shoes.

Their ride back to Russian Hill was made in silence. To Maggie's surprise, it wasn't the offended silence which should have followed her outburst of temper. John seemed thoughtful rather than remote, and after a second glance at his unperturbed profile, Maggie looked straight ahead.

It wasn't until he'd pulled up in front of the apartment and reached across to open her door that she dared meet his gaze again.

"You might as well get out here," he announced. "It's easier than going around back to the garage."

"Will I see you later?" Her eyes looked like pools of despair in the greenish light of the dashboard.

His hand went back to the steering wheel. "I thought

maybe you were too tired."

"No, of course not." She ran the tip of her tongue over her upper lip nervously. "John, I'm sorry I was cross. I don't know why I was so silly."

"Forget it." He closed his car window before going on casually. "You'd better get inside where it's warmer. The air feels more like winter than spring tonight. I'll check with you after I put the car away."

She waited on the apartment steps and watched, hoping that he'd look back from the corner. To her disappointment, he didn't do anything of the sort.

By the time she'd unlocked the door of Agatha's apartment and thrown her wrap over the arm of the couch in the living room, she was ready to burst into illogical, unreasoning, copious feminine tears. And that would be all that was needed to make John leave for the north two weeks ahead of schedule, she decided mournfully.

If he was desolate over her proposal for a sensibly long engagement, he was concealing it admirably. From the way he was treating her now, he'd evidently decided to be "sensible" as well. Probably he'd give her a casual pat on the shoulder when he said good-night. As a matter of fact, he wouldn't even be saying good-night if she hadn't made a point of it.

She shivered and ran her hands over her upper arms. Chiffon wasn't the ideal covering for keeping goose bumps away in a chilly apartment. Agatha had probably opened that darned bedroom window for the friendly spirits again and no one had noticed. She'd have to close it as soon as she saw how Banjo was faring.

The canary turned his head and blinked sleepily at her when she turned on the overhead light in the kitchen. Probably he should have a cover on his cage, Maggie thought, as she reached in to poke a lettuce leaf farther through the brass supports. By then, Banjo had lost interest and was starting to preen his wing feathers.

Maggie's lips thinned to a despairing line as she envisioned the weeks ahead. Waiting for Banjo to sing would be the high point of her daily life. It wasn't a prospect to warrant turning handsprings, or sending up skyrockets. She wondered suddenly if John ever wrote letters. Or whether he was a hopeless masculine creature who thought a postcard every two weeks was all that was necessary.

She asked him point blank when she opened the door to his knock a few minutes later.

His eyebrows shot up in surprise, and then he rubbed the back of his neck with some embarrassment. "I hate writing letters," he confessed. "Never do it unless there's a typist around. Don't worry, though, I'll telephone every time I get into town."

"How often will that be?"

His expression was politely noncommittal. "It depends, Maggie. I probably should have told you that mining engineers don't make ideal husbands . . . our hours are terrible when we're on the job. But then you'll have plenty of time to think about all the hazards while you're home planning the wedding."

Her fingers plucked aimlessly at the fringe on one of Agatha's sofa pillows.

He went on relentlessly in that dispassionate tone. "It's a good thing that you use your head, Maggie. After all, marriage is a serious step and people can't afford to make any mistakes." He stared steadily at her. "Isn't that right?"

"Oh, absolutely," she replied, wishing she still had Agatha's urn so she could throw it at him.

"You've had a rough time today. I'll let you get some rest. Incidentally, I wouldn't wait up for Holly if I were you . . . she's apt to be half the night." He nodded in kindly fashion and moved to the hall door as Maggie's incredulous glance followed. Apparently he wasn't even going to bother with a brotherly kiss on the cheek like Tony. Maybe he thought that logical, modern fiancées abstained from demonstrative gestures and felt goodnights should be exchanged in brisk, no-nonsense fashion. He paused briefly with his hand on the knob. "Night, Maggie. Give me a call when you're ready for visitors in the morning." He went out, shutting the door firmly behind him.

Maggie opened her mouth, closed it, and then opened it again to say, "Damn!" in a loud voice. She thought things over carefully before adding, "Damn . . . damn . . . *damn!*" for good measure. A sofa pillow was slammed against the opposite wall, narrowly missing the picture of an Indian guru who stared coldly down on her. She stared back at him, her lip curling. "That goes for you, too," she snarled. "All men should be phased out of civilization!"

She flounced down on the hard sofa and stared mutinously at the closed apartment door. If John thought he was going to treat her this way before they were married —he was crazy. Going away for weeks at a time—weeks without letters or even a postcard—while she waited for a miserable phone call.

Her flood of self-pity almost overflowed at that juncture, before another ominous thought struck her. All those weeks, when John was alone, he'd be thinking, too. As the days went by, he might very well wonder what he'd ever seen in such a nondescript, ordinary female—the tepid fiancée who received his dutiful phone calls. When his project was completed, he'd probably board a polar flight for a long vacation—alone.

Maggie sighed softly. Despair had replaced her anger long ago. She stared desolately down at her hands, folded on the bouffant skirt material in her lap. Then her eyes widened slightly as they focused on the soft chiffon, and she was on her feet, hurrying to the hallway. She threw open the door so hard that it bounced against the wall behind it. "John," she called urgently and was half-way into the hall before she skidded to a stop by his apartment door.

John was leaning against the plaster staring back at her, his arms folded across his chest. Maggie swallowed in surprise. From his immovable stance, he might have been a statue erected for the occasion. For a moment, she was throbbingly aware of the deserted corridor around them and the old-fashioned fixture at the end of the hall which cast a subdued illumination over their still figures, making shadows of giant-killer proportions on the waxed floor tiles.

Her glance flicked again over John's rocklike figure. Why was he there—waiting? Almost as if he expected her to come or hoped she would. She had to clear her throat before she could speak. "My dress . . . I can't get out of it without someone's help. If you could undo the buttons again . . . please?" Her entreaty finished in a whisper.

John shoved himself erect and motioned her back to the open door of her apartment without answering. She meekly retraced her route with him following closely behind. He shut the door behind them and stood in the middle of Agatha's foyer.

"Come over here to the light. Those damned buttons are so small that I need a magnifying glass," he commanded.

She let her breath out in a soft sigh at his gruff tone. If he'd made a sarcastic remark about history repeating itself, she couldn't have forgiven him.

By the second button, she knew that he wasn't making comparisons with that night in Carmel, and she relaxed perceptibly. For some reason, his fingers fumbled at her movement. Then he went doggedly back to work.

When he reached the third button, she looked across

at the hall mirror and noted the reflection of his dark head, frowning down at her in solemn concentration. Her glance lingered on his tall, lean body—on those discerning gray eyes that made her willpower dissolve whenever they moved over her—on the firm mouth that had been so persuasive last night. His kisses were hard, hungry, possessive. Maggie's heartbeat fluttered, remembering.

John worked his way down without saying a word.

She looked in the mirror again. Why didn't he admit that he was disappointed by her decision to postpone the wedding? It was the only logical explanation for his behavior all evening. She knew something else about that behavior as well—he wouldn't say a word to make her change her mind.

When she felt his fingers on the last button, her instincts surrendered to a feminine prerogative decreed by Eve at the very beginning of time. Maggie turned to face him, slipping her hands inside his coat to keep him close to her.

John's expression was transformed in a second. "Maggie, love—you've changed your mind?"

There was such a lump of emotion in her throat that she could only nod. Evidently that was enough.

"Tell me, Maggie. Tell me now!" His fingers were like steel on her back.

"I love you," she whispered. "I love you so much that it makes me dizzy to be in the same room with you." Her voice faltered. "I can't stand the thought of leaving you."

John smiled faintly. "You should have known I wouldn't let you go off like that. What do you think I am?"

She moved closer, molding her body to the hard strength of his. "Down deep inside I knew I couldn't go anywhere without you. Tomorrow, any time."

"For the rest of our lives," he confirmed. "I felt like that about thirty seconds after I met you." His hands caressed her as he bent to nuzzle the silken hollow of her throat. "You're my life now, Maggie. Without you, I don't even function." Then he didn't bother with words as his mouth covered her parted lips demanding a response she couldn't possibly have denied.

John finally surfaced from that hard embrace long enough to push his starry-eyed fiancée firmly away from him. He managed to take a deep, steadying breath. "Now, dear heart, we'll do things my way—so pay attention. I'll call and get our plane reservations for tomorrow. We'll tell your folks, you can resign from your job, and we'll apply for a marriage license all in one day. You may not have time for much of a trousseau, but—" He broke off with a sudden frown.

For the first time, Maggie became aware that her dress kept her decently covered only by the most liberal standards.

"For God's sake, woman—go put something on," he ordered her absently. "We have a lot of things to settle yet tonight."

Maggie broke into delighted laughter. "I never thought I'd hear you say those words."

"Damned if I don't make you pay later for that, Delilah," he said in a severe tone.

She hesitated safely beyond his reach. "By the way, Mr. Elliott, it's perfectly acceptable for engaged couples to exchange a good-night kiss these days. All the etiquette books say so."

By then, he had the telephone directory in his hand. "Oh, I'd planned to fit one in later on, Miss Rome. Very chaste—very proper. *After* you put some more clothes on and *after* you make the coffee. Now move, angel!"

Maggie blew him a kiss before heading for her dressing room. When she passed Agatha's open bedroom window, the sheer curtains billowed gently . . . once . . .

twice . . . and then hung sedately back in place. Outside, the brisk night air remained strangely undisturbed.

In the kitchen, Banjo suddenly straightened on his perch as the current of fresh air swept through the room. There was a moment's hesitation while he preened his lemon-colored wings. Then, purposefully, he raised his beak and began to sing.

Bestsellers from SIGNET

☐ **BRING ME A UNICORN: The Diaries and Letters of Anne Morrow Lindbergh (1922–1928) by Anne Morrow Lindbergh.** Imagine being loved by the most worshipped hero on Earth. This nationally acclaimed bestseller is the chronicle of just such a love. The hero was Charles Lindbergh; the woman he loved was Anne Morrow Lindbergh; and the story of their love was one of the greatest romances of any time. "Extraordinary . . . brings to intense life every moment as she lived it."—**New York Times Book Review** (#W5352—$1.50)

☐ **ELEANOR AND FRANKLIN by Joseph P. Lash.** Foreword by Arthur M. Schlesinger, Jr. A number 1 bestseller and winner of the Pulitzer Prize and the National Book Award, this is the intimate chronicle of Eleanor Roosevelt and her marriage to Franklin D. Roosevelt, with its painful secrets and public triumphs. "An exceptionally candid, exhaustive . . . heartrending book."—**The New Yorker** (#J5310—$1.95)

☐ **JENNIE, VOLUME I: The Life of Lady Randolph Churchill by Ralph G. Martin.** In JENNIE, Ralph G. Martin creates a vivid picture of an exciting woman, Lady Randolph Churchill, who was the mother of perhaps the greatest statesman of this century, Winston Churchill, and in her own right, one of the most colorful and fascinating women of the Victorian era. (#E5229—$1.75)

☐ **JENNIE, VOLUME II: The Life of Lady Randolph Churchill, the Dramatic Years 1895–1921 by Ralph G. Martin.** The climactic years of scandalous passion and immortal greatness of the American beauty who raised a son to shape history, Winston Churchill. "An extraordinary lady . . . if you couldn't put down JENNIE ONE, you'll find JENNIE TWO just as compulsive reading!"—**Washington Post** (#E5196—$1.75)

Rainbow Romances from SIGNET

☐ **GIFT FROM A STRANGER by Ivy Valdes.** For Jane Gilmore it began with a pair of mismatched shoes and ended with a large legacy and a villa in Sicily. A villa which was to be the scene of many surprises and dangers, and in which Jane learned an unexpected truth about herself. (#P5216—60¢)

☐ **OVER MY SHOULDER by Ivy Valdes.** Linda Patterson, on holiday with her husband and fifteen-year-old son, thought the Bavarian hotel a pretty stopping place. That is, until she learned that behind its painted façade lurked a danger that threatened her life with her husband and her whole future! (#P5215—60¢)

☐ **CHASE A DARK SHADOW by Ivy Valdes.** When Anne Rycroft opens the door to a foreigner seeking her father, the vicar of a small London parish, she finds herself on the threshold of terror and a nightmarish journey to a remote Greek island. (#P5115—60¢)

☐ **THE LAIRD AND THE LADY by Vivian Donald.** When lovely, dark-haired, concert pianist Lorna Forrest goes to visit Ranald MacDonell, laird of Coigach, she finds herself implicated in theft and caught up in the sinister designs of a murder plot. (#P5114—60¢)

☐ **THE QUIET CORNER by Rebecca Marsh (Condensed for Modern Readers).** A world-famous actress stalks out of a Broadway hit and returns home to make the play of her life—for her sister's fiance. (#P5113—60¢)

☐ **MEXICAN INTERLUDE by Pamela Nichols (Condensed for Modern Readers).** A trio from a New York fashion magazine on assignment in Mexico becomes involved with a mysterious stranger who spells love, larceny, diamonds—and attempted murder. (#P5112—60¢)

JOHN D. MacDONALD

A
TAN AND SANDY
SILENCE

FAWCETT GOLD MEDAL • NEW YORK

A Fawcett Gold Medal Book
Published by Ballantine Books
Copyright © 1971 by John D. MacDonald Publishing, Inc.

ISBN 0-449-12969-1

The lines from "A Year's Changes" by Jim Harrison, which appeared in the collection titled *Locations,* published by W. W. Norton & Company, are reprinted courtesy of the author.

Copyright 1968 by Jim Harrison

Manufactured in the United States of America

First Fawcett Gold Medal Edition: January 1972
First Ballantine Books Edition: July 1982
Twenty-seventh Printing: April 1985

In northern Manitoba
a man saw a great bald eagle—
hanging from its neck,
teeth locked in skin and feathers,
the bleached skull of a weasel.

by Jim Harrison
(From "A Year's Changes")

a
tan and sandy
silence

one

On the most beautiful day any April could be asked to come up with, I was kneeling in eight inches of oily water in the cramped bilge of Meyer's squatty little cabin cruiser, the *John Maynard Keynes,* taking his automatic bilge pump apart for the third time in an hour.

The socket wrench slipped, and I skinned yet another knuckle. Meyer stood blocking out a sizable piece of the deep blue sky. He stared down into the bilge and said, "Very inventive and very fluent. Nice mental images, Travis. Imagine one frail little bilge pump performing such an extraordinary act upon itself! But you began to repeat yourself toward the end."

"Would you like to crawl down in here and—"

He backed up a hasty half step. "I couldn't deprive you of the pleasure. You said you could fix it. Go ahead."

I got it apart again. I spun the little impeller blade and suddenly realized that maybe it turned too freely. Found the set screw would take a full turn. Tightened it back down onto the shaft. Reassembled the crummy little monster, bolted it down underwater, heaved myself up out of the water, sat on the edge of the hatch, and had Meyer flip the switch. It started to make a nice steady wheeeeeeng, gouting dirty bilge water into the Bahia Mar yacht basin.

Meyer started to applaud, and I told him to save it until we found out if the adorable thing would turn itself the hell off like it says in the fine print. It took a good ten minutes to pump the water out. Then it went weeeeeeeng-guggle-chud. Silence.

"Now cheer," I said.

"Hooray," he said mildly. "Thank you very much and hooray." I looked at him with exasperation and affection. My mild and bulky friend with the wise little blue eyes, bright and bemused, and with the bear hair, thatch black, curling out of the throat of his blue knit shirt.

"Another half inch of rain last night," I told him, "and you could have gone down like a stone."

He had stepped out of his bunk in the dark after the rain stopped and into ankle deep water. He had sloshed over to my houseboat, *The Busted Flush,* and told me he had a small problem. At three in the morning we had toted my auxiliary pump over and set it on the dock and dropped the intake hose into his bilge. His home and refuge was very low in the water, the mooring lines taut enough to hum when plucked. By first light the *Keynes* was floating high again, and we could turn the pump off and carry it back. Now the repaired automatic bilge pump had taken out the last of the water, but he was going to live in dampness for quite a while.

"Perils of the sea," he said.

I stepped up onto the dock and squatted and began to rinse the grease and bilge water off my hands under the hose faucet. Meyer shaded his eyes and looked toward the *Flush.* "You've got a visitor, Travis. Isn't that what's-his-name?"

I stood up and stared. "It sure is. Good old what's-his-name. Harry Broll. Do you think that son of a bitch has come to try me again?"

"After the showing last time. . . . Was it two years ago?"

"At least."

"I think he's at least bright enough not to try again."

"Not the same way. But he did catch me with one very nice left. True, he broke his hand, but it was one to remember."

"Want company?"

"No thanks."

Harry turned and saw me when I was about fifty feet away. He was big, and he had gotten bigger since I'd seen him last. More gut and more jowls. Not becoming. He wore a pale beige suit, a yellow shirt, and he had a chocolate-colored neckerchief with an ornate, gold slip ring.

He raised his hands in the most primitive gesture of reassurance. Palms out. Sickly smile to go with it. As I came up to him he said, "Hi, McGee." He put his hand out. I looked at it until he pulled it back. He tried to laugh. "Jesus, are you still sore?"

"I'm not sore, Harry. Why should we shake hands?"

"Look. I want to talk to you. Are you busy or anything?"

"What about?"

"About Mary. I know you've got no reason in the world to do me any favors. But this concerns . . . Mary's well-being."

"Is something wrong with her?"

"I don't know. I don't really know."

I studied him. He seemed concerned and upset. He had the pallor of desk work. His black hair had receded since I had seen him last. He said, "I couldn't think of anybody else to come to. I can say please if it'll help. Please?"

"Come on aboard."

"Thanks. Thanks a lot."

We went into the lounge. I had on an old pair of denim shorts and nothing else. The airconditioning cooled the sweat on my shoulders and chest. He looked around, nodding and beaming, and said, "Nice. Real nice. A nice way to live, huh?"

"Want a drink?"

"Bourbon, if you've got it."

"Got it."

"On the rocks."

I put out the bottle and the glass and said, glancing down at my soiled hands, "Ice is in the bin there. Help yourself while I clean up, Broll."

"Thanks. You sure keep yourself in shape, McGee. Wish I had the time. I guess I better make sure I have the time one of these days."

I shrugged and went forward, dropped the shorts into the hamper and stepped into the oversized shower, thinking about Mary and wondering about her as I sudsed and scrubbed away the rest of the grime from the repair job. Miss Mary Dillon when I had known her. Then abruptly —maybe too abruptly—Mrs. Harry Broll. When I put my watch back on I saw that it was nearly four o'clock. Meyer and I were invited for drinks at six aboard the *Jilly III*. I put on fresh slacks, an oyster-white sailcloth sports shirt, my ancient Mexican sandals. On the way back to the lounge I stopped in the galley and put some Plymouth on the rocks.

He was sitting on the yellow couch, and he had lit a small cigar with a white plastic mouthpiece. "It must really be something, being able to just take off any time you feel like it."

I slouched into a chair facing him, took a swallow of my drink, and put it on the coffee table. "You've got a problem, Harry?"

"About that time I made such a damn fool of myself . . ."

"Forget it."

"No. Please. Let me say something about that. Like they say, the first year of marriage is the hardest, right?"

"So they say."

"Well, I knew you and Mary were old friends. I couldn't help knowing that, right? I mean, you and Meyer came to the wedding and all. I wondered how good friends you had been. I couldn't help wondering, but I didn't want to really know. Do you understand?"

"Sure."

"The way it happened, we got into a hassle. It was the first real one we'd had. People shouldn't drink and fight when they're married. They say things they don't want to say. I started saying some pretty ugly things about her and you. You know Mary. She's got a lot of spirit. She took it and took it, and finally she let me have it right between the eyes. I deserved it. She blazed right up at me. She said she'd been cruising with you alone aboard this houseboat, down through the Keys and up the west coast to Tampa Bay, and she'd lived aboard for a month and cooked your food and washed your clothes and slept in your bed, and you were kind and decent and gentle and twice the man I am. So that Sunday afternoon I slammed out of the house and got in the car and came over here to beat on you. I could always handle myself pretty good. I wasn't drunk enough for that to be any excuse. Jesus, I never hit so many arms and elbows and shoulders in my life."

"And the top of my head."

"That's what popped the knuckles. Look. This knuckle is still sort of sunk in. How many times did you hit me? Do you know?"

"Sure I know. Twice."

"Twice," he said dolefully. "Oh, shit."

"I waited until you ran out of steam, Harry. I waited until you got arm weary."

He looked at me in an appraising way. "I wish I'd done more good."

"I had a pair of sore arms. You bruised me up, Harry. And a three-day headache."

"I guess I had to get it out of my system. Do you understand it's still pretty hard for me to come to you to ask for anything?"

"I suppose it might be."

"Mary kept telling me to grow up. Okay. I'm trying to grow up. I'm trying to be a mature, rational human being. Like they say, I've been examining my priorities and my options."

"Good for you. But where do I fit in?"

"Here's what I want you to tell Mary."

"But I—"

"Give me a chance. Okay? Tell her that as soon as the SeaGate project is all set up, I think we ought to get away, just the two of us. A cruise or fly over to Spain, whatever. And tell her that the Canadian girl didn't mean a damn thing to me, that I didn't bring her back down here or ask her down, that she came on her own. And tell her to please get in touch with me so we can talk."

"Hold it! I don't know where Mary is."

His face turned red. "Don't give me such crap. You willing to let me search this houseboat?"

"She isn't here, you damn fool."

"I'll find something of hers. Clothes, lipstick, something."

"Harry. Jesus. Look around all you want."

He settled back in the chair. "Okay. You and Mary knew I'd come here sooner or later. So you haven't been having your fun aboard this boat."

"That's called paranoia, old buddy. When did she leave you?"

"January fifth."

I stared at him in disbelief. "This is the fourteenth day of April. You have a slow reaction time."

"I've been hoping she'd come back or get in touch. Tell her how much I've been hoping. She caught me dead to rights. She went around the house with a face like a stone for nearly two weeks, then when I got home that Tuesday, she'd packed and left. No note, even. I went down the list of her friends and called them. It was humiliating for me."

"I bet."

"Now just one damn minute—"

"What makes you think she'd come to me?"

"I thought about it. I mean, back in January. It seemed like the most likely thing for her to do. I spent a whole weekend hanging around here. You had . . . another friend. So I decided if Mary had come here, she'd found you were busy, gone someplace else."

"She didn't come here, Harry."

"Not right away."

"What is that supposed to mean?"

He leaned forward. "Okay. Where were you at ten o'clock on Friday morning, April second?"

"I haven't the faintest idea."

"You and Mary came off this houseboat at ten that morning, and you went out to the parking lot and got into a white Ford LTD convertible with rental plates. A friend of mine happened to be here and happened to see the two of you get in and drive off. This friend followed you. You went over to the Parkway and turned south toward Miami, and he came back, and he phoned me about it."

"Are you willing to listen a minute? Are you willing to try to listen?"

"All I know is my wife left me and she's sleeping with you, McGee, and I'd like to see you dead."

"The woman I was with is about Mary's height, and her figure is just as good, at least as good as Mary's used to be. Her hair is dark like Mary's. The woman is an old friend. That's her rental convertible, and it's still out there on the lot. With her hair in a scarf and dark glasses, she was all prepared for a trip in an open car. She's here aboard her boat. Her name is Jillian Brent-Archer. I haven't seen Mary since the wedding. Not once, Broll. And that was better than three years ago."

He looked at me. "You're real cute, McGee. Jesus, you're cute. Most of the damn fools in this world would believe you. Are you going to tell Mary what I told you to tell her, what I've begged you to tell her?"

"How can I, when I don't even know . . ."

And the dumb little weapon came out from under his clothes somewhere, maybe from the waist area, wedged between the belt and the flab. A dumb little automatic pistol in blued steel, half-swallowed in his big, pale, meaty fist. His staring eyes were wet with tears, and his mouth was twisted downward at the corners. The muzzle was making a ragged little circle, and a remote part of my mind identified it as .25 or .32 caliber, there not being all that much difference between a quarter of an inch diameter and a third of an inch. There was a sour laugh back in another compartment of my skull. This could very possibly be the end of it, a long-odds chance of a mortal wound at the hand of a jealous husband wielding something just a little bit better than a cap gun. The ragged circle took in my heart, brain, and certain essential viscera. And I was slouched deep in a chair facing him, just a little too far away to try to kick his wrist. He was going to talk or shoot. I saw his finger getting whiter, so I knew it was shoot.

I shoved with my heels and went over backward in the chair. The weapon made a noise like somebody slapping shingles together. My left heel went numb. I rolled to my right, knocked over a small table, fielded the chunky glass ashtray on the first bounce, rolled up onto my knees, and slung it underhand at his head as he came up out of the depths of the yellow couch. I missed him shamefully, and was caught there too close to him as he aimed at the middle of my face from five feet away and tried to pull the trigger. But the slide was all the way back, the clip empty.

I got slowly up onto very wobbly knees as Harry Broll lowered the gun to his side, relaxed his hand, let it fall. My heel tingled. A slug had grooved the hard leather on the bottom of the heel. The lounge smelled like the fourth of July.

Harry's big face wrinkled like a slapped baby, and he took a half step toward me, arms half reaching out for comfort and forgiveness, and then he plumped back down on the couch and bellowed once, a walrus on a lonely strand.

My drink was gone, spilling when the table went over. I moved cautiously, checking myself for any area that might feel dead and damp. That is the bullet feel, dead, damp, and strange, before the torn nerves and muscles catch up and begin screaming. No such areas. I made tall careful steps into the galley, made a new drink. I went back in. Harry Broll sat with face in hands, snuffling drearily. The paper had kept me aware of him over the years. Broll plans new condominium complex. Broll given zoning board exception. Broll unveils shopping plaza concept. Chamber lauds Broll.

I sat opposite him again after putting the chair back on its legs. Looking around, I could count five ejected cartridge cases.

"How old are you, Harry?"

He sighed and mumbled it into his hands. "Thirty-five."

"You look fifty."

"Get off my back."

"You're too soft and too heavy. You sweat a lot, and you're short of breath, and your teeth need cleaning."

He lifted his mottled face and stared at me. "Why are you saying these things?"

"Maybe if you hadn't gotten so sloppy, Mary could have given you a second chance. Or maybe it was already a second chance."

"Oh, no. I don't play around. Jesus, I haven't had the time or the energy. This was the first time, I swear."

"You don't play around, and you don't go around killing people."

"You pushed me too far and—"

"You always carry that thing?"

"No, I—"

"You brought it along in case you felt like killing me?"

"Thank God, I missed you. I'm not thinking right lately. Everything would have gone down the drain. Everything."

"It would sort of spoil my day, too."

"You know, when a man takes a good look at himself, he begins to wonder why. You know? I've been pushing myself hard. Drinking too much, smoking too much. Late nights. Conferences. For what? Damned if I know. For the sake of winning? How did that get to seem so important? But you shouldn't have tried to lie to me, McGee."

"Your friend is an idiot. Mary never came near me. She hasn't phoned me or written me. I didn't know she'd left you. Look, I knew her a long time ago. She was at one of those crisis points in her life. She'd never met you, Harry. Never seen you, never heard your name, never knew she'd marry you. We were friends. We took a cruise down through the Keys and up the west coast, and she got things sorted out. We made love. Not for the first two weeks of the cruise. That wasn't the purpose of it. Once all the knots and springs began to loosen up, then it seemed like a natural thing to have happen. It made pleasure. It was a way of saying hello. Nobody was a victim. She was a very sweet lady, and what I remember best is that we laughed a lot."

"I . . . I have to talk to her before the thirtieth."

"Why the deadline?"

"It's a business thing. Some things to sign. To protect my interest in SeaGate. Of course, if I'd shot you, what difference would it make whether I kept my share of Sea-Gate or not?"

"Will it make a lot of difference when I sign the complaint against you?"

"Complaint?"

"Assault with a deadly weapon. Attempted homicide?"

"You wouldn't!"

"What's to stop me? My undying affection for you?"

He pulled himself together visibly. He wrapped up the emotions and put them on a high shelf. I could almost see the nimble brain of the entrepreneur take over. "We'll both have versions of what happened here, McGee. I'm essentially a salesman. I think I can sell my version far easier than you can sell yours."

"What's your version?"

"I'll let that come as a surprise to you."

I could think of several variations that could leave him looking pretty good. And, of course, there was the usual problem of believability. Does one believe Harry Broll, pillar of the business community, or a certain Travis McGee, who seems to have no visible means of support, gentlemen?

"A man as shrewd as you, Harry, should realize that the guy who gave you the bad information made an honest mistake."

"I know Mary. She'd get in touch with you."

"Would that she had."

"What?"

"A troubled friend is a friend in trouble. I'm right here. She could have come around, but she didn't."

"She made you promise not to tell where she is."

I shook my head. "Broll, come with me. I will show you that rental convertible, and I will show you the lady who rented it and who went to Miami with me and came back with me."

"It's a nice try. You've got a lot of friends. They'd all lie for you. Every one. Think it over. Tell her what I said. She has to get in touch with me."

We stood up. I picked up his little automatic, released the catch and eased the slide forward and handed it to him. He took it and looked at it, bounced it on his big hand, and slipped it into his side pocket. "I better get rid of it," he said.

"If you think you might get any more quaint ideas, you better."

"I was going to scare you. That's all."

I looked him over. "Harry. You did."

"Tell her to call the office. I'm not living at home. It was too empty there."

"If after all these years I should happen to see your wife, I'll tell her."

two

Meyer came aboard *The Busted Flush* at twenty minutes to six, five minutes after Harry Broll left. He was dressed for the small festival at six o'clock aboard Jillian's great big motor-sailer trimaran. He wore pants in a carnival awning pattern and a pink shirt that matched one of the myriad stripes in the awning.

"Goodness gracious," I said.

He put a hand on a bulky hip and made a slow 360-degree turn. "Plumage," he said. "And have you noticed it's spring?"

"If you'd carry a camera around your neck and walk fifty feet ahead of me, nobody would know we were together."

"Faw," he said. "And tush." He went toward the bottle department, saying, "About Mr. Harry Broll . . . ?"

"Who? Oh, yes. Of course. Mr. Broll."

"McGee, don't try me, please."

"You are supposed to walk in here, and instead of giving me a fashion show, you are supposed to snuff the air, look about with darting glances. Then you are supposed to find those six cartridge cases in that ash tray and snuff at them. Then you prowl around and find where all six hit, including the one that's hard to find. It hit right smack in the middle of my model 18 Marantz and killed it as dead as Harry tried to kill me."

Meyer backed to the nearest chair and lowered himself into it. "Six shots?"

"Six."

"With serious intent?"

"Damn well told."

I explained the situation. Meyer listened, looking very troubled.

"Don't sit there looking like an old beagle," I told him. "Harry won't be back."

"Maybe somebody else will."

"What is that supposed to mean?"

"Travis, are you just a little slower than you were a few years ago? Half a step, maybe?"

"I don't know. Probably."

"Why should you get slower and get careless at the same time?"

"Careless?"

"Don't try to kid yourself. You would have stumbled against him or spilled something on him and brushed it off. You would have checked him out and located the gun and taken it away from him."

"This was just old Harry Broll."

"And you are just old T. McGee, trying to pretend you don't know what I'm saying. You could be on the floor with a leaking hole in your skull."

"I can't go around acting as if everybody was going to—"

"You used to. And you are alive. What has given you this illusion of immortality of late?"

"Lay off, Meyer."

"Staleness? People are very good at things they are very interested in. If you lose interest, you are dead. If a Harry Broll can damned near kill you, Travis, what about somebody with a more professional attitude and background?"

"Wouldn't I be more alert?"

"Don't some of them look and act as innocuous as Harry Broll?"

"What are you getting at?"

"If you just go through the motions, Travis, maybe it's time to give the whole thing up. What good is a way of life if it turns out to be fatal?"

"Are you going to support me?"

"Not a chance. Anyway, isn't Jillian first in line?"

"Come *on!*"

"There are worse ways to live."

"Several hundred thousand worse ways, Meyer, but just because Harry Broll. . . . Consider this. Six shots in a very confined space. What's the matter with my reaction time?"

"The trouble is that they were fired at all. He came here once to try to beat your face flat. So two years later he comes around again, and you invite him in to try his luck with a gun. What are you going to dodge next time? A satchel charge?"

"I have to depend on instinct. I did not sense any kind of murderous intent on his—"

"Then your instincts are stale. Listen. I don't want to lose a friend. Go where I can visit once in a while. Exchange Christmas cards. Better than putting a pebble on your gravestone."

"Just because—"

"Don't talk. Think a little. And we should be going."

I shrugged and sighed. When he gets into one of those moods, there is nothing one can do with him. He smells doom. I buttoned up the *Flush,* making certain my little security devices were in operation. The sun was low enough to make a yellow-orange glow across all the white gleam and brightwork of a vulgar multimillion dollars' worth of seagoing toys. Hundreds of millions, in truth. As we walked over I saw the sixty-plus feet of a big new Bertram, grumbling, bubbling, sliding elegantly into a slip. Six thousand dollars a foot. It doesn't take too many of those, too many Matthews, Burgers, Trumpys, Huckins, Rybovitches, and Strikers, to make a row of zeros to stun the mind.

I stopped and leaned my crossed arms atop a cement piling and looked down at a rainbow sheen of oil on twilight waters.

"What's the matter now?" asked Meyer.

"Harry is right, you know."

"To try to kill you?"

"Very funny. He's right about Mary getting in touch. I get the feeling she would. Emotional logic. The last time her world ruptured, I helped her walk it off, talk it off, think it off."

"So maybe she had enough and said the hell with it."

"She is one stubborn lady. Harry is no prize. She married him a little too fast. But she would really bust a gut to make the marriage work. She wouldn't quit. She wouldn't run."

"Unless he did something that she just couldn't take. Maybe it got to her gag reflex. Wouldn't she run then?"

"Yes. I guess so. And maybe she's a stronger person than she was back when I knew her. All Harry said was that he had gotten mixed up with some Canadian girl, a first offense. I know that wouldn't make Mary give any ringing cheers. But I think she's human enough to know it wouldn't be the end of the world or the marriage. Well, he has to locate her before the end of April, or he has big business problems."

"Hmm?"

"Something about signing something so he can keep his interest in SeaGate, whatever the hell that is."

"It's a planned community up in the northeast corner of Martin County, above Hobe Sound where there's no A-1-A running along the beach. It's a syndicate thing, way too big for anybody like Broll to swing by himself."

"How do you know all that stuff?"

"There was a feature story about planned communities in the *Wall Street Journal* a month ago. The local papers have had articles about it for over a year. I believe *Newsweek* had a—"

"Truce. Could a guy like Broll do well in a deal like that?"

"Depends. The ownership structure would be the important consideration."

"Could you find out where he fits and how, and why Mary would have to sign something?"

"I imagine I could. But why?"

"Harry's nerves are bad. He looks bad. He has a money orientation. If he misses out on large money because Mary runs and hides and won't sign, it somehow doesn't sound like Mary. It would be a cheap shot and a dumb shot. She isn't dumb. Whether she stays with him or leaves him, it would be better for him to have money. She's been gone for two months. If he was so certain she'd run to me,

where has he been for two months? Time is running out in
two weeks. So he comes around with shaking hands and a
sweaty shirt and a couple of places he missed while shav-
ing. Time is running out not on the marriage, on the
money. It makes me wonder."

"I'll look into it," he said as we walked.

End of discussion. We had arrived at the area where
they park the showboats, the ones too big to bring around
inside, and thus have to leave them on the river, not far
from the fuel pumps, where two out of every three Power
Squadron types who cruise by can whap them against the
cement with their curling wash. The *Jilly III* is a custom
motor-sailer trimaran out of St. Kitts, owned by Jillian,
the widow of Sir Henry Brent-Archer. It is seventy feet
long with a beam that has to be close to fifty feet. It rides a
bad sea with all the stability of a brick church. Minimal
superstructure to emphasize an expanse of teak deck as
big as a tennis court, with more than half of it shaded by
the big colorful awning tarp her crew of three always
strings up as soon as they are at dockside.

The bar table was positioned, draped in white damask.
A piano tape was playing show tunes with muted discretion over the stereo system I'd helped her buy the last time
she was in Lauderdale. There were a dozen guests assembled, three conversational groups of elegant folk sipping
the very best booze from the most expensive glasses. Jilly
saw us approaching the little gangplank and came a-strid-
ing, beaming, to welcome us aboard.

A lady of unguessable years, who made damned well
certain she gave you no clues at all. If she turned up as a
Jane Doe, DOA, traffic, a hasty coroner could not be
blamed for penciling in the apparent age as plus or minus
twenty-seven. Tall, slender brunette of such careful and elegant grooming, such exquisitely capped teeth, it seemed
safe to assume she was in some area of entertainment. But
she had such a much better tan and better physical condition than most show business people, one might safely
guess her to be, perhaps, a model for beachwear? A lead
in a commercial water ballet?

But a coroner less hasty, more sophisticated, who searched the scalp and elsewhere for the faintest of traces left by superb Swiss surgeons, who slipped the tinted plastic lenses off and studied the eyes closely as well as the backs of the hands, base of the throat, ankles, wrists. . . . He might add a quotient of years in direct ratio to his quality of observation and his experience.

Jilly had a lively and animated face peering out from the careless spill of black hair, all bright questing eyes, black brows, big nose, broad and generous mouth. Ever since I had known Jilly, her voice had cracked like that of a boy in early adolescence, changing from the piercing, songbird clarity of the Irish upperclass countryside to a burring baritone honk and back again. It was so effective it seemed contrived. But a small sailboat had foundered one night in a bad sea, and she had clung to a channel buoy, permanently spraining her vocal cords shouting at the boat traffic until finally she was heard and she and her injured friend were rescued.

"Meyer!" she cried. "My *word,* darling! You're of a surpassing radiance. Travis dear, what happened to him? Did he molt or something?" She linked her arms through ours and croaked, "Come on, dears. Meet the ones you don't know and get smashed soon as you can because I am gallons ahead of you."

The introductions were made. Jillian slipped away to greet more guests. We drank. The sun went down. The night breeze was gentle but cool, and ladies put their wraps back on. The party lights strung from the rigging were properly dim, flatteringly orange. The buffet materialized, as if the table had risen up out of the teak. The music tape was more lively, the volume louder than before.

I found myself inadvertently paired with a smallish, withered Englishwoman with a shrunken face the color of weak tea and hair dyed the color of raspberry ice. A Mrs. Ogleby. I had seen Meyer talking to her towering and cadaverous husband, pumping him about the latest Common Market difficulties. We carried our buffet plates forward where she could sit on a narrow shelflike bench built out from the bow where the rail was solid. I sat crosslegged on the deck with my plate atop the massive bow cleat.

"I understand that you are one of dear Jillian's very favorite Americans, Mr. McGee."

She managed to load the comment with sweetly venomous insinuation. I beamed up at her. "And she's one of my favorite foreigners."

"Really! How terribly nice for her. Actually, Geoffrey and I were old friends of poor Sir Henry long before he married Jillian."

"Then Jillian isn't one of your favorite people, eh?"

She clinked her fork against the plate and leaned forward and peered down at me. "Whatever gave you such an odd idea? She is *very* dear. Very dear to both of us."

"I knew Sir Henry, too."

"Really! I wouldn't have thought you would have known him."

"I was a house guest at St. Kitts for a few weeks."

"But that would have been after he was quite ill, I take it." Her smile was thin and knowing in the light of the nearby party lantern. A truly poisonous little woman.

"No. As a matter of fact, Mrs. Ogleby, Henry and I swam our three miles every morning, went riding or sailing every afternoon, and played chess every evening."

She paused and regrouped. "Before he became ill, Sir Henry had really fantastic energies. How strange we all thought it that he would marry someone that young, after being a widower so long. It seemed odd. But, of course, that was so awfully long ago it is rather difficult to think of Jillian as—"

"Just think of me, dears, no matter how difficult it may be," said Jilly. "Hmmm. What is this you have, Lenore? I didn't see it at all. May I? Mmmm. Shrimp, and what a deliciously fiery sauce! Difficult to think of me as what, Lenore darling?"

When Mrs. Ogleby hesitated, I said, "She was about to pinpoint the date when you and Sir Henry were married."

"Were you, dear? It slips my mind, you know. Was it

just before or just after that fuss with the Spanish Armada?"

"Don't be absurd! I was only—"

"You were only being Lenore, which is part of the trouble, isn't it? Travis, I was married to Henry long long ago. Matter of fact, I was but three years old at the time, and most of the people in the church thought it was some sort of delayed christening. There was talk that it was an unwholesome relationship, but by the time I was fourteen— eleven years later—I looked twenty, and everyone said that it had probably been all for the best. And it was, of course. Lenore, you seem to be finished. Dear, come with me and show me just where you found the shrimp, will you please?"

"But if there is any left, it should be quite obvi—"

"Lenore!"

"Quite. Of course. I shall be happy to show you, my dear Jillian."

"I knew it would make you happy to have a chance to be nice to me, Lenore."

Off they went. Old friends, smiling and chattering.

Twenty minutes later as I was moving away from the bar with some Wild Turkey straight, instead of brandy, Jilly intercepted me and moved me into relative shadow.

"Travis, if you are a truly thoughtful and understanding man, you have your toothbrush hidden away on your person."

"I had the idea the party girl would need her eight hours."

"Have a little mercy, dear. There's but one way to settle down from this sort of bash. You shall divert me."

"I can leave and then come back. You know. Like a house call."

"Is its tender little romantical pride bruised because the party girl thinks love making is therapeutic? To say nothing of being a hell of a lot of fun. Just stay on, dear. Stay by me. Smile like a tomcat with a little yellow feather caught in his whiskers, and soon now we can smile them off and sing out our merry farewells."

"Giving Lenore more food for thought?"

"Thought? Christ, that poisonous bitch doesn't think. She slanders, because she has her own terrible hunger she can't ease in any way. She burns in fire, my darling, and hates and hates and hates. Poor thing. Brace yourself, pet. I want you horribly."

three

I drifted in and out of a placid and amiable doze. Water slapped the triple hulls, whispering lies about how big the seas could really get. I cocked an eye at an upward angle at the battery digital clock fastened to the bulkhead over Jillian's bed. Watched 4:06 turning magically to 4:07. There was a single light on in her stateroom, a rose-colored globe of frosty glass, big as a cantaloupe, standing next to its twin reflection in the dressing table mirror.

It was warm in her stateroom, not unpleasantly so, just enough to leave a humid dew, rosy highlights on our entangled flesh, sprawled and spent, atop a wrinkled dampness of custom sheets in a pattern of green vines with yellow leaves against white.

Jilly lay oddly positioned, her upper torso diagonally across my chest, face in a pillow, cheek against my right shoulder, her slack right arm hooked around my neck. Her long tanned legs were sprawled down there, off to my left. My right arm was pinned, but my left arm was free, my hand resting on the small of her back.

I traced the velvet geographies of that small concave area of the country of Jilly and then made a coin-sized circle of fingernails and thumbnail and made a slow circling motion against her there, a circle as big as a teacup. In time the pattern of her breathing changed. She shifted. She exhaled though slack rubbery lips, making a sound like a small horse.

"Is someone mentioning my name?" she said in a sleepy voice.

"Pure telepathy."

29

She raised her head, clawed her hair out of the way, and peered up at the clock. "Gawd! What year is it? Don't tell me."

She heaved herself up, tugging her arm out from under my neck. She sat up and combed her hair back with the fingers of both hands, yawning widely as she did so. She shook and snapped her head back, settled her hair, then curled her limber legs under her and smiled down at me. "Been awake long, Travis?"

"Off and on."

"Thinking? About what?"

I hitched myself higher on the pillows. "Random things. This and that."

"Tell me about them."

"Let me think back. Oh, I was wondering how it's possible to make this bed up. It's shaped to fit perfectly into the curves of this middle hull right up at the bow and—"

"There are little lever things on the legs down there, and when you push them down, then you can roll the bed back and make it up. You certainly think about fascinating things."

"Then I heard a motor go on, and I was wondering if it was a bilge pump or a refrigeration compressor or—"

"You are trying to be tiresome. Didn't you think about what I asked you?"

"Maybe I did. A little bit. Like wondering why it has to be me."

"If one could know why a person settles upon a particular person, one would know one of the mysteries, wouldn't one? I think it was because of four years ago. I think it started then."

A friend of a friend had put Sir Henry Brent-Archer in touch with me. A problem of simple extortion. I had gone down to the British Virgins and spent three weeks at their spacious and lovely home and found exactly the right way to pry the two-legged lamprey loose, file its sharp teeth off, and send it unhappily on its way. And during the three weeks I had become ever more sensuously aware of Sir Henry's handsome and lively wife. She made sure of that awareness.

"Because I kept it from starting?"

"Was I all that distasteful to you, my darling?"

"Not you. The situation. I liked Sir Henry. In spite of the fact I was working for him on a special problem, I was still a guest in his home. In a man's home you live by his code. It does not have to be typed out and glued to the guest suite door. He did not want me to kick his dogs, overwork his horses, bribe his servants, read his diary, filch his silverware, borrow his toothbrush, or lay his wife. I accepted the obligation when I moved in."

She snickered. "Would you believe that was the only time in the years I was his wife that I ever tried to be naughty?"

"There's no reason not to believe it."

"I was very grateful to Sir Henry. He came along at just the right time in my life. My whole dreadful family was sliding into the pit, and through him I could save them, so I snatched him up quickly. I liked him well enough for half the marriage, liked him a great deal for the rest of it, and started loving him after he was buried. Anyway, on that stupid night I lay and listened to my heart going bump, bump, bump. Then I got up and drenched myself with that lovely scent and put on the little froth of nightgown and crept through the night like a thief and slipped into your bed. And suddenly got lifted out bodily, carried to the door, given a great whack across my bare behind, and shoved out into the hall. I did not know whether to laugh or cry. I did both."

"It was closer than you'll ever know, Jilly."

"So it's you, dear man. The chosen. Relax and enjoy it. Why not? Am I trying to nail you down permanently? Of course, but through your own choice and decision. I give you full disclosure, dear. I have something over eight hundred thousand pounds, carefully managed by nice little Swiss elves. The income is about a hundred and fifty thousand of your dollars a year, and taxes take hardly any. There is the lovely house with the beach, the bay, and the view, and the boats and cars and horses. I am not exactly a junior miss, but I work very hard at myself, and I come from healthy stock. I suspect I shall go on about the same for years and years and years and suddenly one morning wake up as a shriveled, cackling little old witch. All I ask of you is that you come back home with me, darling. Be my houseguest. Be my love. We laugh at the same things. We enjoy the same things. Last trip and this trip we've certainly established . . . physical compatibility. Darling, please! We'll travel when you want to and go where you want to go. We'll be with people when you want to, and they will be the people you want to be with. Please!"

"Jilly, you are a dear and lovely lady—"

"But! I know, dammit. But! Why *not*? Do you even *know*?"

I knew but did not want to tell her. You see many such couples around the yacht clubs and bath clubs and tennis clubs of the western world. The man, a little younger or a lot younger that the moneyed widow or divorcee he has either married or is traveling with. The man is usually brown and good at games, dresses youthfully and talks amusingly. But he drinks a little too much. And completely trained and conditioned, he is ever alert for his cues. If his lady unsnaps her purse and frowns down into it, he at once presents his cigarettes, and they are always her brand. If she has her own cigarettes, he can cross twenty feet in a twelfth of a second to snap the unwavering flame to life, properly and conveniently positioned for her. It takes but the smallest sidelong look of query to send him in search of an ashtray to place close to her elbow. If at sundown she raises her elegant shoulders a half inch, he trots into the house or onto the boat or up to the suite, to bring back her wrap. He knows just how to apply her suntan oil, knows which of her dresses have to be zipped up and snapped for her. He can draw her bath to the precise depth and temperature which please her. He can give her an acceptable massage, brew a decent pot of coffee, take her phone messages accurately, keep her personal checkbook in balance, and remind her when to take her medications. Her litany is: Thank you, dearest. How nice, darling. You are so thoughtful, sweetheart.

It does not happen quickly, of course. It is an easy life.

Other choices, once so numerous, disappear. Time is the random wind that blows down the long corridor, slamming all the doors. And finally, of course, it comes down to a very simple equation. Life is endurable when she is contented and difficult when she is displeased. It is a training process. Conditioned response.

"I'm used to the way I live," I told her.

"The way you live," she said. With brooding face she reached and ran gentle fingertips along the deep, gullied scar in my thigh, then leaned, and touched the symmetrical dimple of the entrance wound of a bullet. She hunched closer to me, bent, and kissed the white welt of scar tissue that is nearly hidden by the scruffy, sun-faded hair at my temple. "The way you live, Travis. Trying to trick the tricky ones. Trying to make do with bluff and smiles and strange lies. Filching fresh meat right out of the jaws of the sharks. For how long, dear, before finally the odds go bad and the luck goes bad once and for all?"

"I'm sly."

"Not sly enough. Maybe not quick enough anymore. I think you've been doing it for too long, darling. Too many years of getting things back for silly, careless people who should not have lost them in the first place. One day some dim little chap will come upon you suddenly and take out a gun and shoot you quite dead."

"Are you a witch? Do you so prophesy?"

She fell upon me, hugged me tight. "Ah no, dear. No. You had all the years when that was the thing you had to do. Now the years belong to me. Is it such a sickening fate you can't endure the thought of it?"

"No, Jilly. No, honey. It's just that . . ."

"Give us a month. No. One week. One insignificant little week. Or else."

"Or else?"

She burrowed a bit, gently closed her teeth onto the upper third of my left ear, then released it. "I have splendid teeth and very strong jaw muscles. If you say no, I shall set my teeth into your ear and do my best to tear it right off your head, darling."

"You just might at that."

"You love to bluff people. Try me."

"No, thank you. One week."

She took a deep breath and let it out. "Lovely! Time in transit doesn't count, of course. Can we leave . . . day after tomorrow?"

"I don't know."

"Why don't you know?"

"I just found out that an old friend might be in trouble. It just seems to me that if she was in trouble, she'd come to me."

Jilly wiggled and thrust away from me and sat up. "She?"

"Frowning makes wrinkles."

"So it does. She?"

"A respectable married lady."

"If she's so respectable, how is it she knows *you?*"

"Before she was married."

"And I suppose you had an affair with her."

"Gee, honey. I'd have to look it up."

I caught her fist about five inches from my eye. "You bahstid," she said.

"Okay. An affair. A mad, wild, glorious liaison which kept us in an absolute frenzy of passion."

Her look was enigmatic. "You are perfectly right, of course, darling. It is none of my business. What's she like? I mean, what physical type?"

"In general, a lot like you, Jilly. Tall, slender brunette. Dark hair, takes a good tan. Long legs, short waisted. She would be . . . twenty-eight or -nine by now. Back when I knew her, she didn't race her motor the way you do. More of a placid, contented person. She really enjoyed cooking and scrubbing and bed-making. She could sleep ten or twelve hours a night."

"You damned well remember every detail, don't you?"

I smiled up into her leaning, earnest face—a small face but strong of feature in the black, bed-snarled dangle of hair. I looked at her limber, brown body in the rose glow of the lamp ten feet away, noting the way the deep tan above and below her breasts decreased in ever more pallid horizontal stripes and shadings down to that final band of pale and pure white which denoted her narrowest bikini top.

"Why are you laughing at me, you dull sod?"

"Not at you, Lady Jillian."

"I am *not* Lady Jillian. That usage is improper. If you are not laughing *at*, then you are laughing *with*. And if you are laughing *with*, why is that I am not amused?"

"But you are, darling."

She tried to keep her mouth severe but lost the battle, gave a rusty honk of laughter, and flung herself upon me.

"I can't stay angry with you, Travis. You promised me a week. But I'll punish you for that dark-haired lady."

"How?"

"On our way to St. Kitts there will be at least one day or night when we'll spend hour after hour quartering into an ugly, irregular chop."

"I don't get seasick."

"Nor do I, my love. It would spoil it if either of us became ill."

"Spoil what?"

"Dear man, when the chop is effective, one cannot stay on this bed. You are lifted up, and then the bed and the hull drop away from you, and when you are on your way down, the bed comes up and smacks you and boosts you into the air again. It is like trying to post on a very bad horse. When that happens, dear, you and I are going to be right here, making love. We'll see how well you satisfy a lady in mid-air. I shall have you tottering about, wishing you'd never met Mrs. Whatever."

"Mrs. Broll. Mary Broll. Mary Dillon Broll."

"You think she should have come to you if she's in trouble? Isn't that a little patronizing and arrogant?"

"Possibly."

"What sort of trouble?"

"Marriage trouble. Her husband cheated, and she caught him at it and left him back in January."

"Good Lord, why should she come galloping to you?"

"It's an emotional problem, and when she had one sort of like it years ago, we got together, and she worked her way out of it."

"And fell in love with you?"

"I think that with Mary there would have to be some affection before there could be anything."

"You poor dumb beast. You're *so* obvious."

"What do you mean?"

"You can't for the life of you comprehend why she doesn't come scuttling back to Dr. McGee's free and famous clinic. Your pride is hurt, dear. I suspect she's found some other therapist."

"Even if she had, I think she'd have let me know the marriage had soured. I get the feeling something happened to her."

She yawned and stretched. "Let me make one thing abundantly clear, as one of your grubby little political types says or used to say. Once we have our design for living, if we have any doleful visits from one of your previous patients, my dear, I shall take a broom to them and beat them through the garden gate and down the drive."

"Don't you think you ought to type all these rules up and give me three copies?"

"You're so damned *defensive!* Good Christ, am I some sort of dog's dinner?"

"You are a lively, sexy, lovely, sexy, well-dressed, sexy, amusing, sexy, wealthy, sexy widow lady."

"And some *very* tidy and considerate men come flocking around. Men with all the social graces and very good at games. Not knuckly, scabrous, lazy, knobbly old ruins like you, McGee."

"So grab one of those tidy and considerate ones."

"Oh, sure. They are lovely men, and they are *so* anxious to please me. There's the money, and it makes them very jumpy and nervous. Their hands get cold and damp. If I frown, they look terrified. Couldn't you be more anxious to please me, dear? Just a little bit?"

"Like this, you mean?"

"Well . . . I didn't exactly mean that. . . . I meant in a more general sense . . . but . . . now that you bring it up.

. . . god, I can't remember now what I did mean. . . . I guess I meant this. Yes, darling. This."

The narrow horizontal ports above the custom bed let a cold and milky morning light into the stateroom at the bow of the center hull of the *Jilly III*. As I looked up, 6:31 became 6:32. Jillian's small round rump, her flesh warmer than mine, was thrust with a domestic coziness into my belly. My chin rested against the crown of her head. Her tidy heft had turned my left arm numb. My right hand lay upon the sweet inward curve of her waist.

Worse fates, I thought. A life with Jilly Brent-Archer wouldn't be dull. Maybe it is time for the islands. In spite of all good intentions, all nervous concern, all political bombast, my dirty two-legged species is turning the lovely southeast coast into a sewer. On still days the stinking sky is bourbon brown, and in the sea there are only the dwindling runty fish that can survive in that poisoned brew.

It happens slowly, so you try not to notice it. You tell yourself it happens to be a bad day, that's all. The tides and the winds will scrub it all clean. But not clean enough anymore. One life to live, so pop through the escape hatch, McGee. Try the islands. Damned few people can escape the smudge and sludge, the acids and stenches, the choking and weeping. You have to take care of yourself, man. Nobody else is going to. And this deft morsel, curled sleeping against you, is a first-class ticket for all of the voyage you have left. Suppose you *do* have to do some bowing and scraping and fetching. Will it kill you? Think of what most people have to do for a living. You've been taking your retirement in small installments whenever you could afford it. So here's the rest of it in her lovely sleep. The ultimate social security.

I eased my dead arm out from under her and moved away. She made a sleep-whine of discontent. I covered her with the big colorful sheet, dressed, turned out the rosy light, and made sure the main hatchway locked behind me when I left.

Back aboard the *Flush* I put on swim trunks and a robe to keep me warm in the morning chill. The sun was coming up out of the sea when I walked across the pedestrian bridge over the highway and down onto the public beach. Morning birds were running along the wet sand, pecking and fleeing from the wash of the surf. An old man was jogging slowly by, his face in a clench of agony. A fat girl in a brown dress was looking for shells.

I went in, swam hard, and rested, again and again, using short bursts of total energy. I went back to the *Flush* and had a quart of orange juice, four scrambled eggs along with some rat cheese from Vermont, and a mug of black coffee.

I fell asleep seven and a half inches above my oversized bed in the master stateroom, falling toward the bed, long gone before I landed.

four

Thursday, when I got up a little before noon, the remembered scene with Harry Broll and his little gun seemed unreal. Six loud whacks, not loud enough to attract the curious attention of people on the neighboring craft. The *Flush* had been buttoned up, the airconditioning on. No slug had gone through glass.

I found where five had hit. At last I spotted the sixth one in the overhead. It had hit tumbling and sideways and had not punched itself all the way out of sight, so by elimination it was the one that had grooved the leather sole of my sandal and numbed my heel.

I had rolled to my right after going over backward in the chair. It gave me the chance to kick a small table over, creating more distraction and confusion, and it also forced him, being right-handed, to bring his arm across his body to aim at me, which is more difficult than extending the arm out to the side. Two into the deck, one into the chair, one into the table, one into the overhead, and one into my stereo amplifier.

So maybe the clip held six, and he had not jacked one into the chamber until he got to the parking lot at the marina. If he'd put one in the chamber and filled the clip all the way, there would have been one left for the middle of my face.

Dead then or a long time in the institutional bed with the drains in place and the pain moving around under the sedatives like a snake under a blanket.

Don't give yourself any credit, Mr. Travis McGee. The fates could have counted to seven just as easily. You had an easy shot at him with the ashtray, but your hand was sweaty and the fingertips slipped. You missed badly.

Meyer could be right. I had depended on instinct. It had been my instinct that Harry Broll had not come to kill me. Then he had done his best, and I had lucked out. So was instinct becoming stale? When it stopped being a precision tool, when it ceased sending accurate messages up from the atavistic, animal level of the brain, I was as vulnerable as if sight or hearing had begun to fail. If soft, sloppy, nervous Harry Broll could almost do me in with a pop gun, my next meeting with professional talent could be mortal.

There was another dimension to it. Once I started doubting my survival instinct, I would lose confidence in my own reactions. A loss of confidence creates hesitations. Hesitation is a fatal disease—for anyone in the salvage business.

There are worse careers than house guest. Or pet gopher.

Too much solitary introspection started to depress me. I was ready for Geritol and cortisone. I pulled all the plugs and connections on the Marantz and lugged its considerable weight all the way to where I'd parked Miss Agnes, my ancient and amiable old blue Rolls pickup. I drove over to town to Al's Musicade. He is lean, sour, and knowledgeable. He does not say much. He took it out back himself and found bench space in his busy service department. I watched him finger the hole in the front of it. He quickly loosened the twelve Phillips screws that hold the top perforated plate down, lifted it off, found more damage, reached in with two fingers, and lifted out the deformed slug.

"Somebody didn't like the programing?"

"Bad lyrics."

"Week from today?"

"Loaner?"

"Got a Fisher you can use."

We walked out front, and he lifted it off the rack, a used one in apparently good condition. He made a note of the serial number and who was taking it out.

I put the borrowed amplifier on the passenger seat beside me and went looking for Harry Broll's place of business. I had seen it once and had a general idea where to find it. I had to ask at a gas station. It was west of Lauderdale, off Davie Road, over in an industrial park in pine and palmetto country. All of it except the office itself was circled by high hurricane fencing with slanted braces and three strands of barbed wire on top. There was a gate for the rail spur and a truck and equipment gate. I could see a central mix concrete plant, a block plant, big piles of sand, gravel, and crushed stone. I could see warehouses, stacks of lumber, piles of prestressed concrete beams, and a vehicle park and repair area. This was a Thursday at one thirty in the afternoon, and I could count only ten cars. Four of those were in front of the office. The office was a long, low concrete-block building painted white with a flat roof. The landscaped grass was burned brown, and they had lost about half the small palm trees planted near the office.

There were too many trucks and pieces of equipment in the park. It looked neat enough but sleepy. BROLL ENTERPRISES, Inc. But some of the big plastic letters had blown off or fallen off. It said:

ROLL E TERP ISES, Inc.

I cruised slowly by. I was tempted to turn around and go back and go in and see if Harry was there and try once more to tell him I'd had no contact whatsoever with Mary for over three years. But he was going to believe what emotions told him to believe.

I wondered how Meyer was doing, using his friends in the banks, brokerage houses, and investment houses to find out just how sweaty Harry Broll might be. The tight-money times and the over-building of condominiums and the pyramiding costs had busted quite a few able fellows lately. Harry probably hadn't come through that bad period without some ugly bruises. I could tell Meyer how idle Broll's place of business looked, if he hadn't found out already.

When I got back to Bahia Mar, Meyer was still missing. I felt restless. I set up the Fisher, hooked up the tape decks, turntables, and the two sets of speakers. It checked out all right. I turned it off and paced. The itch you can't quite reach. Familiar feeling. Like the name you can't quite remember.

I looked up the number for Broll Enterprises and phoned. The girl answered by reciting the number I'd just dialed.

"Maybe you can help me, miss. I'm trying to get a home address for Mrs. Harry Broll."

"In what regard, please."

"Well, this is the Shoe Mart, and it was way back in November we special-ordered a pair of shoes for Mrs. Broll. It took so long she's under no obligation to take them, but they're more a classic than a high-style item, so I figure she probably wants them, but I been drawing a blank on the home phone number, so I thought maybe they moved or something."

"Will you hold on a moment, please?"

I held. It took her about a minute and a half. "Mr. Broll says that you can deliver them here to the office. Do you know where we are?"

"Sure. Okay. Thanks. It'll probably be tomorrow."

I hung up, and once again, to make sure, I dialed the home phone number for Harry Broll, 21 Blue Heron Lane. "The number you have dialed is not in service at this time."

I scowled at my phone. Come on, McGee. The man is living somewhere. Information has no home number for him. The old home number is on temporary disconnect. The new number of wherever he's living must be unlisted. It probably doesn't matter a damn where he's living. It's the challenge.

Okay. Think a little. Possibly all his mail is directed to the business address. But some things have to be delivered. Booze, medicine, automobiles. Water, electricity . . . cablevision?

The lady had a lovely voice, gentle and musical and intriguingly breathy. "I could track it down more quickly, Mr. Broll, if you could give me your account number."

"I wish I could. I'm sorry, miss. I don't have the bill in front of me. But couldn't you check it by address? The last billing was sent to 21 Blue Heron Lane. If it's too much trouble, I can phone you tomorrow. You see, the bill is at my home, and I'm at the office."

"Just a moment, please. Let me check the cross index."

It took a good five minutes. "Sorry it took me so long," she said.

"It was my fault, not having my account number, miss."

"Broll. Bee-are-oh-el-el. Harry C.?"

"Correct."

"And you said the bill went where?"

"To 21 Blue Heron Lane. That's where I used to live."

"Gee, Mr. Broll, I don't understand it at all. All billing is supposed to be mailed to Post Office box 5150."

"I wonder if I've gotten a bill that belongs to someone else. The amount doesn't seem right either."

"You should be paying $6.24 a month, sir. For the one outlet. You were paying more, of course, for the four outlets at Blue Heron Lane before you ordered the disconnect."

"Excuse me, but does your file show where I am getting the one-outlet service? Do you have the right address?"

"Oh, yes sir. It's 8553 Ocean Boulevard, apartment 61. I've got the installation order number. That *is* right, isn't it?"

"Yes. That's right. But I think the billing is for eleven dollars and something."

"Mr. Broll, please mail the bill back in the regular envelope we send out, but in the left bottom corner would you write *Customer Service, Miss Locklin?*"

"I will do that. I certainly appreciate your kindness and courtesy, Miss Locklin."

"No trouble, really. That's what we're here for."

Four o'clock and still no Meyer, so I went out and coaxed Miss Agnes back to life and went rolling on up Ocean Boulevard. I kept to the far right lane and went slowly because the yearly invasion of Easter bunnies was upon us, was beginning to dwindle, and there was too little time to enjoy them. They had been beaching long enough so that there were very few cases of lobster pink. The tans were nicely established, and the ones who still burned had a brown burn. There are seven lads to every Easter bunny, and the litheness and firmness of the young ladies gamboling on the beach, ambling across the highway, stretching out to take the sun, is something to stupefy the senses. It creates something which is beyond any of the erotic daydreams of traditional lust, even beyond that aesthetic pleasure of looking upon pleasing line and graceful move.

It is possible to stretch a generalized lust, or an aesthetic turn of mind, to encompass a hundred lassies—say five and a half tons of vibrant and youthful and sun-toned flesh clad in about enough fabric to half fill a bushel basket. The erotic imagination or the artistic temperament can assimilate these five and a half tons of flanks and thighs, nates and breasts, laughing mouths and bouncing hair and shining eyes, but neither lust nor art can deal with a few thousand of them. Perceptions go into stasis. You cannot compare one with another. They become a single silken and knowledgeable creature, unknowable, a thousand-legged contemptuous joy, armored by the total ignorance of the very young and by the total wisdom of body and instinct of the female kind. A single cell of the huge creature, a single entity, one girl, can be trapped and baffled, hurt and emptied, broken and abandoned. Or to flip the coin, she can be isolated and cherished, wanted and needed, taken with contracts and ceremonies. In either case the great creature does not miss the single identity subtracted from the whole any more than the hive misses the single bee. It goes on in its glistening, giggling, leggy immortality, forever replenished from the equation of children plus time, existing every spring, unchangingly and challengingly invulnerable—an exquisite reservoir called Girl, aware of being admired and saying "Drink me!," knowing that no matter how deep the draughts, the level of sweetness in the reservoir remains the same forever.

There are miles of beach, and there were miles of bunnies along the tan Atlantic sand. When the public beach ended I came to the great white wall of high-rise condominiums which conceal the sea and partition the sky. They are compartmented boxes stacked high in sterile sameness. The balconied ghetto. Soundproof, by the sea. So many conveniences and security measures and safety factors that life at last is reduced to an ultimate boredom, to the great decisions of the day—which channel to watch and whether to swim in the sea or the pool.

I found 8553. It was called Casa de Playa and was spray-creted as wedding cake white as the rest of them. Twelve stories, in the shape of a shallow C, placed to give a maximum view of the sea to each apartment even though the lot was quite narrow. I had heard that raw land along there was going at four thousand a foot. It makes an architectural challenge to take a two-hundred-foot lot which costs eight hundred thousand dollars and cram 360 apartments onto it, each with a view, and retain some elusive flavor of spaciousness and elegance.

Economics lesson. Pay eight hundred thou for the land. Put up two hundred thousand more for site preparation, improvement, landscaping, covered parking areas, swimming pool or pools. Put up a twelve-story building with 30 apartments on each of the floors from the second through the eleventh and 15 penthouse apartments on top. You have 315 apartments. The building and the apartment equipment cost nine million. So you price them and move them on the basis that the higher in the air they are and the bigger they are, the more they cost. All you have to do is come out with about a thirty-three hundred net on each apartment on the average after all construction expenses, overhead expenses, and sales commissions, and you make one million dollars, and you are a sudden millionaire before taxes.

But if the apartments are retailing at an average forty thousand each and you sell off everything in the building except ten percent of the apartments, then instead of being a million bucks ahead, you are two hundred thousand in the red.

It is deceptively simple and monstrously tricky. Meyer says that they should make a survey and find out how many condominium heart attacks have been admitted to Florida hospitals. A new syndrome. The first symptom is a

secret urge to go up to an unsold penthouse and jump off
your own building, counting vacancies all the way down.

As I did not care to be remembered because of Miss
Agnes, I drove to a small shopping center on the left side
of the highway, stashed her in the parking lot, and walked
back to the Casa de Playa.

On foot I had time to read all of the sign in front.

NOW SHOWING. MODEL APARTMENTS. CASA DE
PLAYA. A NEW ADVENTURE IN LIVING. FROM $38,950
TO $98,950. PRIVATE OCEAN BEACH. POOL. HOTEL
SERVICES. FIREPROOF AND SOUNDPROOF CONSTRUC-
TION. SECURITY GUARD ON PREMISES. NO PETS. NO
CHILDREN UNDER FIFTEEN. AUTOMATIC FIRE AND
BURGLAR ALARM. COMMUNITY LOUNGE AND GAME
AREA. ANOTHER ADVENTURE IN LIVING BY BROLL
ENTERPRISES, INC.

The big glass door swung shut behind me and closed
out the perpetual sounds of the river of traffic, leaving me
in a chilled hush on springy carpeting in a faint smell of
fresh paint and antiseptic.

I walked by the elevators and saw a small desk in an alcove. The sign on the desk said: Jeannie Dolan, Sales Executive on Duty. A lean young lady sat behind the desk,
hunched over, biting down on her underlip, scowling down
at the heel of her left hand and picking at the flesh with a
pin or needle.

"Sliver?" I said.

She jumped about four inches off the desk chair. "Hey!
Don't sneak up, huh?"

"I wasn't trying to."

"I know you weren't. I'm sorry. Yes, it's a sliver."

"Want some help?"

She looked up at me. Speculative and noncommittal.
She couldn't decide whether I'd come to deliver something, repair something, serve legal papers, or buy all the
unsold apartments in a package deal.

"Well . . . every time I take hold of something, it hurts."

I took her over to the daylight, to an upholstered bench near a big window which looked out at a wall made of pierced concrete blocks. I held her thin wrist and looked at her hand. There was red inflammation around the sliver and a drop of blood where she had been picking at it. I could see the dark narrow shape of the splinter under the pink and transparent skin. She had been working with a needle and a pair of tweezers. I sterilized the needle in her lighter flame, pinched up the skin so that I could pick a little edge of the splinter free. She sucked air through clenched teeth. I took the tweezers and got hold of the tiny end and pulled it out.

"Long," I said, holding it up. "Trophy size. You should get it mounted."

"Thank you very very much. It was driving me flippy," she said, standing up.

"Got anything to put on it?"

"Iodine in the first aid kit."

I followed her back to the desk. She hissed again when the iodine touched the raw tissue. She asked my advice as to whether to put a little round bandaid patch on it, and I said I thought a splinter that big deserved a bandage and a sling, too.

She was lean, steamed-up, a quick-moving, fast-talking woman in her late twenties with a mobile face and a flexible, expressive voice. In repose she could have been quite ordinary. There was a vivacity, an air of enjoying life about her that made her attractive. Her hair was red-brown, her eyes a quick, gray-green, her teeth too large, and her upperlip too short for her to comfortably pull her mouth shut, so it remained parted, making her look vital and breathless instead of vacuous. She used more eye makeup than I care for.

"Before I ask question one, Miss Dolan—"

"Mrs. Dolan. But Jeannie, please. And you are . . .?"

"John Q. Public until I find out something."

"John Q. Spy?"

"No. I want to know who you represent, Jeannie."

"Represent? I'm selling these condominium apartments as any fool can plainly—"

"For whom?"

"For Broll Enterprises."

"I happen to know Harry. Do the skies clear now?"

She tilted, frowned, then grinned. "Sure. If a realtor was handling this and you talked to me, then there'd have to be a commission paid, and you couldn't get a better price from Mr. Broll. There used to be a realtor handling it, but they didn't do so well, and I guess Mr. Broll decided this would be a better way. Can I sell you one of our penthouses today, sir? Mr. Public, sir?"

"McGee. Travis McGee. I don't know whether I'm a live one or not. I'm doing some scouting for a friend. I'd like to look at one with two bedrooms and two baths just to get an idea."

She took a sign out of her desk and propped it against the phone. "Back in ten minutes. Please be seated." She locked her desk and we went up to the eighth floor. She chattered all the way up and all the way down the eighth floor corridor, telling me what a truly great place it was to live and how well constructed it was and how happy all the new residents were.

She unlocked the door and swung it open with a flourish. She kept on chattering, following a couple of steps behind me as I went from room to room. After quite a while she ran out of chatter. "Well. . . . Don't you want to ask *anything*?"

"The floor plan is efficient. The equipment looks pretty adequate. But the furniture and the carpeting and the decorating make me feel sort of sick, Jeannie."

"A very expensive decorator did all our display apartments."

"Yeck."

"A lot of people are really turned on by it."

"Yeck."

"We've even sold some with all the decor intact, just as you see it. The buyers insisted."

"Still yeck."

"And I think it is absolutely hideous, and it makes me feel queasy, too. It looks too sweet. Cotton candy and candy cane and ribbon candy. Yeck."

"Got one just like this that hasn't been messed with?"

"Down on five. Come along."

We rode down three floors. The apartment was spotlessly clean and absolutely empty. She unlocked the sliding doors, and we went out onto the balcony and leaned against the railing.

"If the answers to the other questions make sense, Jeannie, my friend might be interested, provided you don't show her that one up on eight."

I asked the right questions. Was it long-term leasehold or actual ownership with undivided interest in the land? How much a year for taxes? How much for the maintenance contract? What were the escalation provisions in the maintenance contract? How much did utilities run? Would the apartment be managed, be rented if you wished when you were not using it?

"How many apartments are there all told?"

"Counting the penthouses—298."

"How many unsold?"

"Oh, very few, really."

"How many?"

"Well . . . Harry might cut my throat all the way around to the back if I told anybody. But after all, you are my surgeon, and I have the scar to prove it. We've got thirty-six to go. I've been here a month and a half, and I get free rent in one of the models and a fifty-buck-a-week draw against a thousand dollars a sale. Between the two of us, Betsy and me, we've sold two."

"So Harry Broll is hurting?"

"Would your friend live here alone, Travis?"

"It would just be more of a convenience for her than anything. She lives in the British Virgins. St. Kitts. She comes over here often, and she's thinking about getting an apartment. I imagine she'd use it four times a year probably, not over a week or two weeks at a time. She might loan it to friends. She doesn't have to worry about money."

Jeannie Dolan made a small rueful face. "How nice for her. Will you be bringing her around?"

"If I don't find anything she might like better."

"Remember, this floor plan is $55,950. Complete with color coded kitchen with—"

"I know, dear."

"Wind me up and I give my little spiel." She locked up, and we rode down in the elevator. She looked at her watch. "Hmmm. My long, exhausting day has been over for ten minutes. I read half a book, wrote four letters, and got operated on for a splinter."

"There's some medication I want to prescribe, Mrs. Dolan. If there's an aid station nearby, I can take you there and buy the proper dosage and make sure you take it."

She looked at me with the same expression as in the very beginning speculative, noncommittal. "Well . . . there's Monty's Lounge up at the shopping center, behind the package store."

five

Monty's was no shadowy cave. It was bright, sunny, and noisy. Terrazzo floor, orange tables, a din of laughter and talk, shouts of greeting, clink of ice. Hey, Jeannie. Hi, Jeannie, as we found our way to a table for two against the far wall. I could see that this was the place for a quick one after the business places in the shopping center closed. There was a savings and loan, insurance offices, a beauty parlor, specialty shops all nearby.

The waitress came over and said, "The usual, Jeannie? Okay. And what's for you, friend?" Jeannie's turned out to be vodka tonic, and friend ordered a beer.

In those noisy and familiar surroundings Jeannie relaxed and talked freely. She and her friend Betsy had come down to Florida from Columbus, Ohio, in mid-January to arrange a couple of divorces. Their marriages had both gone sour. She had worked for an advertising agency, doing copy and layout, but couldn't find anything in her line in the Lauderdale area. Betsy Booker had been a dental hygienist in Columbus but hated it because no matter what kind of shoes she bought, her feet hurt all the time. Betsy's husband was a city fireman, and Jeannie's husband was an accountant.

She seemed miffed at her friend Betsy. There was tension there, and it had something to do with Harry Broll. I tried to pry, but she sidestepped me, asked me what I did. I told her I was in marine salvage, and she said she knew it had to be some kind of outdoor work.

Finally I took a calculated risk and said, "If my friend likes the apartment, then I'll see what I can do with Harry

Broll. Hope you don't mind hearing somebody badmouth him. Harry is such a pompous, obnoxious, self-important jackass, it will be a pleasure to see how far down he'll come on the price."

"You said you were friends, McGee!"

"I said I knew him. Do I look like a man who needs friends like that?"

"Do I look like a girl who'd work for a man like that?"

We shook hands across the table, agreeing we both had better taste. Then she told me that Betsy Booker's taste was more questionable. Betsy had been having an affair with Harry Broll for two months.

"Betsy and I were in a two bedroom on the fourth on the highway side, but she has gradually been moving her stuff up onto six into his one bedroom, apartment 61. I guess it hurt her sore feet, all that undressing and dressing and undressing and walking practically the length of the building."

"Bitter about it?"

"I guess I sound bitter. It's more like hating to see her be so damned dumb. She's a real pretty blonde with a cute figure, and she just isn't used to being without a guy, I guess. It isn't a big sex thing going on. Betsy just has to have somebody beside her in the night, somebody she can hear breathing. She makes up these weird stories about how it's all going to work out. She says he's going to make a great big wad of money on some kind of land promotion stock and because Mrs. Broll deserted her husband, he's going to be able to get a divorce and marry Betsy."

"Couldn't it happen like that?"

"With him? Never!" she said and explained how she hadn't liked Harry's looks and had checked him out. Her best source had been the housekeeper at the apartment building. Last November when the place had been finished, Harry Broll had taken over apartment 61. He had an unlisted phone installed. He did not get any mail there.

"It's obvious what he was setting up," Jeannie said. "The world is full of Harry Broll-type husbands. The housekeeper said some Canadian broad moved into the apartment a week later. Harry would take long lunch hours. But he must have slipped up somehow, because Mrs. Broll arrived one day about Christmas time and went busting in when Harry was leaving, and there was a lot of screaming going on. His wife left him, even though Harry had gotten rid of his girlfriend. Then Harry moved out of his house and into the apartment. Betsy saw his house once. He took her there and showed it to her. She said it's big and beautiful. She won't ever get to live there. He'll dump her when he gets tired of her."

She said two drinks would be plenty. I paid the check and took her out and introduced her to Miss Agnes. Jeannie was so delighted with my ancient Rolls that I had to drive her up to Pompano Beach and back. I let her out across from the Casa de Playa. I wondered if I should caution her about mentioning my name to Betsy, who might in turn mention it to Harry Broll, and turn him more paranoid than ever. But it seemed to be too long a chance to worry about and too little damage from it even if it did happen.

She gave me an oblique, quick, half-shy look that said something about wondering if she would ever see me again. I discovered that I would like to see her again. We said cheerful and conspiratorial goodbys. She walked around the front of Miss Agnes, waited for a gap in traffic, and hastened across the highway. Her legs were not quite too thin, I decided. The brown-red hair had a lively bounce. From the far curb she turned and waved, her smile long-range but very visible.

It was dark when I parked Miss Agnes. I walked to F Dock and on out to Slip 18 and made a ritualistic check of the mooring lines and spring lines, then checked to see how the *Muñequita* was riding, tucked in against the flank of *The Busted Flush,* fenders in proper placement to prevent thumps and gouges.

"Don't pretend you can't hear my foot tapping, you

rude, tardy son of a bitch," Jilly said with acid sweetness. She was at the sundeck rail, outlined against the misty stars with a pallor of dock lights against her face.

I went aboard, climbed up, and reached for her but she ducked away. "What did I forget, woman?"

"The Townsends. I told you I accepted for both of us. Don't you remember at all?"

"What did we accept?"

"Drinks aboard the *Wastrel* and dinner ashore. They're over at Pier 66. Old friends, dear. She was the heavy little woman with the good diamonds."

"Oh."

"You're drawing a blank, aren't you?"

"I seem to be."

"Hurry and change and we can join them at dinner. And, dear, not quite as informal as you were at my little party, please?"

"Is she the woman who kept talking about her servant problem? No matter what anybody else was talking about?"

"Yes. That's Natalie. And Charles is hard of hearing, and he's too vain to admit it or buy one of those little electronic things. *Please* hurry, Travis." She eeled into my arms, pressed herself close to me. She smelled very good, and she felt springy and useful. "The sooner we go, dearest, the sooner we can leave their party and come back and have our own little party."

I gave her a good solid whack on the behind and said, "You go ahead and make excuses."

"Ouch! That was too rough, really. You'll be along soon?"

"Jilly honey, I don't know those people. I can't talk to them, and they can't talk to me. I could use up my life with people like that and never know where it went."

"They're my *friends!* I won't permit you to be rude to my friends. You accepted, you know."

"*You* accepted."

"But I expect you to have some consideration for—"

"Don't expect anything from me, Jillian. Sorry I forgot.

Sorry you had to hang around waiting for me. Now go to your party and have a good time."

"Do you mean it?"

"Why shouldn't I want you to have a good time?

"I have *had* it with you, you bahstid!"

"Sorry, Jilly. I just don't go to parties unless I like the people."

She went clicking down the outside ladderway and clacked her way aft and off the *Flush* and down the dock and away into the night. I went below, turned on a few lights, built a drink, ran a thumb down the stack of tapes, picked Eydie, and chunked her into the tape player and fixed volume.

Eydie has comforted me many times in periods of stress. She has the effortlessness of total professionalism. She is just so damned good that people have not been able to believe she is as good as she is. She's been handed a lot of dull material, some of it so bad that even her best hasn't been able to bring it to life. She's been mishandled, booked into the right places at the wrong time, the wrong places at the right time. But she can do every style and do it a little better than the people who can't do any other. Maybe a generation from now those old discs and tapes of Eydie will be the collectors' joy, because she does it all true, does it all with pride, does it all with heart.

So I settled back and listened to her open her throat and let go, backed by the Trio Los Panchos, Mexican love songs in flawless Mexican Spanish. She eased the little itch of remembering just how good my Irish lady had smelled, tasted, and felt.

A lot of the good ones get away. They want to impose structure upon my unstructured habits. It doesn't work. If I wanted structure, I'd live in a house with a Florida room, have 2.7 kids, a dog, a cat, a smiling wife, two cars, a viable retirement and profit-sharing plan, a seven handicap, and shortness of breath.

God only knows how many obligations there would have been once we were living in the British Virgins. Sing to me, Eydie. I just lost a pretty lady.

Through the music I heard the bong of my warning bell. I put on the aft floods and trapped Meyer in the white glare, blinking. I turned them off and let him in. I could not use Eydie for background music, so I ejected the tape and put a nothing tape on and dropped the sound down to the threshold of audibility.

Meyer said, "I was here an hour ago, and there was a beautiful, angry lady here, all dressed up, with someplace to go but nobody to go with."

"Fix yourself a knock. She decided to go alone."

"I bet."

"I am a crude, selfish bastard, and she is through with me."

He came back with a drink. He sat and said, "They tell me that a ring in the nose bothers you for the first week or so and then you never notice it again."

"Until somebody yanks on the rope."

"Oh, she wouldn't do that without good cause."

"Who the hell's side are you on?"

"She'll be back."

"Don't put any money on it."

"Speaking of money . . ."

"Harry Broll?"

"Yes, indeed. I had a long, tiring day. I talked to twenty people. I lied a lot. This is what I put together. It is all a fabric of assumption and supposition. Harry Broll is a small- to medium-sized cog in the machine called Sea-Gate, Inc. It is Canadian money, mostly from a Quebec financier named Dennis Waterbury, and New York money from a syndicate there which has been involved in other land deals. They needed Broll because of his knowledge of the local scene, the local contacts, legal shortcuts, and so on. It is a privately held corporation. They are going public. The offering price has not been set yet, but it will be about twenty-six or twenty-seven dollars a share. Most of the shares will be offered by the corporation, but about a third of the public offering will be by the present shareholders. Harry will be marketing a hundred thousand shares."

Cause for a long, low whistle. Old Harry with two and a half mil before taxes was a boggling picture for the mind to behold.

"How soon does he get rich?"

"Their fiscal year ends the last day of this month. The national accounting firm doing the audit is Jensen, Baker and Company. They will apparently get a guaranteed underwriting through Fairmont, Noyes. I hear that it is a pretty clean deal and that SEC approval should be pretty much cut and dried after they get the complete audit report, the draft of the red herring."

I stared at him. "Red herring?"

"Do you know what a prospectus is?"

"That thing that tells you more than you care to know about a new issue of stocks or bonds?"

"Yes. The red herring is the prospectus without the per share price of the stock on it or the date of issue. And it is a complete disclosure of *everything* to do with the company, background of executives and directors, how they got their stock, what stock options they may hold, what financial hanky panky, if any, they've ever been involved in. Very interesting reading sometimes."

"Nice to see an old acquaintance get rich enough to afford a hell of a lot of alimony."

"When a company is in registration, they get very secretive, Travis. Loose lips can sink financial ships."

"What would he want Mary to sign? He said it was to protect his interest in SeaGate."

"I wouldn't have any idea."

"Can you find out?"

"I can try to find out. I suppose the place to go would be West Palm. That's where the administrative offices of SeaGate are. That's where they are doing the audit, starting early so that they can close the books as of April thirtieth. It would be futile to try to pry anything out of the Jensen, Baker people. But maybe somebody in the Sea-Gate organization might talk. What did you do today?"

I told him. It was complicated and a lot of it was wasted time and effort, so I kept to the things that had worked.

Then I got to my big question. I had been bouncing it off the back of my mind for an hour, and it was going to be a pleasure to share the trauma with someone else.

"Here is this distrait husband, Meyer. He says he doesn't chase women. The Canadian girl was an exception, a big mistake. He wants me to tell Mary he wants her back. They'll go on a nice trip together. He is so rattled and upset he takes out his little gun and tries to kill me. Suppose he had. His two and a half mil would do him no good at all. And Mary could do him no good by coming back. Okay. He stashed his Canadian tail in apartment 61 at his Casa de Playa, and it was right there that Mary caught him. Harry got rid of the girlfriend. Mary gloomed around for a time, and then she left him. He wants her back. He's sending messages through me, he thinks, to get her to come back to him. Let's say she decides to go back. She goes to their house and finds it closed up. She knows he has the apartment. So she'd go there next, and she'd find him all cozied up there with a blonde named Betsy Booker. Draw me some inferences, please."

"Hmmm. We'll assume that the Booker woman is living in Broll's apartment with him, and the signs of her presence are too numerous to eliminate with short warning. Thus, when Broll came to see you, he either was very sure that Mary *would* not come back to him or that Mary *could* not come back to him. Or, possibly, if Mary could come back to him and decided to come back to him, he would have an early warning system to give him ample time to get the Booker woman out of the apartment and maybe even move back to Blue Heron Lane. This would imply that he knows where she is and has some pipe line to her. In either case, there would be considerable insincerity in his visit to you. Yet a man playing games does not pause in the middle of the game to murder someone out of jealousy. So we come to a final postulate which is not particularly satisfying. We assume that he is and was sincere but is too comfortable with his current living arrangement to want to think it through and see how easily it could spoil his second chance with Mary."

"He's not that dumb. Dumb, but not *that* dumb."

"Logic has to take into account all alternatives."

"Would you consider eating Hungarian tonight?" I asked him.

"Considered and approved."

"Poker dollar for the tab?"

"Food and drink, all on one."

six

The way you find Mary is the same way you find anybody.
Through friends and neighbors. And patience. Through
shopping habits, money habits, doctor, dentist, bureau-
cratic forms and reports. And more patience.

You reconstruct the events of three and a half and four
years ago and try to remember the names and places, the
people who could be leads. You find out who Mary used
to be, and from that maybe you find out where she is.

To start with, she was Tina Potter's friend. Came down
to see Tina and Freddie. Came down from Rochester,
New York. It was just a visit, and then she got her own
place. Had some money, some kind of income. Didn't
have to work. Came down because she had just been
through a jolting and ugly divorce action. She'd gotten her
maiden name back by court order. Mary Dillon. Dillon
and Dolan. I seemed to be working my way through the
Ds. D for divorce.

A quiet young woman. We all got to like her. She had
been putting the pieces of herself back together very very
nicely. Then something happened. What the hell was it?

At last I remembered. Tina Potter had come over to the
Flush late one afternoon and asked me if I could sort of
keep an eye on Mary. Freddie had a special assignment in
Bogota, and Tina would go with him only if she was sure
somebody would watch over Mary. The incident which
had racked her up had been the accidental death of her divorced husband a few days before. A one-car accident on
a rainy night somewhere near Rochester. Left the road
and hit a tree.

I remembered Tina's earnest face as she said, "Two-bit psychology for whatever it's worth, McGee. I think Mary had the idea, hidden so deep she didn't even realize it, that one day her Wally would grow up and come back to her and then they'd have the kind of marriage she thought they were going to have the first time around. So with him dead, it can't ever be. She's trying to hang on, but it's very white-knuckle stuff. Would you mind too much? She trusts you. She can talk to you."

So I had spent a lot of time with Mary. Beach walking, driving around, listening to music. But if she laughed, she couldn't be sure it wouldn't turn into tears. She had no appetite. The weight loss was apparent. A drink would hit her too hard.

I suggested the aimless cruise. Get away. No destination. Mary knew by then it wasn't a shrewd way of hurrying her into the sack, because had that been the target, it would have happened one of the times when her guard was way down. She agreed without much enthusiasm, provided she could pay her share of the expenses and do her share of the chores aboard.

After two weeks she had really begun to come out of it. At first she had slept twelve and fourteen hours a night, as if her exhaustion was of the same kind that happens after an almost mortal wound. Then she had begun to eat. The listlessness had turned to a new energy. She could laugh without it turning to tears.

One day when we were anchored a dozen miles north of Marathon, among some unnamed islands, I took the little *Sea Gull* outboard apart, cleaned it, lubricated it, reassembled it, while she zipped around out there in the sailing dinghy, skidding and tacking in a brisk bright wind. When she came back aboard the *Flush* she was wind blown, sun glowing, salty, happy, and thirsty. Before she went off to take her very niggardly freshwater shower, she brought me a beer. She told me she hadn't felt so good in a long long time. We clinked bottles in a toast to a happy day. She looked, smiling, into my eyes, and then her eyes changed. Something went click. They widened in small shock and surprise, then looked soft and heavy. Her head was too heavy for her slender neck. Her mouth was softer. Her mouth said my name without making a sound. She got up and left me, her walk slow and swaying, and went below. It had been awareness, invitation, and acceptance all in a few moments, all without warning. I remember hastily fastening the last piece of the housing back onto the small motor and deciding that I could test it and stow it later. The lady was below, and there was a day to celebrate, a cruise to celebrate, a recovery to celebrate.

So try Tina and Freddie Potter. Long gone, of course. Scrabbled around in the locker where I throw cards and letters. Found one a year old. Address in Atlanta. Direct-dialed Atlanta information, then direct-dialed the Potter house. Squeals of delight, then desolation that I wasn't in Atlanta. Freddie had just gone off to work. She had to quiet the kids down, then she came back on the line.

"Mary? Gee, I guess the last I heard was Christmas time, Trav. She wrote kind of a short dreary note on the back of a New Year's card. She sounded pretty depressed, so I wrote her, but I didn't hear from her. What's the matter? Why are you looking for her?"

"She left Harry Broll early in January."

"That doesn't surprise me much. I never could understand why she married him. Or the first one, Wally, either. Some women seem to have to pick losers every time. Like some women pick alcoholics every time. But . . . I'd think she'd get in touch with you or with us. But you know Mary. Doesn't want to be a burden to anyone."

"How about family?"

"Well, there was just her mother up in Rochester, and she died two years ago. That was all she had, Trav. Gee, I can't think of who you could ask. But I'd think she'd have some friend she'd talk to. A neighbor or something."

She couldn't contribute anything more. She wanted me to let her know when I found out where Mary was, and she wanted me to come to Atlanta and stay with them and tell them all the news about everybody around the marina.

I couldn't use the Rolls pickup to visit the neighbors

along Blue Heron Lane. There aren't any cover stories to fit that set of wheels. And housewives are very edgy these days. They have little peep holes set into the doors and outdoor intercom speakers and little panic buttons to push if they get too nervous. Respectability is essential. Nothing eccentric please.

So I borrowed Johnny Dow's Plymouth sedan, and I wore pressed slacks, a sincere jacket, an earnest shirt, and a trustworthy necktie. I carried a black zipper portfolio and a dozen of my business cards. I am Travis McGee, Vice President of CDTA, Inc. It is no lie. Meyer incorporated the company a few years ago, and he keeps it active by paying the tiny annual tax. CDTA means nothing at all. Meyer picked the letters because they sound as if they have to mean something. Commercial Data Transmission Authority. Consolidated Division of Taxes and Audits. Contractors' Departmental Transit Acceptance.

In my sincere, earnest, trustworthy way I was going to hit the neighborhood on this hot Friday morning with a nice check which I had to deliver to Mrs. Harry Broll in settlement of her claim and get her to sign a release. I used one of the checks Meyer had ordered. It was on an actual account. Of course, the account was inactive and had about twelve dollars in it, but the blue checks were impressively imprinted with spaces for his signature and mine. He borrowed a checkwriter from a friend in one of the shops, and we debated the amount for some time before settling on a figure of $1,093.88.

"Good morning, ma'am. I hate to bother you like this, but I wonder if you can help me. My name is McGee. Here is my card. I've got out a check payable to Mrs. Harry Broll in full payment of her claim of last year, and I have a release here for her to sign, but the house looks as if they're off on a long trip or moved or something. Could you tell me how I could find Mrs. Broll?"

It was not a long street. Three short, curving blocks. Large lots, some of them vacant, so that the total was not over twenty-five homes right on Blue Heron Lane. The Broll house was in the middle of the middle block on the left. The canal ran behind the houses on the left hand side, following the curves. Dig a canal and you have instant waterfront.

I made the logical moves. I parked the Plymouth in the Broll driveway, tried the doorbell, then tried the neighbors, the nearest ones first.

"I can't help you at all. We moved in here three weeks ago, all the way from Omaha, and that house has been empty since we moved in, and from any sign of neighborliness from anybody else around here, all the houses might as well be empty, if you ask me."

"Go away. I don't open the door to anyone. Go away."

"Mrs. Broll? Someone said they split up. No, we weren't friendly. I wouldn't have any idea where you could find her."

At the fourth front door—the fifth if you count the place where nobody answered—there was a slight tweak at the baited end of my line.

"I guess the one to ask would be Mrs. Dressner. Holly Dressner. She and Mrs. Broll were all the time visiting back and forth, morning coffee and so forth. That's the next house there, number 29, if she's home. She probably is. I didn't hear her backing out."

After the second try on the doorbell I was about to give up. I could hear the chimes inside. No answer. Then the intercom speaker fastened to the rough-cut cypress board beside the front door clicked and said, "Who is it? And, for God's sake, just stand there and talk in a normal tone of voice. If you get close to the speaker and yell, I won't understand word one."

I gave my spiel, adding that the lady next door told me she would be the one to ask. She asked me if I had a card, and she had me poke it through the mail slot. I wondered why she sounded so out of breath.

I heard chains and locks, and she pulled the door open and said, "So come in." She wore a floor-length terry robe in wide yellow and white stripes, tightly belted. Her short, blond, water-dark hair was soaked. "I was in the pool. Daily discipline. Come on out onto the terrace. I'm too wet to sit in the living room."

She was a stocky woman with good shoulders and a slender waist. She had a tan, freckled face, broad and good humored, pale lashes and brows, pretty eyes. The terrace was screened, and the big pool took up most of the space. Sliding glass doors opened the terrace up into the living room. The yard beyond the screening and beyond the flowerbeds sloped down to a small concrete dock where a canopied Whaler was moored.

She invited me to sit across from her at a wrought iron table with a glass top.

"Try that on me again, Mr. McGee. Slowly. Is this the check?"

She picked it up and put it down and listened as I went through it again. "A claim for what?" she asked.

"Mrs. Dressner, it's company policy not to discuss casualty claims and settlements. I'm sure you can understand why."

"Mr. McGee, may I ask you a personal question?"

"Of course."

"How come you are so full of bullshit?"

I stared at her merry face and merry smile. But above the smile the hazel eyes were expressionless as poker chips.

"I . . . I don't quite understand."

"Go back to Harry and tell him that this didn't work, either. What does he think I am? Some kind of idiot, maybe? Goodby, Mr. McGee."

"This isn't for Harry. This is for me."

"So who the hell are you?"

"How friendly are you with Mary anyway?"

"Very very very. Okay?"

"What happened to her when Wally got killed?"

She frowned at me. "She came apart. She flipped."

"And a man took her on a boat ride?"

"Right. And the way she talked about him, that's the one she should have played house with instead of Harry Broll."

"I almost thought about it seriously."

"You?"

"Travis McGee. *The Busted Flush.* Cruised the Keys

and up the west coast to Tampa Bay. Taught her to sail. Taught her to read a chart. Taught her to navigate."

She put her determined chin on her fist and stared at me. "That *was* the name. You, huh? So what's with the funny games, coming here with your funny card and your funny check? If you knew we're close friends, why not start honest?"

"I have not seen her or talked to her in over three years, Holly. And don't jump on my knowing your first name and try to make anything out of it. The woman next door clued me."

"Hitting the whole neighborhood?"

"One at a time. Mary is . . . low-key intense. She hides a lot of herself. She doesn't make friends easily. But she needs people, so I thought she'd have to have a friend in the neighborhood. A friend, not an acquaintance. Right?"

"So right, McGee. Coffee and tears. Most women bug me. Mary doesn't. I . . . still don't feel right about you. About taking you for granted. It *could* be some kind of a trick. I want to ask you things, but I can't think of anything to ask that you couldn't have gotten from Harry."

"He's trying to find her."

"You know it! I thought the silly son of a bitch was going to try to shake it out of me."

"When was this?"

"A couple of weeks ago. He'd had a couple. He got all weepy. He insisted I had to know where Mary is."

"Do you know where she is?"

"McGee, I know why Harry wants to find her. He wants her to come back to him and sign something and live happily ever after."

"It might be an ugly shock if she did come back."

"How?"

"She'd find the house empty, and she'd go look for Harry at the Casa de Playa, where he just so happens to be shacked with a divorcing blonde named Betsy Booker. In apartment 61."

I couldn't read her expression. "So?"

"So isn't that where Mary found him with the Canadian?"

"Only two people could have told you that. Or three. Harry, Mary, or Lisa—the Canadian quiff."

"Wrong."

"The hell you say."

"I got it out of Betsy Booker's best friend, Jeannie Dolan, also from Columbus, who got part of it from Betsy and part of it from the housekeeper. Jeannie and Betsy take turns manning the sales desk at the Casa de Playa."

I saw her buy it and give a small nod. "So help me. That rotten Harry. Jesus! The way I read it, Lisa was not the first. Just the first she caught him with. He really is one sorry bastard."

"How did she find out?"

"She thinks it was one of the girls in his office or a girl he'd fired, trying to make things rough for him. She got a phone call. The person on the other end whispered. Mary said it was spooky. Something very much to the point. 'Mrs. Broll, your husband has loaned apartment 61 in his new building to Lisa Dissat, and he'll be taking another long lunch hour today so he can drive out there and screw her.' So she drove out and hid somewhere until he arrived and went upstairs. Then she went up to the sixth floor and waited around until the door opened and he started to come out. She took a quick run at the door and knocked it open and charged past him and found the bareass Canadian getting ready to take a nice nap. I take it there was a certain amount of screaming going on for a while."

"Then Harry got rid of the girl friend?"

"She was packed and out of there the next day. Back to Canada, Harry told Mary. He confessed his sad story. He had gone to Quebec for business conferences with his Canadian partners. He had to dictate new agreements. They sent the secretary to the hotel. They worked very late. He was too tired to think clearly. She was pretty and available. It went on for the three days he was up there. He came back. Two days after he was back, she phoned him at his office from Miami. She had quit her job and followed him back to Florida. So he told Mary that while he was trying to talk Lisa into going back, he put her up at the apartment. I guess he was having a hard time convincing her. He talked from the end of November till two days before Christmas. That's a lot of long lunches and a lot of evening conferences."

"But Mary didn't leave him until January fifth."

"Harry told you that?"

I laughed. "I thought the silly son of a bitch was going to try to shake it out of me, too. This was just the other day. And he got weepy."

"So you're finding her for him?"

"May I ask you the same personal question you asked me?"

"Okay. Okay. I'm sorry. Why then?"

"For myself. Pride, I guess. Harry thought if she was really in trouble, she would come running to me. And the more I think about it, the more logical it seems. That she would. Besides—" I stopped suddenly.

"What's the matter?"

"When was Harry here, did you say?"

"Oh, two weeks ago."

"Can you pin it down to a day?"

"Let me go take a look at my kitchen calendar and see."

She came back and said, "Less than two weeks ago. It was a Monday morning. April fifth."

"He told me someone had seen Mary with me on April second. He was wrong, of course. Why would he come after you instead of me if she was seen with me?"

"Maybe he hadn't been told about it before he came to see me," she said.

"And maybe he was trying to get you to admit she'd moved in with me or some damn thing. What difference does it make anyway? He didn't act as if he was thinking very clearly."

"Mary was thinking about getting in touch with you. She was sitting in my kitchen wondering out loud if she should. That was after she'd decided to take off. Then she decided it would be better to have some breathing space in between, some time to herself first. I thought she would have written you long before now. It's over three months."

"She writes you?"

"Don't get too cute, McGee."

"Okay. Do you know where she is?"

"Yes."

"And she is okay?"

"I have no reason to think she isn't. If I was Mary, I would be relishing every damn moment. The farther from Harry, the better."

"That's all I wanted to know, Mrs. Dressner. That she is okay. I had to hear it from somebody I could believe."

"Hey! You're spoiling the fun. You're supposed to worm the whole story out of me. Or try to."

"It's Harry who has to know where she is. Not me."

"Friend McGee, I am not about to get you two men confused, one with the other."

"So she is a long distance from here. And should be relishing every moment. Right?"

"I've gotten some comedy post cards."

"I believe you. There are people you believe and people you don't. I don't need to know any more than I know right now."

She looked rueful. "Everybody believes me. Everything I'm thinking shows. I've got one of those faces. I'd make a rotten spy. Hey, sit down again. I haven't offered you anything. Coffee, tea, beer, booze? Even some lunch?"

"No thanks."

"Believe me, I'm glad to have anybody show up here. This is one of the days when the house gets empty somehow. David—my husband—has been gone all week. He'll be home tomorrow, probably about noon. He's gone a week or more out of every month. Our two little gals are tennis freaks, so who sees them at all when the weather is like this? I miss hell out of Mary, I really do. You could choke down some terrible coffee at least. Pretend it's delicious, and I'll tell you where Mary is. Even if you don't have to know."

She brought coffee from the kitchen to the glass-top

table on the screened terrace. Moving around had loosened the hitch in the terry belt, and when she bent to pour my coffee, the robe suddenly spilled open. She spilled coffee, clutched frantically, put the pot down, and gathered herself together and tied the robe firmly, her face dark red under the freckles. It was obvious she had not contrived it.

"Some people are solitary drinkers. I'm a solitary skinny dipper."

"It's habit forming," I said.

She got paper towels and mopped up the spilled coffee and filled my cup the rest of the way. She sat and stared at me, lips pursed. Finally she said, "Thank you."

"For?"

"For not jumping to any conclusions, for which I could not exactly blame you. Good God, I tell you my husband is away, my kids are playing tennis, I'm lonesome. I beg you to stay for coffee and then damn near drop my robe on the floor."

"Some days are like that."

"I like the way you can smile without hardly changing your mouth at all. It's kind of all in the eyes. Mary said you're a doll. She said big and brown and sort of beat-up looking. But you're bigger and browner than the idea I had of you. About Mary. That was a sordid scene at the Casa de Playa. It shook her. Friendship is friendship, but you don't tell your friends what to do when it comes to big emotional decisions. Through Christmas and the rest of December she spent a lot of time over here. I let her bounce it all off me. She was thinking aloud, arguing it out. Taking one side and then the other, while all I did was say 'um.' But I could tell which side was winning. Finally she said that if she hadn't already had one divorce, she would definitely decide to leave Harry. It was a lousy reason to stick around, just to avoid being divorced twice, which has a kind of ring of failure to it, failure as a person or as a woman. So she was going to leave him and go away and, to be real fair, think it all through. But the way she felt, she'd probably sue for divorce after the waiting period. I waited for her to really make her mind up, and then I questioned her to make certain she was sure, and finally I told her about a little problem I had once with her husband. There'd been a party down the street and the four of us, the Brolls and the Dressners, had walked back together, a little tight. They came over here for a nightcap. There were supposed to be falling stars. It was in the paper. I wanted to see them. We put out the lights on the terrace, and I stretched out on a sun mattress beside the pool, right over there, to watch up through the screening overhead. David went to the kitchen to fix drinks, and Mary changed her mind about what she wanted and went in the kitchen to tell him. Harry was on a sun mattress near mine. All of a sudden he rolled over and put his big old cigar mouth on mine and pressed me down with his big belly and ran his big paw up under my skirt and started groping me. I froze with shock for about one second, and then I gave a big snap of my back like a huge fishing shrimp and bucked him into the pool in all his clothes. It turned into a big joke. He said he'd gotten up and tripped and fallen in.

"When I told Mary about it, she was furious with me for not telling her sooner. I told her I hadn't told David, because he would have tried to beat Harry to death. I said that now she'd made her mind up, I could tell her about what Harry pulled that time. Frankly, what I was doing was trying to lock her into her decision to drop that jerk forever. Having her own money made it easy for her to get away. She got it from her trust officer at the Southern National Bank and Trust in Miami. Cash. A lot, I think. She didn't want Harry tracing her through credit cards or personal checks. She told me she didn't want to hear his voice or see his face once she left. Not for a long time anyway. We sat right out here one afternoon, a warm day for early January, and we looked at the travel folders she'd picked up from some little travel agency where she wasn't known. She wanted to go to the islands. Between the two of us we decided that Grenada looked the best, and it was certainly far enough, way down there at the bottom of the West Indies, almost as far as Trinidad. So the travel agency sent wires and cables and got her set up at what looked like a very plush place, the Spice Island Inn. She's sent me those joke greetings. Four or five, I guess. Airmail takes eight days! That place is a real hideaway."

"Harry told me she left on January fifth. He said he came home from work and she was gone."

"I think it was an impulse. She wasn't going to leave until Thursday or Friday. I was out most of that afternoon. Maybe she tried to say goodby. I guess she probably drove down to Miami and stayed in a hotel or motel until her flight left."

"I wonder what she did with her car?"

"I think she was going to leave it at Miami International."

"Which is two fifty a day, no matter how many days, so she is up to a two-hundred-dollar parking charge."

"McGee, the lady had decided to go first class all the way. That is what ladies do when they get mad enough."

"What would Harry be wanting her to sign?"

"I haven't the faintest idea."

"Good coffee."

"Come on! It tastes like stewed tire patches."

She walked me to the door. She got ahead of me and leaned back against the door and looked up quizzically. She stood a little taller than my elbow. "McGee, I just wondered. It seems like a hell of a lot of trouble you went to. The business cards and the funny check and the sales talk."

"No big thing, Holly. The cards and the checks were in the cupboard. I have to hunt for people sometimes. You learn to use something that works."

"Why do you hunt for people?"

"I do favors for friends."

"Is that a line of work with you?"

"I really wouldn't know how to answer that question."

She sighed. "Heck, I thought I could solve a problem for Mary. She never *was* able to figure out what it is that you do for a living."

"Salvage consultant."

"Sure. Sure."

When I glanced back, she was standing on her shallow front steps, arms crossed. Her hair was beginning to dry and to curl a little. She smiled and waved. She was a sturdy, healthy woman with a very friendly smile.

seven

I was on the beach by three o'clock that Friday afternoon and that was where Meyer found me at a few minutes to four. He dropped his towel, sat upon it, and sighed more loudly than the surf in front of us or the traffic behind us.

There were nine lithe maidens, miraculously unaccompanied by a flock of boys, playing some game of their own devising on the hard sand in the foamy wash of the waves. It involved an improvised club of driftwood, a small, yellow, inflated beach ball, one team out in the water, and one on the beach. Either you had to whack the ball out over the heads of the swimmers before they . . . or you had to hit it past a beach player who then. . . . Anyway, it involved a lot of running, yelping, and team spirit.

"A gaggle of giggles?" Meyer said, trying that one on me.

My turn. "How about a prance of pussycats?"

"Not bad at all. Hmmm. A scramble of scrumptious?"

"Okay. You win. You always win."

He slowly scratched his pelted chest and smiled his brown bear smile. "We both win. By being right here at this time. All the strain of a long, difficult, and futile day is evaporating quickly. Meyer is at peace. Play on, young ladies, because from here on out life will be a lot less fun for most of you."

"Grow up and be earnest and troubled?" I asked. "Why does it have to be that way?"

"It doesn't. It shouldn't be. Funny, though. They take all those high spirits, all that sense of fun and play into one of the new communes, and within a year they are doleful wenches indeed. Somber young versions of American Gothic, like young wagon train mothers waiting for the Indians to ride over the ridge. And their men look like the pictures of the young ones slain at Shiloh. Idealism in our society is pretty damned funereal."

One of the players looked up the beach and gave a quick wave and then went churning into the water to capture the yellow ball.

"One of my constituents," Meyer said comfortably.

"You are a dirty old man."

"You have a dirty mind, McGee. I could not bring myself to ever touch the child. But in all fairness it does enter my mind. Lovely, isn't she?"

"Exquisite."

"Her last name is Kincaid, and I do not know her first name. She is known to everyone as Breadbox. She has an incredible appetite. She's an economics major at Yale. Quite a good mind. Her father grows tobacco in Connecticut. She drove down in a five-year-old Porsche with two other girls. This summer she is going to work in a boutique aboard a cruise ship. She has a dog at home named Rover, which seems to have come full circle and is now an 'in' name for a dog. She is getting over a romance which ended abruptly and does not want to become interested in another man for years and years, she says. Tennis used to be her sport, but now she prefers—"

"So all right already, Meyer. Damn it."

"I think she was waving at someone behind us."

"What?"

"I never saw the child before in my life. I was just putting together into one package some of the things some of the other young ladies have told me."

"Have you been drinking?"

"No. But if you'd like to . . ."

With as little warning as a flock of water birds, the nine maidens dropped the club and went jogging north along the beach, one of them clutching the yellow ball.

Meyer said, "I did not do well today, Travis. Just a few

small items. Dennis Waterbury is in his mid-thirties, bland, shrewd, tough, quick, merciless—and completely honest. He gives his word and keeps it."

"Listen. I was able—"

"Let me deliver my few crumbs first. Harry Broll's cost on his one hundred thousand shares was ten dollars a share, and his money and the money the others put in was used to acquire the land, prepare sites, build roads, start the utility construction, water, waste processing, and so forth. A very golden opportunity for a man like Broll to get his foot in the door with people like Waterbury and friends. But in order to make it big, he had to pluck himself pretty clean, I imagine, and borrow to the hilt. Put up one million and drag down two million and a half. The odds are splendid, the risk low enough."

"About Mary, I—"

"I can't seem to find out what she would have to sign. She wouldn't have to sign anything in connection with the stock. It's in his name. She isn't on his business paper."

"Mary is alive and well and living in Grenada."

"In Spain?"

"No. The island."

"Dear chap, the one in Spain is Gran-AH-duh. The island is Gre-NAY-duh. The British corrupted it with their usual mispronunciation of all place names."

"You've been there?"

"No."

"But you know a lot about it?"

"No. I happen to know how to pronounce it. One has to start somewhere."

"Let's swim."

After about ten minutes Meyer intercepted me fifty yards from the beach, to ask, "How come you could find that out and Harry can't?"

"I found the only person who might really know for sure, aside from the travel agent. A neighbor lady, who shows her good taste by disliking the hell out of Harry Broll. She thought for a while Harry sent me. I softened her up. She makes terrible coffee."

"Did Harry try to pry it out of her, too?"

"Yes. Nearly two weeks ago. With tears. Without the gun. But rough. She said she thought he was going to try to shake it out of her."

Meyer nodded and went gliding away, head up, in that powerful, slow, and tireless breast stroke that somehow makes me think of a seal when I see his head moving by.

When I came out of the water, he was sitting on his towel again, looking petulant, a rare mood for Meyer.

"Something bothering you?"

"Illogical actions and illogical emotions bother hell out of me, Travis. His wife has been gone over three months. How about checking accounts, credit cards?"

I explained about the trust account and her taking cash so that she couldn't be easily traced by her husband. He said he knew one friendly face in the trust department of Southern National, but of course it would be Monday before he could learn anything there.

"Why bother?" I asked him. "I'm satisfied. We know where she is. I don't give a damn how jittery Harry Broll gets."

We walked back across the bridge together, squinting toward the western sun setting into its usual broad band of whisky soup. "I guess it doesn't matter in any case," Meyer said.

"What doesn't matter?"

"What happens to anybody. Look at the cars, McGee. Look at the people in the cars, on the boats, on the beach, in the water. Everybody is heading toward their own obituary notice at precisely the same speed. Fat babies, and old women like lizards, and the beautiful young with long golden hair. And me and thee, McGee. At tick-tock speed moving straight toward the grave, until all now living are as dead as if they had died in Ancient Rome. The only unknown, and that is a minor one, is how long will each individual travel at this unchanging, unchangeable pace?"

"Good God, Meyer! I was going to buy you dinner."

"Not today. This is not one of my good days. I think I'll open a can of something, go walking alone, fold up early. No need to poison somebody else's evening."

Away he trudged, not looking back. It happens sometimes. Not often. A curious gaiety, followed by bleak, black depression. It was a Meyer I seldom see and do not know at all.

Friday night. I took my time building a drink, showering, dressing, building a refill. Dark night by then, and a wind building up, so that the *Flush* moved uneasily, creaking and sighing against her lines, nudging at her fenders. I felt restless. I was wondering where to go, who to call, when Jillian came aboard.

She clung tightly and said she had been utterly miserable. She looked up at me with two perfect and effective tears caught in her lower lashes, her mouth quivering. The Townsend party had been desperately dull, really. She shouldn't have tried to force me to go. She shouldn't try to force me to do anything. She realized that now. She would not do it again, ever. Forgive me, Travis darling, please. I've been so lonely and so ashamed of myself etc., etc., etc.

Once forgiven, all the lights came on behind her eyes, and the tears were flicked away. Mood of holiday. She had been confident of reconciliation, she had brought hairbrush and toothbrush. And all the urgencies a girl could muster.

In the morning a rare April rain was coming down hard, thrashing at the ports beside the half acre of the captain's wrinkled and rumpled bed, bathing us in gray ten o'clock light.

"Is your friend in trouble?" she asked.

"Who?"

"That respectable married lady friend, of course."

"Oh. No, she's fine. It turns out she's hiding from her husband. She went down to Grenada."

She lifted her head. "Really? Henry and I went down there on the first really long cruise we took in the Jilly III. The Grenadines are one of the great sailing areas of the world. And the yacht basin at St. George's is really marvelous. You see people from everywhere, really. Yacht Services is very helpful."

"She's staying at the Spice Island Inn."

"Quite expensive. Is she alone down there?"

"Apparently."

"She can get into all kinds of delicious mischief if she wants. If she's even half attractive, she won't be lonely. The air is full of spice and perfume down there, dear. It's a fabulously erotic island. Always so warm and lazy, with the hot hot sun and the hills and jungles and the beaches. Quite near the equator, you know."

"I didn't know."

"Well, it is. Don't you think we should go there one day?"

"I guess so."

"You don't seem exactly overwhelmed with enthusiasm."

"Sorry."

"Are you going back to sleep, you wretch?"

"Not with you doing what you're doing."

"This? Oh, it's just a sort of reflex thing, I guess. Darling, if you're no longer worried about your friend, could we be ready to aim the *Jilly* toward home on Tuesday? I can get her provisioned on Monday."

"What? Oh, Tuesday. I guess so."

"You don't seem to keep track of what I'm saying."

"I guess I'm easily distracted."

"You're easily something else, too."

"What did you expect?"

"I expect, my dear, if we put our minds to it, we might make the Guinness Book of Records. Cozy? A nice rain always makes me very randy." After a moment she giggled.

"What's funny?"

"Oh, I was thinking I might decide we should go to Grenada during the rainy season, dear."

"Ho ho ho."

"Well . . . it amused *me*. When I feel this delicious, I laugh at practically anything. Sometimes at nothing at all."

The unusual cold front which had brought the rain ahead of it moved through late on Saturday afternoon. She went back to the *Jilly III*. She said she had a thousand things to do before we sailed on Tuesday. She said to come over on Sunday, sometime in the afternoon. She said

I could bring along some of my clothes and toys then, if I wanted.

She left and I locked up again, hot showered, and fell into a deep sleep. I woke at ten on Saturday night, drank a gallon of water, ate half a pound of rat cheese, and dropped right back down into the pit.

I woke with a hell of a start at four on Sunday morning, and thought there was somebody coming aboard. Realized it had been something happening in a dream. Made a grab for what was left of the dream, but it was all gone too quickly. Almost a nightmare. It had pumped me so full of adrenalin there was no hope of going back to sleep. Heart bumped and banged. Legs felt shaky. I scrubbed a bad taste off my teeth, put on jeans and boat shoes and an old gray sweatshirt, and went out onto the deck.

A very silent night. No breeze. A fog so thick the nearer dock lights were haloed and the farther ones were a faint and milky pallor, beyond tangible gray. I could hear slow waves curl and thud against the sand. The craft on either side of the *Flush* were shrouded in the fog, half visible.

Meyer's gloomy message had been delivered none too soon. Everybody else had been tick-tocked to the grave, leaving one more trip to complete—mine. Then, far away, I heard a long screeeeee of tormented rubber and a deep and ugly thud with a small accompanying orchestration of jangles and tinkles. The thud had been mortal, tick-tocking some racing jackass into his satin-lined box, possibly along with the girl beside him or the surprised folk in the other car.

A few minutes later I heard the sirens, heard them stop at what seemed a plausible distance.

So stop thinking about this and that, McGee, and think about what you don't want to think about, namely the lush future with the rich widow.

I climbed to the sun deck and went forward and slouched behind the wheel and propped my heels atop the instrument panel, ankles crossed.

That old honorary Cuban had simplified the question all to hell when he'd said that a moral act is something you feel good after. Conversely, you feel bad after an immoral act. But what about the act that is neither moral nor immoral, Papa? How are you supposed to feel then?

Look, we are very suited to each other. There is a lot of control either way on both sides, so timing is no problem at all. She pleases me. She knows how to intensify it. I like the textures and juices, spices and rhythms of her, all her tastes and tastings. We truly climb one hell of a hill, Papa, and when we fall off the far side together, it is truly one hell of a long fall, Papa, and we land truly and well and as zonked out as lovers can get. We laugh a lot. We like to hold each other afterward. We make bawdy jokes. She has a lot of body greed and finds me a satisfying stud. In her gratitude she takes a lot of extra effort to keep things varied and interesting. So?

There's this little problem. I go into the head, Papa, and look at this battered and skewed beach-bum countenance of mine, reflected in the mirror, and my eyes look dull, and my mouth looks slack, and I am wearing the remnants of a doggy little smirk. I know she is in there, a-sprawl on the bed, drifting in and out of her little love doze, and I look truly and well at myself in the mirror, and I do not feel good about anything or bad about anything. I just feel as if I had made one of those little diagonal lines you use to keep track. You know—four little vertical lines side by side and then the diagonal that crosses them out and ends the group.

In the mirror my nose looks too big, and my skin looks grainy. I wear the doggy little grin. The smells of her cling to my body. There is the feeling of marking something off on a long score sheet. Something well and truly done that will have to be well and truly done for whatever years we both have left, because that is the bargain. Chop that cotton, tote that bale, plow that little acre of God.

What about it when you don't feel good and you don't feel bad? When you just feel that it's done for this time and done reasonably well, and later on the slack dangle of flesh will turn tumescent, and it will and can be done again, just as well as the last time? With proficiency, determination, patience, understanding, power and skill. Isn't lovemaking as good a way as any to pass the time for the rest of your life? It tones the body, and it's acceptable exercise, and it makes two people feel good.

If I don't grasp the opportunity, somebody will find some quick and dirty way to let the sea air through my skull.

I'm overdue. That's what Meyer says, and that's what my gut says in a slow cold coil of tingling viscera. Overdue, and scared, and not ready for the end of it yet. The old bullfighters who have known the famous rings and famous breeds despise the little country corridas, because they know that if they do not quit, that is where they will die—and the bull that hooks their steaming guts out onto the sand will be a poor animal without class or distinction or style.

An animal as ordinary as Harry Broll.

I shifted position, dug the keys out of the pocket, and found the keyholes in the instrument panel. It is one of the tics of the boatman, turning on the juice without starting up, just to check fuel levels, battery charge. By leaning close, I could read the gauges in the pallid light.

Maybe it isn't just the woman. This woman. Or a passing of time. It is the awareness, perhaps, of the grasshopper years, of always pushing all the pleasure buttons. The justification was a spavined sense of mission, galumphing out to face the dragon's fiery breath. It had been a focus upon the torment of individuals to my own profit. Along with a disinterest in doing anything at all about all those greater inequities which affect most of us. Oh, I could note them and bitch about them and say somebody ought to do something. I could say it on my way to the beach or to the bed.

Who will know you were ever around, McGee? Or care?

Wait a minute! What am I supposed to be doing? Making up the slogan I shall paint on my placard and tote in the big parade? A parade is a group, and I'm not a group animal. I think a mob, no matter what it happens to be doing, is the lowest form of living thing, always steaming with potential murder. Several things I could write on my placard and then carry it all by myself down empty streets.

UP WITH LIFE. STAMP OUT ALL SMALL AND LARGE
INDIGNITIES. LEAVE EVERYONE ALONE TO MAKE IT
WITHOUT PRESSURE. DOWN WITH HURTING. LOWER
THE STANDARD OF LIVING. DO WITHOUT PLASTICS.
SMASH THE SERVOMECHANISMS. STOP GRABBING.
SNUFF THE BREEZE AND HUG THE KIDS. LOVE ALL
LOVE. HATE ALL HATE.

Carry my placard and whistle between my teeth and
wink and smirk at the girls on the sidewalk watching the
nut with his sign.

Am I supposed to go out with my brush and yellow
soap and scrub clean the wide grimy world?

If you can't change everything, why try to change any
part of it, McGee?

The answer lit up in the foggy predawn morning, right
over my head. A great big light bulb with glowing fila-
ments, just like those old timey ones over in Boca Grande
in the Edison place.

Because, you dumbass, when you stop scrubbing away
at that tiny area you can reach, when you give up the illusion you are doing any good at all, then you start feeling
like this. Jillian Brent-Archer is another name for giving
up your fatuous, self-serving morality, and when you give
it up, you feel grainy, studlike, secure, and that doggy little
smirk becomes ineradicable.

You are never going to like yourself a hell of a lot, T.
McGee, so what little liking you have must be conserved.
To become Jilly's amiable useful houseguest and bedguest
would turn you into something which you are not—yet
have an uncomfortable tendency to become.

You retain the fragile self-respect by giving Them the
increasingly good chance of ventilating your skull or
scragging you through the heart. There have been some
rotten little scenes with Jilly, but the next one will be the
most memorable of all.

So Mary Broll is okay. And there is a good lump of
cash money stashed behind the fake hull in the forward
bilge of the *Flush*. But it would be a good time, a very
good time, to go steaming out and find the plucked pigeon

and clean up its little corner of the world by getting its feathers back—half of them, anyway. Get out there on the range and go down to the pits and stand up for a moment and see if they can pot you between the eyes. If they miss, maybe you'll get your nerve back, you tin-horn Gawain.

eight

Sunday I did not feel up to facing the predictable fury of Lady Jillian. She wanted me aboard for drinks Monday evening. Time enough, I told myself.

Meyer came over to the *Flush* on Monday morning at about ten thirty. I was punishing myself for recent sensual excess by polishing some neglected brightwork on the instrument panel, using some new miracle goop that was no more miraculous than the old miracle goop.

Without preamble he said, "I phoned the trust department of the Southern National Bank and Trust Company and told the girl to put me through to somebody who could give me a trust account number. When another girl answered, I said that my name was Forrester, and I was with Merrill Lynch. I said we had received a dividend which apparently should have been sent to Mrs. Harry Broll's trust account. I wanted to advise New York and mail the check along, and to prevent further confusion, I wanted the trust account number and the name of the trust officer handling that account. Mary Dillon Broll or Mrs. Harry Broll, 21 Blue Heron Lane, and so forth. She told me to hold, and in a minute or two she came back and said the number was TA 5391, and the trust officer was Mr. Woodrow Willow."

"Interesting, but—"

"I asked her to put me through to Mr. Willow. When he came on the line I introduced myself correctly and told him that I was a personal friend of Mrs. Broll, and she had told me before going away on a trip that he handled her

85

account TA 5391. He said that was correct. He sounded guarded. Properly so. I told him that Mrs. Broll had asked me to give her some advice regarding rephasing her accounts to provide a maximum income, as she anticipated some possible change in her personal status."

"You are getting very crafty lately, Meyer."

"Please stop rubbing those damned dials and look at me. Thank you. He sounded huffy then and said they were perfectly competent to give all necessary investment advice. I told him I knew that and that was why I had called him. I certainly didn't want to usurp their authority and responsibility. I said I seldom make portfolio recommendations any more, only for old friends and at no fee, of course. I said that women often become confused about the way a trust account is set up. I said I understood she had discretion over it, that she could determine what she wanted bought and sold and so direct them. He said that was indeed the case. He sounded wistful, as if he wished it weren't true. I said that I had been trying to get in touch with her in order to clear my ideas with her before coming in to discuss them with him. I said her husband had been unable to help me. I said her house was closed, and her neighbors did not know where she had gone. I asked if he could help me. He said she had phoned him early in January and had come in and drawn out all the accumulated interest and dividends, a sizable amount, and told him she was going away for a month or six weeks. She did not know where. He said he wished he could help me."

"A month or six weeks?"

"Yes. Over three months ago."

"She could have decided to stay longer, you know."

"That's what Woodrow Willow said. He said she was quite upset when she came to see him. He said he could guess why she might be thinking in terms of independent income. So I said that, of course, maximizing income would enable her to live comfortably, but with a woman that young, inflation protection was important."

"Did it work?"

Meyer displayed an uncommonly wolflike smile. "He

hesitated and I heard a desk calculator rattling and humming, and then he said that with her equities reinvested in income holdings, she'd have a pretax income of from twenty-five to twenty-seven thousand. So I told him that we should probably think in terms of eighteen to twenty or, in case of substantial alimony, consider tax exempts. He said he'd be delighted to talk to me about it, but of course he would have to have clearance from her to discuss her affairs. I said I realized that. He said he expected to hear from her very shortly, before the end of the month. Travis, I couldn't push him any further."

"I can see that. He was all set to snap shut at any moment. You got a hell of a lot out of him. Congratulations."

"I braced myself and took a risk. I said, 'Oh, yes, of course. To sign those things for Mr. Broll.' He hesitated and then said, 'It's inconvenient for her to come here in person. So she told me when she came in what Mr. Broll was asking of her. It's something that they did once before, and it was paid off. I had her sign the note. The loan was later approved by the loan committee and the board. A sizable loan, secured by the assets in her trust, with her signed authorization to me to deposit the loan proceeds in Mr. Broll's personal checking account. The effective date of the loan was to be April fifteenth, last Thursday. He requires the funds before the end of the month. She requested me to get it all set up but not to go ahead with it until she gets in touch with me and tells me to proceed or to destroy the signed documents and forget it. That's why I expect her to be in touch with me soon.' Travis, I remember you telling me to always press the luck when it is running your way. So I told him that I had heard that Broll was getting very agitated about getting the note and the authorization signed, so I imagined that Mr. Broll had been in touch with him. Mr. Willow has a very weary laugh. He said he hears from Mr. Broll almost constantly. He said he saw no reason to tell Mr. Broll everything was signed and ready to go, awaiting only authorization from her. I got the impression Harry tried to bulldoze him, and Mr. Willow got his back up. Then he began to realize he had told me more than he should. I could *feel* him pulling back. So I jumped in and said that actually the documents aren't signed until she says they are signed. Until then it is an approved line of credit, and if she doesn't care to use it, she doesn't have to. I told him he was quite correct, and I could feel him trying to persuade himself I was not working for Harry Broll. I hope he did."

I put the cap on the miracle goop and swabbed up the few white places where it had dribbled on the varnish, miraculously removing the gloss. I spun the helmsman's seat around and looked at Meyer.

I said to him, "You are pretty damned intense about something I don't understand. We don't know whether Mary wants him to have that money or not. We know she's in Grenada, knowing he's sweating it out, and she's probably enjoying it every time she thinks about it. We know that Harry is getting so frantic he's losing control. He isn't thinking clearly. Are you?"

"She's been gone over three months now. Harry is living in a way that means he doesn't expect her to come back. You thought she'd get in touch with you if she was in trouble. She didn't. Who saw her leave? What travel agency did she use?"

I reached into the back of my mind and swatted something down. It had been buzzing in circles back there. I picked it up off the floor and looked at it. "Meyer, once on that cruise years ago we bought provisions and got a lot of green stamps. I think it was in Boca Grande. They got wet and got stuck together. Mary soaked them apart. It soaked all the glue off. She dried them between paper towels. Then she got a green stamp book and some Elmer's, and she glued them into the book. Meyer, she didn't even *save* green stamps. Another thing. We spent a lot of time anchored out, as far from marinas and boat traffic and shore sounds as we could get. So she kept turning off the generator, the airconditioning, even the little battery transistor radio. She made great things out of the leftovers from yesterday's leftovers. She's not stingy. If you asked for her last dime, she'd borrow two bits somewhere and give you thirty-five cents. But she has a waste-not, want-not twitch. I kidded her about it. She didn't mind. But it didn't change a thing. Holly Dressner told me Mary planned to leave her car at the Miami airport. Okay. Would Mary pay two and a half a day indefinitely? Ninety days is two hundred and twenty-five dollars. Not Mary. No matter how upset. She'd find out the rates and turn around, drive a few miles, make a deal with a gas station or parking lot, and take a cab back and catch her flight."

"If she had time."

"Unless she changed a lot, she'd get there two hours ahead when the ticket desk says one hour. She'd have time."

"So we should go look for her car?"

"Holly should be able to tell me what to look for."

"Travis, I don't want to seem efficient, but why don't we phone Mary in Grenada? I would rather go below and drink one of your Tuborgs and listen to you fight with the island operators than drive to Miami."

I struck myself a heavy blow in the forehead with the heel of my hand, said a few one-, seven- and ten-syllable words, and we went below.

I started at eleven thirty, and by the time I got the desk at the Spice Island Inn, I was in a cold rage. It was a radio link, and nobody seemed to give a damn about completing it. I had mentally hung Alex Bell and Don Ameche in effigy several times.

At last I got the faint voice of a girl, saying, "Spice Island Inn. May I help you?" It was the singsong lilt of the West Indies, where the accented syllables seem to fall at random in strange places.

"Do you have a Mrs. Broll registered? A Mrs. Harry Broll?"

"Who? I am sorry. What last name, sir?"

"Broll. Bee-are-oh-el-el. Broll."

"Ah. Broll. There is no Mrs. Harry Broll.

"Was she there? Did she leave?"

"There is a Mrs. Mary Broll. She is here since many weeks."

"From Florida?"

"Yes. She is here from Florida."

"Can you put me through to her, please."

"I am sorry."

"Do you mean you can't?"

"There is the instruction, sir. Mrs. Broll does not take overseas calls. Not from anyone, sir."

"This is an emergency."

"I am sorry. I can write down for her your name and the number of your telephone. I cannot say if she returns the call. She does not wish to be disturbed by telephone calls from overseas. If you can give me your name?"

"Never mind. Thank you for your help."

"I am sorry." She said something else but it faded away into an odd, humming silence. There were loud clicks. Somebody else said, "Code eighteen, route through Barbados, over."

I said, "Hey! Somebody."

The humming stopped and the line went dead as marble. I hung up. I stood up and stretched. "Mrs. Mary Broll has been there for a long time, but she doesn't take overseas calls."

"In case one might be from Harry, I suppose."

"That takes care of it. Right, Meyer?"

"I suppose so."

"It was your idea. I phoned. She's there."

"I know. But . . ."

"But?"

"The known facts now seem contradictory."

"Meyer, for God's sake!"

"Now listen to me. She wants to hide from her husband and think things out. She does not want to take any overseas calls. What would it cost her to get the operator and the desk clerk to deny that she's even registered? Ten Biwi dollars each, ten U.S. dollars total? No more, certainly. If she was sure her husband couldn't trace her, then the only call she *could* get would be from her friend Holly Dressner, and she would want to take a call from her I'd think. If she set it up so that he *can* find out where she is, then the refusal to take calls would mean she wants him to fly down, and the bait would be the loan he needs."

"First you simplify things, Meyer, and then you complicate the hell out of them. I don't know what to think now."

"Neither do I. That's my problem."

"So we drive to Miami anyway?"

Holly was home, and she was very helpful about the car. "It's one of those Volks with the fancy body. Oh, dear. What in the world are they called?"

"Karmann Ghia."

"Right! Two years old. Dark red. Hard top. Believe it or not, I can give you the license plate number even. We were shopping, and we went to the place you get the plates together, and mine is about the same weight, so we were in the same series. Hers was one digit more than mine, so hers is 1 D 3108."

We drove down to Miami in Miss Agnes, and I jammed her through the confusions of the cloverleaves and put her in one of the new airport parking buildings, halfway up the long wide ramp leading to the third level, nosing her against the wall between two squatty Detroit products which made her look like a dowager queen at a rock fest. A mediocre hamburger, gobbled too hastily on the way down, lay like a stone on the floor of my stomach.

I pointed out to Meyer how our task was simplified. Apparently there was some kind of stone-crushing plant in operation not too far from the open parking garages. The longer any car had been parked there, sheltered from the rain, the more white powdered stone dust it had all over it. And Mary's would be one of the whitest of all.

There were more than enough ramps and levels and separate structures. Finally, on a top level on the side furthest from the entrance and exit ramp, I saw Karmann Ghia lines, powdery white as a sugar doughnut. Even the plate was powder white, but the bas relief of the digits made it readable as I neared it: 3108. Three months of sitting and accumulating stone dust and parking charges.

Meyer drew in the dust atop the trunk. It would have been a childish trick except for what he drew. A single large question mark. I wiped the windshield with the edge of my hand and bent and peered in. Nothing to see except a very empty automobile.

A police sedan drifted up and stopped close behind the Ghia. "Got a problem?" the driver asked. His partner got out.

"No problem, officer."

"Your car?"

"No. It belongs to a friend."

The driver got out. "And you can't quite remember the name of your friend, I suppose?"

I gave him my earnest, affable smile. "Now why'd you think that, officer? This belongs to Mrs. Mary Broll, 21 Blue Heron Lane, Lauderdale, for sure."

"Girl friend?"

"Just a friend, officer."

"Doesn't your friend have anything to say?"

Meyer said, "I was not aware that you were addressing me with any of the prior questions, officer. I happen to have here—"

"Easy. Bring it out real real slow."

"I happen to have here a page from a scratch pad which, if you will examine it, gives the name of the owner and the license number and description of the vehicle."

The nearest officer took the note and looked at it and handed it back. "Repo?"

"What?" Meyer asked. "Oh. Repossession. No. We happened to be parked here, and we knew Mrs. Broll has been gone for three months, and we wondered if she'd left her car here."

The other officer had gotten into their car. I heard his low voice as he used the hand mike. He waited, then got out again. "Isn't on the list, Al," he said.

"Parked here, you say. Now both of you, let me see

some ID. Slow and easy. Take it out of the wallet. Keep the wallet. Hand me the ID. Okay. Now you. Okay. Now show me your parking ticket. What kind of a car?"

"Officer, it is a very old Rolls Royce pickup truck. Bright blue. It's over there in that other—"

"I saw that, Al. Remember? That's the one I had you back up and see if it had the inspection sticker."

It stopped being confrontation and began to be conversation. "Nobody," said Al, "but nobody at all is going to arrive here in that freak truck to pull anything cute. Okay. For the hell of it, why were you wondering if this woman left her car here?"

"Not so much if she left it here, but to see if she was back yet. We were just wondering. If we didn't find it, maybe she left it someplace else, or she came back from her trip. But we found it, so that means she's still on her trip."

"She stays away too much longer, she can save money by forgetting the car." They got in and glided away without saying goodby or looking back. I guessed they cruised the garages from time to time, checking their hot car lists. It would make a good drop after a stolen car had been used for a felony. Leave it, walk across to the upper or lower level, leave the airport by cab or limousine. Or airplane. Or by private car previously stashed in the parking garage.

Meyer was very quiet, and he did not speak until we were approaching Miss Agnes. He stopped and I turned and looked back at him and strolled back to where he was standing.

"Are you going to break into tears?"

"Maybe. If you were as anxious to find your wife as Harry is, if it's financially important as well as emotionally important, wouldn't you report her missing and give her description and the description of her car with the tag number to the police?"

"I would think so."

"Then the number would be on their list, wouldn't it?"

"Yes. I mean, yes, damn it."

"And because you are thinking what I am thinking and because we happen to be right here, wouldn't it be a good time to find out about airline connections, McGee?"

"For two?"

"I have to finish my paper on the Eurocurrency which replaced the dollar. I promised the conference program chairman."

nine

I should have boarded my early afternoon BWIA flight to Barbados with stops at Kingston and San Juan, thoroughly, if not visibly, bloodied by Jillian. This was Tuesday, and I should have been sailing the sea not the air.

Cowardice is a very curious ailment. The attacks occur when you do not expect them. Instead of saying the rehearsed words, I heard myself say, "Jilly dear, the matter of the old friend has come up again. I wouldn't want to go cruising down to St. Kitts with that hanging over me. I wouldn't be able to stop thinking about it and wondering. It will take a few days ..."

"Darling, I want you to be able to keep your mind on your work. Exclusively. Besides, the five-day forecast is foul. It might work out very nicely."

"No tantrum?"

"What sort of woman do you think I am, dear? That's hardly flattering, you know. All evidence to the contrary, I am not a spoiled little bitch who goes about whining and screaming and drumming her heels. I'm grown up, you know. And more patient than you imagine. I have waited quite a while to have you all to myself."

"This shouldn't take very long."

"I'll be here when you return, dear Travis. Grenada?"

The habit of caution took over. It is an automatic reflex. Never tell anybody anything which they might in turn tell the wrong person. "No. That information is obsolete. San Juan."

"Of course. By this time, Grenada must be well emptied

95

out. She could have more fun in Puerto Rico. Are you and she going to have a lot of fun, Travis? Just like old times?"

"I'm not planning to. But you never can tell."

"Really! You are the most—"

"You keep asking the wrong questions. It's a bad habit."

"As bad as giving the wrong answers."

For a moment the tantrum was on the edge of happening, but she forced it back, visibly, forgave me, kissed me a lingering farewell.

Now five miles over Cuba, I wondered if it would have been better for both of us if I had made it clear I was never going to become her tame houseguest. I wondered if it had been cowardice or if I was really, underneath, the kind of miserable son of a bitch who likes to keep something in reserve in case he happens to change his mind.

Our captain, being a pleasantly enthusiastic host, invited us to look down at Cuba. I was following the McGee rule of international travel and was in first class, alone in the window seat, the bulkhead seat on the starboard side. It was British West Indian Airways, BWIA, and the leg room in the bulkhead seats on the 727 is good.

A clear and beautiful day. The tilled-field geometry of Cuba looked like the geometry of any other of the islands, from five miles up. We moved across the southern coastline, and the shallow sea was a hundred shades, from the pale pale tan of shallow sand through lime and lavender to cobalt.

"Sir?" the clear, young voice said. She was a small, dusky stewardess with a high forehead, a blue-eyed stare of calculated innocence, a dark spill of glossy black hair. Her skin was a matte texture, and it was one half-shade lighter than milk chocolate. She was the one with the absolutely great legs I had noticed when I had clambered onto their airplane. "You are going to . . ."

"Barbados."

"Ah, yes. Thank you, sir. Can I get you something to drink?"

"The last time I was on BWIA there was fresh orange juice. Do you still—"

"Oh, yes."

"With vodka then, please?"

"Oh yes, right away, thank you." She twinkled at me and spun away, the short skirt flirting and snapping. It is changing in the islands, same as everywhere. The conservative island politicians and the white businessmen try to tell you there is no racism, that black and white are treated alike and live amiably together in happy understanding and compassion.

But if you are observant, you notice that the more desirable the job, particularly the jobs women hold—stewardesses, cashiers in banks, clerks in specialty shops, hostesses in restaurants—the more likely they are to be bleached by past miscegenation. There are some true blacks in those positions, of course, but in a far lower ratio than exists in the general population. Look at the cleaning women, the canefield workers, the laundry workers, to find the purest blacks in the islands. And the blackest blacks are, of course, probably seventy-five to eighty percent of the population of the West Indies, the Bahamas, the Windward and Leeward islands. The other twenty percent is a perceptible lightening of color, shade by shade, all the way to unleavened white. Regardless of all protestations, the whiter you are, the better you live. Blondes have the most fun. One of the most thoroughly ignored aspects of the Cuban Revolution is how happily the black Cubans embraced the new order. Though the percentage is smaller in Cuba than elsewhere through the Caribbean, the pattern of discrimination was the same. Black Cuba was entirely ready for anything at all which promised equality in education, jobs, and health care. It didn't have to be Khrush or Mao. They would have built statues to a big green Martian if it could have delivered on the promises.

The curious and immediate and personal result of the color prejudice in the islands was that my pale chocolate stewardess with the great legs identified with me. We were both part of the ruling cabal. There could be an earnest friendliness in her unlikely blue eyes, an uninhibited flirtatiousness.

Another little girl of exactly the same color, but a citizen of the US of A and working, say, for Eastern on a domestic run, would have been working hard on an Afro hairdo, would have given me the precise number of millimeters of smile as prescribed by Eastern, would have been entirely correct, but her eyes would have been as empty as the ice of a long winter, concealing nothing more personal than a propagandized hostility, a prepackaged contempt, an ability to see me only as a symbol of oppression, not as a living creature walking two-legged on the same untidy world, trying to live through the weird years with a little bit of grace and care.

Too bad, somehow. The real guilt is in being a human being. That is the horrible reality which bugs us all. Wolves, as a class, are cleaner, more industrious, far less savage, and kinder to each other and their young.

When she came back with the screwdriver, she leaned one round delicious knee on the empty seat beside me and reached and put the glass and napkin on the small, built-in service area between the seats. I could read her name tag. Mia Cruikshank.

"Mia?" I said.

"Yes, sir?"

"I just meant . . . it's a pretty name."

She made a droll mouth. "Better than what it was, I think. Miriam. Mia is smashing compared to that."

"Smashing indeed."

So we went humming down across the blue seas under the blue skies of vacationland at approximately nine hundred feet per second, which is the muzzle velocity of the .45 caliber Colt automatic pistol, an ugly and cumbersome weapon. Our happy captain pointed out this and that. We stopped at Kingston and San Juan and points south. We lost more passengers than we took on. Each island had its quota of red tape, so that the stops were long.

Mia kept me happily supplied with drinks and food, and we found it easy to smile at each other. We stood together when the sun was low, on the little platform at the top of the rolling stairs at the little airport on St. Lucia.

"You are remaining at Barbados, sir, or continuing?"

"To Grenada tomorrow morning."

"Oh, yes. That is so lovely an island. Of course, Barbados is very nice, too. Just one night is a short time to stay."

"I didn't want to stay there at all."

"I know. There is no way. You fly with us or Pan Am to Barbados or Trinidad, from Miami everyone arrives too late for the last flight to Grenada. It has to be by daylight, of course, in the small aircraft. Where will you stay in Barbados?"

"I thought I would check it out after I get there."

"Oh, yes. The season is over. There is room everywhere. But really, there was room in most of the places during the season too this year. We did not carry so many people to Barbados this year."

"Why not?"

She glanced back over her shoulder and moved closer to me, lowered her voice. "I am not a rich, important person who owns a hotel, so perhaps they know what they are doing. But, sir, suppose this was in the season and you are traveling with a lady and you try to make a reservation for the two of you in Barbados, just to stay in a hotel room overnight to continue on in the morning. In your money, in US dollars, to stay at the Barbados Hilton, it will be seventy dollars for one night, and there will be ten percent service charge added to that, so that it will be seventy seven dollars. Even were you to stay at the Holiday Inn, sir, it will be fifty-five plus ten percent, or sixty dollars and fifty cents."

"Without meals? You have to be kidding."

"Oh, no. You see, sir, they will only make reservations for you on the Modified American Plan, which includes breakfast and dinner, even when it is clear you will have dinner aboard this flight and leave so early the next morning there is perhaps time for coffee and rolls. This is happening in all the islands, sir. It is perhaps the worst in Barbados, the worst of all. It is a fantastic greed. It is like some terrible animal out of control, so hungry it feeds upon itself and is killing itself. I should not say so much."

"I won't turn you over to the tourist board, Mia."

"Oh, thank you." She hesitated and scowled. "There is something I am trying to think how to say. It is really what is wrong now with the islands. It is why each year there will be fewer people coming to these lovely places."

"It's a shame."

She turned to face me directly and looked up at me. "Seventy-seven dollars is over a hundred and fifty dollars in our currency. In Biwi dollars. A house servant in Barbados *might* make fifty dollars, Biwi, a month. A waiter or waitress *might* make seventy-five dollars, Biwi, a month. So how does a human person feel serving or cleaning up after another human person who pays two or three months wages for one single night in a room? Sir, it is like such a terrible arrogance and thoughtlessness. It makes hate, sir. It makes contempt. So the cleaning is done badly, and the serving is done very slowly and badly, and there are no smiles. Then, sir, the person who is paying too much because the hotel owners are so greedy, he becomes very angry because, if he pays so much, the service should be of the very best, and everything should be very clean. When he is angry, then he seems to be more arrogant and rich and thoughtless, sir. Hate and anger back and forth, it is a terrible thing. There is no pleasure in work and no pleasure in vacationing here, and that is why each year, like this year, there will be fewer and fewer tourists, jobs, money. It is wicked. I keep thinking to myself, what can be done —what can be done? It is like the goose, sir."

"The goose?"

"The goose they killed to get at the golden eggs." She looked at her watch. An official was trotting up the stairs. "Now we will be going, sir."

After liftoff she gave me a final drink, and she and the other girls did their desk work and policed their area and changed to their ground uniforms. She had time to give me some advice. She told me that the nearest hotel to the airport was a five-dollar taxi ride, Biwi. The Crane Beach. She said the rooms were very small and primitive, but the beach was beautiful, and the food was excellent. She said the management was surly, and the waiters insolent, but it was only for overnight, and it would be almost empty. Besides, the Barbados Hilton and the other hotels were a lot closer to Bridgetown, and so were ten to fifteen Biwi dollars one way from the airport. In most of the islands it appears that committees of taxi drivers determine airport locations.

"Just laugh at whatever they want to charge you at the Crane Beach, sir. The season is over. Put down ten dollars, Yankee, and tell them the service charge percent is included, not extra. They will show you a rate schedule and tell you it is official and they cannot change it. Just laugh. They will take the money and give you a room. It is not so easy to get a taxi in the morning early from there. Just tear a Yankee dollar in two pieces and give half to the taxi driver and tell him when to come in the morning. He will be certain to return. Do not tip anyone at that hotel. They are shameless, and it is all included in the price of everything anyway."

I was genuinely grateful to Mia. I thanked her and said, "I hope I will get a chance to tell you how I made out."

"Perhaps, if you fly BWIA back to Miami, I will serve you again. How long shall you be in Grenada, sir?"

"A few days. Any idea where I should stay?"

"Oh, no. I do not know that island so well. This is not a vacation for you. Business, yes?"

"How do you know?"

"I think I can tell if a man is not one who would take a vacation alone, sir. Good luck, sir."

My taxi man arrived the next day three minutes before the stipulated hour. He smiled broadly when he saw me standing in the early morning light outside the hotel gates with my single piece of carry-on-luggage. He decided that it was a splendid idea, the half of the paper dollar. It left each of us with an investment to protect. He had brought some tape, and he put his dollar back together before we started off. His name was Oswald, and he was a thin old man with several gold teeth. He drove his elderly white Plymouth with that kind of care which is more involved with not breaking anything than not hitting anybody.

I took LIAT, a BWIA subsidiary, to Grenada, a direct flight of about forty minutes. It was an old Avro with the rows shoved closer together to increase capacity, so that the little oval windows did not match the seat positions. Two big propjet Rolls Royce brutes powered the small aircraft. The stewardess was about the same size and shape as Hubert Humphrey. The pilot had Walter Mitty dreams of being a fighter pilot. It was an interesting takeoff and an even more interesting landing.

At Grenada's grubby little airport I once again had to show my driver's license and turn over that card form which serves as embarkation and debarkation permit, depending on how you fill out the blanks.

And then came a fascinating ride in a taxi. The island is only twenty-one miles long and twelve miles wide. The airport is about as far as it could possibly be from the principal town, St. George's. The morning ride took one full hour, and I would not have wanted my man to have tried to shave five minutes off the elapsed time. I helped with the brakes so continuously that my right leg was nearly paralyzed when we finally came down out of the mountains to sea level. The driver—he gave me his card —was Albert Owen, and he had a Chevrolet assembled in Australia with a suspension system designed for the Outback of Australia. He had put fifty-three thousand incredible miles on it on that improbable road system, using up God only knows how many sets of brake linings. Drive on the left. Average width of road—one and a quarter lanes. No shoulders. Blind corners. Big lumps, deep potholes, children, dogs, pigs, donkeys, bicycles, trucks, buses, motorcycles. So honk the horn almost continuously, shift up and shift down, swerve, leap, squeal, slide, accelerate—and all the time Albert Owen was hollering back over his shoulder at me, pointing out bah-nah-nah tree, almond tree, sugar cane, sar. Over there mammy apple, coconut plahntation sar, cocoa, also you are seeing nutmeg, sar. Many spices.

Once when a small insane truck came leaping at us on the wrong side around a bend, Albert swerved smartly. It missed us by the thickness of a coat of paint. Albert laughed and laughed. He said, "That is one foolish driver, sar. He nearly mosh us."

But nobody actually did mosh us. It was hard to believe they were not trying. Were the fates to put Albert down on any weekday morning on the Palmetto Turnpike heading into Miami with the inbound torrent, the terror of it might put him into a dead faint. A Miami cabdriver suddenly transported into Albert's mountains might conceivably run weeping into the jungle.

People certainly did go about moshing people. The dead cars amid the lush vines and wild shrubs were proof enough of that.

Albert asked me where my reservation was as we plummeted down toward the town and blue late-morning sea beyond. I said I had none but would look about a little. He said there were no problems this time of year. There had been trouble with the government water supply. When the hotel cisterns had run out, many people had left. Now the water was on again, but there were not so many tourists as on other Aprils. I found out that the Grenada Beach Hotel was the place most centrally located on Grande Anse, the two miles of crescent beach just south of the town, looking westward. I asked him if he would wait there for me. We made certain financial negotiations.

I left my single piece of luggage with him. He parked in the vehicle circle outside the main doors. I walked in and through an open lobby area and found a thatched bar off to the left, open to the outdoors, looking out across a long expanse of green lawn and tall, graceful coconut palms toward the garden of beach umbrellas, toward the bright colors of beach chairs and towels on the distant sand.

A bored bartender in a red coat appeared from some unknown hiding place, yawning. He made me a delicious rum punch with grated nutmeg afloat on it. He asked for my room number, and I paid cash for my drink, then gifted him with some of the Biwi I had picked up at the moneychanger's booth in the temple of Miami International. He brightened visibly, and I asked him if he had a phone back there, and he said he did, and he said he would be glad to phone the Spice Island Inn for me. He did so and handed me the phone.

"What number is Mrs. Broll in, please? Mrs. Mary Broll?"

"Ah . . . yes, she is in cottage 50, sir. Shall I ring her for you?"

"No thank you," I said and hung up.

I finished my drink very very slowly. It is a very strange reluctance, a curious hesitation that can immobilize you at such a time. You are eager to prove to yourself that you've been quite wrong, that you've taken too many small things and built them up into a fantasy structure that cannot be true.

Yet, if by some chance the fantasy proves to be reality, most of the game is still left to play, and an ugly game it can be.

It could be a delicious surprise. I could see the shape of Mary's familiar mouth, the wide and startled eyes, and then the rush of pleasure, the embrace.

"The Spice Island Inn is close by?"

"That direction. Very close. A small walk, sir. Two minutes."

But in the hot tropical blaze of April a man in slacks and sport shirt, socks and shoes would be as conspicuous on that beach, I found, as in a Mother Hubbard at a nudist camp. I went back through the hotel and found Albert dozing in the shade. I woke him, and we got into the broiling taxi and rode south to the entrance to the Spice Island Inn.

Meyer and I had tried to cover all eventualities in the long planning session we'd had before I left. In the islands there appeared to be so little interest in any verification of identity that the risk factor seemed very minor indeed. If we were wrong, I was going to feel a little foolish. But if we were right, there was a chance I could feel something beyond mere foolishness.

And so, in Albert Owen's back seat I switched the cash money, all of it, from one wallet to another and became

Gavin Lee. Known as Gav. Known as Mr. Lee. This follows Meyer's theory that when you pick a new name, pick one that has the same basic vowel sounds. Then you will react if you hear somebody behind you say your assumed name.

I was going to carry my own suitcase in. Albert did not think that was appropriate. The desk was very cordial. Nothing creates such a flavor of genuine, heart-felt welcome as a nearly empty hotel. They showed me the rates. They told me I had a choice of plans. They showed me a map of the place with all manner of accommodations. What would please Mr. Lee, the ostensibly vacationing land developer from Miami, Scottsdale, Acapulco, Hawaii, Palm Springs, and Las Vegas? Well, I'm kind of curious about those with the private pool. These here on your map. Just this row of them, eh? How about this one right here on the end? Number . . . I can't read it upside down. Thank you, 50. Full. Are all these full then? Just 50, 57, and 58. Well, in the middle then, as far from the occupied ones as . . . 54? I can see there are two bedrooms, but I don't see any one bedroom ones with the walled garden and the pool, so. . . . Now what will it be on . . . a European Plan? After a few days I may change, depending on how the dining room is here. Of course. I'm sure it's marvelous. All right. Quote me on a per day. . . . That's $28, single? That's US? Hmmm. Plus ten percent service charge and five percent tax, which is . . . $32.34 per day. Look, I'm carrying a bit more cash than I intended. Would you mind taking this hundred-dollar bill for three days in advance? And I'll bring you an envelope to put in the safe.

I paid Albert off and told him I would keep his card and I would certainly get him to drive me back to the airport some day. A bellhop led me down a long long path to the newest line of attached bungalows, the ones with the pool in the garden. The row was a good two hundred and fifty yards from the hotel proper. He demonstrated the airconditioning, the button to push for food service, the button to push for drink service.

Then he went away. I was left in silence, in the shadowed coolness of the tourist life.

Drive the clenched fist into palm. Pock!

"Be here, baby. Just *be* here!"

ten

The row of tall attached cottages with a double peak on the roof of each one was set at a slight angle to the beach, so that architecturally they could be set back, one from the next, to provide total privacy for the individual walled gardens where the small swimming pools were.

The row of cottages was back a hundred feet and more from the beach. Between the front gates of the cottages and the beach itself was a private expanse of sand, landscaped palms, sea grapes, almond trees with sun chaises spotted about at intervals far enough apart for privacy.

I put on swim trunks and took up a position on a chaise fifty feet from my front gate, turning it in such a way I could watch the gate of number 50. By then it was past noon. The tropic sun had such a hefty sting I knew that even my deep and permanent tan would not be immune, not without a little oil and a little limitation on the exposure time.

At twenty minutes to one the gate opened, and a young woman came out. She was of medium height, delicately and gracefully built. Her dark hair was quite long, and she had a white band above her forehead clipping it in place. She seemed to be somewhere in her twenties. I could not make a closer guess at that distance. She wore eccentric sunglasses with huge round lenses in dark amber. She wore a don't-swim-in-it bikini fashioned of white elasticized cord and swatches of watermelon-colored terrycloth. She was two shades darker than Mia Cruikshank, a perfect and even tan which could only have come from untold hours of total discipline and constant care.

A man came out with her. Youngish, lithe, laughing and saying something which made her laugh. Awesomely muscled, moving well so that muscles bulged and slid under the red-bronze tan. A Riviera swimming outfit, little more than a white satin jockstrap. She walked a few steps and then turned in a proprietary way and went back and tested to see if the gate was locked. She looked in her small white Ratsey bag, apparently to make sure that her key was there. Then they walked toward the hotel.

My heart had turned heavy, and there was a taste of sickness in my throat. But you have to be certain, terribly certain. Like a biopsy. Make absolutely sure of the malignancy. Because the surgery is radical.

I gave them five minutes and then followed the same route. I found them in another of the ubiquitous thatched bars, having a drink at a shady table and still laughing. A cheerful pair. I went to the bar and ordered a drink. When I had a chance, I asked the bartender if the woman at the table was a certain Lois Jefferson. He looked troubled. He said he knew them by the numbers. Just a moment, please. He went to the other end of the bar and came back with a signed drink tab. Mary D. Broll. Number 50. He showed it to me. I thanked him, said I was wrong. I winked at him and said, "But that is not Mr. Broll?"

He had a knowing smile. "It is just a friend. He has been a friend for a week, I think. He works, I think, on a private boat. That is what I hear. It is easy to make friends here."

I picked my drink up and moved along the bar to a stool that was about a dozen feet from their table. I turned around on the stool, my back to the bar, and looked at her with obvious and amiable and very thorough appreciation. She was worth appreciating, right from her brown, slender, tidy little ankles right on up—not too quickly—to a ripely cushioned little mouth, dark eyes set at an interesting tilt, a broad, immature, and vulgar little nose.

She put her glasses back on and leaned over and said something to her nautical friend. He put his drink down and turned around and stared back over his shoulder at me. I smiled and nodded at him. He had a Prince Valiant haircut, and his hair was the dark molten shade of some golden retrievers. His face had a tough, pinched, disadvantaged look which did not go with the Valiant hair or the beachboy body. I do not make any judgments about hair length, mine or anyone's. I own some Sears electric clippers with plastic gadgets of various shapes which fit on the clippers to keep you from accidentally peeling your hair off down to the skull. I find that long hair is a damned nuisance on boats, on the beach, and in the water. So when it gets long enough to start to make me aware of it, I clipper it off, doing the sides in the mirror and the back by feel. The sun bleaches my hair and burns it and dries it out. And the salt water makes it feel stiff and look like some kind of Dynel. Were I going to keep it long, I would have to take care of it. That would mean tonics and lotions and special shampoos. That would mean brushing it and combing it a lot more than I do and somehow fastening it out of the way in a stiff breeze. Life is so full of all those damned minor things you have to do anyway, it seems nonproductive to go looking for more. So I go hoe the hair down when it attracts my attention. The length is not an expression of any social, economic, emotional, political, or chronographic opinion. It is on account of being lazy and impatient. No reason why the male can't have long, lovely, dark-golden hair if he wants it. But it is a personal decision now, just as it was during the Crusades and the Civil War.

He kept staring right at me, and I kept smiling at him. So he got up fast and rolled his shoulders as he covered the twelve feet to stand in front of me, bare feet spread and braced.

"Chief, stop the birddog routine. You're annoying the lady."

"Me? Come *on* now! Don't let her kid you. Lois and I have known each other for a long time. She knows I like to look at her. Always have. And I know she likes being looked at. Right, dear?"

"You're out of your tree, chief. Knock it off. She isn't Lois."

I stood up. "She's Lois Jefferson. Believe me!" I edged

by him as he tried to block me away from the table. "Lois, honey. It's Gav Lee, for God's sake. It was a good joke, but let's not run it into the ground."

She took the glasses off and looked up at me. "Really, I'm not Lois. I'm Mary Broll. Really."

I boggled at her. "Not Lois Jefferson from Scarsdale? Not Tom's wife?"

It sucked in the fellow nicely. He was all alerted for games. When you roam in public with an item like that woman, you keep the guard way up. "Honey," he said, "how about this clown? You get it? Tom Jefferson. Thomas Jefferson. Stop annoying us, chief, or I'll call the—"

I turned on him. "Really. Would it put too much of a strain on you to have a little common courtesy? Her husband has always had the nickname Tom, for quite obvious reasons. His real name is . . ." I turned back to her. "What *is* Tom's real first name, dear?"

She laughed. "But I am really *not* your friend!"

I stared at her. "That can't be possible. It's the most fantastic look-alike. . . . You wouldn't believe. . . . Miss Broll, would you—"

"Mrs. Broll."

"I'm sorry. Mrs. Broll, would it be rude of me to ask you to stand up for just a moment?"

"I guess not."

"Now just one goddamn—"

I turned on him again. "What harm can it do, Mr. Broll?"

She stood up beside her chair. I moved closer to her, and I stared into her eyes from close range. "By God, I *am* wrong. I would never have believed it. You are a little bit taller than Lois, and I think your eyes are a darker shade, Mrs. Broll."

"Now go away," the man said.

As she sat down she said, "Oh, shut up, Carl. You get so boring sometimes. The man made a mistake. All right? All right. Please forgive Carl, Mr. . . . ."

"Lee. Gavin Lee. Gav to my friends."

"I don't see any friends of yours around here," the man said.

She gave me a very pretty and well-practiced smile. "Gav, this rude animal is Carl Brego. Carl, shake hands nicely with Gav, or you can damned well take off."

I saw the little tightening around his eyes and knew the childish bit he was going to try. So when he put his hand out, I put my hand into his much too quickly for him to close his hand to get my knuckles. I got my hand all the way back, deep into the web between thumb and finger. Then I could just maintain a mild, firm clasp and smile at him as he nearly ruptured his shoulder muscles trying to squeeze my hand to broken pulp.

"Sorry about the little misunderstanding, Carl," I said. "I'd like to buy you two nice people a drink."

He let go of my hand and sat down. "Nobody invited you to join the party, chief."

He had fallen into that one, too. He was scoring very badly. I said, "I don't expect to sit down with you, Carl. Why should I? I was going to go to that table way over there and have my own drink over there and send two to this table. You act as if I'm trying to move in on you. How far would I get, Carl? As you are not Mr. Broll, then this lovely lady is a friend of yours. You are having lunch together. Just the two of you. If I were having lunch with her, I would be very ugly about anybody trying to move in. I just think you overreact, Carl. I made a little mistake. You keep getting rude for no reason. But I'll still buy those drinks. I was thinking of it as an apology, not a ticket to the party."

So saying, I gave the lady a little bow and marched on over to my distant table and told the waiter to give them anything they might want. I sat with my back toward them.

It did not take her long. Four minutes, I think it was, before he appeared beside my chair, standing almost at attention.

"Excuse me. Mrs. Broll would be very happy if you would join us for lunch."

I smiled up at him. "Only if you are absolutely certain you don't mind, Brego."

It hurt his mouth to say it. It hurt his whole face. "Please join us, Mr. Lee."

All through lunch I knew Brego was waiting and planning. When I saw that he wasn't at all upset that I was living just a few doors—or a few gardens—away from his pretty friend, I could almost guess the kind of routine he had figured out.

And during lunch I had managed to steer the conversation in a direction that gave me a chance to awaken more than a flicker of interest in her eyes and at the same time gave her a chance to shove a little blade into Carl Brego and give it a twist.

I said, "I take little flyers in island property sometimes. Actually, that's why I'm here. Some associates said I ought to take a look at this one. Anyway, usually I like to pyramid, but quite a while ago I got into Freeport up in the Bahamas at the right time and got out at exactly the right time with much more than I'd expected, so I thought I'd give myself a little present. So I bought this great big, ridiculous brute of a schooner in Nassau and had the yard that sold it to me hire aboard a crew, and I actually set out for *this* island. But the guest I invited aboard for the trip became terribly seasick. We made it as far as Great Inagua and got off, both of us, at Matthew Town and arranged passage from there back to civilization. I had the crew take the boat back to Nassau. As I remember, my acountants told me the net loss was something like thirteen thousand dollars after I'd had the yard resell the schooner. But it would have been cruel and unusual punishment to have made the young lady sail one more mile."

Something behind her dark eyes went ding, and a cash drawer slid open in her skull. She counted the big bills and shut it again and smiled and said, "Carl knows all about yachts. He sails one around for a very fat rich lady, don't you, darling?"

"That must be very interesting," I said.

"He's waiting on Grenada until she arrives with friends," the woman said. "You know. Like a chauffeur, parked somewhere."

"Knock it off," Carl said in a small humble voice.

"Please?" she said.

"Please."

And that made it even more imperative. I decided I was reading her well enough to see that she knew the direction the tensions would take and would give the ceremony a chance to get under way at the first opportunity. And would want to watch.

When we got to her gate, there was no one in sight. The breeze had stopped. Sweat popped out immediately on all three of us. I felt it run down my back.

"Do come in, Gav," she said. "Do join us."

She was starting to unlock the gate. Carl said, "So it's enough already."

"Enough?" she said blankly. "Enough?"

"Honey, the guy is taking a cheap shot, and I'm going to run him off."

She licked her mouth. "Carl, sweetie, why do you have to be—"

"You can go in out of the heat, or you can stay and watch how it's done, Mary. Either way I run this smartass off."

"Any special direction?" I asked.

"Pick the one you like best, chief," he said with a jolly grin of anticipation. "Start now and save yourself grief."

"Take your best shot, Brego." He took it. I was worried that he might know too much about what he wanted to do. If he did, it was going to take a long time in the hot sun, and if he didn't, it could be reasonably quick.

He did a little bounce, a little prance. He pawed with the clumsy, measuring left and then came leaping in, following up on the right hook that he had brought up from about five feet behind him, practically at ground level. He did not know what he was doing. People who know do not go around taking the chance of hitting the solid bone of skull or jaw with the bare fist. A broken hand is incapacitating. It takes a long, tiresome time to heal. He wanted to pop me one and let the momentum carry him into me so he could get his hands and arms on me and put those muscles to work. He gave me lots of time for a decision. If I fell back away from it, he was going to tumble onto me. That way I might get a thumb in my eye before I could unwind and unravel him. The footing in the soft sand was a little uncertain for savate. So I moved forward, a little to my right, to take me inside that long, sweeping hook.

I felt it go around me, and I let his momentum then drive me back. I drove both hands, fingers spread, into his long hair, I clenched hard and went down pulling him on top of me but getting my knees up against my chest in time. One shoe slipped off his sweaty body, but the sole of the other stayed in place against his belly, and momentum gave me enough leverage to push him up and over. It was a good, high kick, and he spun well. By then I was on my back with my hands straight up over my head.

He hit the soft sand flat on his back with one hell of a whump. It exploded the air out of his lungs. I was up first, and I moved into position, waiting for him. He got up slowly, gagging for air. As he pushed up, I cranked his arm around behind him and put my other hand on the nape of his neck and ran him into the weathered boards of the garden fence, quite close to the woman. He splintered a board with the top of his head. She squeaked and chewed her fist. I dragged him back by the ankles, face down. I picked him up and stood him on his noodle legs and slapped him until he started to come around. Then I bent him over and ran him into the fence again. I dragged him back again, and I turned his feet until he rolled over onto his back. I slapped him where he lay, and when he stirred and his eyes came into focus, I levered his mouth open by bracing the heel of my hand against his chin. I packed his mouth full of soft hot sand, from the back of his throat to his pretty, white teeth. He came sputtering and gagging onto his hands and knees and coughed himself sick. I grabbed the hair and pulled his head up and back.

"Nod if you can understand me, Brego." He nodded. "Do you want me to break any bones? Do I have to do that?" He shook his head. "She isn't your woman any more. Understand?" He nodded. "Now I am going to start kicking your ass. You better head for the beach. If I ever see you back here, I'll break some bones."

I went around behind him and got a pretty good soccer kick into it, using the side of my foot. On the upswing. It slid him onto his face. He came scrambling up with more energy than I expected, but I got him again just as he got his feet under him and his hands free of the sand. Three running steps and he landed on his face again but didn't spend any time resting. He got up and went into a wobbly scuffling run, fists against his chest, not daring or wanting to look back.

I watched him and then turned and looked at the woman. She gave me a very uncertain smile. There was an unhealthy skin tone under that deep lovely tan. "I . . . I thought you were going to kill him."

"Kill him? What in God's name for?"

"Well . . . it was so quick and so terrible."

"He won't be back, Mary. Are you going to miss him, particularly? You going to be lonesome?"

"That would depend, wouldn't it?"

"Is there any of his stuff in there?"

"Not much. A few things."

"Anything worth his coming back after?"

"I wouldn't think so. No."

"Now you can invite me in again."

Her color was back. "You take a hell of a lot for granted."

I put a knuckle under her chin and tilted her face up and looked at it inch by inch, a long and interested search. "If you want, girl, I can throw you back, like an undersized mackerel. The world is full of Carl Bregos. It's up to you."

She twisted her chin free. "I guess I wouldn't want to be thrown back, Gav. I guess it wouldn't fit my image. Was there really a Lois Jefferson?"

"If you think there was."

"I don't think so."

"Then there never was such a girl."

"Poor Carl. Do you always get what you want?"

"I usually get what I *think* I want."

She tilted her shoulders one way, her hips the other. Her look was challenge. "And sometimes you find out you didn't really want it after all. Me, too. Win a little, lose a little, huh?"

"If you wanted Brego, you'd still have him. I wouldn't have gotten to say more than two words to you."

"Like I was saying when we were so rudely interrupted, you want to come into my house? It's hot out here when the wind quits."

So we went in, and I wondered why I could find no trace of a Canadian accent. She had to be Lisa Dissat.

eleven

Though the plantings were different, the patio furniture of a different style and arrangement, the pool and the cold water shower head were placed just as in my rented garden. I went to the shower and turned it on and sluiced off the sand that had caked thickly on my sweaty back and on my left side where I had rolled to get up quickly. The woman stood and watched me and then took a big, striped beach towel from a stone bench and brought it to me as I stepped out of the spray and turned the shower off.

As I dried myself, I realized how sexually aware of her I had become. Physical readiness. All her honey-brown curves and cushions were there, appropriate, ready for use.

It is such an old old thing, the pattern of male conflict that wins the female. It is deep in the blood and the secretions, a gut knowledge. We are mammals still caught up in all the midbrain mechanisms of survival. The bison female stood long ago and watched the males thud their brute heads together, tear up the sod with their hooves, watched the loser lope heavily away, and then she waited patiently to be mounted by the victor. The stronger the male, the stronger the calves, and the better protected the calves would be during the long months of helplessness. The victorious male, turning from battle to the prize of battle, would be physiologically ready to mate her and have no question about her readiness.

I knew the musky readiness of the woman. She told me in the way she stood, in the way she looked at me, in the shape of her placid mouth. Maybe ten percent of what we can say to each other is with words, and words can conceal as easily as they can reveal. The rest of it is body language, our cants, tilts, postures, textures.

And who can prove there is not an actual telepathic signal being transmitted? Tiny electrical discharges occur in the living mind in great and complex profusion. Strong emotion, tautly focused, may send out an impulse so strong it can be read. Hate, fear, anger, joy, lust . . . these all seem contagious beyond all objective reason. I knew she was so swollen, so moist, so ready, that if I trotted her into the shadowy coolness of the apartment and into her bed, there would be no time or need for foreplay, that she would cling and grind and gasp and within a minute begin to go into a climax.

The violence had caught us up in the first act of the fleshy ceremony, and I wanted to take that quick, primitive jump so badly I felt hollowed out by the ache of it. Bed was her country. That was where, after the first great surge, she would take command. I would become what she was accustomed to and lose any chance of keeping her off balance. I shook myself like a big tired Labrador after a long swim, balled the damp towel, and flipped it at her face. She moved in her slow sensuous dream, getting her hand partway up before it hit her squarely in the face. It fluttered to the floor.

"Hey!" she said, frowning. "What's that for?"

"Pick it up!"

"Sure," she said. She picked the towel up. "What are you sore about? Why are you getting ugly and spoiling the fun?"

"He was supposed to hammer me to bloody ruin out there. That was supposed to be the fun. Thanks a lot."

She came toward me. "Darling, you've got it all wrong. I was getting *bored* with him! I was *so* glad you came along."

"Sure, Mary. Only I know the Bregos of this world. They don't start anything they don't think they can win. Their cheap women chouse them into it because they like the blood. You set me up by reacting to me. If you'd cooled it, there'd have been no fight. He was going to smash me around and that was going to turn you on for him, so you'd hustle him into your sack for a quick hump. A little midday entertainment. No thanks."

She leaned forward from the waist, face contorting, voice turning to a squalling fishwife. *"Goddamn* you! *You* moved in on us with all that crap about me looking like somebody else. *You* thought I was worth the chance of getting your ass whipped. Don't slam the gate on the way out, you son of a—"

Her lips started to say the obvious word, but I had fitted my big right hand to her slender throat, just firmly enough to cut off her wind, not firmly enough to crush any of the tender bones and cartilage. The ball of my thumb reached to the big artery in the side of her throat under the jaw hinge, and my first and middle finger reached to the artery on the left side of her throat.

Her eyes went wide, and she dropped the towel and put her nails into the back of my hand and my wrist. I pinched the arteries gently, drastically reducing the flow of blood to the brain. It gave her a gray-out to the edge of fainting. Her eyes went out of focus, and her mouth sagged. When I let up, she tried to kick me, so I pinched again. Her arms fell slack to her sides. When I released the pressure, adjusting my hand enough so that she could breathe, she raised her hands and then hung them upon my wrist.

I smiled at her, pulling her a half-step closer and said, "If you get loud and say nasty things, dear, if you get on my nerves, I can hold you like this, and I can take this free hand and make a big fist like this, and I can give you one little pop right here that will give you a nose three inches wide and a quarter inch high."

"Please," she said in a rusty little voice.

"You can get a job as a clown. Or you can see if you can find a surgeon willing to try to rebuild it."

"Please," she said again.

I let go of her and said, "Pick up the towel, love."

She coughed and bent and picked it up and backed away. I turned away from her and went to the cottage apartment and pulled the door open and went in. I went to the kitchen alcove and checked the bottle supply. I heard her slide the glass door shut again.

I fixed some Booth's with Rose's lime juice and a dash of bitters, humming softly but audibly. I took my glass over to the couch and sat and smiled at her and said, "Did I ever tell you I read minds?"

"You must be some kind of a crazy person." It was not said as an insult. It was said softly, wonderingly.

I pinched the bridge of my nose and closed my eyes. "Many messages are coming through. Ah, yes. You are wondering if you can get the hotel management to throw a net over me and get me out of here. No, dear. I think they would believe me instead of you. If they make life difficult, I could go down to the harbor and find your friend Brego and bounce him up and down until he agrees to write out a personal history of your touching romance and sign it. Then I could go find your husband and peddle it to him. It would cut the heart out of any alimony payments."

"I just want you to—"

"Where and when did you meet Brego?"

"On the beach. Over a week ago. My neck hurts."

"Of *course* it hurts a little! How could I do that without giving you a sore neck? Let me see. What else is in your mind? You're wondering if I'm going to lay you and if I'll be nicer to you afterward. The answer to both questions, dear, is: time will tell."

She went over to the kitchen bar. Ice clinked into a glass. She came back with a drink and sat on a hassock five feet away from me. Her eyes looked better. Her confidence was coming back. She squared her shoulders, tugged the bikini top and bottom into better adjustment, tilted her head, and risked a meager smile. "I guess all that lunch talk about land investments was a lot of crap, huh?"

"What makes you think so? It's what I do."

"You don't act like it's what you do. Like the way you were with Carl and with me, Gavin. I mean . . . well, it's like you enjoyed hurting."

"Well . . . let's suppose there's a man with a good idea where a new interstate is going or a new jetport, and suppose we teamed up, and you had some nice long weekends with him, and he clued you about where to buy the raw land. Mary, I just couldn't stand having you get tricky with me about something like that. I wouldn't want to worry about you selling that information to somebody else. I'd have to have you so trained for the work that if I just stare at you for ten seconds, you start to have the cold sweats and the gags. Hurting is purely business. I guess I enjoy anything that helps make money."

She thought that over, sipping, frowning. "But it's not as if I was going to work with you, Mr. Lee."

"Time will tell."

"You keep saying that. Well, I'm not going to work with you or for you. For that kind of work you're talking about, what you want is some kind of a hooker, it seems to me."

"Does it seem like that to you? Really? I wouldn't say that. You're built for the work. You have just enough cheap invitation in the way you look and the way you handle yourself to keep a man from wasting a lot of time on unnecessary preliminaries."

"Now wait one goddamn minute—"

"Are you still with Brego? No. Then shut up."

"I'm sorry. Don't get sore."

"Fifty bucks makes you a hooker. For five hundred you're a call girl. Five thousand makes you a courtesan."

"What's that?"

"Never mind. But when we move the decimal point one more place, your end of the arrangement is fifty thousand. That makes you a career woman."

The pointed tongue moved slowly across the underlip. She swallowed and said, "I've got my own thing going, thanks."

"Alimony is a cheap hustle."

"It all depends."

"On how much he's got? On the evidence? On the law?

It has to be a cheap hustle, because when there's enough money involved, there's more profit from going in some other direction."

I had wanted to test just how deep the hardness went. Her eyes changed. She slopped some of her drink onto her bare knees, wiped it off with her hand. "That's crazy talk."

"Not for careful people who've got the right contacts."

"For me, no thanks. I just wouldn't have the nerve, Gav."

I got up and moved around, carrying my drink. I did not know where to take it from there. I could guess that she had been ordered to keep to herself in Grenada but had finally gotten so bored she had become reckless and picked up Brego. Now the Brego game had mushroomed into something a lot less comfortable for her. If she could live quietly at the inn for the length of time she was supposed to, she could get away with it. She wasn't too much shorter than Mary or too much younger. Dark hair. All American women look alike to the help.

I hadn't wanted to let myself think about Mary. From the physical description the housekeeper had given Jeannie Dolan, this woman was the Canadian, Lisa Dissat. If she was here, Mary was dead. I had the beginnings of an idea. I went back to the conversations at lunch. Neither the first name of her supposed husband nor her Stateside residence had come up.

After mental rehearsal and rewrite I sat once again and looked placidly at her and said, "The way you spell that last name is bee-are-oh-el-el?"

"Yes."

"Kind of unusual. It rings a bell someplace. Mary Broll. Mary Broll. It's been bothering me ever since I met you in the bar."

"Why bother with it? Want me to fresh up your drink?"

"Got it!"

"Got what?"

"Where'd you register from? One buck will get you five it's the Fort Lauderdale area. Sure! We had a syndicate set up a couple of years back and we wanted a builder in the Lauderdale area who could put up a hotel and marina complex in a hurry. Heavy-set fellow name of Broll. Big. Not old. Frank? Wally? Jerry? . . . Harry! Damn right. Harry Broll."

"Maybe there's more Brolls than you know, Gav."

"Bring me your purse, honey."

"What?"

"Go get your purse. Your pocketbook. Your handbag. Bring it to dear old Gavin Lee so he can look at your ID, dear."

She gave me a broad, bright smile, and her teeth chattered for a moment before she got herself under control. "Okay. My secret is out. You are speaking of the man I used to love."

"How long have you been married to him?"

". . . Nearly four years."

"Any kids? No? Lucky. Kids seem to get the rough end of the stick. Bring me the purse, honey."

"Why should I? I told you, didn't I?"

"Honey, if we stop getting along, we're going to have to hurt your neck a little until we get squared away."

"Please. It makes me sick to my stom—"

"Get the purse!"

She brought it to me. I found the billfold. I examined the identification. I looked at the signature on the driver's license. I knew my Mary had signed it, and I knew, looking at it, that she was dead.

"Honey, go over to that desk and take a piece of paper and sign your name on it. Mary D. Broll. And bring it back here to me."

"Who *are* you? What do you want?"

"I am the fellow who sat across the table from Mary D. Broll at Le Dome of the Four Seasons in Lauderdale two years ago last month. There were about ten of us at that dinner. Harry was making the big gesture, trying to sucker us into letting him build for us. I spent the evening trying to make his wife. She wouldn't give me a clue. I always have a better memory for the ones who get away. Here's her signature right here. Go over there and forge it for me, honey."

"Who *are* you?" she demanded, close to tears.

I gave her a broad, egg-sucking smile. "Me? I am the fellow who all of a sudden owns himself a whole woman, right from dandruff to bunions and everything in between. Broads like you don't play games like this unless there's money in it. And now it's *our* money, dear. I am the fellow who is going to get it all out of you, and I am going to beat on you until you convince me there's nothing left to tell. Me? Hell, baby, I am your new partner."

"Please. Please. I can't tell you—"

"The little lady in this corner is getting one chance and one chance only, to go over to the desk and sign her real, true, legal name to a piece of paper and bring it back to the gentleman. And if it turns out that it is not her real true name, it is going to be one of those long afternoons. We're going to have to stuff a towel in the little lady's mouth so the screaming won't spoil anybody's vacation."

She walked to the desk, her back very straight. She wrote on a piece of paper and brought it back and handed it to me and began to weep. She covered her face and ran for the bedroom. Damned few women look well from a rear elevation, running away from you in a bikini. She was not one of them. She had written her name neatly. It was a schoolgirl neatness. Lisa Dissat.

I slowly crumpled the sheet of hotel paper. I felt tired. I got up and walked back to the bedroom where she lay upon the unchanged sheets she and Brego had stained, sweated, and rumpled. She was on her side, knees hiked up, clenched fists tucked under her chin. She made sucking sounds, whining sounds. Fetal agony.

In the better interrogations there is always a good guy and a bad guy. I had been the bad guy. Time to change roles. I went into the bathroom and took a hand towel and soaked it in cold water. I wrung it out, took it to the bed, sat on the side of the bed, and cupped my hand on her shoulder and pulled her toward me. She resisted and made protest sounds, then let herself roll onto her back.

I hitched closer and gently swabbed her face and forehead. Her eyes went wide with astonishment. The last thing she had expected was gentleness. She snuffled. Her face looked touchingly young. Tears had washed away the challenge and the hardness.

"Have you got anything with you to prove your name is Lisa Dissat?"

"N-no."

"And you're pretending to be Mary Broll?"

"Yes. But I—"

"Does Broll know you're impersonating his wife?"

"Yes."

"Were you having an affair with him?"

"Yes."

"Where's the real Mary Broll?"

". . . I don't know."

"Lisa?"

"I didn't know what he was going to do! I *didn't!*"

"Lisa!"

"I couldn't have changed anything."

"Just say she's dead, Lisa. Go ahead."

"I didn't know he—"

"Lisa! Say it!"

"She's dead. Okay. She's dead."

"Harry killed her?"

She looked startled. "Oh, no!"

"Who killed her?"

"Please, Gavin. If he ever knew I told anybody—"

"You're in a real box, dear. You can worry about what's going to happen in the future, or you can worry about what's going to happen in the next ten minutes."

"I don't even know if he really meant to."

"What's his name?"

". . . Paul. Paul Dissat. He is . . . my first cousin. We worked for the same man. In Quebec. Mr. Dennis Waterbury. Paul got me the job there. I'm a secretary. I was a secretary. Paul is an accountant. He is . . . very trusted. I think he might be crazy. Really crazy. Maybe he really planned to kill Harry's wife. I don't know. I don't even know if he knows."

"How much money is involved?"

"An awful lot. Really, an awful lot of money."

"Stop crying."

"I want to talk about it, and I don't want to talk about it. I've been scared for so long! I *want* you to make me tell you all of it, but I'm afraid to tell you."

twelve

It was a very long afternoon for both of us. But longer for Lisa Dissat, because from time to time she tried to get cute. But the more she tried it, the more conditioned she became, and the more quickly she would correct herself.

At last I was able to bring the complex, wandering, fragments of the story into reasonably sharp focus.

Paul Dissat had hungered for a long time to share in some of the large profits Dennis Waterbury made on his varied operations and investments in resort lands, oil and gas drilling programs, new urban office structures, tanker leasing, and so on. Paul Dissat was well paid. There were staff bonuses when things went well. Paul Dissat was shrewd enough to realize that without investment capital he had no chance of participating in the profits and that if he used his skills to tinker with the records of the various corporations and their shifting, changing bank balances, sooner or later an audit would catch him.

He was single, she said, and did not look like anybody's idea of an accountant. Bachelor apartment, sports car. She said he was a superb skier, proficient at downhill racing and slalom. She said that three years ago, when she was twenty-three, she had run up bills she was unable to pay. She was afraid of losing her job. She had phoned Paul. She had not seen him in several years. He had taken her to dinner and back to his apartment and made love to her. He had paid her overdue accounts and arranged for her to be employed by Waterbury. After they had been intimate many times, he had told her of his plan to share in some of the fat profits from Waterbury's operations. He would arrange the necessary leverage through her. He said he would let her know when the right opportunity came along.

He arranged for her to seduce the particularly unattractive minor partner in one of the Waterbury developments and to pretend infatuation. Paul prompted her during the affair, telling her what her lines should be. Eventually, in order to safely end the affair without Lisa going to his wife, the man deposited a substantial amount of cash in her savings account. Paul told her that the cash was the proceeds from the stock in a Waterbury enterprise that the man had sold to get the money to buy her off. Paul had taken all of the cash except a thousand dollars.

They had done it once again prior to her affair with Harry Broll and made a little more than the first time. Paul explained to her that a man who has suddenly made a substantial profit tends to be generous with a mistress who is becoming too demanding and possessive.

I wanted to know why she kept so little of the take and let her first cousin have all the rest. She said it was because she was in love with him. At first.

"The third one was Harry," she said. "I went to the hotel and took dictation. Just like the first two men. Ten minutes after I looked at him in a certain way and told him how real brilliant he was, I was helping him take off my bra, because his hands were shaking so bad. Then after Harry went back to the States, Paul made me quit my job and follow him. I didn't want to. He said this could be the big one, worth a big risk. So . . . I did what he said. Harry got jumpy when I phoned him last November from Miami. He was glad, but he was nervous, too. I told him I had followed him because I was so in love with him I couldn't live without him, and I was putting my future in his hands."

Harry had set her up in the apartment in the Casa de Playa. At about that time Paul Dissat had been transferred to the administrative offices of SeaGate, Inc. in West Palm Beach, just as he had planned and expected. SeaGate was a large, complex situation with very complicated financing and special tax problems. Paul had been involved in it from the beginning.

"I called Paul once, but he got very angry. He told me to keep on following orders. The orders were to make myself just as agreeable as I possibly could, to make Harry as happy as possible, to really work on the sex part of it and do anything and everything to give him so much pleasure he'd never be able to get along without me. That wasn't easy, because Harry worked hard and he didn't keep in shape and didn't have much energy left for bed. But after I learned what turned him on the most, it got better for both of us. I had to pretend to be passionately in love with him. You know, it wasn't such a bad life. Go shopping, go out on the beach, get your hair done, watch your weight, do your nails, take naps. Not a bad life. Then a few days before Christmas, Paul wanted to know when Harry would be with me, definitely. I said I could make sure he'd come in the middle of the day on the twenty-third and spend an hour and a half with me. He told me not to be surprised if Mrs. Broll showed up. I couldn't understand what Paul was trying to do. He told me to shut up and do what I was told. She came barging in as Harry was leaving. Better looking than I'd thought from what Harry had told me about her. She called me some things, and I called her some things, and she went away crying."

Harry Broll had then become very upset. He had told Lisa Dissat that he needed her, that he wanted to get a divorce from Mary and marry her, but he couldn't do that yet. He had to make up with Mary, humble himself, promise never to see Lisa again. He said he had to do that because without her financial backing he was going to miss out on his great opportunity at SeaGate. He said he had to move her out of the apartment and be very careful about seeing her. He said it might last until May, but then he could leave Mary and marry her.

On the night of January fourth, shortly before midnight, Harry came to Lisa's motel, where he had moved her after taking her out of the apartment. He was drunk. He said that he and Mary had a terrible fight, and she was leaving him. As soon as Harry had passed out, Lisa phoned Paul to report, as required, any new development. Paul drove over to the motel, left his rented car there, borrowed Harry's car and house keys, and told Lisa to undress the unconscious Harry and keep him quiet for as long as she could manage.

"He wouldn't tell me what he was going to do. He acted all . . . keyed up, excited, on top of the world. He came back at daylight. He seemed very tired and very relaxed. He helped me get Harry up. Harry was confused. He knew Paul, of course, because of SeaGate and knew he was my cousin. But that was the first he realized that Paul knew about Harry and me. Paul pretended to be very upset about the affair, I guess to keep Harry off-balance. The three of us went back in Harry's car to Harry's house on Blue Heron Lane. Paul kept telling Harry he was in trouble. Paul made me wait in the living room. He took Harry into the bedroom. Harry made a terrible sound. A kind of bellowing groan. I heard heavy footsteps running, and then I heard Harry throwing up. When Paul brought him back into the living room, all cleaned up, Harry was like a sleepwalker. Paul kept saying it was an accident, and Harry kept saying anything like that just couldn't be an accident, and Paul kept telling him that everything could be worked out for the best if Harry would just pull himself together. Paul had me make coffee, a lot of it."

Mary had, of course, been interrogated by Paul Dissat and murdered by Paul Dissat when he finally had everything he needed—the air reservations and tickets from the travel agency, the hotel reservation, the complete details of her arrangement with her trust officer, the fact that only one friend knew where she was going and why: Holly Dressner at 27 Blue Heron Lane, a few doors away. And he had the ninety-two hundred dollars in cash she had drawn from the income account of TA 5391. Mary was half packed for the trip. She had bought resort clothes. At Paul's order Lisa finished the packing, hunting through Mary's belongings for what she thought she would need.

"It was weird with her on the bed all covered up. I tried some of the stuff on in her dressing room. She was a little hippier than I am. I mean some of the things were a size ten when I'd be better off in an eight. Harry was like a very sick person. He couldn't seem to get himself out of it. Tears kept rolling down his face. Once he just sort of hung on me. He grabbed me and put so much weight on me he nearly rode me right down on to the floor. He was asking me something, mumbling about how could Paul do that, how could he. They had a terrible argument later on. I couldn't hear most of it. It was about what to do with her body. Harry said he couldn't stand having her buried on the place. There was something about the seawall and a transit mix truck. Paul told Harry she was going to be buried right on the property, then Harry would not go back on any promises, ever."

She was given her orders, and Paul made her repeat them until there was no chance of her forgetting them. Drive to Miami International. Find accommodations for the night of the fifth and sixth. Stay in the room. Use Mary's ticket on the seventh. Use Mary's driver's license as proof of birthplace when needed. Use her immunization certificate if needed. Use her hairstyle. Wear big dark sunglasses. Travel in her new clothes. Go to Grenada. Register as Mary Broll. Live quietly. Keep to yourself. Send some post cards to Holly Dressner. Pick the kind which do not require a message. Sign with a little drawing of a smiling face.

"I *did* try to keep to myself. But, God, I've been here a long long time, Gav. I really have."

"What do you do next? What are Paul's orders?"

"On Monday, next Monday, I'm supposed to send a cable. Paul dictated it to me." I made her get it. It was to Woodrow Willow at Southern National in Miami. PROCEED WITH LOAN AS ARRANGED EARLY JANUARY. HAVE ADVISED HARRY BY PHONE. HOME SOON. MARY BROLL.

Harry's part in it would be to phone Woodrow Willow that same day, Monday, April twenty-sixth, and tell him that Mary had reached him by overseas phone call from Grenada to tell him she had cabled Willow to go ahead, tell him not to worry, tell him she would be home soon.

He would inform Willow that Mary had given him the name of the travel agency she had used and had told him that her neighbor, Mrs. Dressner, had known all along where she was.

Very nice. If Willow felt like double-checking after he got the cable, he could call the travel agency and call Mrs. Dressner.

"Can't they check back on an overseas call?" I asked.

"Sure. That's why I call him at his office next Sunday afternoon. I've got the number. He'll have a secretary there. It will be person-to-person. Mrs. Broll calling Mr. Broll. That's for afterward, in case they do a lot of checking."

"Checking what?"

"I'm reserved to leave here on Monday, the third of May. Paul just didn't have time to work everything out before I left. But the way he wants it to happen, Mary Broll will have some kind of accident. He's going to get a message to me telling me what to do. I just . . . leave everything of hers and arrive back home as myself somehow. Maybe a towel and a beach bag left on the beach, and nothing missing but a swim suit and a cap."

"Where does the money come from?"

"The way I understand it, Gav, Harry invested seven hundred thousand in SeaGate. The letter of agreement said that on or before April thirtieth, he has to pay in another three hundred thousand to make one million dollars. There is a block of stock escrowed for him and a note escrowed, saying SeaGate owes him seven hundred thousand plus interest. It is an . . . indivisible block. He takes it all and wipes out the money SeaGate owes him and pays three hundred more. If he doesn't, he just gets his seven hundred back with interest, and the hundred thousand shares go to increase the number of shares the corporation is selling to the public and to reduce the number the stockholders will offer. There is no way in the world Harry can get that money except from the bank on a loan on Mary's trust. He can't get an extension, and he can't cut down the number of shares he'll take. And he is borrowed to the hilt everywhere else."

"So he had to keep Mary alive for about four months after she died?"

She shivered. "Or lose a big profit, a million and a half."

"How much to your cousin?"

"He said a million. He didn't say that in front of Harry. I think he could get it all out of Harry." She frowned. "The thing about Paul, he stopped giving a damn *what* he does. It doesn't matter to him any more. It scares me. Once when I was little, a deaf boy took me to the movies, and he laughed when nobody else was laughing. Paul is like that now, sort of."

"And I suppose Harry has been making a big fuss, storming around, shaking up Mary's friends, demanding they tell him where they're hiding her."

"Maybe. I don't know. I guess it would make him look better later on, if people could testify to that. I don't know how he is. I keep wondering how he'll sound on the phone."

Her voice dragged. Her face looked puffy with fatigue. Her eyes were irritated because of the many times the tears had come. There wasn't much left of the day. She said, "Can we go for a walk on the beach? Would that be okay, Gavin?"

She got up and got a gaudy print dashaki and pulled it over her head, pushed her hair back into semiorder, put her big glasses on. "Gee, I feel emptied out, as if it's out of my hands somehow. I should be scared, but I'm too beaten down to be scared. You're in charge, Gav. You've taken over. I don't know where we're going, but you're running the ship."

It was so nicely done I had my mouth all set for the bait and the hook. Poor little victim of a sordid conspiracy, clinging to the first man who'd give her the benefit of the doubt.

Sweet little immature face and a busy, nimble little butt and all the conscience and mercy of a leopard shark. Let me be your little pal, mister. Nobody else has ever understood me but you. She had slipped up on one little detail, but it was a bad slip. She let me see how she must have looked trying on Mary's new resort clothes while Mary lay dead. Probably Lisa turned this way and that, looking in the mirror, smoothing her rear with the backs of her hands, wishing the damned dead woman had bought the cute clothes one size smaller. She tried on clothes while the men argued in the next room. "Look at it this way, Broll. You had a look at her an hour and a half ago. They'll want to know why you waited so long before reporting it. What do you tell them?" While Lisa hummed and bit her lip and frowned at herself and wondered if the colors were right for her.

thirteen

We walked up the beach in the orange and gold light of tropic sunset. The tide was moving out and the packed sand was damp and firm under our tread, a coarse, yellow-brown sand. The sun was behind us setting into the sea just out beyond Long Point. Far ahead, beyond the rocks that marked the end of Grand Anse beach and beyond St. George's harbor, was the toy-town look of the town at evening, spilled up the green slopes, small formal shapes with windows looking toward the sea.

We walked past the Grand Anse Hotel, the Grenada Beach Hotel, the Holiday Inn. Cars had come down to the public areas to park under the sea grapes and the almond trees. People swam in the relative cool of twilight, and people walked the long broad promenade of packed sand. Sloops and ketches and multihull sailboats were anchored off the two-mile crescent of beach. A fast boat was pulling a limber black girl on water skis between the anchored sailboats. Behind us was the blinding dazzle of the sun's path on the quiet sea, and our shadows ahead of us were long in a slanting pattern against the damp sand.

"You were going to talk, I thought?"

"I am. I am." She moved closer, linked her arm through mine, hugged it against her body, and looked up at me. "I have to, I guess. Do you know how things can happen to your life that . . . don't fit it somehow? Then everything else isn't real. When you forget, then everything around you is real again, but what happened doesn't seem as if it could have ever happened. Do you know what I'm talking about?"

"Not yet, girl. Not yet."

"I guess in my own way I was as numb as Harry was. It seems like ten years ago, practically."

"Didn't you think it was pretty damned stupid for Paul to kill Mary Broll? Didn't you tell him it was stupid?"

She had to wait until we had passed a group of people strolling at a slower pace than ours. She indicated a stubby cement pier at the far border of the Holiday Inn property. It projected only to the surf line and seemed to have no purpose other than as some sort of groyne to retain the sand. We went up the slope of beach, stepped up onto it, and walked out to sit near the end, our backs to the sunset.

She laced her fingers in mine, tugged at my hand, and rested it palm upward against the smooth, round brown of mid-thigh. She frowned toward the town.

"I've thought about it and thought about it, Gavin. I guess it got to be pretty obvious to Paul that an affair with me wasn't going to be enough leverage on Harry. Harry and his wife weren't getting along so great anyway. There wasn't anything real important to expose, you might say. So why did he tip off Mary Broll so she'd catch me and Harry together? Why did he make sure she *would* catch us? Why did he tell me to yell at Mrs. Broll and make a big scene out of it? Motive, right?"

The point was well taken. Mary would certainly confide her problem to someone. The scene at the apartment had attracted so much attention that even Jeannie Dolan heard about it later. Of late, Harry had been blustering around, threatening people, trying to locate his dead wife.

If the police were tipped, dug for Mary, and found her, even the most inept state's attorney could put together a case F. Lee Bailey couldn't successfully defend.

"So, Lisa, you think Paul had decided to kill her when he made the phone call to her. Does that make sense? He didn't know then she'd decided to go away. He didn't know then what she'd arrange about the loan. She could have left without any warning at all. He'd have to be some kind of warlock, reading the future."

"I know. I think about it until my head starts to hurt, and then I give up."

"Did you think he'd ever kill anybody?"

"You don't go around wondering whether people you know can kill other people, do you? I knew he was mean. I knew how nasty he could get. I knew there was something kinky about him, the way he got something special out of sleeping with me and then making me sleep with those older guys. It was something to do with him never getting married, I think. We look alike, like brother and sister. His eyes are the same as mine, the same dark dark brown and long black lashes and—see?—the left one set straight, and the right one slanty. His mouth is like mine, a lot of natural red to the lips, and the mouth small, and the lower lip heavy and curling out from the upper lip. We both look younger than we are, but that's always been true of the whole family. Aside from that there isn't the least thing feminine about him. Even my eyes and mouth don't look girlish on Paul, somehow. Except when he's asleep. That's strange, isn't it? I'd watch him sleeping, and then his eyes and lips would look the most like mine and make me feel strange. He is big! He's almost as tall as you are and as big through the chest. But he moves a lot quicker. I guess I mean his normal way of moving is quicker. Nobody is quicker than you were with Carl. Jesus! You looked kind of dumb and sleepy, as if you couldn't believe he was really going to beat on you. Then you were something else."

"I want to know more about Paul. How old is he?"

"He'll be coming up onto thirty-seven, I think in July. Yes. Other companies have tried to hire him away from Mr. Waterbury. So I guess he's a good accountant. He stays in great shape all year. He does competition slalom in the winter and tennis in the summer. His legs are tremendously powerful, like fantastic springs."

"An exercise nut?"

"With weights and springs and pulleys and things. And a sun lamp that travels by itself from one end of you to the other and turns itself off. He's real happy about those legs.

One funny thing, he's as dark as I am, and he has to shave twice a day when he goes out in the evening, but on his body, except for those places where everybody has hair, he hasn't any. His legs have a really great shape, and there isn't any hair on them or his chest or his arms. The muscles are long and smooth, not bunchy. When he tenses them, his legs are like marble."

"You called him kinky."

She frowned and thought for a little while. I saw the point of her tongue slowly moisten the curve of underlip. "No. That isn't the right word. The whole sex scene isn't a big thing with him. I mean it's there, all right. It was something we would do. You know, when he couldn't unwind and get to sleep, he'd phone me to come over to his place down in the city. We were five blocks apart. He makes me feel . . . I don't know . . . like one of his damn exercise machines, something with a motor and weights and springs, so that afterward he could put it in his exercise log. Ten minutes on the rowing machine. Eight minutes on the Lisa machine."

"I can't really get the picture of you two."

"What's so difficult, honey?"

"You move to Quebec and change jobs because he tells you to. You come over whenever he phones you. He tells you to seduce Mr. X and then Mr. Y and tells you how to extort money from them, and he takes most of it. He tells you to seduce Harry, quit your job, and follow Harry to Florida, and he tells you to come here and pretend to be Mary. You are awfully goddamn docile, Lisa."

"I know. I know. Yes. It's funny about him. He's just so absolutely positive you're going to do what he tells you to do, it's a lot easier to do it than try to say you won't."

"Did you ever try to say you wouldn't do something he asked you to do?"

"God, yes! In the very beginning, before he even got the job for me. I was at his place, and he asked me to get him something from across the room. I was sitting at the table, and I said something like 'You're not a cripple, are you?' He got up and went behind me and hit me on top of the head with his fist. I blacked out and fell off the chair and cut my chin. It did something funny to my neck, pinched a nerve or something, and I was in bed for three days with it, practically in agony. He was a darling. He waited on me hand and foot. He was so sweet and considerate. I guess . . . it's easier to do what he says, because you have the feeling that neither of you knows what he'll do if you say no. At work he's another person."

"How do you feel about the way you're crossing him?"

"It keeps making me feel as if I'm going to throw up."

She looked up at me with a piquant tilt of her dark head. It's funny," she said. "I never saw you before today. Then you scared me so. You really did. Now you're so nice and understanding. I can really talk to you. About everything."

Her fingers were laced in mine, and she pressed down on my hand, holding the back of my hand against the round, tan thigh, slowly swinging her dangling leg as she did so. I felt the smooth working of the thigh muscles against the back of my hand. It was a sensuous and persuasive feeling. She was a pretty piece, making her constant offer of herself in any way that she could.

"Why trust me?" I asked her.

She shrugged. "I don't know. I guess I'm trying to. I guess I can't go it alone, no matter what it is. I appreciate you didn't mark me up any. I mean I hate to get belted in the face where it shows. It cuts a person's mouth inside, and there's a big puffy bruise and maybe a mouse comes under a person's eye. It's a bad thing to do to a girl. She goes around ashamed."

"Paul belted you?"

"Sometimes."

"But you trust him?"

"He's a blood relative. Maybe I shouldn't trust him at all. He's strange. He really is. It doesn't show. You have to know him."

"I keep thinking of how boxed in you are."

"How do you mean?"

"Suppose after you go back, Harry is picked up for killing his wife. They have her body. It's certainly no big problem finding the girlfriend and proving you were there.

With that starting point, Lisa, how long before the state attorney's investigators learn about the impersonation? Would you want to explain on the stand why you took her money, her tickets, her reservations, her clothes, and her car?"

There was a sudden sallowness. "Come *on* now. Don't, honey! Jesus! I don't like jokes like that. We're in this together, aren't we?"

"Are we?"

"What do you *want* of me? What more do you want that I'm not ready and eager and willing to give, dear?"

"Do you think Cousin Paul is going to give you a short count on the money again?"

"If he gets the chance."

I pulled my hand away from her. "Now what would keep him from having the chance? Me?"

"Darling, please don't try to confuse me."

"How am I confusing you?"

"Well . . . you said you own me now, and you said there had to be money in it. So I guess you'll go after the money. I guess you'd have to have my help."

"Doing what?"

"That would be up to you, dear."

"To figure out how you can help me get rich?"

"That's the name of your game, I thought."

"Maybe Paul's game is over."

"How do you mean?"

"Harry Broll is not a complete idiot. Why couldn't he have gone quietly to the police and managed to sell them the truth? So they lay back and wait for you to return and for Paul to make his move, and scoop you both up."

"Damn! I forgot to tell you about the letter I wrote Paul. He was right there when I wrote it. He found Mary Broll's personal stationery for me to use. He told me what to write. I had to do it over because he said it was too neat the first time. I dated it January fifth. It said that Paul had been right and I never should have gotten involved with Harry. It said Harry had done something terrible while drunk and had gotten me to his house afterward to help him but I couldn't. I said I was frightened and I was going away and to wait until I got in touch with him. He held it in front of Harry and made him read it. Then he had me seal it in an envelope and put a stamp on it and address it to Paul's place in West Palm Beach. Paul put it in his pocket to mail as soon as he could."

The sun was gone. The world was darkening. The sky was a dying furnace, and the sea was slate. We walked back the way we had come but more slowly.

"Gavin?"

"Shut up, Lisa. Please."

The beach was almost empty. The outdoor torches had been lighted at the Spice Island Inn. Birds were settling noisily to bed, arguing about the best places. Canned music was coming over all-weather speakers, a steel band playing carnival calypso.

When we reached her gate, she said, "Now can I say something? Like, please come in?"

"I want to sit out in the breeze, thanks. Over there."

"Join you?"

"Sure."

"Bring you a drink, maybe?"

"Thanks. Same as before."

I sat deep in a chaise, legs up, trying to work it out in every possible combination and permutation. With Mary Broll dead, Woodrow Willow was supposed to slam the lid on that trust account. Harry was probably the beneficiary under her will, possibly a coexecutor along with the bank. But had she died in early January, even in a traffic accident, the chances of processing the estate quickly enough for Harry to get his three hundred thousand before April thirtieth were very damned remote. She had to die later on.

So what if Meyer and I had not had all those vague feelings of uneasiness? What if we had accepted my phone call as being proof enough that she was alive and well and living in Grenada?

Then it would have worked like a railroad watch. The timely loan. The news of pending reconciliation. Enough supporting information for Willow to consider the cable legitimate authorization. Then the ironic tragedy. Estranged wife on the point of returning home to her contrite husband, missing in mysterious drowning incident. Search is on for body. However . . .

"Here you go," she said. I thanked her for the drink. She had brought one for herself. She sat on the side of the chaise, facing me. I moved my legs over to make room. The stars were beginning to come out. I could see that she had brushed her hair, freshened her mouth. The bright, block print dashaki had deep side slits, and she adjusted herself and it, either by accident or design, so that the side slit showed the outside of a bare thigh and hip as high as the waist, a smoothness of flesh in the dying day that was not interrupted by the narrow encirclement of bikini I had seen there before.

"You certainly do an awful lot of thinking," she said.

"And here I am, dear, alive and well."

"But you have been terribly terribly hurt a few times, Gav."

"The times when I wasn't thinking clearly."

"Do I keep you from thinking clearly? I'd sure like a chance to try. Would you mind if I ask you politely to please make love to me?"

"What are we celebrating?"

"You're *such* a bastard! Gavin darling, I feel very very insecure about a lot of things. I've been alone a long time. Now I want somebody to hold me tight and make love to me and tell me I'm delicious. For morale, I guess. Why do you even make me ask? It doesn't have to be any big thing, you know. It doesn't have to take up a hell of a lot of your time. Hitch over just a little bit, darling, and let me . . ."

The way she started to manage it—to lie down beside me and hike her dashaki up and tug my swim trunks down and simultaneously hook one brown leg over me—certainly wasn't going to take up a great deal of anybody's time, the way she was going at it.

I pushed her erect and pulled the trunks back up. "Very flattering. Very generous. But no thanks."

She laughed harshly and picked her drink up off the sand near her feet. "Well, comparing you to Carl, I can say this. You've got a different kind of attitude. If I hadn't uncovered proof, I'd be wondering about you."

"I'm busy pretending I'm Paul, wondering how he has it all worked out."

"Different strokes for different folks."

"I hang back and make sure Harry Broll follows orders. I check with him about the Sunday afternoon phone call from you. On Tuesday morning, the twenty-seventh, I will get in touch with Mr. Willow, in my capacity as an employee of SeaGate, to verify that Mr. Broll will indeed have the funds to pick up his escrowed block of SeaGate shares. I am assured. The money comes through. And I am very very busy right through the thirtieth and through the weekend, because that is the end of the fiscal year for SeaGate. Right?"

"I guess so, dear."

"Then I have to do something about Cousin Lisa. She's expecting a message from me. I'll have to deliver it in person."

"To tell me what to do next?"

"Old Harry is twitchy about his dead wife. And Lisa is twitchy about Harry's dead wife. Harry and Lisa could testify against me if they ever join forces. Lisa is wearing the dead woman's rings. I just have to arrange a nice quick safe way to meet her in the islands and blow her face off and blow her dental work to paste. Then there's no mystery about a body. I can settle down and separate good old Harry from every cent of his gain and every cent he has left over when that's gone. When Harry is empty, it will be time to lay him to rest, too. By accident. Just in case."

I reached an idle hand and patted her on the shoulder. She remained quiveringly still, then was suddenly up and away, to come to rest five feet from the chaise, staring at me.

"No! No, Gavin. He's my first cousin. No."

"He couldn't do that?"

"Absolutely not. Not ever. Not any way."

"Then why are you so upset?"

"Anybody would be upset, hearing something so horrible."

"You know you are supposed to fake Mary Broll's death. There's less chance of a hitch if somebody plays the part of the body. You've been Mary Broll since January. Why switch now?"

"Don't be such a bastard!"

"It's the way I have to read him from everything you've told me. A quirky guy but very logical. A good improviser. If one logical plan doesn't develop the way he wants it to, he thinks up an alternative just as good or better. And . . . Lisa dear, just what the hell good are you to him? The end of usefulness. He knows there's a chance you'll make new friends who'll hear about how you died and get very upset about it and might run into you in an air terminal somewhere a year from now. All you are is a big risk, and an unnecessary risk."

"Shut *up!*"

"Think about it."

"I *am* thinking about it."

"It wouldn't be *my* style, but I have to admire it in a way. It ties up the loose ends. No way out for Harry. Or you."

She found her drink had been kicked over. "Ready for another?"

"Not yet, thanks."

"Want to come in?"

"I'll stay here awhile."

"Be back soon, dear."

fourteen

Though Lisa Dissat was not gone for more than ten minutes, it was full night when she came back, a velvet beach under a brilliance of stars. There were lights behind us from the Spice Island Inn cottages. The lights made a slanting yellow glow against the sand.

She sat beside me again. She had changed to tailored white shorts, a dark blouse with a Chinese collar and long sleeves. She smelled of perfume . . . and Off. The white fabric was snug on the round hip that pressed warm against the side of my knee.

"Took off your instant rape suit, eh?"

She pulled her shoulders up slightly, and her drink made the sounds of ice as she sipped. "I guess you made me lose interest."

"Are you a believer now?"

"Up to a point. I can't see any percentage in taking dumb risks. You are the loose end Paul doesn't know about. I guess I can be the bait in the trap. But we have to be awfully awfully careful. He's very sensitive to . . . what people are thinking. We can't give him any chance at all."

"How do you mean that?"

"If it's like you say, if that's what he's going to try to do, then he'll have it all worked out so there won't be any risk in it, hardly any at all. So if he really wants to kill me, we have to kill him instead, darling."

"Your very own first cousin?"

"Don't be a stinker, please. What other choice is there?"

"Then what?"

"Then we have to get me back into the States in some safe way. I guess there's no reason why I couldn't go back in as Mary Broll, come to think of it. What harm would it do?"

"None, if you don't try to keep on being Mrs. Broll."

"If he isn't thinking about killing me like you say, then we'll have to play it by ear."

"All goes well, and you and I are back in the States. Then?"

"We just go and see Harry. That's all. I'll tell him that unless he gives us lots and lots of money, he's going to have lots and lots of trouble. And you can beat him up if he tries to bluff us."

"How much money?"

"I don't think we should make him really desperate or anything. I think we should leave him with enough so he'll think he came out of it pretty well. I think we could ask for half a million dollars."

"Each?"

"No, dear. He has to pay taxes on the whole thing, you know. I think with the holding period before the sale to the public, it will be long term. Yes, I know it will. He should get his money next December. Hmmm. His taxes will be a half million. That leaves him two million, and I know he owes four hundred thousand and he will have to pay back the three hundred thousand. So out of his million and three, we'll take five hundred thousand, darling, and he'll have eight hundred thousand left. It would be neater if we took six hundred and fifty and left him six hundred and fifty, don't you think?"

"A lot neater. And you want half?"

"What I want and what you'll let me have aren't the same, are they?"

"They could be with cooperation all the way."

"Moving money like that around without leaving traces that people can find later is very hard. Do you know anything about that kind of problem? I'd think you would."

"If Harry Broll will hold still for the bite, yes."

"There's no problem, Gav honey. None."

"Leaving only Paul."

She finished her drink, bunted me with her hip. "Scrooch over some, honey. Make room. No funny stuff this time, I promise."

She turned, lay back, and fitted her head to my shoulder, swinging her legs aboard.

After a while she said, "Want to order dinner in my place or yours, dear?"

"I don't know yet."

"I'm not hungry, either. Gee, look at all the damned stars. Like when I was a little kid, the night sky looked glittery like this."

"Where was that?"

"Way up in French Canada on the St. Lawrence, north of Riviere du Loup. A little town called Trois Pistoles. Ten thousand saints, ten thousand churches all over that country. Convent school, uniforms, vespers, acts of contrition, the whole scene. I ran away when I was fifteen. With my best friend, Diane Barbet. We got across the border and into the States. Things got kind of messy for us. You survive or you don't, I guess. I don't know what happened to Diane. I think about her sometimes. A guy in Detroit helped me really go to work on my hick Canuck accent. Movies, television, radio, and using a tape recorder. I think in English now, except if something startles the hell out of me or scares me. I get scared in French. Another man sent me to business school. To learn to be an executive secretary. That was in Cincinnati. He was a real old guy. He picked me up. I was hitchhiking. He took me home. He lived alone—his wife had been dead two years. He wanted me to stay there with him and pretend I was his grand-niece so the neighbors wouldn't turn him in. I wanted somebody to send me to school so I could be a secretary, so it worked out okay. He bought me pretty clothes. I was eighteen by then. He bought me a little car, even. He was retired. He cooked and kept the house clean and did the laundry and made the bed. He even ironed my things that needed it, and he rinsed out stuff. I was really pretty rotten to old Harv. He was forty years older than me. That is a lot of years. When he got on my nerves, I wouldn't let him touch me. I cut off the supply. He didn't really want me too often or give me much trouble. I finished school and got my certificate and got a job. The way I was living, I could put it all in the bank, and I did. I came home one evening, and he was on the floor in the utility room. His whole left side had gone dead. His eye drooped and spit ran out of the left side of his mouth, and he couldn't speak. He just made terrible noises when he tried. I packed all my things into the trunk of my car, and then I called the hospital. I parked in the next block and walked back to make sure they found him and put him in the ambulance. I went to a motel. I finished out the week after I gave notice. I got my money out of the bank. I left and went down to Mobile and sold the car there. You can sell cars easy in Alabama. Then I flew home to Canada and got a good job in Montreal. I kept missing old Harv. I still miss him, I guess. It was a pretty good way to live, you know? I wasn't very nice to him. If I had it to do over, I'd be a lot nicer. I'd never hold out on him the way I did. It never cost me a thing to make him feel good.

"Anyway, I had a wonderful life in Montreal. There was a great bunch of kids there. And then I fell really *really* in love. When my guy took off with a girlfriend of mine, I did what I always do when I hurt. Buy, buy, buy. Shoes, clothes, wigs. I like money. I guess I spend it to hurt myself. You know? I knew I was in real trouble unless somebody bailed me out. So I went up to Quebec and saw Cousin Paul. I think I could have gone the rest of my life without the kind of help *he* gave me. Hey, look!"

"Shooting star."

"I know. But such a big, bright, slow one, huh? It lasted forever."

"Did you make a wish?"

"Was I supposed to? Would it work?"

"The way to make a wish come true is to wish for something you're going to get anyway."

"Is it okay to wish a little late?"

"Go ahead. It wasn't my shooting star."

"Okay. I wished." My arm was around her. She turned in a twisting motion that slipped her breast into my hand.

Under the thin fabric of the blouse she wore no bra, and in seconds I felt the nipple growing and hardening. "Does that give you a clue, friend? Something I'm going to get anyway?"

I sat up, raising her with me, slid my hands onto her waist, picked her up, and dropped her onto the sand beside the chaise.

"Ow! That made me bite my tongue, you son of a bitch!"

"Just be a good girl and stop trying to hook me on the product. It's there anytime I want it. Stop pushing it."

She stood up. "Don't be too damned sure it's going to be served up on a damn tray when you decide to ask for it, Gav. And I wasn't trying to hook you on anything. I just think it's friendly and nice to get laid. It isn't a big thing, is it? And it got me going, what I was talking about."

"Old Harv, for God's sake?"

"No, you dummy! The money. Big gobs of money, just thinking about it makes me feel all hollow and crawly inside, and I guess it's so much like the feeling you get when you know you're going to get laid, it works the same way."

"Go take a cold shower."

"You're terribly nice to me. You're oceans of fun. I'm going to walk up and down the beach and think about blizzards and icicles and catheters and having my teeth drilled. That takes me off the edge fast."

"I should think it would."

So she went walking out there, clearly visible, scuffing barefoot through the foamy water that came running up the wet slope after the thud of each slow, small wave. A girl walking slowly, slow tilting swing of hips, legs shapely and dark below the white glow of the shorts.

She had deftly pushed a lot of my buttons. She had worked on proximity, touch, forthright invitation. She had talked in areas that accentuated sexual awareness. She smelled good, felt good, kept her voice furry and intimate. I knew she wasn't being made wanton and reckless by my fabulous magnetism. We were moving toward an association, possibly profitable. For maximum leverage within that association of two, she wanted to put that weapon to work which had profited her in the past, probably in every relationship except the one with her cousin.

I was another version of good old Harv, whom we last saw on the floor with spit running out of his mouth. She'd pushed Harv's buttons and got her secretarial training and a car and a lot of clothes. Her libido certainly wasn't out of control. It was just a useful thing for her to do, a nice little inexpensive favor for her to grant, and if it clouded the recipient's judgment, eventual profit from the relationship might improve.

Were I a great ape, a giant anthropoid, munching stalks torn from the jungle, and able to lead her to forgotten treasure, Lisa would take her best shot at making everything friendlier and nicer. As she said about Harv, it wouldn't cost a thing to make that big monkey feel good.

But knowing how and why the buttons are pushed doesn't diminish the physiological aftereffects of the button pushing. The tumescence is noticeable. The palm of the hand retains the shape of the breast—the precise size, warmth, and rate of erection. The eyes watch the slow walk, creating an increase in the heart beat and rate of respiration and blood pressure and surface body temperature, as the conditioned mind anticipates the simple progression of events of calling to her, bringing her close, shucking her out of the shorts, pulling her astride, and settling her properly for that sweet, grinding task that would end so quickly the first time.

The buttons tripped certain relays. I had to go back into the mind, into central control, and reset those relays, compensate for the overload, switch the current back to those channels designed for it.

I went searching through the past for the right memory, the one which would most easily turn growing desire to indifference.

I thought a memory of Miss Mary Dillon long ago aboard *The Busted Flush* would do it. There were more than a few, but they would not come through vividly enough to achieve turnoff.

Lisa made it so damned easy, so completely available,

there was no importance to it. And with no importance to an act, why did it matter whether or not it happened? Why did McGee need some cachet of importance in this world of wall-to-wall flesh in the weekend livingroom where the swingers courteously, diligently, skillfully, considerately hump one another to the big acid beat of the hifi installation, good from 20 to 20,000 cycles per second?

Is McGee still impaled upon some kind of weird Puritan dilemma, writhing and thrashing around, wrestling with an outdated, old-time, inhibiting and artificial sense of sin, guilt, and damnation? Is that why he couldn't accept the lifetime gift Lady Jillian offers? Is that why he has this sickly, sentimental idea that there has to be a productive and meaningful relationship first, or sex degrades? So bang the doxy, because easing the ball-pressure is reason enough.

Who needs magic and mystery? Well, maybe it is magic and mystery that an Antarctic penguin will hunt all over hell and gone to find the right pebble to carry in his beak and lay between the funny feet of his intended, hoping for her favor. Maybe sex is a simple bodily function, akin to chewing, sneezing and defecation. But bald eagles fly as high as they possibly can, up into the thinnest air, making the elegant flight patterns of intended mating all the way up, then cleave to each other and fall, fall, fall, mating as they fall fluttering, plummeting down toward the great rock mountains.

The way it is supposed to work nowadays, if you want to copulate with the lady, you politely suggest it to her, and you are not offended if she says no, and you are mannerly, considerate, and satisfying if she says yes.

But the Tibetan bar-headed goose and her gander have a very strange ceremony they perform *after* they have mated. They rise high in the water, wings spread wide, beaks aimed straight up at the sky, time and time again, making great bugle sounds of honking. The behaviorists think it is unprofessional to use subjective terms about animal patterns. So they don't call this ceremony joy. They don't know what to call it. These geese live for up to fifty years, and they mate for life. They celebrate the mating this same way year after year. If one dies, the other never mates again.

So penguins, eagles, geese, wolves, and many other creatures of land and sea and air are stuck with all this obsolete magic and mystery because they can't read and they can't listen to lectures. All they have is instinct. Man feels alienated from all feeling, so he sets up encounter groups to sensitize each member to human interrelationships. But the basic group of two, of male and female, is being desensitized as fast as we can manage it . . .

"What the hell is there about me that turns you off?" Lisa demanded. She had walked up the slope to stand by the chaise, blotting out a Lisa-shaped abundance of stars as she looked down at me with a faint angle of pale yellow light laying across her cheekbone and lips.

"I was wondering what you'd do if I picked up a pebble in my beak and put it between your feet."

"I've heard of a lot of ways guys get kinky, but that is—"

"Why do you want reassurance from me? Take my word for it. You are a fantastic piece of ass. Ask practically anybody."

"I don't know. I haven't checked it."

She stood there for a few seconds in silence. Then she said, "If you ever do want some, friend, you're going to have to take it away from me, because that's the only damned way in this world you're ever going to get any."

"Goodnight, Lisa."

She walked away from the shoreline, a silhouette moving toward the yellow lights.

fifteen

Thursday I was up early. Awakening in a new place makes the day of arrival seem unreal. There had been no Carl Brego, no Lisa Dissat trying to be Mary Broll, no Lisa Dissat striding angrily away from me in the hot, buggy night. I went to my cottage after she left, swam in my minipool, two strokes per lap, changed, and went to the open dining room. The food was good, the service indifferent. There were some beautiful people there. A fashion photography team. Some yacht people. Some twosome guests had tried to get as far as possible from wherever they didn't care to be seen together. Some guests were ritualistic sun worshipers who had been there for many many weeks, using the intense tropic sun to add each day's tiny increment of pigmentation at the cost of blinding, suffocating, dazed hours and quarts of whatever oil they happened to believe in. Johnson's or coconut or olive. They were working toward that heady goal of becoming a living legend in Bronxville or Scranton or Des Moines.

"Tan? You think that's a tan? So you didn't see Barbie and Ken when they got back from Grenada that time. Dark? I swear to Christ, in a dark room all you could see were white teeth. And Barbie's diamonds."

I took a cab into town, memorizing landmarks all the way. I negotiated the rental of an Austin Moke. A Moke is a shrunken jeep with a very attractive expression, if you look at the front of it and think of the headlights as eyes. It looks staunch, jaunty, and friendly. It is a simplified piece of machinery. Stick shift which, like the wheel on the right, you work with the left hand. The horn, a single-

153

note, piercing beeeeep, is operated by pressing in on the turn indicator with the right hand. A quick whack with the heel of the hand is the approved method. Four speeds forward, small, aircooled engine, pedals so tiny that if you try to operate one with your bare feet, it hurts like hell. Canvas top nobody ever folds down in the hot season, and all they have in Grenada are two hot seasons, one wet and one dry.

With the tourist season almost over, there were a lot of them in stock. I picked one with a lot of tread, and the rental man and I walked around it and tested lights, horn, directional signals, windshield wiper (singular). He wanted his total rental in advance, which is standard for the area. While we dickered, I practiced getting in and out of the damned thing. I'd learned in Grand Cayman and Jamaica that with the length of my legs there is only one possible way. Stand beside vehicle on right side. Bend over at waist. Reach across body and grasp steering wheel with right hand, while simultaneously lifting left leg, inserting it into vehicle so that foot comes to rest on floor well beyond pedal area. Swoop your behind onto the seat and pick up right leg and lift over high broad sill (which contains gas tank). In driving position both knees are bent sharply, spread wide apart. Steering wheel fits between knees, and lower part of legs must angle in to assure foot contact with pedals. Adjust to inevitability of frequently giving oneself a painful rap on the left leg while shifting.

We arrived at a mutually agreeable fee of five Yankee —ten Biwi-dollars a day for a one week rental or any period of less than a week. I buy the gas. I will phone him when I leave and tell him to pick it up at the Spice Island Inn. I promise not to leave it at the airport. I tell him I would not drive it over that road to the airport for a hundred dollars a mile. Can I drive safely on the left side of the road? I suggest that perhaps no one in Grenada can drive safely on any side of the road. But yes, I have so driven on other islands of this British persuasion.

We accomplish the red tape, he gives me a free map of St. George and environs. I note that, as expected, there is at least one half-pint of gas in the five-gallon gas tank. I edge carefully into the tourney and immediately am nearly bowled over and over by a small pale bus with a name across the front of it. The name is: I AM NOTHING.

After I have bought petrol and felt my way back into the center of town, avoiding too intimate a contact with a large gaudy city bus called LET IT BE ME, I park my Moke and wait until I am certain my legs will work. ("You will enjoy browsing in St. George's along the narrow, quaint streets.")

I changed another wad of Yankee dollars into Biwi at the Bank of Canada, picking that one from among all the shiny banks downtown, from Chase to Barclay's to the Bank of Nova Scotia, because there was a faint aroma of irony in the choice. The girl standing behind the money-changing counter was very dark, very thin, and totally antagonistic—so much so, there was no chance of ever making any kind of human contact with her unless you were her identical anthracite color.

I asked some questions and was directed to a big busy supermarket called EVERYBODY'S FOR EVERYTHING. As long as I had kitchen facilities and I could make my own ice cubes, it seemed useful to set up shop. Gin, rum, fruit juices from Trinidad, mixes, and a couple of large substantial drink glasses. I am a fussy old party about glassware. Nothing takes the pleasure out of drinking like the tiny dim glasses supplied by hotels and motels. I always buy heavy glasses, always leave them behind. Tiny glasses turn drinking from a pleasure rite to a quasialcoholic twitch.

The final purchase was on impulse at a shop I saw on the Carenage on the way home. A great big planter's hat of straw with a batik band. Put a man in a rental Moke with advertising painted on the side of it and put a funny hat on him, and he is a tourist. All tourists look alike. Regardless of age, sex, or the number of extra lenses for their cameras, they all look alike.

I found my way back out to Grand Anse to hotel row, and I found an overland way to get the Moke close to my cottage. I carried my box of stuff in. From the moment I had awakened until the moment I finished putting the stuff away and sat down, I had not let myself think about Mary, Lisa or the mechanics of impersonation.

It is a useful device. If you keep things in the front of your mind, you worry at them like a hound chomping a dead rabbit. Throw problems in the back cupboard and keep them there as long as you can. The act of stirring around seems to shuffle the elements of a problem into a new order, and when you take it out again, there are new ways to handle it.

I tossed my sweat-soaked shirt aside. The airconditioning felt good on my back and shoulders. Okay. Mary is dead. I want Paul Dissat. I want him very badly. The money is the bait, and Lisa is the bait in another sense. I want very badly to convince Paul and Lisa and Harry Broll that, if given a choice, they would elect retroactive birth control. I want them so eager to be out of it they'd dig their own graves with a bent spoon and their finger-nails.

Secondly, as a professional, as a salvage consultant in areas of considerable difficulty, I want to come out of this with a little salvage for myself. If I walk away without a dime, with only expenses I can't reasonably afford, then I lose all respect for myself as a con artist. I would have kicked the hell out of their little wagon just to avenge one hell of a woman, Mary Dillon. Pure emotionalism is bush league.

So? So I do not advise Mr. Willow not to make the loan on Mary's securities. They go to Harry eventually anyway. That is, if Harry happens to be still around. The money has to be loaned to Harry, and Harry has to pick up his block of stock in time and get himself in position to make a great deal of money when the public issue comes out. But that is a long long time for me to wait for my money. I shall use the leverage to extract a reasonable chunk from Paul, maybe from Harry, maybe from both, before I set them to work with those bent spoons.

It may be enough to have Harry and Lisa dig their graves deep with the sides and ends properly squared off and stand in them without the slightest morsel of hope left.

Then I walk away and leave them standing there. But Paul is something else.

Program: Lisa must perform exactly as instructed, make her phone call to Harry, and send the cable to Mr. Willow at the bank. I want her to be desperately anxious to tell me all the details of any contact by Paul Dissat. Then I will prepare to greet him. Here. There. Somewhere.

I pulled on my salty swim trunks and put on my big tourist hat and went looking for the lady. She was not in cottage 50. I trudged around, squinting into the hot glare, and found her on a sun cot at the top of the slope that led down to the beach proper. She was face down. The bikini was yellow today. The top was undone, and she had rolled the fabric of the bottom so that it was about as big around as a yellow lead pencil where it cut across the tanned cheeks of her behind. She was glossy with oil. Her towel was on the sand. I sat on it. Her face was turned away.

"You wanna buy nice coconut, Miss lady? Peanuts? Nice spices?"

She slowly turned her heat-stricken, slack-mouthed face toward me. "I don't want any—" She shaded her eyes, squinted. "Oh. It's you."

"Me. Absolutely correct. Me, himself."

"Who needs you?"

She lay with her face turned toward me, eyes closed. "You need me," I told her.

"Not any more. Thanks a lot. But not any more."

"I don't mean that kind of need, honey. I'm talking about financial need. Commercial necessities."

"Thanks loads. I think I'd better take my chances with Paul."

"That should be a lot of laughs for both of you. I wrote an interesting letter last night."

She forgot her top wasn't latched. She sat up fast. "What kind of a letter? Who to?"

"What's the local policy about the tits on tourists?"

She picked up the top and put it on. "I know what *your* policy is, friend. You ignore them. What kind of a letter?"

"Double envelope. A sealed letter along inside the

sealed letter. If he doesn't hear from me on or before May tenth, he opens the second letter."

"Then what?"

"He takes action."

"*What* action?"

"Oh, he just gets in touch with the right people at the SEC and says that it looks as if one Mr. Harry Broll bought himself into SeaGate, Inc. with a final three hundred thou fraudulently obtained and that this fact might not be uncovered by the accounting firm preparing the material for the red herring and they should check with a Mr. Willow regarding evidence as to whether or not Mrs. Broll was alive at the time he released funds at her earlier request. My friend is an attorney. He knows all the steps in the new registration folk dance. Delicate, these new issues. They can die of a head cold."

"Oh God! Why'd you think you couldn't trust me?"

"Who said anything about that?"

"Isn't that why you did it?"

"Lisa, Lisa, Lisa. What if we miss? Suppose your dear cousin nails us both, lays us to rest in a ceremonial boat, lights the pyre and sends us out to sea. The last few moments would be a lot more enjoyable knowing Cousin Paul would never make a profit on the deal."

She swallowed hard and looked unhappy. "Don't talk about things like that." I knew that behind her sun squint her brain was ticking away, weighing and measuring advantages. I reached under the sun cot and retrieved her big sun glasses from the magazine on which they lay and handed them to her.

"Thanks, dear," she said, putting them on. "Sure. I see what you mean. And if he catches us sort of off base, it could maybe be handy to tell him about your lawyer friend."

"Yes. I think so. If he gives me a chance."

"Can't you see why I thought you did it on account of me?"

I thought it over. "Well, I suppose I can in a way. If you *did* decide he represents a better chance, you could tip him off about me and he could . . . tidy up the situation."

She turned over and put her feet down on the sand near my legs. Her hairline was sweaty. Trickles of sweat ran down her throat, and a little rivulet ran between her breasts and down across her belly to soak into the narrow yellow bikini. Her knees were apart, and the cot was so short-legged that her knees were on the same level as her breasts. Her eyes were even with the top of my head.

She leaned toward me, forearms on her knees, and said in a cooing voice, "You know, you act so weird about me, about us, that I'm afraid I'm going to keep on misinterpreting the things you say. We're going to keep on having misunderstandings. I waited a long time last night for you to come over to my place to say you were sorry."

I looked at her. Bright sunshine is as cruelly specific as lab lights and microscopes. There was a small double chin, caused by the angle of her head. There was a scar on her upper lip near the nostril. Her hands and feet were small, square and sturdy, nails carefully tended. Her posture made a narrow tan roll of fat across her trim belly. Her slender waist made a rich line that flowed in a double curve, concave, convex, into the ripe tan hip and thigh. She sat with her plump parts pouched into the yellow fabric, heavy and vital. Stray pubic hairs, longer than the others, curled over the top of the bikini and escaped at the sides of the crotch, hairs the color of dull copper.

Sweat, muscles, flesh, hair, closeness. So close the tightness of the yellow pouch revealed the cleavage of labia. This was the magic and mystery of a locker room, steam room, massage table, or of a coeducational volleyball game in a nudist colony. This was jockstrap sex, unadorned.

"Lisa, I guess we have to say things so carefully we won't have misunderstandings."

"Maybe I got the wrong impression yesterday. You wouldn't be queer, darling?"

"No more than any other true-blue American lad."

"Some kind of trouble? You can tell Lisa. Prostate, maybe? Or some kind of irritation?"

"I'm in glowing health."

"Honey, are you so strung out on some great broad that

you just don't want to make it with another girl? I could understand that. I've been through that."

"Nobody I've met lately has gotten to me."

Her mouth firmed, and her throat turned darker. "Am I some kind of pig woman it would turn your stomach to—"

"Whoa! It's just a little rule of mine. Save the dessert until last."

Her mouth softened into a sudden smile. "Dessert? Darling, I am also homemade soup, meat and potatoes, hot rolls and butter, and your choice of beverages. I am mostly meat and potatoes."

"There's another reason for waiting, Lisa."

"Like?"

She was ready again, I decided. Like training a mule. A good, solid blow between the eyes, and I should have her total attention.

"It's kind of a sad story, dear."

"I love sad stories. I love to cry and cry."

"Well, once upon a time there was this lovely, delicate little blond lady, and she and I were partners in a complicated little business deal. We took our plans and problems to bed, and talked them over during rest periods. I freaked over that little lady. She loved to make love. Then our business deal went sour. It fell apart. That was too damned bad because it was a nice piece of money for both of us. Well, one day a month later we romped all day together, happy as children, and that night I took her out in a boat, a nice runabout, out into the Atlantic. It was calm and beautiful, and I made her sit on the side rail, and I aimed a Colt .45 with the muzzle an inch from her pretty brow and blew the top of her head off. I wired the spare anchor to her waist and let her go in a half-mile of water, and the moon was so bright that night I could see her for a long way as she went down. Now you can cry."

Her mouth sagged open. She put a hand to her throat and in a husky whisper said, "Jesus H. Christ!"

"That idiot girl thought that by sleeping with me she was buying insurance, in case I ever found out she had gone behind my back and made her own deal for half again as much as she would have made as my partner. She was so convinced of it, she was starting to smile when I pulled the trigger. You're not crying."

"Jesus H. Christ!"

"You said that before, Lisa. After that I decided it's bad policy. I made the punishment fit the crime, but I hated myself. You know? I used to think of that little blonde a lot. It used to depress me. It seemed like a waste, all those goodies sinking to the bottom of the sea."

"What *are* you?"

"Me? I'm your partner, Lisa. And we trust each other, don't we? Nobody is going to try to be cute. But . . . just in case . . . let's save all the goodies until after we've made the money score?"

"T-that suits me, Gavin," she said. She clapped her thighs together so smartly they made a damp slapping sound. "L-later. I . . . I got to go for a minute. I'll be back."

"I'll probably be swimming."

She went off toward her place, walking slightly knock-kneed, head bowed and shoulders hunched.

An imaginary letter and an imaginary blond partner. I could imagine that dear imaginary girl sinking down down through the black water, hair outspread, getting smaller and smaller and more and more indistinct until she was gone out of my imaginary life forever. Poor kid. Gavin Lee was a mean son of a bitch. It made me almost want to cry. Now the Lisa-McGee contest could be declared no contest. The lady wasn't going to come out for the third round. She was cowed. She was going to do as she was told. She was going to have as much sex drive from here on as a harem guard. And at the first word from her cousin she was going to come on the run to tell me all about it.

That evening she was so prim it was as if she had never left the convent school. We walked on the beach and got back to the cottages just after dark. We went to her place. She unlocked the gate. We went in, and she screamed as the two dark shapes jumped me. It got very interesting. They both knew a lot more about it than Carl Brego had.

If they had been ready and willing to kill, they had me. But they weren't. And that gave me a better chance than I thought I was going to get.

I took punishment and gave it back. Whistling grunts of effort. Slap and thud of blows. Scuff of feet. I took one on the shoulder, off balance, and fell and rolled hard and came up near a yellow light bulb. A half-familiar voice said, "Hold it! I said *hold* it, Artie! I *know* this joker."

The voice was suddenly very familiar. "Rupe, you dreary bastard, what are you trying to do?"

"A favor for a friend. Lady, if you can get some Kleenex and some rubbing alcohol or some gin, I'd be obliged. And turn on some lights around here."

I told Lisa it was all right. She turned on the garden lights and the inside lights. She had some alcohol and a big roll of paper towels. All three of us were breathing hard. We were all marked, one way and another.

I said, "Mary, this is an old friend of mine. Rupert Darby, a sailing man. Rupe, Mary Broll."

"Pleased to meet you, Mary. And this here, Mary, is Artie Calivan. Artie is mate on the *Dulcinea,* and I'm hired captain. And this big rawboned bastard it's so hard to get a clean shot at, Artie, is an old friend of mine from way back. Trav McGee."

"McGee?" Lisa said blankly.

"It's a kind of joke name, honey," I said. "It comes from an old limerick. Trav rhymes with Gav for Gavin. And McGee rhymes with Lee."

If it had just hung there, I couldn't have brought it off. But Rupe came in very smoothly. "I'd like to recite you the limerick, Miz Mary, but it's just too dirty to repeat in front of a lady. I use that old name on Gav when I'm trying to get his goat. I think I've got one tooth here that isn't going to grow back tight again, dammit."

I looked at his mate. "You brought along a big one."

"Seems he was needed. I needed two like him."

"You were doing fine with just one of him. But *why?*"

"Oh, that damn Brego. What did you think? He whined all day about how us hired captains ought to help each other out, and he said this big fellow, quick and mean as a sneak, had filched his piec—excuse me, Miz Broll, his lady friend. So finally I said to Artie here, let's take the dinghy and run over there to the inn and bounce this tourist around some. Had no idea it was you, Tr—Gav. None at all. Sorry. But not too sorry. First time I haven't been half asleep in two weeks."

I dabbed at a long scratch on my jaw and moved over to Lisa and put my arm around her waist. "Honey, have you got any message you want these fine men to deliver to Mr. Brego?"

"Rupe? Artie? Would you tell him that Mrs. Broll suggests he stop by again and try his luck with Mr. Lee?"

Rupe laughed. "Sure."

"Would you mind taking some of his things back to him?"

"Not at all."

"Let me go gather them up. It won't take a second."

Rupe sent the young man down to keep an eye on the dinghy. Rupe and I sat in a shadowy corner of the garden.

"What happened to the *Marianne?*" I asked him.

"Two bad seasons, and the bank finally grabbed her. I don't really mind a hell of a lot. I work for good people. Good wages."

"Thanks for the nice job of covering."

"That? Hell, that's what a good hired captain starts with or learns real fast. When somebody clues you, don't stand around saying 'Huh?' Run with the ball. No point in asking you what's going on. I certainly know something is going on, and that broad in there must be part of it. She looks good enough, but there's better on the island. Any time you have to scruff up a clown like Brego to grab yourself that kind of ass—"

"Like you said. There's more than meets the eye."

"By God, Trav, you know something? That was fun off and on."

"Glad you enjoyed it. How's Sally?"

"Fine, last I heard. She went back to her folks. She married a widower fellow with four kids. Our three plus his four makes a lot of family."

"Sorry to hear about that, Rupe. I really am."

"It hurt some. But I hate the land and everything on it. I hate a tree, and I hate a mountain. The only death worth dying is by drowning. With the licenses I've got I'll stay on the water all the rest of my time. When our oldest girl drowned, that did it for Sally. That finished her, up, down, and sideways. No more oceans. Next time I write the kids I'll put in a note to her saying I saw you. She always liked you, Trav."

Lisa came out with a brown paper bag and gave it to Rupe. "This won't be too much trouble?"

"Not one bit, Miz Mary."

"Thank you so much. Excuse me, but is that mate of yours a mute?"

"Artie just doesn't have very much to say."

We both walked Rupert down to the dinghy. He stowed the bag aboard, and they picked the little boat up and walked it out past the gentle surf, scrambled in, and started the little outboard and headed back toward the yacht basin.

"*Imagine* that Carl sending them to beat you up!"

"They gave it a good try."

"Did they hurt you, darling?"

"Hardly at all. A month in bed and I'll feel like new."

"I mean really."

"Honey, the adrenalin is still flowing. So the pain is suppressed. Tomorrow morning when I try to get out of bed I'll know how much damage they did."

"Rupe has really enormous hands, doesn't he?"

"And very hard, too."

"And that gigantic boy is *really* handsome. Did you notice?"

"I wasn't thinking in those terms. Want to eat in the dining room?"

"Let's order it sent to my place. It's so much nicer, really. We can fix our own drinks and be comfortable. I won't make any passes, Gavin. None at all."

She kept her word. Long after we had dined, when the nightcap was down to the dregs, she came over to me and bent and peered at my face, teeth set into the softness of her under lip.

"You are going to have one great big mouse right on that cheekbone, friend."

"I can feel it."

She straightened up. "I can't read you, McGee."

"McGee? Who he?"

"Like the limerick. Tell me the limerick, huh?"

"Tell the truth, I can't remember it."

"Was it real dirty?"

"Not very, as I remember. But insulting."

"Funny, you knowing him. I would have thought he would have told Carl you were an old friend. Carl would have told him your name, Gavin Lee, and described you and all."

"Lee is a common name."

"Gavin Lee sure the hell isn't. And how many people are your size anyway?"

"Lisa honey, what are you trying to develop here?"

"I don't know. Is there anything you ought to tell me that you haven't?"

"Can't think of a thing."

"What are we going to do after we get rich, dear?"

"Live rich."

"Like this place?"

"And Las Brisas at Acapulco. And Cala de Volpe on Sardinia. The Reina Cristina in Algeciras."

"In where?"

"Spain, near Gibraltar."

She sat on the couch a couple of feet from me, eyes hooded, mouth pursed. "Will we travel well together when we're rich?"

"Get along?"

"Do you think we will?"

"We'll have to try it."

"Are you terribly dog-in-the-manger about things?"

"Like what?"

"If we had something going for us and I happened to

see somebody like Artie Calivan. As long as I didn't over-do."

"Get the guests?"

She shrugged. "When they come in pairs, dear. And both exciting."

"I don't like to set policy. Take each situation on its merits. Okay?" I put my glass down and stood up. Winced. Flexed my leg. It was going to stiffen up very nicely during the night. She walked me out to the garden gate. I kissed her on the forehead and told her to dream about being rich. She said she had dreamed about that ever since she could remember.

sixteen

I came bounding awake in the middle of the night from a dream so horrible I couldn't remember any part of it. I was drenched with icy sweat and trembling badly.

The dream made me recall lying to Lisa about sending a letter. A letter would be a comfort. I couldn't wait until morning. Leonard Sibelius, Esq., attorney at law.

The sealed letter inside was about the same, but the cover letter for the sealed letter varied. I asked him to read the sealed letter if he did not hear from me by the last day of May and then give it to some colleague wise in the ways of the SEC and the NASD.

After the lights were out again and the letter tucked away, I thought of how ironic it would be if Harry Broll ended up being defended by Lennie Sibelius on a charge of murder, first. Lennie would get him off. He would extract every dime Harry had ever made and put a lock on every dime Harry might make in the future, but he would get him off.

I felt myself drifting off and wondered what the hell there had been in that nightmare that had so thoroughly chilled my blood.

I was up early again on Friday and made another exciting run into town. I stopped at the main post office and sent the letter to Lennie by air, special delivery, registered mail. I drove through the one-way tunnel that leads from the Carenage area under Hospital Hill to the Esplanade and the main part of downtown. The *Queen Elizabeth II* was in, and it was her last visit of the season. She had spewed about two thousand passengers into the town and onto the beaches. The ones in town were milling around, arguing with each other about the currency and looking for the nonexistent duty-free shops and being constantly importuned to hire a nice taxi and see the sights. The big single-stack ship was anchored out with fast launches running back and forth like big white water beetles.

I ambled around and admired one out of every forty-three tourist ladies as being worth looking at and did some minor shopping of my own, then tested my skill and reflexes by driving back to the Spice Island Inn.

It was on that twenty-second day of April that I risked two lives instead of merely my own and drove Lisa out toward the Lance aux Epines area and had lunch at the Red Crab—burly sandwiches on long rolls, icy Tuborg beer, green salad—eaten outdoors at a white metal table by a green lawn in the shade of a graceful and gracious tree. After lunch we went exploring. We stopped and looked at the sailboats moored in Prickly Bay. I drove past large, lovely houses, and we got out of the Moke at Prickly Point and walked down the rocky slope and looked over the edge at the blue sea lifting and smashing at the rocks, working away on caves and stone sculpture, biting stubbornly and forever at the land. A curiously ugly species of black crab, big as teacups, foraged the dry sheer stone just above the reach of wave and tide, scrabbling in swift hundreds when we moved too near.

I studied my map and found, on the way back, a turn that led to a stretch of divided highway, probably the only bit of it on the little island. Weeds grew up through cracks. It was the grand entrance to the site of what had been the Grenada Expo of several years ago. I had heard that few visitors came. Many of the Expo buildings were never completed. The ones which had been finished lay under the midafternoon hum of sun's heat, warping plywood shedding thin scabs of bright holiday paint. Some faded, unraveling remnants of festive banners moved in a small sea breeze. We saw a VIP lounge where the doorsill brush grew as high as the unused and corroded doorknobs. Steel rods sprouted from cement foundation slabs where buildings had never stood. We found a huge and elegant motel, totally empty, completely closed, yet with the lawns and gardens still maintained by the owners or the government.

I drove down crooked little dirt roads, creaking and swaying at two miles an hour over log-sized bumps and down into old rain gullies you could hide bodies in. She clung and laughed, and we made it down an angled slope to a pretty and private little stretch of beach where the almond trees and the coconuts and the sea grapes grew closer than usual to the high tide mark because of the offshore protection of some small islands.

I parked in the shade. We walked on the beach and found one of the heavy local skiffs pulled well up between the trees, with red and blue and green paint peeling off the old weathered wood. She hiked a haunch onto the gunwale, near the hand-whittled tholepin, braced herself there with one knee locked, the other leg a-swing. The breeze moved the leaves overhead, changing the patterns of sun and shade on her face and hair, on her yellow-and-white-checkered sun top, her skimpy little yellow skirt. The big lenses of her sunglasses reflected the seascape behind me. She sucked at her cigarette, looked solemn, then tilted her head, and smiled at me.

"I'm trying to figure out why it should be so much fun, just sort of churning around in the heat of the day," she said.

"Glad you're enjoying it."

"I guess it's because it's like a date. Like being a kid again in Trois Pistoles and going out on a date. It's a feeling I haven't had in a long long time. It's sort of sweet, somehow. Do you know what I mean, Gav?"

"Not exactly."

"Ever since I left when I was fifteen, I've been with guys I've either just been in bed with or am just about to get into bed with or both. And if it was a guy I'd already had or one I was going to have, if we were alone in a funny, private place like this, we'd be knocking off a stand-up piece right here. I was thinking I don't want you to try anything, because it would take away that feeling of being on a date. There's something funny and scary about it, like being a virgin again. Or maybe it's you that's scary to me, about that girl sinking in the ocean. I dreamed about her. Jesus! You really did that? Really?"

"It seemed like a good idea at the time."

She slid off the gunwale and snapped her cigarette into the surf line. She bent and picked up a coconut in the husk and threw it with a shotput motion. She was wiry, and she got surprising distance with it.

"So this is just a little bit of time when nothing happens and we just wait, Gavin."

"For your cousin. After you make the phone call and send the cable."

I leaned on the boat. Some palm fronds had been tossed into it. I lifted them and saw the battered metal fuel tank for the missing outboard motor, and I saw a spade with a short handle, sawed off where it had broken and decided it was a clumsy, improvised paddle. Clumsy but better than none at all. With all that weight and freeboard she would be a bitch to try to paddle against wind or tide.

"Head back?" I asked.

"Can we keep on being tourists, dear? Let's look at that map again."

We went back to the Moke, studied the map and decided to try the road out to Point Saline and look at the lighthouse. It was a road so wretched that by the time we were halfway I had decided only a jeeplike vehicle such as a Moke could make it. Then around the next hairpin corner I was shouldered into the shrubbery by three taxis coming back from the lighthouse, whamming and leaping over the ruts and broken paving, chock-full of tourists off the *QE2*.

My gratis map had little paragraphs on the back of it about local wonders, so just short of the lighthouse hill we stopped and dutifully got out to walk for a moment on the white sand beach of the Caribbean, then crossed the road and went down a path for about fifty yards to walk on the black sand beach of the Atlantic. Then I roared the Moke up the twenty-degree slope to the lighthouse.

The attendant was there, obviously eager to be a guide, obviously eager for bread. We climbed the several flights to the glass enclosed top. The treads were very narrow, the steps very steep. Lisa was directly ahead of me, and I was staring at the backs of her knees as we climbed.

It was a view so breathtakingly, impossibly fabulous that it became meaningless. It was like being inserted into a living postcard. It does no good to stand and gawk at something like that. The mind goes blank as soon as you see it. Tourists take pictures and take them home and find out they have postcards. If they put Helen in front of the view, they have a postcard with Helen in it. The only way a person could accommodate himself to a place like that would be to live there until he ceased to see it and then slowly and at his own pace rediscover it for himself. When I found out what the attendant had to do to keep that fifty-mile light operating, I was happy to place some Biwi in his hand.

Lisa was quiet on the way back. When we were nearly back to the deserted Expo site, I glanced over at her and saw the tear running down her quiet cheek, coming out from under the sunglasses. I pulled over in a shady spot and said, "Hey!"

"Oh God, I don't know, I don't know. Leave me alone."

"Sure."

Glasses off. Dab eyes, snuffle, sigh, blow nose. Fix mouth. Put glasses back on. Light cigarette. Sigh again, huffing smoke plume at windshield.

"Everything is supposed to be so great," she said. "Everything is some kind of a trick. Every time. Some kind of flaky trick, no matter what it is. Fifty-mile lighthouse! Good God! What the hell is a Fresnel lens?"

"A Frenchman invented it long ago. It focuses light into a beam."

"Nothing is ever what you expect. That's what got to me, Gav. A fifty-mile lighthouse and all there is up there is a mantle like off a Coleman lantern and not a hell of a lot bigger, and that poor scrawny black son of a bitch that has to get up every two hours all night long and run up there and pull on some goddamn weights like a big grandfather clock so his fucking light keeps turning around for another two hours. Fresnel! They fake everything in the world."

"What kind of a big deal did They promise you, Lisa?"

She pulled the glasses off and looked at me with reptilian venom and coldness. "They told me, friend, to sing in the choir, love Jesus, do unto others, pray to God, live a Christian life, and then live in heaven in eternal bliss forevermore. They forgot to explain that the choirmaster would give me free private voice lessons when I was fourteen and by the third lesson he'd have his finger up me. They didn't tell me that if I didn't report him, I'd lose out on all that eternal bliss. They didn't tell me that I wouldn't want to report him, because then he wouldn't have a chance to do it again. They didn't explain about it being the temptation of the flesh and how finally you get to the place where you either make a true confession or you run away. They were running their big lighthouse and making it look wonderful, shining its light all over the world to save souls. But it was just a gas mantle and weights and chains and a weird lens. The real thing they teach you without even knowing it is: do unto others before they do it unto you."

"My my my," I said in a gentle wonder, and the tears came again. She got them under control at last.

"Will you laugh at me if I tell you what I *really* want to do with the money, Gav?"

"I don't think I will."

"I want to join an order. I want to give the money to the order. I want to take a vow of silence. I want to kneel on stone floors and pray until my knees bleed and I faint. I don't ever want to be screwed again the rest of my life or be even touched by any man. I want to be a bride of Christ. Now laugh yourself sick."

"I don't hear anybody laughing."

"You think I'd go over the wall in a week, don't you?"

"Do you?"

"If I can find the guts to start, I'll never leave. Never.

You're doing all this to me by making me feel the way I did a long long time ago. A lot of men ago. A lot of beds ago."

"I don't think people stick with projects they start because they think they should start them. That's image making. People stick to their truest, deepest gratifications, whether it's running banks, building temples out of beercans, stuffing dead birds, or telling dirty jokes. Somewhere early you get marked."

"I got it early. Stations of the Cross. Easter. Christ is risen. At about twelve I felt so marvelously pure. Jesus loved me, that I know."

"So you fight it all your life or go back to it. Either way, it is a deep involvement."

She found her glasses on the floor, picked them up and said wearily, "You know so goddamn much, don't you? You know something? You've got a big mouth. A great big mouth. Let's get back on the beach where I belong."

seventeen

That random afternoon had turned Lisa Dissat off in a way she either couldn't explain or didn't care to explain. It amounted to the same thing. We became like neighbors in a new suburb, nodded and smiling when we met walking to or from the main hotel building or up and down the two-mile beach or back and forth from sun cot to cottage.

I saw some of the cruise ship men, crew and passengers, take their try at her now and then when she walked the long wide beach alone. I saw male guests at our hotel and the other beach hotels make their approach, each one no doubt selecting the overworked line he thought might be most productive. They would fall in step with her, last about a half dozen steps before turning away. I followed her a couple of times and kept count. Prettier young women in bikinis just as revealing walked the beach unaccosted. It was difficult to identify those characteristics which made her such a frequent target. It was something about the tilt and position of her head, in relation to the shape in which she held her mouth while walking. It was challenge, somehow. A contempt and an arrogance. Try me, you bastard. Try your luck and see how good you are. Do you think you're man enough to cope, you bastard? There was both invitation and rejection in the roll of her hip. To describe everything that happened to tilt, curve, and musculature in one complete stride from start to finish and into the next stride would have taken a seventeen syllable word. Provocative, daring, and ineradicably cheap. That was what Rupe had seen so quickly, wondering why I risked even a bruised knuckle to take ass like that away from Carl Brego. It was what I had seen when she sat with Brego for a drink and lunch.

It was a compulsive cheapness. I could not believe that it was deliberate in the sense of being something she had thought out. It had to be something she could not help doing, yet did not do out of some physical warp or out of any flaw in intelligence or awareness.

She had been uncommonly determined to give herself to me. It had been too early an effort. She wanted to be used, not loved. She wanted to be quickly tumbled and plundered. It was what she expected and what she wanted, and it was that need which exuded the musky, murky challenge.

I have a need to try to put people together out of the pieces they show me. The McGee Construct-A-Lady Kit. For those on a budget we suggest our cheaper, simpler Build-A-Broad Kit.

Once you Build-A-Broad, it pleases you more than it did before you took it apart and examined the components.

She had ripened young. They had drilled virtue into her so mercilessly that when she was seduced she believed herself corrupt and evil. Purity could not be regained. So she ran away and had spent a dozen years corrupting because she believed herself corrupt, debauching because she had been debauched, defiling because she was the virgin defiled.

When you cannot like yourself or any part of yourself in mind or body, then you cannot love anyone else at all. If you spend the rest of your life on bleeding knees, maybe Jesus will have the compassion to love you a little bit. She had been destroyed twelve years ago. It was taking her a little while to stop breathing.

I kept in close touch with her. She heard nothing. I killed time restlessly. So Saturday I got a clear connection and talked to Meyer. I told him to check out Paul Dissat in the SeaGate offices in West Palm. I had to spell the name in my own special kind of alphabet before he was sure of it. Detroit Indiana sugar sugar Alabama teacup.

"Dissat? Paul Dissat?"

"Yes. And be damned careful of him. Please. He bites."

"Is Mary there? Is she all right?"

"She's fine."

After all, what else could I say? Time to talk later.

Later on Saturday I drove until I finally found the way to Yacht Services. I parked the Moke and went out on the long dock and found the *Dulcinea*. She was a custom motor sailer, broad of beam with sturdy, graceless lines. Rupe Darby and Artie kept her sparkling, and she looked competent.

Artie had gone over to the Carenage in the dinghy to do some shopping. Rupe asked me aboard and showed me the below decks spaces, the brute diesels, all the electronics. He was fretting about the delivery of some highly necessary engine item. It was supposed to come in by air. They couldn't leave without it, and he didn't want to be late meeting his owners at Dominica. He hoped to be out by Wednesday.

I asked about Carl Brego, and he told me that Brego's rich lady had arrived with friends, and they had left early that morning for two weeks sailing the Grenadines.

A sunbrown and brawny woman in blue denim shorts and a dirty white T-shirt came along the dock and waved and smiled. She had a collie ruff of coppery gold hair, a handsome weathered face. Rupe invited her to come aboard and have some coffee with us. She did, and we sat in the shade of the tarp rigged forward. She was Captain Mickey Laneer, owner and operator of the *Hell's Belle,* a big businesslike charter schooner I could see from where we sat. Mickey had a man's handshake and a state of Maine accent.

"Trav, Mickey here has the best damned charter business in the islands, bar none."

"Sure do," she said, and they both chuckled and chuckled.

"Could be out on charter all the time," Rupe said.

"But that would take all the fun out of it, too much of the same thing," Mickey said.

"She charges high, and she picks and chooses and doesn't have to advertise. Word of mouth," Rupe said, and they kept chuckling.

"Five hundred bucks a day, US, and I don't take the *Belle* out for less than five days, and I won't carry less than three or more than five passengers. Price stays the same."

"That's pretty high," I said.

"I keep telling her she ought to raise the rate again."

"Would you two mind telling me why you keep laughing?"

Mickey shoved her hair back, grinning. "Rupe and I just enjoy life, Mr. McGee."

"She does a good trade with business meetings. Three or four or five busy, successful executives, usually fellows in their thirties or early forties, they come down to relax, get some fishing in, get a tan, do a little dickering and planning. You know."

"Why is everybody laughing but me?" I asked.

"She takes male passengers only, Trav."

I finally caught up. "I get it. Your crew is all female, Captain?"

"And," said Rupe, "all nimble and quick and beautiful and strong as little bulls. They range from golden blond— a gal who has a masters in languages from the University of Dublin—to the color of coffee with hardly a dab of cream. Eight of them."

"Seven, Rupe. Darn it. I had to dump Barbie. She was hustling a guest for extra the last time out. I've warned them and warned them. After I provision the *Belle*—the best booze and best food in the Windwards—I cut it down the middle, half for me and the boat, half for the gals. So on a five day run, they make better than three hundred, Biwi. Everyone from golden Louise all the way to Hester, whose father is a bank official in Jamaica."

"You need eight crew to work that thing, Mick?"

"I know. I know. We're going out Monday for ten days. Four fellows from a television network. Nice guys. It'll be their third cruise. Old friends. That means my gals will be topless before we clear Grand Mal Bay."

"And bottomless before you get opposite Dragon Bay and Happy Hill."

"Could be, dear. Louise flew up to Barbados today. She says she has a cute chum who loves sailing. It's a way for a certain kind of girl to combine her favorite hobbies and make a nice living. I don't take hard-case types. I like polite, happy girls from nice backgrounds. Then we have a happy ship."

She got up and said, "A pleasure to meet any of Rupe's old friends, Travis. Hope you'll sail with us sometime. Rupe has."

"Mickey invited four of us captains to a free five-day cruise last year."

"I had a cancellation," Mickey said, "and we were all wondering what to give the other captains for a Christmas present. Well, nice to meet you."

After she was on the dock, she turned and waved and said, "Tell him our motto, Rupe."

He chuckled. She walked lithely away. He said, "Mickey likes you. In her line of work she gets to tell the men from the boys in a hurry."

"What's the motto?"

"Oh. It's on her letterhead. 'Make a lot of lovely new chums every voyage.' "

"Enjoy the cruise?"

"Oh, hell yes. By God, it is different. There's rules, and Mickey enforces them. None of her gals get slopped. Any and all balling is done in the privacy of your own bunk in your own stateroom, curtains drawn. No pairing off with any special gal, even for a whole day. If a gal is wearing pants, long or short, it means hands off. Otherwise, grab whatever is passing by whenever you feel like it. The gals don't make the approach. The things you remember are like standing aft with a big rum punch in a fresh wind with Micky at the wheel really *sailing* that thing, putting on all the sail it'll take, and those eight great bareass gals scampering around, hauling on those lines, trimming sail. And like being anchored in a cove in the moonlight, the evening meal done, and those gals singing harmony so sweet it would break your heart right in two. Great food and great drinks and good fishing. Everybody laughs a lot aboard the *Belle*. Between all they got to do, those gals put in a day full of work for a day's pay. I can't understand that damned stupid Barbie. Why'd she want to try some private hustling? Her old man must own half the state of South Carolina. Barbie's been a sailboat bum all her life. And she gets this chance to make a good living doing the two things in this world she does best and enjoys most, sailing and screwing, and she blows the whole deal. It's hard to understand. Anyway, we were out five days, and it was like being gone a month, I swear. It's . . . it's something different. If you ever see the *Belle* coming in here or leaving, you wouldn't figure it out. Those gals look like some kind of Olympic people training for a race. Nimble and slender and tough and . . . fresh faced. Scrubbed. You know?"

On Sunday Lisa agreed without much argument to arrange her call so that I could hear both ends of the conversation. She placed it from the cottage. We had to wait a long time before the desk called back and said they had her party on the line. I sat close beside her, and she turned the phone slightly so we could both hear, my right ear and her left.

It was Harry's nervous, lying voice. "Mary, honey? Is that you, Mary darling?"

"Yes, dear. Can you hear me?"

"Talk loud. You sound a million miles away, honey. Where are you? I've about gone out of my head with worry."

I hoped he sounded more convincing to his secretary than he did to me. Lisa followed her prepared script, telling Harry to let Holly Dressner know she was all right and that she had phoned. She said she was afraid he'd find the travel agency she'd used. The Seven Seas. Down in Hallandale. Mrs. DeAngela had been very nice and helpful.

"Are you going to come home? To stay?"

"I think so, Harry. I think that's best, really."

"So do I. When, honey? When will you be home?"

"I've got reservations out of here May third. But don't

try to meet me. I don't know when I'll get in. And I'll have my car. By the way, you don't have to worry about the money. Not any more. I'm going to cable Mr. Willow tomorrow to activate the loan and put the money in your account, dear."

"I've been getting pretty nervous."

"I can imagine. I guess I wanted you to sweat a little."

And on and on and finally it was over, and she hung up. She gave me a strange look and then wiped beads of sweat from her upper lip and throat.

"It spooked me."

"I know."

"If I'd been Mary, I certainly wouldn't arrange a loan for that son of a bitch. I don't see much point in that phone call, really. There's enough without that."

"His secretary will make a good witness. Mary Broll is alive and well and in Grenada. She'll be home May third. She can say she was there when Mrs. Broll called her husband. Probably Harry will have his secretary get Mrs. Dressner on the phone and make sure his secretary hears him give her Mary's message."

"I don't have to send her any more cards. If I was supposed to, Paul would have told me. He thinks everything out."

"It's a good way to be, if you like to kill people."

"It's weird. You know? I've thought and thought about what you said, Gav. The smart thing for him to do would be kill me. Get word for me to meet him on the way back. Some other island. Arrange something. But I just can't believe he would. We're from the same town. We're family. I keep having this dream about him. He's standing watching me sleep, and I sneak my eyes open and find out he isn't really looking at me. He's looking the other way, and he has a mask just like his face that he wears on the back of his head. He's pretending to watch me, but he's looking at something else I can't see. When the dream wakes me up, I'm cold all over."

"We won't have long to wait, Lisa. After you send the cable to Willow tomorrow, you're no use to him."

"Stay close to me, huh?"

I reassured her. I wouldn't let the bad man get her. She'd be safe.

Sure.

eighteen

I was up very early on Monday morning when the sun was still behind the green mountains. I swam. The tide was low and getting lower, still running out. I went back to take my shower before dressing for breakfast.

By then, of course, he had talked with Lisa long enough to discover I was one of his priorities. He had immobilized her and come after me. Usually I am pretty good at surprises. Some sense I cannot describe gives me a few microseconds of lead time, and when I get that kind of warning, the reaction time seems to be at its best. Perhaps it is hearing or the sense of smell at subliminal levels.

I don't know where he hid. There were good places in the garden. He could have crouched behind the bar in the service area or behind some of the bigger pieces of furniture in the living room. He worked it out well. He saw me go swimming, and he nipped over the wall unobserved. I'd locked the gate but not the sliding door. He could assume I would come inside to take my shower, and I would have no reason to close the bathroom door. Standard procedure is to reach in and turn the handles until you get the roaring water to the right temperature, and then you step in. It is a moment of helplessness, and there is a useful curtain of sound.

I remember that when I got the water temperature the way I wanted it, I straightened to strip the swim trunks off. The whole back of my head blew up, and I went spinning and fluttering down through torrents of white, blinding light.

182

I know what he probably used. I made things easy for him. I had picked up the piece of driftwood in the surf a few days before. It was iron hard, less than a yard long, a stick an inch and a half in diameter with a sea-polished clump of root structure at the end of it the size of a large clenched fist.

Because he did not give a particular damn whether he killed me or not, he waited for the water roar, then came prowling into the bathroom with the club cocked, poising like a laborer to sledge a stake into hard ground.

The brain is a tender, gray jelly wrapped in membrane, threaded and fed with miles of blood tubes down to the diameter of thread. The gray jelly is a few billion cells which build up and discharge very small amounts of electric impulses. The whole wet, complex ball is encased in this bone, covered with a rubbery layer of scalp and a hair thatch which performs some small shock-absorbing service. Like the rest of the body, the brain is designed to include its own spare parts system. Brain cells are always dying at a rate dependent on how you live but are never replaced. There are supposed to be enough to last you. If a stroke should kill all the cells in the right hemisphere involved with communication—hearing and speaking, reading and writing—there is a fair chance of dormant cells in the left hemisphere being awakened and trained and plugged into the other parts of the system. Researchers can run a very thin electrode into an animal brain and hit a pleasure center and offer a chimp two levers—push one, and he gets a little electrical charge that makes him feel intense pleasure; push the other, and he gets a banana. The chimp will happily starve to death, pushing the pleasure lever. They can make a rabbit dangerously savage, a cat afraid of mice. They can put electrodes against your skull and trace pictures of your brain waves. If you have nice big steep alpha waves, you learn quickly and well. People who smoke a lot have stunted alpha waves. People who live in an area with a high index of air pollution—New York, Los Angeles, Birmingham—have rotten little alpha waves that are so tiny they are hard to find. No one knows yet why this is so. It may be a big fat waste of everybody's money, time, and energy sending kids to school in Los Angeles, Chicago, and lately, Phoenix.

Anyway, if you take a club to all this miraculous gray tapioca with a good full swing and bash the back of the skull a little to the right of center where a right-hander is likely to hit it, it is not going to function at all for a while, and then it is going to function in some partial manner for a varying period of time, which could be for as long as it lives. If you have any blood leaking in there and building pressure between the bone and the jelly, then it is not going to live very long at all.

Even if there is a perfect, unlikely, one-hundred-percent recovery, it is going to take a long time to gather up the scattered pieces of memory of the time just prior to the blow and the time just subsequent to the recovery of partial consciousness. The memories will never be complete and perfect. Drop one of those big Seeburg jukes off the back of a pickup truck, and you are not going to get any music at all, and even if it can be fixed, the stereo might not ever work too well.

Forget the crap about the television series hard guy who gets slugged and shoved out of a fast moving car, wakes up in the ambulance, and immediately deduces that the kidnapper was a left-handed albino because Little Milly left her pill bottle on the second piling from the end of the pier. If hard case happens to wake up in the ambulance, he is going to be busy trying to remember his own name and wondering why he has double vision and what that loud noise is and why he keeps throwing up.

Assembling the bits of memory into some kind of proper order is a good trick, too.

Here's one fragment. On my left side, curled up in a cramped, tilting, bouncing place where things dug into me. Very hot. Some fabric pasted to me with sweat. Head in a small place full of blue light. Something abrasive under my left cheek. Arms immovable, hands dead. Motor grinding. A woman making a keening sound somewhere near, a thin long gassy cry, over and over, not in fear, in pain, in sorrow—but as if she were practicing, trying to imitate something, like a broken valve in a steam plant. Blackout.

Another: being jounced and joggled, hanging head down, bent over something hard digging into my belly. Thighs clasped. By an arm? One brute son of a bitch to carry me that way in a walk, but this one was jogging! Begin shallow coughing that announces imminent vomit. Immediately dropped heavily into sand. Gag, choke, and drift back into the gray void.

There were others, more vague. Some were real, and some were dreams. The brain was trying to sort out the world and it took bits of input and built dreams. On patrol, clenching myself motionless against stony ground while the flare floated down, swinging a little, moving over to burn out against the shoulder of the hill that closed off the end of the valley they were using. A brilliantly vivid fragment of old nightmare of Junior Allen surfacing behind the cruiser, tough jowls wedged into the gap of the Danforth anchor.

Then along came a more detailed one that continued so long the brain was able to go to work on it, sorting out evidences of reality, comparing them to evidences of fantasy. I awoke slowly. I was sitting on sand, leaning back against something that felt like the trunk of a tree. My arms were fastened around behind me, painfully cramped. I tried to move them and could not. I tried to move my hands, wiggle my fingers, and I could feel nothing.

I stared down at familiar swim trunks and down the brown length of my very own legs with the curled hair sun-bleached to pure white against the brown hide. A quarter-inch-in-diameter nylon cord had been tied to both ankles. It had been pulled so tight it bit into the skin. My feet were puffed. There was a two-foot length of cord from ankle to ankle. My legs spraddled. A sea grape tree grew up out of the sand in the middle of the triangle formed by my spread legs and the ankle-to-ankle cord.

It took time to work it out. It was unlikely I had been there so long the tree had happened to grow there. Do trees grow slowly? Yes. Very slowly. Okay, could I have been fitted over the tree somehow? Long, careful thought. No. Too big. The ankles had been tied after they had been placed on either side of the tree. By me? No, the cord was too tight. My feet were swollen and blood dark. By somebody else then. Untie the cord? Not with arms I couldn't move and hands I couldn't feel. Remove tree? No way. I was supposed to stay there. No choice about it. I turned my head to the left, slowly, slowly. I was in shade. Out there the sand blazed under a high sun. Blue waves, small ones, moved in toward the sand and lifted, crested white, slapped and ran up the sandslant and back into the next wave. I turned my head the other way as slowly and looked to my right.

A man was sitting there. He was sitting on a small, inflatable blue raft I had seen afloat in Lisa's pool. He had a weathered brown basket made of strips of woven palm frond, and he was pressing it back into shape and working new green strips of frond into it. He sat crosslegged, intent on his task. He had a trim cap of dark curls. He had dark eyes and long lashes. He had a plump red mouth. He wore white boxer shorts. He wore a gold cross on a chain around his neck. He wore a wristwatch with a stainless steel band and a complicated dial. That was all.

As he tugged and pulled at the stubborn fronds, a lot of useful-looking muscles bulged and writhed and slid around under the smooth skin of arms and shoulders. He rose effortlessly to a standing position and turned the basket this way and that. It was crude. Conical. Half-bushel size. His legs were slender, but the long muscles looked springy and powerful.

A name tugged at the edge of my mind until finally I could fit my sour mouth around it. An articulated croak. "Paul."

He looked at me. There is a way you look at people, and there is a way you look at objects. There is a difference in the way you look at objects. You do not look at your morning coffee cup, at a runover toad in your driveway, or at a flat tire the same way you look at people. This was the way a man might look at a flat tire that he was going to have to attend to in a little while. Not like the owner of the car but like a service station attendant. Damage appraisal, estimate of time required.

I managed another word. "Untie." I was becoming a chatterbox. He looked back down at his basket repair job. I couldn't understand why he wouldn't talk to me. Then gray mists came rolling in from some swamp in the back of my head, and the world faded away . . .

I was being shaken awake. I was going to be late for school. I was picked up and placed on my feet. I squinted into a dazzling world and saw Paul looking at me. I was leaning back against a palm bole, weak and dizzy. I looked down and saw the familiar length of cord from ankle to ankle. Where could my sea grape tree have gone? I could not imagine.

Paul pulled me away from the tree and turned me to face the sea. He walked me carefully, holding onto my upper arm with both hands, helping me with my balance. I had to take short steps. There was very little feeling in my feet. He guided me at an angle down the beach, the trees at my left, the sea at my right. We were out in the hot glare, away from the shade of the trees. He stopped me and said, "Sit." He helped me ease down onto the sea-damp brown sand, facing the basket I had seen him repairing. It was upside down on the sand, like a crude clown's hat. A wave slid up the sand and took a light lick at the edge of the basket and at my right foot.

With the slow grace that accompanies ceremony, Paul reached and plucked the basket away. It was a magic trick. Lisa's severed head was balanced upright on the sand, facing the sea. Magicians can fool you with things like that. He stood easily in front of her and extended his right foot and put his bare sandy toes against her left temple and slowly and gently turned the head so that it faced me. As he did so he spoke a rapid, guttural, unmusical French.

Lisa rolled mad and empty eyes toward me, eyes that looked through me at something on the other edge of the

world beyond me and creaked her jaw wide and made a
thin, gassy, aspirated scream, gagged for air, and screamed
again.

He squatted, turned her head back, slid his palm under
the chin to uptilt her face, spoke down at her, the French
rapid but gentler, almost tender, chiding her.

A wave slid up and under him, and the edge of foam
slapped the lower half of her face. She gagged and
coughed. He stroked her dark, soaked hair back from her
forehead with a tender and affectionate gesture, patted her
cheek, said something else to her which ended with one
word I understood. *Adieu.*

He moved toward me, and as he did so, I saw a bigger
wave coming. She seemed to see it, too. She squeezed her
eyes shut and clamped her mouth shut. It slapped against
my hip. It washed completely over her head and reached
six feet behind her and paused, then came sluicing back,
leaving two small divergent ridges in the sand from the
nape of her neck toward the sea, shaped like the wake of a
boat. The sea had combed her hair forward, left it pasted
down over her face.

He lifted me easily onto my feet, turned me to face up
the slope of sand, urging me on. By dint of great mental
effort I put three words together. "She can't see." Meaning, if she can't see, she can't see the wave coming the next
time.

"Never mind," he said. His English was good, but there
was a trace of the French-Canadian accent which Lisa had
eliminated entirely. As we walked up the beach, I saw the
old boat and remembered the day with Lisa. So she had
guided Paul to this secluded spot. I saw the spade with the
short handle stuck into the dry sand near the trees. Easy to
dig a hole big enough for Lisa. With her knees against her
chest, her ankles tied to her wrists, it wouldn't take much
of a hole at all. I saw the Moke beyond the trees, on that
rough little sand road, parked almost where I had parked
it on that day of the lighthouse.

He helped me through the thick, dry sand and eased me
down in the shade with my back against a rough tree

trunk. "Dig her out?" I said. I was getting pretty good with three-word sentences.

He sat on his heels, began picking up handfuls of dry sand and letting it trickle out of the bottom of his fist. "It's too late. Not that it would make any difference. I shouldn't have used the basket. She hated the basket. She begged me not to use the basket. But I had to be sure she told every last thing. But something broke in her head. After she lost all her English. Something gave way. I thought seeing you might put her back together. I guess it was the basket. I'll be more careful with you."

I looked out at Lisa. I saw the biggest wave yet of the incoming tide. It did not curl and smash down at the packed sand until it reached her; then it bounced high off that dark roundness sparkling in the sun, the way a wave will bounce off a small boulder along the shore.

It was hard to believe it was Lisa. From the back only the dark hair showed. Her head looked like some large nut covered with a dark growth that had fallen from a tropical tree and rolled down, coming to rest in the incoming tide.

"If she holds her breath at the right time, she could last a long time, perhaps," he said. "But she is dead. Just as you are dead."

"And . . . Mary?"

There was a slight Gallic shrug. "That was bad luck. I went to her to try to convince her to leave Harry for good. Why should a woman like that have been loyal to a man like that? I wanted her to run, because without her, Harry would have to find three hundred thousand somewhere else. I have that much. I was going to squeeze Harry for half his stock. Waterbury should have let me buy in. Then nothing would have ever happened."

"Bad luck?"

"She tried to run. The house was dark. I caught her, and we fell badly. Very badly. It was an ugly situation. She knew who I was. I couldn't call an ambulance, could I? She knew how bad it was. I had to find out a lot from her while she could still talk. She was stubborn. I had to . . . amplify the pain to make her speak." He frowned. "I thought it would sicken me to do that. But it was a strange pleasure in a little while. As if we were lovers. So that is bad luck too, I suppose, to learn that about oneself. Gratification is expensive and very dangerous, eh?"

He stood up, clapped his hands to remove the loose sand. "And it was the same pleasure with Lisa, and we will discover if it is the same with a man, too. I should not care to dig a hole big enough for you, Mr. McGee."

"McGee?"

"I am very good about details. Harry described you well enough. Mary is dead. Lisa is dead. McGee is dead. But we must find out who you sent the letter to and what it said. We shall improvise, eh? There is a tire pump and a jack in the tool compartment of that ugly little vehicle. Something will come to mind. There will be enough time to proceed slowly and carefully."

He walked up toward the car, a hundred feet away. The equation was very simple. No unknowns. I could spend the afternoon on this hideaway beach as Paul Dissat whiled away the lazy hours with a question-and-answer game with the penalty for wrong answers and right answers precisely the same. Improvised agony.

Or I could try to stand up. That was the first step. If I couldn't, there wasn't any point in wondering about step two. If I could stand up, then I had to see if I could walk down the beach and into the sea. I had to hurry, but with short steps well within the range of my constraining nylon cord, and I had to keep my balance. The third part of it was getting into the water at just the right place. I had seen the place when I had been out there near Lisa's head in the hot sun.

There is no such thing as an undertow. Not anywhere in the world. All you ever find is a rip. To have a rip, you have to have a partial barrier parallel to the beach. It can be a sandbar or a reef. The barrier has to be underwater. There has to be a hole or channel through it. A great volume of water comes in on wind and waves and tide over the barrier, rushing toward the beach with waves marching right along behind each other, hurrying in. Then that big volume of water has to get out to make room for the water coming in. So it goes flowing out through the hole or channel. A big volume and a narrow deep hole makes one hell of an outgoing current. It is sort of fan-shaped, wide at the beach end, narrowing toward the gap in the barrier, and going faster and stronger as it gets narrower.

You can read a rip on a sandy beach from the way it boils up the sand in a limited area and makes a foam line out toward the gap. If you get caught in one, you swim parallel to the beach until you are out of it, then turn toward the beach. Fight it and you can panic and drown, because they usually go faster than any man can swim.

I got up, scraping some hide off my back on the palm trunk. I went down the beach slope, stamping my feet wide for balance. The beach and the sea kept tilting, misting, merging, flowing. In nightmare slowness I passed the round, black, hairy thing, saw it vividly for just a moment. A wave had come in and covered it entirely. The top of it was a few inches under momentarily motionless water, at rest when a wave had come all the way in and gathered itself to run back out. Her black hair was fanned out, and in that instant of sharpened, memorable vision I saw the spume of sand drifting out of her open mouth, like a strange cartoon balloon, a message without sound. A sandy, tan farewell.

Paul was shouting above the wave noises. I was off balance, leaning forward. A wave slapped my chest and straightened me up. I took a deep breath and lunged forward. I counted on the exceptional buoyancy of the water, the high salinity of the dry season. I had to know if I was in the rip. I managed to roll and float and look back at the beach and saw him and the trees and the raft and the Moke moving into the distance at six or eight miles an hour. It was a good rip, and I hoped it was a long gap in a barrier reef, that the reef was well offshore, and that it would move me out into a current that would take me away from there. Any direction at all. Out to sea and drown while laughing at how Lennie Sibelius was going to nail Paul Dissat, nail him and sweat him and find out how it happened. All of it.

The swell had built nicely, and it was going to play hell

on him, trying to find me bobbing around in all that blue and white sparkle. If the hands are dead, it is less burdensome to drown, but you try not to drown if you can help it. I could arch my back and float high, my ears full of the drum sounds of the sea, a wave slapping me in the face now and then. Lift my head, pick a direction, and go kicking along. When all the luck has gone bad, do what you can.

nineteen

It was a good rip that carried me way out and put me into a sea current that seemed to be taking me due north at a hell of a pace, increasing speed the further out I got. The water was warm, and the sky was squinty bright, and I was gently lifted and dropped in the swell. It had been a good way to live, and given a choice of dying, it was as good as any that came to mind. I wanted to stay aware of the act of dying as long as I could. I wanted to touch it and taste it and feel it. When it is the last sensation left, there is a hunger to use all of it up, just to see what it is like at the very end, if it is peace or panic.

I kicked my bound legs slowly and easily. When I lifted up, I could no longer pick out the beach area where Lisa had died. I looked to the southwest and saw the checkerboard pattern of the town of St. George's to the northeast growing more easterly as I floated farther. Finally, I began to see more and more of Grand Anse beach as I drifted further out from shore, and it came into view beyond Long Point. When all of the beach was visible, I estimated that I was two miles from land. I saw the bright sails moving back and forth in the bay when a wave lifted me high. I could not guess how long I had been floating because I kept fading into a semidazed condition very much like sleep. The sun was so high I guess it was past noon.

There was a change in the direction of the current. I believed it had begun to carry me northwesterly, but I was too far from any reference points to be sure. I was opposite the town by then, and as near as I could estimate, I was just as far from the town as I was from Point Saline.

When I could no longer see much of the town, see only the green mounded hills, I knew I was at least three miles offshore, possibly four.

I came out of a daze and saw a tall ship bearing down on me about a mile away. There was just enough angle so I could make her out as a three-masted schooner, and she had all the canvas on her, all the fore and aft sails flying, tilting her on a long reach.

I knew it could be reality or fantasy, and the smart money would bet on fantasy. I guessed she had come out of St. George's, and from my estimate of the wind, if she was headed north to the Grenadines, she would stay on that course until she was far enough out to come about and put her on the opposite tack for a single long run that would clear all of Grenada and head her for Carriacou.

I felt remote, as if working out a problem that had nothing to do with me. My arms had no feeling. I moved up and down on big, slow, blue swells. The crests were not breaking. I kept kicking myself back to an angle where I could watch her, see the boil of white water at her bows. My chance of being seen was one in ten thousand, even if she passed by me fifty yards away.

But then I had an idea. I suppressed it because it was going to involve a lot of effort and any effort did not really seem worthwhile. There would be fishermen aboard, people who always scanned the sea even when there is no hope of stopping for a chance at whatever quarry they see. The big fish smash the water, whack it to foam, send the spray flying. Go to work. Make a fuss. Give them something to spot. Hard to do. Double up and snap. Get the bound legs up and whack them down. Get into a spin, writhing and turning the body, kicking. Duck under and come out and kick as high as you can. Dizziness then. Sickness. Vision going. A sound of sails slatting, lines creaking, a thin cry. Sound of an outboard nearby. Hands grasping, lifting me. Fall onto hardness, onto oil stink, fish smell, and vomit up quarts and quarts of sea water . . .

Then came that burlesque of fantasy, an ironic parody of the seafarer's paradise. I was on a low, broad hatch cover, and I could feel the motion of a ship under me. I squinted up into brightness to see, clustered close around me—all their lovely faces somber, all their girl voices murmuring of concern—the sirens of all the legends, seawind stirring their tresses, their lovely skin in shades from antique ivory to oiled walnut. They were close around me, a multitude of them, prodding and massaging calves, ankles, and puffy feet—forearms, wrists, and swollen hands.

One lifted my dead left hand, and I stared at it with remote interest. It was a dark purple rubber glove, over-inflated, with deep dimples where the knuckles had been.

Suddenly I screamed. It astonished me. I am not the screaming type. There was a pain in my right hand equivalent to having all the fingernails yanked off simultaneously. Pain shoved me far enough into sudden darkness so that the raw scream seemed far away and I could think of it as an angry white bird, clawing and flapping its way out of my open throat.

I came out of blackness in time to get myself braced for the next pain. It was again in the right hand, and as it faded, I got a big one in the left hand, which caught me off-balance and so I roared. The enchantresses moved back a little, looking down at me in worried speculation. They were all in little sleeveless blouses in bright colors, no two alike, all in little white shorts.

Captain Mickey Laneer came into view and perched a haunch on the hatch cover beside my hip. She wore a khaki shirt and a baseball cap. "What the hell have you been trying to do to yourself, McGee?"

"Hello, Mick. Lost an argument."

"Somebody throw you overboard?"

"Ran away, got into a rip, floated out from shore."

She stared at me. "From shore? Jesus! You could be a little bit hard to kill. Gals, this is an old and good friend of our old and dear friend, Rupert Darby, captain of the *Dulcinea*. Say hello to Travis McGee." They said hello in smiling musical chorus.

"McGee, clockwise around you, starting with Julia in the yellow shirt, meet Teddie, Louise, Hester, Janey, Joyce, Margot, and Valerie. Teddie, get to the helm on the double and tell Mr. Woodleigh he's falling off to port, for chrissake, and bring him back on. Janey, Mr. McGee needs a big mug of black coffee with four ounces of Fernandez rum in it. Margot, you help me get Mr. McGee onto his feet, and we'll put him in my cabin while we run back in."

I started to say something to her, then had to clamp down on the pains. Very savage pain but not as bad as the first ones.

"Speak to you privately, Mickey?"

"Move back, gals."

"Somebody is going to make very damned sure I drowned. It could revise their plans if I didn't. They'll keep a watch on the hospital. They could get to me there, I think. It's a bad risk."

"McGee, I like you. But I can't get involved in anything. The government pretends I don't exist. They like the money I bring in. The black power types talk about me forcing blacks into prostitution. Bullshit! Hester is the only almost pure black, and there are three less than half. Every girl has freedom of choice, believe me. Any publicity of any kind, any infraction, they hit me with a heavy fine. Enough to hurt without driving me out of business. Don't kill the goose. But don't let her get fat. You need hospital attention for the head and the hands. So I'm going to come about and have a nice run back and turn you over to Rupe to put you in the hospital. I've got four good, regular customers aboard who've paid their money for a ten-day cruise. Sorry."

I started to fade out and couldn't have pulled myself back in time if a sudden pain hadn't hit my right foot, as if an electric icicle were being shoved through it.

"Mick. I'm . . . sorry, too. Rupe heading up to Dominica Wednesday. Take me up to Grenadines, set up a meet, transfer me. Reach him on radio?"

"Yes but, dammit—"

"Take me back, and I blow your tired businessman cruises right out of the water, captain. Sorry as hell. You probably fulfill a pressing need. No pun. Official complaint to your lady governor, if I have to. And the premier. And the *Miami Herald*."

"McGee, I like you less and less. You are a bastard!"

"Only when I have to be."

"But, damn you, you could *die* on me!"

"Sort of a risk for both of us."

"Valerie? VAL! Get it on over here, girl. This big ugly son of a bitch going to die on me? She was a nurse, McGee."

Valerie was of that distinctive and very special mix you see in Honduras. Mayan, Chinese, and Spanish. She looked at my hands and she had me roll onto my belly while she checked the back of my head. Her touch was firm enough to hurt but gentle enough to let you know the hurt was necessary.

They helped me onto my back again, and she bent close and thumbed my eyelids up and looked gravely into one eye and then the other, back and forth, several times.

"Well?" Mickey said impatiently.

"Eet wass a terrible blow on the head. I don't know. The pupils are just the same size. Probably no fracture because the skull is solid and thick right there. Concussion. Could be bleeding in the brain, captain."

"How do we tell? What do we do?"

"One girl has to be with him every minute, and what she has to do all the time she is with him is count his pulse for one full minute and write it down. Count his respiration for one full minute. Write it down. Over and over. One hour is the most a girl can do that and be accurate. Half-hour is better."

"So we set up half-hour shifts."

"Then she must write down a column of figures. Suppose it is like . . . 71, 70, 72, 69, 71, 70, 69. Fine. Then it is 70, 69, 67, 68, 66, 67, 65 . . . right then the girl on duty finds me and finds you, and we get a seaplane alongside to take him to a hospital. They'll have to open his skull and see if the clot is shallow enough so they can take it out and keep him alive."

"My hands?" I asked.

"They'll hurt like hell," Valerie said. "Like living hell. But you'll be fine. No nerve damage. No dead tissue. Good circulation, so that even something that tight couldn't cut it all off."

The pain hit again as I was fading, but it just held me on the edge, and when it stopped, I went the rest of the way on down. Blurred memories of being carried, of choking on hot, pungent coffee, of hearing the hiss of water along the side of the hull. Then memories of it being night time, feeling that slow swing and turn of an anchored vessel, hearing faint music from topside, of moving in and out of sleep and seeing girls, sometimes the same one, sometimes a different one, solemnly and intently taking my pulse, lips moving, writing on a pad, then staring back and forth from my chest to a watch, counting respirations, writing it down. A Coleman lantern was hung from the overhead with an improvised shade which left the bunk in relative shadow and filled the rest of the small cabin in harsh brightness.

I awoke to a gray morning light in the cabin. The lantern was out. A slender, dark-haired girl sat taking my pulse. She had a narrow, pretty face, sallow skin. Her forehead and the end of her nose were sunburned.

"Where are we?"

"I'm counting."

"Sorry. Tell me when you're through."

"You made me get mixed up."

I let her count, write it down. "We're at anchor in a cove by some pretty little islands north of Grenada. They're called the Sisters. Now I have to count your breathing."

"Who are you?"

"Joyce. I'm new. Hush, please."

"From Barbados, eh?"

It startled her. "How'd you know that?"

"I can even remember the words. You are Louise's 'cute little chum.' She flew up and talked to you about the job."

She blushed. "Yes. Let me count, please."

"Dear girl, do your counting, and then I have to get up and use the head."

She wouldn't let me without going and bringing Valerie back to check me over and give permission. I felt shaky and frail. When I came back from the nearby head, clutching at everything handy, Valerie was sitting on the bunk looking at the notebook tabulations, and Joyce was standing near her. They got out of my way, and I sighed as I got in and lay back.

"Now we can take you off the continuous count, I think," Valerie said. "Do you feel dizzy? Do your ears hum?"

"No."

"I think we'll take a count every fifteen minutes. Joyce, your hour will be up in . . . ten minutes. Stay another hour, okay? I'll have Margot take over from you at seven thirty, and you can go help with breakfast then."

"You're a good nurse," I told Valerie. "Isn't there a shortage of nurses around the islands?"

She was so still for a moment her pretty face looked like a temple carving. Her Indian blood was more apparent. "Oh, yes. A shortage of nurses. And damn lots of patients. And not so many reasons for keeping them living, I think. The children die. The old ones come back, over and over, trying to die."

She spun and left quickly. I tried to smile at Joyce. Maybe I managed it convincingly enough. I think she smiled back as her face tilted and blurred and faded into gray-black. I had to say something to assure Joyce and myself I was not going sour on them.

"What did you do in Barbados, dear?" My voice seemed to come from the bottom of a brass barrel.

"Does it matter?" she said from the far end of a hundred-yard corridor.

"I'm interested. I'm curious. That's all."

She began to emerge out of the humming mists and the metallic distances. I saw her face again, shifting as if underwater, then firming up. "Are you all right?" she asked, frowning. I felt her fingertips moving on my wrists, seeking the pulse.

"I'm fine."

"You looked different. Your eyes were funny. I work in a boutique in Bridgetown. My husband worked at the desk in a couple of the good hotels. We could live on what we made if we were careful. Maybe he got tired of being careful. He left over a year ago, and I have no idea where he is. What else do you want to know? I'm English and Portuguese mostly with a bit of colored. I make about two hundred and seventy-five to three hundred, Biwi, a month in the season and a lot less when the tourists are gone. I can't quite live on it. I've sold the things Charles and I owned, like the music system we got on hire-purchase and was all paid for, and I let them come and take the things which weren't paid for. The last thing I let go, the last thing worth selling, was my little sailboat my father built for me before he died when I was twelve." Her words were coming faster and faster, and she had stopped searching for the pulse. Her thin fingers were wrapped around my lacerated wrist. "It was the only thing I could use to get away, to be someone else, and I took it out in a gale before I let it go, telling it to drown me, but it would not . . ."

"Hey, now," I said.

Her eyes had filled. "I mean there is no end to it, Mr. McGee. I've been a decent woman. I have no family at all. A fat political gentleman wants to give me a cottage in a development he owns. There has been one girl every two years, I understand. He is quite old. They each end up with a cottage and some sort of small pension. I imagine a long street of them with the years marked on little signs in the little yards, with all of us sitting on our little porches . . ."

"Joyce, honey. There, honey."

Kind words started the flood. She put her forehead down into the bend of my elbow, and the stifled sobs wracked her thin body. I stroked her hair and made soothing sounds. I identified my own feeling of guilt. I had not really wanted to know about her life and her problems. I had been talking in an effort to keep the brassy mists from sucking me under. But the words had opened her up, and it had come spilling out.

She pushed herself away, stood with her back to me, blew her nose. "Why should you give a damn?" she said in a choked voice. "Why should anybody?"

"Is this cruise what your friend Louise described?"

She turned, snuffled, sat wearily in the chair. "Oh, yes.

Louise didn't lie. She called a spade a spade. It's a ten-day trial, you might say. I will do deck duty, scut work, help with the food, drinks, laundry, scrubbing, and all that. But I don't have to be . . . available unless I decide to be and tell Captain Laneer first. The men really seem quite nice. I can keep my clothes on, thank God. Louise said it took her three days to get used to pottering about the decks and below decks entirely starko. I think it would take me forever, and even then I couldn't adjust. The girls are so much nicer than I imagined. But an entirely naked woman is not really erotic, do you think? Of course, in a cold wind or offshore insects or one's time of the month or coming into port, clothes are definitely required." She had a brooding look, frowning down at her knuckles. "It's rather difficult for one to imagine being quite ready for it. I mean if one has taken a bucket of scraps aft after cleaning fish, it is so abrupt to be suddenly tweaked, then taken by the hand, and led below." She roused herself and looked slightly startled. She had been voicing her internal monologue. "I go on, no?" She forced a wan smile. "At any rate, once the ten days are ended, I shall either go back to the boutique to stay or go back to quit my job and pack. I shall fret about it later, not now. Valerie told me that it would be good for you to get as much sleep as you can now. Can you sleep, dear?"

I could. I slept and slept and slept. The dull ache in hands and feet and head did not inhibit it. In too many of the sleep periods Lisa was way down below the velvet black, waiting for me on the bright beach, the severed head propped on the delicate bones of the jaw, smiling at me.

It was another morning, and Mickey Laneer brought me a stone mug of coffee, nudged me awake, and put the coffee in my hand after I had hitched up, knuckled grainy eyes.

"You are some kind of a sleeper," she said.

"A long swim with your hands and feet tied will do it every time. We moved again, didn't we? Where are we, and what day is it?"

"Anchored in the lee of Frigate Island at eight o'clock on the morning of Thursday, April twenty-ninth."

"Thursday! But couldn't you get in touch with—"

"He'll be off to the west of here about opposite us at fourteen hundred. We'll make a radio check on him an hour beforehand. No sweat. We'll run out and intercept and put you aboard *Dulcinea.*"

"I've been a lot of trouble to you and your crew, Mick."

Her smile was sour. "Better this kind than the kind you were going to lay on me if I ran you back in."

"Hard feelings, captain?"

She grinned, punched me on the side of the thigh. "My four passengers haven't made any complaints. Maybe because I run the only game in town. The gals have loved playing nurse. By doing it your way—with you having the grace not to die on me—I've kept my friendship with Rupe. And I put a high value on it. No, McGee. Except for having to give up my own cabin, no hard feelings. How do you feel anyway? Strong?"

I checked and tested. "Better than I should."

"You look good. If you feel strong enough, I can send you down a little sample of our recreation program here aboard the *Hell's Belle*. Courtesy of the management. Name your favorite nurse, man."

"Joyce?"

The taut smile was gone. "Now you really are a smartass, you know that? I know damned well you know that girl's arrangement aboard, because she told me about talking to you."

"I thought maybe she'd made her decision."

"And you were curious? I wouldn't want you aboard long. You'd make too much mischief. Nobody puts any kind of pressure on that kid. She works it out for herself. She makes her own decisions."

"What will she decide?"

Mickey Laneer stood up, looking weary and cynical. "She'll decide that every other choice she has is worse. I'll send your breakfast."

Teddie brought my breakfast. She was the big, creamy, Minnesota Swede who had learned her sailing on Lake Superior. She was the one who giggled. Her hair was sea-weathered to a harsh spill of pure white hemp. From the bulge of bland forehead down to the clench of prehensile toes, she was tanned to the shade of macaroons. She giggled as she presented the tray with the menu she had devised. Two giant rum sours. A stack of toast. A platter of flying fish, perfectly sautéed and browned, crisp and sweet. A big enameled coffee pot and two of the stone mugs. She latched the door, giggling, and we had breakfast. She took the tray over to the table and came back, giggling. In the moist hollow of her throat, from earlobe to collarbone and across the socket in front, around to the other earlobe, she smelled exactly like fresh cinnamon and Pears' Soap.

The rendezvous was made about fifteen minutes past two, an estimated seven miles due west of Frigate Island. I convinced Mickey that there was no need to use the tender to transfer me. It was a freshening breeze, the sea running sparkling high. I said that though I didn't want to test my skull by diving, I could certainly swim a little. Rupe put the *Dulcinea* dead in the water, rocking in the trough, and hung the boarding ladder over. Mickey at the helm took the *Belle* across the *Dulcinea's* stern, laying her over so that as I sat on the lee rail and swung my legs around to the outboard side, my feet were but inches from the water.

I dropped and swam the fifty or sixty feet to the *Dulcinea,* bringing from the *Belle* no more than I had brought aboard—the swim trunks, leaving behind somewhere in the sea the scraps of nylon cord they had cut out of my flesh.

There was no hand extended to help me when I clambered aboard the *Dulcinea.* Rupe and Artie stood staring at the *Belle,* jaws slack, leathery paws dangling. Mickey saw no need to change the uniform regulations for an old friend like Rupe. Mickey showed off by taking the *Belle* fifty yards past us, coming about smartly, working hell out of her girls, and then coming back aslant, waving as she angled across our bows on a northeast course not over forty feet away. The girls shouted, grinned, laughed, and waved.

"Fool woman," Rupe said. "All sailor, that fool woman. Artie. Artie? ARTIE!"

"Huh? Me?"

"Bring in that boarding ladder and stow it right this time."

"Boarding ladder?"

"ARTIE!"

"Oh. Sure. Yessir, Rupe. Right away."

Rupe put the diesels back in gear, opened them up to full cruise, checked the chart and gave Artie the compass course, and left him at the wheel. We went below.

"Now what the *hell* is this all about, Trav?"

"It'll take some time."

"Time is what we've got the most of."

twenty

Rupe loaned me the money to get home, and Artie loaned me the clothes, a set of fresh khakis that fit better than I would have guessed from looking at him. I had to buy straw sandals at Kingstown on St. Vincent. Customs and immigration clearance was at San Juan, and I had an interesting time there. People are supposed to have papers and luggage, a wallet and a toothbrush.

They wanted to take my citizenship away from me. I told them it was a little misfortune at sea. I told them we could make some collect phone calls. When I said a magic name they could call collect, they came to attention. They almost smiled. That was on Sunday, the second day of May. I pulled the home number, unlisted, out of the damaged recesses of memory and got his wife, then got him. He talked to the boss immigration fellow, and when they were through, the boss immigration type felt a compulsion to pump my hand and call me sir and ask me if there was any little thing he could do, anything at all.

Before my flight left, I tried Meyer again, and this time he was aboard his boat, and when he heard and recognized my voice, he said in a shaky voice, "Thank God. Thank God." I told him what I needed and what to do and not to be so sentimental, anyway.

It was a bright, clear day to fly across the Bahamas and the incredible tones and shades of the Bahama flats. I wanted to think but not very much. I wasn't very sure about being able to think things through. I wanted to depend on Meyer. The weather across my internal landscape wasn't very good. Patches of gray, like drifting clouds, obscured things I wanted to see. And sometimes in a waking state I would have the same feeling, the same jolt as when you awaken from sleep. For a little while I would not know where I was or where the plane would land.

I got off that flight and walked through the lower level and out to vehicle pickup, and there was Meyer, bless him, standing beside a dark blue rental Ford as ordered. A very anonymous car. I told him he had better do the driving, as I was not entirely sure of the circuitry in my head. He drove. I talked. We selected a ma-and-pa motel on the way into Lauderdale on Route 1, and he got me a room in the back with an airconditioner that sounded like an air hammer breaking up paving. I finished the story in the room.

I unpacked the stuff Meyer had brought from the *Flush,* using that spare key I gave him, which he keeps hidden aboard the *Keynes.* He had packed some Plymouth, which seemed a kindly gesture. He went and got ice from the machine, and we drank from sleazy disposable glasses that looked as though they were about five-room-guests overdue for disposal.

I sat on the bed, sipping the clean, cool taste of juniper. Meyer paced and paced. He would stop in front of me to ask questions. "I'm not clear on one point. You *did* write the whole thing to Lennie Sibelius, telling him to get moving, open the inner envelope if you hadn't checked in by the end of May?"

"I did. But I told Lisa the tenth of May. I wrote to Lennie later. And I did not tell her who I wrote to, of course."

"She believed you?"

"She very definitely bought it. And she told Cousin Paul everything he wanted to know. Assumption: he believed her the way she believed me. But by the time he found out about the letter, he'd gone too far with both of us to start making deals. His next step was to make me talk to him. And he could have. I'm stubborn, Meyer. Need I mention it? The pain threshold is high, as measured on the dolorimeter. But I could have gotten so anxious to talk I would have fallen all over myself. He scares me. What was your reading on him?"

"Humble beginnings. Very bright, very reliable. Full scholarship to McGill. Went back to his village to work for the man who helped him. Worked for that man about three years, and then one of Waterbury's companies acquired the benefactor's business in a merger situation. Waterbury was impressed by Paul Dissat and took him into the Quebec headquarters. Dissat is thirty-six, single, conservative, devout Catholic. He doesn't drink or smoke. He's apparently managed his own savings very shrewdly. Handsome. Very fit. Superb skier and superior tennis player."

He paced and I sipped, and the airconditioner kept up its whangbangroaring, leaking condensation down the blue concrete-block wall.

He stopped in front of me, using his lectern mannerisms. "He functions very well in a highly pragmatic profession. He is perfectly aware of cause and effect. He can weigh the degree of risk he is willing to take. He will assume that the man who gets your letter will be competent. Can his whole plan stand determined investigation? No. Even without a link as weak as Harry Broll enough could be learned to bring it before a grand jury. What would this sort of scandal do to the SeaGate stock offering? It would come out that a fraud had been committed to get funds from a bank to pay for a preoffering block of stock. Waterbury could not afford to proceed. Both Jensen, Baker, and Fairmont, Noyes would recommend the applications be withdrawn. This would all happen, if your letter exists, with or without Paul Dissat on stage. See where I'm going?"

"I think so."

"With no public issue to raise money through the sale of stock, SeaGate comes to a shuddering halt. Harry's indivisible block becomes worthless. I can think of a Dissat-like solution."

"Grab the three hundred thousand from Harry?"

"Yes. But don't burn the bridges. Not all the way. Kill Harry because he is the last useful witness left alive. Then take a leave of absence on an emergency basis, somewhere out of touch. Lay back and listen. If there is no letter at all, if it was a bluff, then come back after the deadline and pick up the project again."

I toasted him. "To you, Meyer. If he has left already, I get the letter back from Sibelius, and we wait for him to reappear. If he's still here and working closer to the deadline of the tenth and if he hasn't gotten around to Harry, we pluck Harry away from him and take Harry to a private place and have a long chat about Mary and Lisa."

"If he has left, or is preparing to leave, and wants a door ajar so that he can get back just in case, then he'll have given Waterbury some sort of cover story, I imagine."

"Can we arrange a secret meeting with Waterbury?"

"Travis?"

"Why are you looking at me like that?"

"If we can't find Harry Broll anywhere and if Paul Dissat is still around and if Harry never did buy that block in SeaGate, even if Mary's body is dug up and identified, there's no way you can get Paul indicted. You probably can't even get him fired."

"He's got pretty legs."

"I don't want you to do some damned idiot thing."

"Long black eyelashes, Meyer. Red lips."

"Travis!"

"Maybe I want to dance with him. Maybe I want to whisper in his ear. But I don't want to have him come to me. You see, he's a careful man. He knows I'll come back if I didn't drown. That's why I told you to be careful about being seen going aboard the *Flush*. Am I overreacting?"

"No. You are not overreacting."

"Don't let him get to you, Meyer, when he starts looking for that letter."

"I've never seen you like this."

"He scrambled my brains. We should get away. I know a great cruise we could take."

"A cruise! A cruise?"

"It's different. I'll tell you about it later."

"Do that. There's been no report of Mary Broll's death from Grenada. It's taking a long time."

"A guest is charged for the cottage whether she uses it or not and charged for the food whether she uses it or not. And in the absence of a body it is the kind of island where, if a lady gets invited aboard a yacht for cocktails or up into the hills to an estate for cocktails, a lady could decide to spend a week being entertained. It is, shall we say, an impulsive place. A carefree isle."

"I phoned Mr. Willow last Wednesday. He got the cable from Mrs. Broll on Monday, and he talked with Harry Broll on Monday. On Tuesday morning he activated the loan papers and deposited the funds in Broll's personal account. I thought you'd like to know. That's when I started trying to get you on the phone. Wednesday, Thursday, Friday, Saturday. It was . . . pleasant to hear your voice."

"Paul sent the cable in her name. No problem. I should have realized how easily he could do that." I looked at Meyer's watch after first staring at my empty wrist for the thousandth time. "Five o'clock on Sunday afternoon. About the only thing we can do is try to find Harry."

"How?"

"There is a name in the back of this scrambled skull. All the file cards are spilled on the floor. Let me crawl around back there for a minute."

I retrieved the red-brown hair, pale green eyes, the vital and expressive face, the lean, quick-moving body. I let her walk around and smile, and then I knew her. "Jeannie Dolan of 8553 Ocean Boulevard." I hitched along the bed and got her number from information and called her.

"Who?" she asked in a sleepy voice.

"McGee. The guy with the blue Rolls pickup."

"Hey! It's you! I'd about decided I hadn't made any kind of dent on you at all. And that doesn't help a girl's pride. Where are you? Ask me out and then sweat out about three minutes of girlish reluctance and then come and get me, huh?"

"I am going to do exactly that later on, but right now I can't do any stirring around."

"Oh! Are you sick?"

"Not too sick to take you out, Jeannie. But I am trying to give the impression of being out of town. For good reasons."

"Okay. I'm not even talking to you. I will go around saying, 'Whatever happened to good old whosis?' "

"You are one nice lady."

"Rrrr*right!*"

"For reasons I may tell you some day, right now I want to know how goes the course of true love and romance and convenience. Betsy and Harry."

"It isn't exactly a script Ali McGraw is going to want to star in. Right now Betsy is teed pretty good. He was real jumpy and mean last week, and Wednesday morning early, like five, he got a phone call. It woke her up, but she fell asleep, and then he's shaking her awake. It's just getting to be daylight, and he's dressed, and he's packed a suitcase. He tells her he's going away on business. By the time the front door slams, she has asked him where he's going and when he'll be back about three times—no answer. I told her I think she has been handed the personally engraved, natural-bristle brush and maybe she should move back down here onto four with me. She's been calling his office and getting brushed off there, too. She drove out there a couple of times, but there was no sign of his car. Maybe he is away on business. But it showed no consideration, the way he left."

"Sold any condominiums?"

"Not to that friend of yours. She never showed up. If she really exists."

"You are very suspicious of people."

"If you'd ever met my husband, you'd know why. He could walk into a phone booth and leave by a side door."

"I'm a sneaky type too, Jeanne."

"That's nice. It's what I'm used to."

"I'll be calling you soon."

"You do that, hon. Bye."

Meyer and I talked, establishing the new parameters. But it was like the game of guessing which fist contains the chess pawn. Harry had enough animal caution to know that if things went wrong for Paul Dissat, it was runaway time for Harry. So if it was Paul who phoned him, maybe Harry had started to run. Conversely, Paul would know Harry was shrewd enough to know when to run, and so if Paul gave Harry cause to run, he would make certain Harry wouldn't be able to.

"The money will be the clue," Meyer said. "The first thing in the morning, as soon as the bank is open. I don't think it was paid over to SeaGate. And I don't think it's still in the bank."

"How do you manage that?"

Meyer smiled an unexpectedly unkindly smile. "By almost giving Woodrow Willow a coronary. He deserves a jolt. One should not be able to con a trust officer out of any assets held in trust."

"I'm coming along."

"Do you think you—"

"In the disguise you're going to go out and buy me at Happy Sam's Giant Superstore Open Always Practically."

"And on the way back here I buy pizza and beer to go?"

The lobby of the Southern National Bank and Trust Company takes up half of the ground floor of their new building on Biscayne. It is like three football fields. People at the far end are midgets, scurrying around in the cathedral lighting. The carpeting is soft and thick, dividing the lobby into function areas through the use of colors. Coral, lime, turquoise. The bank colors are pale blue and gold. The girls wear little blue and gold bank jackets with the initials *SNB* on the pocket, curled into a fanciful logo, the same logo that's stitched into the carpet, mosaiced into the walls, embossed on the stationery, and watermarked into the checks. The male employees and officers up to ambassadorial rank wear pale blue and gold blazers. Everybody has been trained to smile at all times. The whole place looks like a huge, walk-in dental advertisment. There is probably also a bank song.

Meyer dropped me a block away, and while he found a parking space, I strolled back to the bank and went in. I wore a Hawaiian shirt, a straw ranch hat with a red band, a drugstore camera around my neck, sunglasses with big pale orange lenses.

A guard moved in from the side and asked if he could help me. I said I was meeting the little woman here because she had to cash a travelers check, probably to buy some more of those damn silly hotpants, and where would she go to cash travelers checks. He aimed me across a hundred yards of carpeting, under a forty-foot ceiling. Nobody else looked at me. Tourists are invisible, except to the man trying to sell them something. Otherwise, they are as alike as all the trees in the park. Only a botanist knows there is any difference between trees. Or an applegrower.

I kept moving, because if I stood still, one of the guards would come over and ask me if he could help me. I did not know how long it would take. Meyer said he would come in from the north side corridor after going up to the trust department and coming back down with Mr. Willow. Also, I kept moving because I wanted to make certain that by no ten-thousand-to-one chance was Cousin Paul doing a little banking business this hot, windy Monday morning. Sometimes his face would be completely gone from memory, and that would frighten me. Then it would pop back like a slide coming into automatic focus.

At long last I saw Meyer coming toward me, striding right along, and I guessed that was Mr. Woodrow Willow a half step to the rear. I watched Meyer. He was going to rub his nose if he wanted me to join the act. He looked through me and did not see me at all. Woodrow Willow was not what I expected. This was a young man, tall, fresh-faced, snub-nosed, round-headed with the same mouth old Walt used to draw on his chipmunks. I sauntered after them, and caught up when they talked to a man who had his own big blond desk in a solitary, private thirty-by-thirty area of coral carpet right out in the midst of everything. The man used a phone. Soon a rangy woman came over walking like one of those heel-and-toe competitors, elbows pointed outward. She listened. She picked up the phone. A far younger girl came, carrying a ledger card. She jogged. Every part of her jogged.

After she left, Meyer shook hands with the man at the desk, and Meyer, Willow, and the rangy woman walked all the way across to a line of teller's stations on the far side of the bank. The rangy woman spoke to a slender girl with brown hair. Then she spoke to a man patrolling behind the cages. The slender girl closed her window and came around and out onto the bank floor. Meyer turned toward me and rubbed his nose. The rangy woman was leaving.

I walked up, and Meyer said, "Mr. Willow, this is my associate, Mr. McGee. McGee, may I present Miss Kathy Marcus."

"Who *is* this person?" Willow said in a voice of despair. "Good God, I had no idea you were going to bring in—"

"A place where we can talk?" Meyer said. "Just to have Kathy tell us in her own words before we get into anything else. Then we won't be taking up so much of her time."

"Take a lot," she said. "I've got a three-dollar short that's driving me up the wall."

"We'd better use one of the small conference rooms upstairs," Willow said.

Upstairs was 1910 banking, as opposed to the 1984 version in the lobby. Oak paneling, green rugs, leather libraries. The computers were hidden off-stage. Park your Mercer under the elm trees and come in and talk about buying a block of Postal Telegraph.

There were six chairs around the table in the small conference room. There were two framed prints of clipper ships and a seventeen-pound glass ashtray on the polished walnut. As soon as the door was shut, I shed the ranch hat, shades, and camera.

"Enjoying your stay?" Kathy asked me with a quick wink.

"Little gal, when I come across those Everglades in that big old airconditioned Greyhound bus, I said to the little woman, I said, Mother, we shoulda—"

Kathy guffawed, stopping me. Willow rang the big glass ashtray with his pipe in authoritarian tempo, silencing everybody. "Please! This is a very serious matter. If I have

your attention, Miss Marcus, we would like to find out to
what extent you are involved—"

"Whoa, friend," she said sharply, no laughter in her
voice or her level stare.

"Now you will *listen* to me, Miss Marcus! I was saying—"

She got up and went to the door and smiled and said,
"When you go home to the wife and kiddies tonight, Woodie, tell her that nice Miss Marcus quit the bank and went
right down the street to another bank. Some loyalty, huh?"

"Come back and—"

"Woodie dear, the banks are so hard up for anybody
who is worth a damn, it's pathetic. They've been hiring
people here if they're ambulatory and feel warm to the
touch. And I am one very damned good teller, and I have
been here four years, and I am not now, nor have I ever
been, *involved* in anything hanky or panky."

"Please, come back and—"

"Woodie dear, you just can't have it both ways. You
can't call me Kathy and fun around with me when we're
alone in an elevator and give me a friendly little grab in
the ass and a chummy little arm pressure on the tit and
then expect me to sit meek and mild in front of these gentlemen and take some kind of accusatory shit from you. No
thanks. I'll tell them downstairs who ran me out of this
bank."

"Kathy," he said.

With her hand on the knob she looked at him with narrowed eyes and said, "That's a start at least. Say the rest
of it."

"I'm sorry. I didn't mean to imply—"

"Do you want me to come back and sit down, Woodie?"

"Please. I would appreciate it very much."

She came slowly back to the chair, sat, and smiled and
said, "If these men had been strangers, Woodie, I would
have let you go on being a jackass, and I would have
cooked you later. But I'm among friends. Friends who rescued an eerie blonde from the oldest floating houseparty in
the world."

"I remember already," Meyer said.

I looked at her more closely. "Delmonica Pennypacker?"

"Just a little name I made up for my vacation. Anyway, as I understand it, Woodie, you want a play-by-play account of cashing the check for Mr. Harry Broll."

Woodrow Willow was coming out of shock. He cleared his throat and told how a Mr. Winkler, a vice president of the bank, had received a telephone request last Wednesday at closing time from Harry Broll, stating that he would be in at about eleven on Thursday to cash a check for three hundred thousand on his personal account. He wanted to make certain the bank would have cash available in hundred-dollar bills. This is not an unusual request in an area where large real estate deals are made.

Kathy took over and said, "The way our system works, everything has to go through teller records, or we're out of balance. The cashier is Herman Falck, and I suppose Mr. Winkler told Herm to have the cash on hand. Herm told me he would run it through my balance, and he said Mr. Broll would probably bring in a dispatch case for the money. That amount would fit with no trouble. We run a minimum cash balance in the drawer at all times to make the place less appealing to the knockover boys. We signal the vault for more cash or to come make a pickup when we get too fat. They come zipping in a little electric money cart.

"So at ten after eleven Herm brings these two men over to me. I put out my closed sign so that a line won't build behind them. He takes the dispatch case from the man with Mr. Broll and hands it around to me. Mr. Broll gives me the check, and Herm initials it. Then Herm goes back and brings the cash cart behind the cage. It's just a matter of packing the sixty wrapped stacks of hundreds into the case. A black plastic case, imitation lizard. I counted them out as I packed them. Five, ten, fifteen, on up to three hundred. The case was below eye-level looking from the floor of the bank. I snapped the snaps and slid it up onto the counter, and the other man took it, and they walked away."

"Had you ever seen Mr. Broll before?" I asked.

"I think so. He looked sort of familiar. Maybe I waited on him. The name seems familiar."

"How did he act?"

"Well, I guess he's really a pretty sick man. I don't think he could have managed without the other man helping him."

"In what way did he seem to you to be sick?"

"Well, he was very sweaty. His complexion was gray, and his face was wet. He kind of wheezed. Like asthma sometimes. He didn't have much to say. Usually, men joke about lots of money when they put it in or take it out. They joke with me because I'm all girl, I guess. His friend had to kind of support him walking to my window, I noticed. Mr. Broll walked slowly, a little bent over and taking small steps. His friend was very nice to him. Considerate."

"What did his friend look like?"

"Younger. Dark curly hair. Tall. Middle thirties, I'd guess. A very nice voice. Some kind of accent. Marvelous clothes. Conservative mod. But he was too pretty for my taste. Husky pretty. Great eyelashes. He called Mr. Broll 'Harry,' but Mr. Broll didn't call him anything. Let me help you, Harry. Here, let me take that, Harry. Come on, there's no hurry, Harry. Take your time, old man. It took them a long time to walk to the main doors. The fellow helped Mr. Broll and carried the dispatch case. I watched them. They didn't go right out. I guess Mr. Broll felt faint, because they stopped and sat down in that lounge area left of the main doors. It made me uneasy. You like to see three hundred thousand get to where it has to go and get locked up again. They sat side by side on the couch. I could see the fellow leaning toward Mr. Broll and talking quietly and confidentially. I saw Mr. Broll put his hand over his eyes. The other man pulled it away and took his handkerchief and wiped Mr. Broll's face, wiping the sweat away, I guess." She frowned. "Maybe I shouldn't say this, but the whole scene had a funny flavor. It seemed faggoty to me, like a wife with a sick husband. . . . No. The other way around. A youngish husband with kind of a fat, sick old wife he doesn't really love but feels sort of affection and gratitude and . . . a sense of duty to, if I don't sound flippy."

"Not flippy at all."

"I was busy, and when I looked again, they were gone. I would guess it was about twenty minutes before noon when they left the bank together."

Willow said, "Would you say Mr. Broll was drunk or drugged?"

She thought it over. "No. He kept his eyes sort of squinted up. He knew what he was doing. He just seemed . . . fragile. As if he was in terrible pain. As if he had the world's worst bellyache and was wondering if he was going to pass out with it. And . . . he smelled sort of sour. He was wrinkled, and he had beard stubble. I wondered if he'd been traveling all night or he'd slept in his clothes. I suppose it *could* have been the world's worst hangover."

"Thank you, Miss Marcus," Willow said. "Uh . . . Kathy."

"That means take off, huh?"

"With our thanks, Kathy," Meyer said. "You are a bright girl and a good observer. And if it ever becomes possible to tell you anything about this whole matter, we will."

"Thank *you*," Kathy said. She paused at the door and said, "McGee, do you still have that wild floating pad?"

"The Busted Flush. Slip F-18."

"I'll come visit. If you haven't gotten married up."

"Come visit, Kathy. Bring your swim pants."

"I'll bring a bowl of Greek salad. I make one hell of a Greek salad."

When the door shut, Willow said, "Good help is so terribly hard to find and hard to keep that one has to . . . uh . . . put up with a degree of impertinence that . . . uh . . . "

"Like she said, Woodie," I told him, "it's a lot easier to get respect from the pretty ones if you don't keep grabbing them by the ass in the elevator. Right, Meyer?"

"Absolutely right. An executive can't have it both ways."

"Keep the pretty ones at a distance," I said. "Grab the dog-faced ones by the ass. Then you have a happy bank."

"A contented bank," Meyer said.

"Goddammit," Willow yelled. "Tell me what this is all about!"

Meyer said, "I'll ask you the same question I asked you before, Woodrow. Could you swear that you were absolutely, positively certain that Mary Broll was alive when you processed that loan?"

"The answer is still the same. But why are you asking the question?"

"I'll ask you another. What was Harry Broll going to use the money for?"

"To buy the SeaGate stock, to pay the balance due of three hundred thousand. Don't look at me like that. It's legal, you know. It is illegal to borrow money to buy *listed* securities."

"He'd lose a great opportunity if he didn't buy the block of stock?"

"Oh, yes! Really great."

"Would he have to have cash to buy that stock, Woodrow?"

"Of course not! A certified check would—"

"Do you think he bought it?"

"I don't know."

"Can you think of any way of finding out?"

"Don't go away."

We were left alone. Meyer sighed. I told him he was pushing Woodie around beautifully. All he did was sigh again. When Meyer gets the silents, he isn't very good company.

twenty-one

As Meyer drove conservatively back toward Lauderdale in fast traffic, he said, "We can summarize what we know, if you think it will help."

"You do it, and I'll tell you if it helps."

"We do not care whether Harry Broll was running from Dissat or hurrying to meet him. Immaterial. Dissat had him from some unknown hour early Wednesday morning until they walked into the bank Thursday at ten after eleven. By three o'clock Wednesday afternoon Harry Broll was forced to make the phone call to Mr. Winkler about the large cash withdrawal. Dissat had to then sustain Broll on that depressed level where he could make his appearance at the bank without creating suspicion, yet would have no interest in appealing for help. Total emotional and physical defeat. A person reduced to Harry Broll's condition is beyond feeling terror. Only despair. The only part left would be the details of disposal, or if he'd already planned how to do it, to go ahead with it. If it required darkness, he would have to have a place to take Broll to wait for night, or better yet, a place to immobilize him safely so Dissat could put in an appearance elsewhere. If we are building the structure of limitation, the parameters of time and space, we need to know if Dissat appeared at the West Palm office on Wednesday, and if he did, the time spent there."

"And where he is right now," I said. "When I wonder where he is right now, I wonder if he's crouched on the floor behind us. That's what he does to me, Meyer. Sorry. He was so *pleased* with himself, so damned *delighted* when he reached out with his bare toes and turned her head so she looked at me with those empty, crazy eyes. It was a funny kind of innocent pleasure, as if he had no idea there was anything really wrong about it. He was like a little kid who'd built a kite that would fly, and he wanted me to tell him how great it was. He tried to talk tough. Movie tough. But it was like something that had to be said. An obligatory part of the ceremony. After that we were going to share something, he and I. Some special personal important relationship. Dammit, I can't say it so that you can understand how it was."

"He fits the pattern of a certain kind of damaged personality I have read about, Travis. He could be called the activated sociopath sadist. Bright, healthy, energetic, competent. Excellent in areas requiring ritual. Mathematics, accounting, engineering. Quite cold inside. Tricky. Unable to concede the humanity of people around them because, having no basis of comparison, they think all of us have their same dry and barren soul. They are loners. They can charm when they choose. Sexually stunted, inhibited, often impotent. When Mary tried to escape from him and he caught her and they fell badly and injured her seriously, that activated him. Now he knows what he wants. He wants inventive episodes like the one with Lisa. The money will be meaningful only in how many such episodes it will buy. He isn't aware of evil. Only of being caught. You have to think of him as a bored child who suddenly discovers that it is wonderful fun to go to the pet store and buy a mouse and bring it home and do things to it until it is dead. Life is no longer boring. It is full of rich and wonderful excitement. The mouse shares the experience, so he feels fond of the mouse for as long as it lasts. You could say that the child loves the mouse to the extent he can feel love."

"Jesus!"

"I know. Stroking Lisa's forehead, drying Harry's sweaty face, are imitations of emotion. We can imagine he spoke tender words to Mary because she was pleasing him, giving him release. He's not a madman in any traditional sense. He cannot feel guilt or shame. If caught, he would feel fury and indignation at the game ending too soon. He'll go to great lengths to stay free, unsuspected. His career is a lot less important to him than it used to be. My guess is he'll be gone by the deadline, the tenth, a week from today."

We rode in silence for a time. "Meyer? How did you get that Woodie Woodchuck to snap to attention?

"By reminding him that he had informed me of the approximate value of the assets in one of his trust accounts without any authorization from the trust customer or the senior trust officer. Banks take all confidential relationships very seriously. He soon said he would be very happy to help me find out all about the three hundred thousand."

"How did he find out Harry had forfeited his option?"

"I don't know. Probably phoned a contact at SeaGate and asked what value, as collateral, Harry's hundred-thousand-share block would have. The stuff is too closely held to have an OTC quote."

"Couldn't he have borrowed against the stock he was going to get?"

"Not if he had already done so."

"Sick condominiums and a sick construction business. How about the seven hundred thousand he's supposed to get back from SeaGate?"

"If it went into land improvements at the site, then I guess he'd have to wait until the public issue money comes back to SeaGate."

"So that goes to pay off other debts, and then Harry's business quietly fades away and dies?"

"Reasonable guess."

"He had to take Harry somewhere and keep him there. Harry and Harry's car. Transportation problems, Meyer. Logistics and tactics. If he took him to wherever he lives—"

"A cluster apartment complex at West Palm on the bay shore. Rental apartments. Not likely."

"I suppose you have his phone number?"

"You asked me to check him out. Remember?"

"And your overall impression?"

"A very dull fellow, competent and humorless."

"You know the name of the cluster apartments?"

"I'd rather not say it. Palm Vista Gardens. D-2."

"The first phone booth after we get off the pike, please."

He parked at a gas station by a shiny row of vending machines under a roof made of plastic thatch, incredibly green. I phoned from the hotbox provided by Gen Tel out on the cement wasteland. I hoped Palm Vista Gardens was big enough to have a rental and administration office on the premises. It was. The lady's voice came right from the resonant bridge of her Indiana nose.

"Yes, maybe you *can* help me. Have you got any furnished one-bedroom vacancies?"

She was not a well-organized lady. She tended to ramble. She gave information and then with cries of dismay retracted it and called herself names, mostly "old fool."

She finally discovered that one of their renters, "a nice young man" who had been on the special month-to-month basis with one month in advance (an arrangement they made with the "nice young people" from that new Sea-Gate company) had come in on the last day of April, just last Friday, and given his notice. He said he was vacating in a week. And that would make it . . . the eighth? No. The seventh. Yes. Next Friday. They could start showing it again the following Monday if there wasn't too much to be done. That was number D-2, which meant apartment 2 in cluster D. Just stop at the office. But don't wait too long. They go very quickly to nice young people, providing they don't have any pets. Or any babies, of course. I wondered how they felt about noisy goldfish, the kind that do a lot of leaping and splashing and churning around.

I tried to blot out all rational thought with a lot of peripheral items. Goldfish. Lead-free gasoline. Diminishing aquifer. I walked to the car, realizing I had left the cheap camera on the back seat. An essential part of my tourist costume. Meyer stood beside the rental car, drinking a can of orange pop, and it suddenly seemed insane that Meyer wore no tourist disguise. Paul Dissat knew exactly who I was and where I lived. And if he had gone to Bahia Mar and poked around as such a thorough chap would, he would have learned that Meyer was associated with me in certain obscure but apparently profitable ventures. Though believing me safely drowned off Grenada's lovely beaches, he might conclude that it was a very good chance my letter of self-insurance had been sent to Meyer to stow in a safe place. And so, as a percentage play . . .

It worked on me to the point that Meyer stared at me and said, "What the hell is wrong, Trav?"

My mouth wasn't going to work. Alarm is contagious. He trotted around and got behind the wheel, whipped us out into the traffic flow with a good imitation of teenage technique. At last I managed two words. "No hurry."

I saved the rest of it for my rackety motel unit. I tried to smile at Meyer. "Pure chicken. Sorry. I just don't know what the hell is . . ." Then I felt the sudden and humiliating sting of tears in my eyes and turned quickly to blink them away before Meyer could see them.

I stood with my back to him, staring out between the slats of the battered tin blinds at the side wall of a restaurant and a row of trashcans haloed with bluebottled buzzing. I spoke too fast and chuckled where there was no need, saying, "It's the old bit of the brave and noble hunter, gliding silently through the jungle, following the track of the big black panther, and slowly beginning to realize that the panther is also a-hunting and maybe he's flattened out on top of that thick limb up ahead or behind that bush over there or in the shadow of that fallen tree, with just the tip of his thick glossy black tail moving and the shoulder muscles rippling and tightening under that black hide. I'm spooked because I kept telling myself the son of a bitch would be gone by now, but he isn't going until Friday, and—"

"Travis. Come on. Slow down."

Can't ever really fool ol' Meyer. I sat on the bed. We're all children. We invent the adult facade and don it and try to keep the buttons and the medals polished. We're all trying to give such a good imitation of being an adult that the real adults in the world won't catch on. Each of us takes up those shticks that compose the adult image we seek. I'd gone the route of lazy, ironic bravado, of amiable, unaffiliated insouciance. Tinhorn knights of a stumbling Rosinante from Rent-A-Steed, maybe with one little area of the heart so pinched, so parched, I never dared let anything really lasting happen to me. Or dared admit the flaw. Maybe in some crazy way Paul Dissat was a fun-house mirror image of me, a warped McGee with backspin, reverse English.

The adult you pretend to be convinces himself that the risk is worth the game, the game worth the risk. Tells himself the choice of life style could get him killed—on the Daytona track, in the bull ring, falling from the raw steel framework forty stories up, catching a rodeo hoof in the side of the head.

Adult pretenses are never a perfect fit for the child underneath, and when there is the presentiment of death, like a hard black light making panther eyes glow in the back of the cave, the cry is, "Mommy, mommy, mommy, it's so dark out there, so dark and so forever."

Cojones are such a cultural imperative, the man who feels suddenly deballed feels shame at reentering the childhood condition. Papa Hemingway will never take him fishing. George Patton will slap his face.

In all my approximately seventy-six inches of torn and mended flesh and hide, in all approximately fifteen-stone weight of meat, bone, and dismay, I sat on that damned bed and felt degraded. I was unmasked as a grotesque imitation of what I had believed myself to be.

Frowning, I tried to explain it in halting fashion to Meyer. "You talked about . . . the reflexes slowing, the warning system not working, the instincts inaccurate when . . . the only reason Harry Broll didn't kill me was because he lacked one more round in the clip. Then in Grenada I didn't even think of being careful . . . didn't sense his presence, got such a shot in the skull bone my head is still blurred. Meyer, people have been a few steps ahead of me other times. I've played pretty good catchup. This time I have this feeling that there's no way. He's going to stay out in front, and if I get too close, he'll turn around and take care of the problem. Maybe I've gotten too close already, and I have ten more minutes or ten more hours."

"Travis."

"I know. I'm scared. It's like being very very cold. I can't move well, and I can't think at all."

"So I do the thinking?"

"I wish you would. Don't go back to your boat. I have a very ugly hunch about your boat."

"We have to talk to Dennis Waterbury in absolute privacy, and I have to make contact in such a way that he will trust us to the limited extent that rich and powerful people can trust anyone."

"Can you do it?"

"I don't know. I have to try to reach some people by phone. In Montreal and Toronto and Quebec."

"Start trying."

"If I can get through to someone he knows and trusts, who can tell him I am reputable, not a shakedown artist, then we are going to give him whatever lead time we can spare before I go to the law."

"With what?"

"With enough. Woodrow Willow's contact said Broll didn't buy the stock. So there's a missing three hundred thousand and a missing Harry Broll. If they dig around the seawall at Blue Heron Lane, they'll find Mary's body. Kathy Marcus and the other bank people could pick Paul Dissat out of a lineup. Maybe it will sink the SeaGate public issue without a trace. Even if Dissat never took a penny from the Waterbury enterprises, a breath of scandal can make the accounting firm and the underwriters back off."

"So why don't we go to the law? Why do we screw around with Waterbury if we've got all this?"

"Think about it, Travis. Think about it."

I instinctively fingered the place on the back of my skull where I had been so soundly thumped. Meyer was right. SeaGate was a very large thing, and Dissat was an operating officer in the SeaGate power structure. The lower echelons of the law would never go cantering into battle on the say-so of an apparently unemployed beach bum and a semiretired and eccentric economist. It was a two-county operation with both state and federal implications. Lower echelons would take the eccentric pair into skeptical custody and sweat them both.

Suppose you go to the top level, such as approaching the United States attorney in the area and suggesting he refer the problem to the FBI for investigation because of possible violations of the criminal code insofar as banking regulations are concerned. Then the approach would be made so tentatively—due to the SeaGate clout and the dubious source of the tip—that Dissat would be alerted, and he would disappear into his large countryside or ours.

First, you sell Dennis Waterbury on the idea that his boy, Paul Dissat, has been a very very bad boy lately and any publicity given his activities can founder the SeaGate plans. You convince him and give him some facts he can quietly check. You speak to him in absolute privacy and secrecy. Then, when *he* picks up the phone and relays his unhappy suspicions to the highest level, Dissat will be pounced upon first and investigated later, giving Waterbury additional time to plug up the holes and protect the upcoming public issue from scandal.

I said, "Okay. Do you think I'll ever be able to think things out for myself any more? Or will you have to be on permanent standby?"

"I think they start you on baskets and work up to needlepoint."

"I am supposed to laugh. All right, Meyer. Ha ha ha. Make your phone calls. What if the bastard won't listen even if we can get him alone?"

"Men who are rich have times when they don't listen. Men who are quite bright have times when they don't listen. Men who are both bright and rich *always* listen. That is how they got the money, and that is how they keep it."

"Then do we go to Canada, or does he come here?"

"He's here now. I found that out when I was learning all I could about Paul Dissat. Waterbury is in a guest cottage on a Palm Beach estate. The owners are in Maine now, but they left enough staff to take care of Waterbury. Pool, tennis courts, security system, private beach."

He started making calls. He had to push the thermostat high enough to kill the compressor before he could hear. I lay a-doze, hearing his voice come from metallic distances, sounding like the voices of grownups when I had been a child half-asleep in a moving car or train.

twenty-two

He found an old friend at last, a Professor Danielson in Toronto, who knew Waterbury well and was willing to try to set it up. Meyer gave Danielson the motel number and unit number and asked to have Waterbury phone him as soon as convenient. If Danielson found that Waterbury was unable or unwilling to phone Meyer for a secret meeting, Danielson would phone back.

Nothing to do but wait and try to digest a roast beef sandwich which lay in my stomach like a dead armadillo. The motel television was on the cable. We turned the sound off and watched the news on the electronic printer, going by at a pace for a retarded fifth grader, white on black printing with so many typos the spelling was more like third grade than fifth.

The woes of the world inched up the screen. Droughts and murders. Inflation and balance of payments. Drugs and demonstrations. Body counts and new juntas.

Spiro was dead wrong. The trouble with the news is that everybody knows everything too fast and too often and too many times. News has always been bad. The tiger that lives in the forest just ate your wife and kids, Joe. There are no fat grub worms under the rotten logs this year, Al. Those sickies in the village on the other side of the mountain are training hairy mammoths to stomp us flat, Pete. They nailed up two thieves and one crackpot, Mary. So devote wire service people and network people and syndication people to gathering up all the bad news they can possibly dredge and comb and scrape out of a news-tired world and have them spray it back at everybody in constant streams of electrons, and two things happen. First, we all stop listening, so they have to make it ever more horrendous to capture our attention. Secondly, we all become even more convinced that everything has gone rotten, and there is no hope at all, no hope at all. In a world of no hope the motto is *semper fidelis,* which means in translation, "Every week is screw-your-buddy week and his wife too, if he's out of town."

The phone rang, and Meyer sprang up and cut off the compressor and took the call. He made a circle of thumb and finger to tell me we had gotten through the corporate curtain. He listened for several minutes, nodded, and said, "Yes, thank you, we'll be there." Hung up.

"A Miss Caroline Stoddard, Mr. Waterbury's private secretary. We're to meet with him out at the site at Sea-Gate. We go through the main entrance and follow little orange arrows on sticks that will lead us to the storage and warehouse area. There are two small contracts going on now out there. Earth moving and paving. They stop work at four, and the crews leave. The area is patrolled at night, and the guard shift starts at eight at this time of year. Mr. Waterbury will meet with us at an office out there in the end of one of the warehouses behind the hurricane fencing near the vehicle park and the asphalt plant. We can find the place by looking for his car. If we meet him out there at five, we should have plenty of time for uninterrupted talk."

We got to the area a little early, so we drove down A-1-A for a little way, and when we found a gap in the sour commercial honky-tonk, Meyer pulled over. Down the beach there was a cluster of fat-tire beach buggies, some people swimming. Meyer and I were walking and talking over our plans when a chunky trail bike came growling up behind us, passed us, and cut in and stopped, and a fellow with enough black beard to stuff a small pillow glowered at us and gunned the bike engine. He looked very fit and unfriendly.

"You've got a problem?" I asked.

"You are the guys with problems. How come there are

so many of you characters so cramped up you got to come creeping around to stare at naked people?"

"Where, where, where!" Meyer said, smiling. "If it's required, I'll stare. But as a rule, it's dull. If you have some graceful young girls cavorting, that is an aesthetic pleasure for a certain amount of time. Doesn't sand get into the working parts of that thing?"

Meyer is disarming. Maybe a completely frantic flip, stoned blind, could run a knife into him. Otherwise, the belligerent simmer down quickly.

"It's sealed so it doesn't happen too bad. But you can mess it up if you try. I thought you were more guys with binoculars, like the last pair. See, if you walk down this way far enough, then you can see around the end of the buggy and see the girls."

Meyer said, "Excuse me, but I was of the impression that the current belief is that the flaunting of the natural body cures the woes of society by blowing the minds of the repressed."

"A lot of people think that way. But we're opposed to the brazen display of the body and public sexuality. We're here on a pilgrimage mission for the Church of Christ in the Highest. And we have permission to camp on this part of the beach while we're bringing the word of God to the young people in this area."

"Wouldn't it be a lot easier to cover those girls up?" I asked him.

"Four of our sisters have got the crabs, sir, and they are using the salt water and the sunshine to cure them. The drugstore stuff didn't work at all, hardly."

Meyer said, "I have worked and studied in primitive countries, and I have caught about every kind of body louse a bountiful nature provides. And I have yet to contract a case that did not respond immediately to plain old vinegar. Have your girls soak their heads, armpits, and their private parts in vinegar. It kills the crabs and kills the eggs, and the itching stops almost immediately."

"You wouldn't kid me?" the beard asked.

"It is the most useful and generally unknown information in the modern world."

"They've been going up the walls. Hey. Thanks. And God bless you guys."

He roared away. I told Meyer he was fantastic. Meyer said that my continual adulation made him uncomfortable, and it was time to see The Man.

We turned around, and where A-1-A curved west, away from the Atlantic beach, Meyer drove straight, down a road that was all crushed shell, ruts, and potholes, and marked private. Soon we came to the entrance pillars, a huge billboard telling of the fantastic city of the future that would rise upon the eleven square miles of sandy waste, where no child need cross a highway to get to school, where everything would be recycled (presumably vitiating any need for cemetery zoning), where clean industry would employ clean, smiling people, where nothing would rust, rot, or decay, where age would not wither nor custom stale the fixed, maniacal smiles on the plastic faces of the future multitude who here would dwell.

Once past the entrance pillars we were on a black velvet vehicle strip (trucks stay to right, off blacktop) which restored to the rental Ford the youth and ease it had lost during a few months, a few thousand miles of being warped, rocked, and crowded by the dozens of temporary owners.

We followed the small, plastic orange arrows and saw some yellow and green and blue arrows on yard-tall sticks marching in other directions, forming a routing code for workmen, planners, delivery people. A small sign in front of a wilderness of dwarf palmetto said starkly: SHOPPING PLAZA E 400,000 SQ. FT. ENCL. Yes, indeed. A multi-level, automated, air-controlled, musicated selling machine, where—to the violins of Mantovani and the chain gang shuffle of the housewife sandals—only those processed foods would be offered which the computer approved of as being saleable in billion-unit production runs.

We turned away from the sea and against the glare of the high western sun saw the construction headquarters, the belly and stack and hoppers of a portable asphalt plant, saw the trucks and spreaders, piles of aggregate, loader, and loading ramp. That area outside the warehouse and office compound enclosed by hurricane fencing was deserted, as if a flock of Seabees had slapped blacktop on it and been airlifted out. There was a big, vehicle gate in the hurricane fencing, and it stood wide open. In the fenced area were some above-ground fuel tanks and pumps for the vehicles, outdoor storage of some unidentifiable crated items, a generator building, and six small prefab steel warehouses backed up against a truck loading dock. A dark green Lincoln Continental limousine was parked by the next to the last warehouse.

Meyer parked nearby, and we got out. Meyer said in a low voice, "He'll be tempted to think it's some kind of a shakedown. Give us money, and we'll keep quiet about Dissat and let the public issue go through. But Danielson says Waterbury is honest by choice, not as a matter of necessity or operating policy."

There were three crude steps up to the crossbraced plywood door. It stood a few inches ajar, the hasp folded back, a thick padlock opened, hanging from the U-bolt in the door frame.

I gave the door a couple of thumps with the underside of my fist. It made a nice booming sound in the metal structure.

"Hello?" said a pleasantly feminine contralto voice, elusively familiar. "Are you the gentlemen who phoned? Come in, please."

It was dim inside. There were no windows at the end where we entered, only at the far end. We were on an elevated area with a floor made of decking with steps leading down to the slab floor of the warehouse proper. The office was at the far end. The air was very thick and still and hot in the warehouse portion, but I could hear the whine of airconditioning in the enclosed office at the far end.

"I'm Caroline Stoddard," she said. "So nice to see you again, Mr. McGee."

I located her off to the left, standing down on the lower level. At first I thought she was one very big secretary in some kind of slacks outfit, and I blinked again, and my eyes adjusted, and it was Paul Dissat. That odd feeling of having heard the voice before was because of the slight residual accent.

"Be very nice," he said in his normal voice, "and be *very* careful. This is a new automatic nailer. They use it to knock the forms together for footings and pilings and so on. That hose goes over there to that pressure tank, and the compressor is automatic, and the generator is on."

It seemed heavy, the way he held it. He turned it to the side and triggered it. It made a hard, explosive, phutting sound, and nails zinged off the concrete and whanged the metal wall twenty feet away. He turned it toward us again.

"I'm a bad shot," he said. "But these things spray. At more than six inches they begin to turn. They'd make a ghastly hamburger of your legs, I think. I don't know why I've always been a poor shot. I'm well coordinated otherwise. Harry was a fantastic marksman. I guess it must be a natural gift."

"Fantastic marksman?" I asked numbly.

"Didn't you know? You could throw three cans in the air, and with that silly little popgun of his he could hit each one of them twice before they hit the ground without even seeming to aim, just pointing at them by some kind of instinct."

"When he came to see me—"

"He was coming apart. I was having trouble keeping him quiet. He had to make some mock show of being terribly concerned about Mary so that later people could testify he was almost out of his mind with worry. He said you moved so quickly and startled him so badly, he nearly hit you in the foot."

"Where is Mr. Waterbury?" Meyer asked in a tired and wistful tone.

"Playing tennis, I should imagine. This is his time of day for it. Cool of the evening. When word came this morning of the request for information from Mr. Willow, I called him back and after a little hesitation he told me one McGee and one Meyer had initiated the request. Don't keep edging sideways, McGee! It was really a shock. I thought you dead. From drowning or brain damage. You pranced like a sick, ugly stork, and you went floating out at a incredible speed. You are very lucky and very hard to kill."

"Where is Mr. Waterbury?" Meyer asked.

"You are a bore," Dissat told him. "I went to his eminence and told him I had confidential information that two sharpshooters were going to try to get a private audience with him and try to frighten him into parting with money. I gave him the names. He told me to handle the problem. I handle a lot of problems for the man. When the information came in from Toronto, he had me take the call. Don't you think limousines allay all suspicions? They're so symbolic. Sit on the floor slowly and carefully, Travis. That's very good. Now, Meyer, make a wide circle around behind him and come down the steps. Fine. Walk over to that coil of wire on the floor next to the pliers and stretch out on your face with your head toward me. *Very* good. Now, Travis, you can come down and go around Meyer and kneel on the other side of him. Hold it. Now I want you to wire your friend's wrists together and then his ankles. The better job you do, the better all three of us will get along."

It was a heavy-gauge iron wire, quite soft and malleable. It was such dim light I felt I could do a fairly sloppy job. Dissat moved back to the wall, and an overhead bank of daylight fluorescent tubes winked on.

"You're doing a lot more talking, Paul," I said. "All keyed up, aren't you? All nerves?"

"Pull that strand tight. There. That's fine. Let's say I'm more talkative because you're more receptive. Would you like to know how the wave action affected Lisa's body?"

"I bet it was fascinating."

"It was. I sat and watched the whole thing. After the waves were breaking way in beyond where she was, the outgoing wash started to scoop the sand out from around her until she was almost uncovered. Finally she toppled over onto her left side. Then the waves began digging the sand out from under her, settling her lower and lower and flowing and forming around her as it began covering her. The very last thing I saw of her was her right shoulder, and it looked like a little, shiny brown bowl upside down on the smooth sand. And then that disappeared, too. I imagine that on all beaches the sea is a scavenger, burying the sad, dead things and the ugly litter every time the tide comes and goes. Now one more turn *under* the other wrist and then twist it and cut it. Good!"

I wished the pliers were heavier. I rehearsed the motions in my mind. Whip the arm up and hurl the pliers at his face, falling forward at the same time to give the throw more velocity and also shield Meyer from the expected hail of nails. I could scramble forward and take the nails in the back and get to his ankles and yank his feet out from under him, provided no nail went head-deep into the spine. And provided he didn't swing the muzzle down fast enough to drive a close pattern into my skull.

I hesitated, thinking how badly I had missed Harry with the ashtray, and while I hesitated, Dissat moved, making plier-throwing a much worse risk.

He shifted the heavy nailer, swinging the pneumatic hose out of the way, much as a singer manipulates the mike cable. In the bright fluorescence he looked almost theatrically handsome. He was like a color still shot for those strange ads Canadian Club used to use. (I never knew how challenging it would be to hold two men captive with an automatic nailing device until I tried it.)

"Talkative?" he said. "Perhaps. Relief, I suppose. I've made a decision and simplified the future. Harry's money and mine make enough, you know. I've sent it to safe places. You two are the last loose ends. I'm taking sick leave. Actually, I'm retiring. Maintaining two identities compounds the risk factor. I told you in Grenada what I learned about myself from Mary Broll and poor Lisa. Now I shall have a chance to devote all my time to exploring it further. Very thoroughly. Very carefully. Mostly it's a matter of selecting people who might logically disappear of their own accord. I suppose the challenge excites me. So I talk a great deal, don't I? There's nothing I can reveal you can't guess, so it's not a help to you, is it? We shall explore the matter of the letter you sent from Grenada. As a matter of form. It isn't really important whether I learn about it or not, so I don't have to be awfully careful, do I? To keep everything tidy, I might leave with a traveling companion. A certain Mrs. Booker. Betsy. Would you know about her? Never mind. His ankles are finished? Walk backward on your knees. Further. Further. Right there. Sit down there, please, and wire your own ankles together, leaving a length of wire between them, the same length as the nylon cord that day on the little beach."

One uses any small frail idea. From handling the thick, soft wire I guessed that if one bent it back and forth enough times, it would snap. So I took a couple of turns around my ankles, tight enough to keep the wire from turning on my ankle. I made the binding turns, squeezed the wire knots with the plier jaws, nipped away what was left. With luck, management, and timing the wire might part at the squeezed place after enough steps.

He moved to stand over Meyer. He bent over and held the business end of the nailer almost touching the base of Meyer's spine. "I have this on single fire, McGee. Or single nail. If you can wire your own wrists nicely, I'll be so pleased with you, I'll give up the pleasure of finding out just how he'd react to one nail right here. Use ingenuity, McGee. Do a nice job. After Grenada, I take no chances with you."

I did a nice job. I was even able to nip off the extra wire by wedging the pliers between my forearm and the flooring. By holding my wrists together, exerting pressure, I could make it look as if there was no slack at all. Cheap little tricks never do any good at all, except to give the trickster false hope when he needs it.

Dissat came lithely over, bent, and inspected, kicked the pliers away with the edge of his foot. He grunted with satisfaction and walked over and put the nailer down beside the pressure tank, then swung and flexed his arms. "It got much too heavy," he said. He picked up a short, thick piece of metal. I thought it was steel pipe with a dull, gleaming finish, but as he walked toward Meyer, flipping it and catching it, I guessed from the way he handled it that it had to be very light metal, probably aluminum bar stock. It spun and smacked neatly into the palm of his hand each time.

"I don't even know what we use this for," he said. "There's a lot of it in the last warehouse. I've been taking an inventory personally, to check on pilferage of materials, small tools, and so on. That's where I kept Harry, in that warehouse. This piece just happens to have perfect weight and balance. I picked it up by accident the first time. After that, every time I picked it up, old Harry would start rolling his eyes like a horse in the bull ring."

He bent suddenly and took a quick swing, very wristy, and hit Meyer on the back of the right leg, just above the knee. It made an impact sound halfway between smack and thud. Meyer bucked his heavy frame completely off the floor and roared.

"See?" Paul said. "Heavier stock would crush bone and tissue, and lighter stuff would merely sting. I experimented with Harry and went a little too far. I whacked him across his big belly once too often and possibly ruptured something in there, God knows what. For a time neither of us thought he could walk into the bank for the money."

"I'll trade Meyer for all you want to know about the letter."

He looked at me owlishly. "*All* of Meyer? Alive and free? That's naive, you know. Meyer is dead, and you are dead. There's no choice now. I *could* trade you, say, the last fifteen minutes of Meyer's life for information about the letter. He would approve a deal like that when the time comes. But what would be the point? I'm not that interested in your letter, really. I learned a little bit from Mary and more from Lisa and a little more from Harry. Now I can check what I learned and learn a little more. Why should I deprive myself?"

"Why indeed?" Meyer said in a husky voice.

"I like you both," Paul said. "I really do. That's part of it, of course. Remember, Travis, how Lisa became . . . just a thing, an object? It moved and made sounds, but Lisa was gone. I made the same mistake with Harry but not until the very end. The problem is to keep the person's actual identity and awareness functioning right to the end. Now we have to get Meyer out of here. Get up and go bring that hand truck, Travis, please."

I got the truck, and at Paul's request I bent and clumsily wedged and tugged and lifted my old friend onto the bed of the truck. Meyer ended up on his right side. He squinted up and me and said, "I have this terrible pun I can't seem to get out of my head, like one of those songs you can't get rid of. Let's hope his craft is ebbing."

"How is your leg?" I asked him.

"Relatively shapely, I think, but considered too hairy by some."

"Are you trying to be amusing?" Paul asked.

Meyer said in his public speaking voice, "We often notice in clinical studies that sado-sociopathic faggots have a very limited sense of humor."

Dissat moved to the side of the truck, took aim, and clubbed Meyer right on the point of the shoulder, and said, "Make more jokes, please."

Meyer, having exhaled explosively through clenched teeth, said, "I hope I didn't give the wrong impression, Dissat."

"Are you frightened, Meyer?" Paul asked politely.

"I have a lump of ice in my belly you wouldn't believe," Meyer said.

Instructed by Paul, I rolled the hand truck along the warehouse flooring, turned it, and backed laboriously up a ramp, pulling it up. He unlatched a big metal door with overhead wheels and rolled it aside. The white sunlight had turned yellowish outside as the world moved toward evening, but it was still bright enough to sting the eyes. I wheeled the truck along the loading dock and down a steeper ramp where it almost got away from me.

I pushed the truck along the concrete roadway, the steel wheels grating and clinking. I became aware that with each stride I could feel less resistance to bending in the wire joining my ankles, and I was afraid it would snap before I wanted it to. I took shorter steps and changed my stride, feet wider apart to put less strain on the wire. We went through the big gates in the fence and over toward the asphalt plant. Dissat told me to stop. He put a foot against Meyer's back and rolled him off the hand truck. We were in a truck loading area with a big overhead hopper. The concrete was scabbed thick, black, and uneven with dried spills of asphalt tar. Paul motioned me away from the hand truck and pushed it back out of the way. Above us was the hopper and a square, bulky tank that stood high on girder legs.

"Do you see that great big wad of wasted asphalt over there, Travis? Meyer is facing the wrong way to see it. Vandalism is always a problem. Last Thursday night some hippies apparently came over from the beach, and for no reason at all they dropped at least two tons out of the holding tank. That's the big, square tank overhead. It's insulated. Just before the shift ends, they run what's left in the plant into the holding tank. It's hot enough to stay liquid all night in this climate, and in the morning while the plant is being fired up and loaded, the trucks draw from the holding tank. But last Friday morning they couldn't drive the trucks under the hopper until they got a small bulldozer over here to blade that solidified hunk of warm asphalt away from where I'm standing. It's all cooled now, of course. And our old friend, Harry Broll, is curled right in the middle of that black wad, snug as nutmeat in the shell."

I remembered being taken on a hunt when I was a child and how my uncle had packed partridge in clay and put the crude balls into the hot coals until they baked hard. When he had cracked them open, the feathers and skin had stuck to the clay, leaving the steaming meat. Acid came up into my throat and stayed, then went slowly back down.

I swallowed and said, "And the patrol checks here tonight and finds more vandalism?"

"You belabor the obvious, McGee. They'll have to blade your hydrocarbon tomb, big enough for two, over next to Harry's. It's hotter now, of course, in the holding tank than it will be by morning." He moved over to the side. "This is the lever the foreman uses. It's a manual system. If I move it to the side . . ."

He swung the lever over and pulled it back at once. A black glob about the size of your average Thanksgiving turkey came down the chute, banged the hanging baffle plate open, and fell—swopp—onto the stained concrete, making an ugly black pancake about four feet across, very thin at the perimeter, humped thick in the middle. A couple of dangling black strings fell into the pancake from overhead. A tendril of blue smoke arose from the pancake. Meyer made a very weary sound. Pain, anger, resignation. The pancake had formed too close to him, splattering a hot black thread across his chin, cheek, and ear. In the silence I heard the faraway flute call of a meadowlark and then the thunder rumble of a jet. I smelled that sweet, thick, childhood scent of hot tar.

When Meyer spoke, his voice was so controlled it revealed how close he was to breaking. "I can certify. It comes out hot."

"Hardly any aggregate in it," Paul said. "It cools and hardens quickly. Travis, please turn Meyer around and put his feet in the middle of that circular spill, will you?"

I do not know what started the changes that were going on inside me. They had started before the meadowlark, but they seemed related somehow to the meadowlark. You used to be able to drive through Texas, and there would be meadowlarks so thick along the way, perched singing on so many fenceposts, that at times you could drive through the constant sound of them like sweet and molten silver. Now the land has been silenced. The larks eat bugs, feed bugs to nestlings. The bugs are gone, and the meadowlarks are gone, and the world is strange, becoming more strange, a world spawning Paul Dissats instead of larks.

So somehow there is less risk, because losing such a world means losing less. I knew my head was still bad. It was like a car engine that badly needs tuning. Tromp the gas and it chokes, falters, and dies. It has to be babied up to speed. I had a remote curiosity about how my head would work with enough stress going on. Curiosity was changing to an odd prickling pleasure that seemed to grow high and hot, building and bulging itself up out of the belly into the shoulders and neck and chest.

I knew that feeling. I had almost forgotten it. It had happened before, but only when I had turned the last card and knew the hand was lost, the game was lost, the lights were fading. I had been working my wrists steadily within the small slack I had given myself, bending a tiny piece of connecting wire back and forth, and the bending was suddenly easier as the wire began to part.

The hard, anticipatory joy comes not from thinking there is any real chance but from knowing you can use it all without really giving that final damn about winning or losing. By happenstance, he'd made a bad choice of wire. And maybe the twisted child was so eager to squash his mice, he might give one of them a chance to bite him.

The wrist wire broke as I put my hands on Meyer to move him. "Can you roll?" I asked in a voice too low for Paul to hear. Meyer nodded. "Roll on signal, to your left, fast and far."

"What are you saying!" Paul Dissat demanded. "Don't you *dare* say things I can't hear!"

"Careful, darling," I told him. "You're going into a towering snit. Let's not have any girlish tantrums."

He quieted immediately. He picked up his chunk of aluminum. "That won't do you any good, and it isn't very bright of you to even try it. You disappoint me when you misjudge me. You take some of the pleasure out of being with you again." I looked beyond him and then looked back at him very quickly. I couldn't be obvious about it.

The instant he turned I broke the ankle wire with the first swinging stride. He heard me and spun back, but by the time he raised the aluminum club, I was inside the arc of it. I yelled to Meyer to roll clear.

My head went partly bad. I knew I had turned him back into a kind of corner where the girder legs of the holding tank were crossbraced. I was in gray murk, expending huge efforts. It was a stage. Somebody was working the strings of the big doll, making it bounce and flap. At times its doll chin bounced on my shoulder. It flailed

and flapped its sawdust arms. I stood flatfooted, knees
slightly bent, swaying from left to right and back with the
cadence of effort, getting calves, thighs, rump, back, and
shoulder into each hook, trying to power the fist through
the sawdust and into the gristle and membrane beyond.

Pretty doll with the graceful, powerful, hairless legs,
with the long lashes, red mouth, and hero profile. Sawdust
creaked out of its throat, and Raggedy Andy shoebutton
eyes swung loose on the slackening threads.

Soon a blow would burst it, and it would die as only a
doll can die, in torn fabric and disrepair. I had never killed
a doll-thing with my hands before.

Somebody was shouting my name. There was urgency
in the voice. I slowed and stopped, and the gray lifted the
way a steamed windshield clears when the defroster is
turned on. I backed away and saw Paul Dissat slumped
against a crossbrace, one arm hooked over it. There was
not a mark on his face.

I backed away. I imagine that what happened next happened because he did not realize what punishment to the
body will do to the legs. He was conscious. I imagine that
from belly to heart he felt as if he had been twisted in half.

The shapely, powerful legs with their long muscle structure had carried him through the slalom gates down the
long tricky slopes. They had kept their spring and bounce
through the long sets of tennis. So perhaps he believed
that all he had to do was force himself up onto those legs
and run away on them.

He tried.

When his weight came onto them, they went slack and
rubbery. He fought for balance. He was like a drunk in a
comedy routine. He flailed with both arms, and his left
arm hit the load lever, and he staggered helplessly toward
the thick, gouting torrent of asphalt from the overhead
hopper. He tried to claw and fight back away from it,
screaming as I once heard a horse scream, yet with an upward sliding note that went out of audible range, like a
dog whistle. But it entrapped, ensnared those superb and
nearly useless legs and brought him down in sticky agony.
I ran to try to grab him, yank him out of that black, smok-

ing jelly but got a steaming smear of it across the back of my hand and forearm. I turned then and did what I should have done in the first place, went for the lever and swung it back to the closed position. The last sight I had before I turned, was of Dissat buried halfway up his rib cage, hands braced against the concrete slab, elbows locked, head up, eyes half out of the sockets, mouth agape, cords standing out in his throat, as the black stuff piled higher behind him, higher than his head.

I yanked the lever back and spun, and he was gone. A part of the blackness seemed to bulge slightly and sag back. The last strings of it solidified and fell. It was heaped as high as my waist and as big as a grand piano

I remembered Meyer and looked over and saw him. He had wiggled into a sitting position, his back against a girder. I took a staggering step and caught myself.

"Pliers," Meyer said. "Hang on, Travis. For God's sake, hang on."

Pliers. I knew there wasn't time for pliers. The gray was coming in from every side, misting the windshield as before. I found my way toward him, fell, then crawled, and reached his wrists. I bent the wire, turning it, freeing it. I saw a sharp end bite into the ball of my thumb, saw blood run, felt nothing. Just one more turn and then he could . . .

twenty-three

I was not entirely asleep and not yet awake, and I could not remember ever having been so completely, perfectly, deliciously relaxed. The girl voices brought me further across the line into being awake.

Rupe had said how very sweet their voices were, how touching, how heartbreaking, aboard the *Belle*. Their harmony was simple, their voices true and small.

"What a friend we have in Jeeeeee-zusss. All our sins and griefs to baaaaaaaare."

I wondered why the extraordinary crew of the *Hell's Belle* should select a number like that. Yet there was the tidy warmth of Teddie's thigh under the nape of my neck, a sweet, firm fit. Fabric over the thigh. I opened my eyes, and it was night. Light came slanting and touched the girl faces, touching their long, hanging hair. I realized I was on a blanket, and there was the unmistakable feel and consistency of dry sand under the blanket. Teddie's face was in shadow. I lifted a lazy, contented arm and put my hand over the young breast under thin fabric so close above my face. It had a sweet, rubbery firmness.

She took my wrist and pushed my hand down and said, "No, brother." They had stopped singing the words of the song. They were humming the melody. "He has awakened," the girl said. It was not Teddie's voice. They stopped singing.

A man's voice said, "How do you feel, brother?"

I raised my head. There were five or six of them in a

244

glow of firelight. Bearded, biblical men wrapped in coarse cloth. I had been hurled out of my historical time and my place.

I sat up too quickly. I felt faint and bent forward to lower my head down between my knees.

A hand touched my shoulder. Meyer said, "I was trying to get you to a doctor and ran off into the sand. This one here is their healer, and he—"

"I was a third year medical student when I heard the call. I'm the healer for the tribe on this pilgrimage mission."

I straightened and looked into a young bearded face. He nodded and took my pulse and nodded again. "We got that tar off your arm and hand with a solvent, brother, and treated your burn and dressed it."

My arm was wrapped with gauze. There was a bandage on my thumb. I turned my head and saw the beach buggies and several campers. A baby was crying in one of the campers.

I lay back very carefully. The thigh was there, cozy as before. The face leaned over me and looked down. "I will comfort you, brother, but no more grabbing me, huh?"

"No more, sister. I thought I was somewhere else with someone else. A . . . different group of girls."

"On a pilgrimage, too?"

"In a certain sense of the word, yes."

"There is only one sense, brother, when you give your heart and your soul and your worldly goods and all the days of your years to the service of almighty God."

"Did your . . . healer put vinegar on my burns?"

She giggled. "That's me you smell, brother. Blessed providence sent you and your friend to us this afternoon before I flipped right out of my tree. If it isn't sacrilege, my sisters and I are enjoying a peace that passeth understanding ever since."

I tried sitting up again, and there was no dizziness. One of the sisters brought me a cup of hot clam broth. She wore a garment like an aba, made out of some kind of homespun. She too smelled of vinegar. There was a crude cross around her neck with green stones worked into it. The automatic slide projector in my head showed me a slide entitled "The Last Known Sight of Paul Dissat in This World." A small gold cross hung free around his straining throat.

After I drank the broth, I tried standing, and it worked reasonably well. They were not paying any special attention to me or to Meyer. We were welcome to be with them. Feel free to ignore and be ignored. Listen to the sweet singing, taste the broth, and praise the Lord.

I found the vinegar girl and gave her back her cup with thanks. Meyer and I moved away from the fire and from the lights in the campers.

"I panicked," Meyer said. "I got the rest of the wire off me and threw you in the damned car and drove like a maniac."

"Where is the car?"

"Up there on the shoulder. It was in deep. They pulled it out with a beach buggy."

"What about that limousine?"

"Good question. Joshua and I went back in there on his trail bike. The keys to it were on the desk in the office. We put the trail bike into the trunk. I locked everything in sight, and we were out of there before seven thirty. I took the long way around, and we left it at the West Palm airport, keys in the ash tray. Call it a Dissat solution. By the way, I made a contribution to the pilgrimage mission collection plate in both our names."

"That's nice."

"One of the wrapped stacks of hundreds from the Southern National. Initialed. Unbroken. There were four stacks in a brown paper bag on the desk in the warehouse office."

"What did Joshua say?"

"Thanks."

"No questions about the kind of help you asked of him?"

"Just one. He said that before he took the name of

Joshua, he had clouted cars to feed his habit. He said all he wanted to know was whether, if we had committed a sin, we repented of it. I said that even though I didn't think of it as a sin, I was going to pray for forgiveness. That's when he nodded and said thanks and riffled the stack with his thumb and shoved it into the saddlebag on the trail bike. I walked out of the airport parking lot, and he drove the bike out and waited for me down the road from the airport. Long way around coming back here, too. I had the idea you'd be dead when I got here."

"Meyer?"

"Yes?"

"Get me home. Get me back to the *Flush*. Please."

"Let's say goodnight to the tribe."

I did a lot of sleeping. I was getting to be very good at it. I could get up at noon, shower, work up a big breakfast, and be ready for my nap at three. The gray fog rolled way back into the furthest corners of my mind. People left me alone. Meyer made certain of that. He passed the word. McGee has pulled the hole in after him. And he bites.

Meyer would come over during that part of each day when I was likely to be up and about.

We'd walk over and swim. We would come back and play chess. I did not want to be among people. Not yet. So he would cook, or I would cook, or he would go out and bring something back.

The longer we delayed the decision, the easier it was to make. The random parts fell together in a pattern we could find no reason to contradict. Harry Broll had grabbed his three-hundred-thousand loan in cash and fled with Lisa, the girlfriend he had promised to give up. Except for some irate creditors nobody was looking for him diligently. Harry's wife had been reported missing in the Windward Islands, presumed drowned while swimming alone. Paul Dissat was missing too, possibly by drowning, but in his case it would more likely be suicide, emotional depression, and anxiety over some kind of disease of the blood. He had requested sick leave.

Jillian had been astoundingly sweet and helpful and had even lived up to her promise to ask no questions. She had flown down to Grenada and stayed a few days and with the knowing assistance of an attorney friend had obtained my packet from the hotel safe and my other possessions from their storage room.

The favor was, of course, Jilly's concession to apology, to regret. When she and her new friend got back from Grenada, she came over with him to give me back my belongings. They had a drink with us, and they did not stay long. Meyer arrived before they left.

"I keep forgetting his name," Meyer said later.

"Foster Cramond. Still a close personal friend of both his ex-wives."

"Rich ex-wives."

"Of course."

"Likable," Meyer said judiciously. "Good manners. No harm in him. Good at games, what? Court tennis, polo, sailing. Splendid reflexes. Did you notice the fast draw with that solid gold lighter? Twelfth of a second. Interesting phenomenon when they looked at each other."

"What? Oh, you mean the visible steam that came out of her ears? And the way he went from a sixteen collar to an eighteen? Yes. I noticed."

"Travis, what was your reaction when you met her new friend?"

"Relief at not running into some big fuss about breaking my word to visit her for a week. And . . . some indignation, I guess. In all honesty, some indignation."

"And you wished you could change your mind again?"

I let his question hang in the air for a long time, for three moves, one involving tightening my defense against his queen's bishop. I found a response that created a new problem for him. While he was studying it, I leaned back.

"About changing my mind. No. My instincts hadn't turned bad when Harry came here. He had no intention of shooting me. So let's suppose I'm slower by a half a step or a full step. Maybe I'm old enough and wise enough to move into positions where I don't need the speed. The only thing I know is that I am going to run out of luck in the future, just as I have in the past. And when I run out, I am going to have to make myself some luck. I know that what counts is the feeling I get when I make my own luck. The way I feel then is totally alive. In every dimension. In every possible way. It wouldn't have to be Jillian. I could lay back, watch the traffic, select a rich lady, and retire myself to stud. But that would be half-life. I have an addiction. I'm hooked on the smell, taste, and feel of the nearness of death and on the way I feel when I make my move to keep it from happening. If I *knew* I could keep it from happening, there'd be no taste to it at all."

Meyer gave that a lot of thought, and then he gave the game a lot of thought. Finally he said, "When in doubt, castle." He moved his king into the short corner, the rook standing guard. "Travis, I am very very glad that you were able to make us some luck. I am glad to be here. But . . ."

"But?"

"Something else is wrong with you."

"I dream some rotten things. I've got my memory almost all straightened out. Picked up nearly all the cards off the floor and put them back in the right order. But I have real rotten dreams. Last night I was buying a shirt. The girl said it was made in the islands, and they weren't sized correctly and I should try it on. When I put it on and came out, I realized that it was exactly the same print that Lisa had worn that first night I knew her. A dashiki. As I started to tell the girl that I didn't want it, she came up to me quickly, and she reached out, and she snapped something onto the front of the shirt. It made a clack. It was a big, round, white thing, too heavy for the front of a shirt. I turned it around, and I saw that the sound had been the lower jaw of a skull being closed with the fabric caught between the teeth. It was a very white, polished, delicate skull, and at first it looked feral, some predator's skull. Then I knew it was Lisa's skull. I tried to get the girl to take it off, but she said it went with that particular shirt. No other shirt. Just that one. And I woke up."

"Good Christ," Meyer whispered softly.

"But usually I don't dream at all."

"Be thankful. Travis. Is something else wrong?"

"Yes."

"Do you have the words for it yet?"

"I think it's getting to the point where there will be words for it. When there are words, I'll try them on you."

"Are you going to check me with that knight? Go ahead. See what happens if you do."

On the following Sunday afternoon, a Sunday late in May, Meyer and I were over on the beach. When the wind died, it got uncomfortably hot in the sun, so we moved to a bench in the shade. I watched two lovely ladies approaching along the beach, consciously keeping shoulders back and tummies in as they strode along, laughing and talking. Elegant lassies. Total strangers. They were walking across the edge of my life and right back out of it, and I would never know them or touch them nor two million nor ten million of their graceful sisters.

"Maybe I can put that problem into words now. But it's just a try. Maybe you can be patient?"

"How often do you see me impatient?"

"This starts with a word Rupe Darby used down in Grenada. A phrase, not a word. It designates a condition. Womaned out. He meant it in the physical sense. Total sexual depletion to the point where you think you never want to see another woman. I think I'm womaned out in a different way. All my love life is pre-Grenada, and that was a lifetime ago."

"So. Womaned out but not in a physical sense."

"God, no. Those two who just went by created the intended reaction. And I keep remembering how neat and warm the thigh of the little Jesus singer felt under the nape of my neck. Physical capacity is just dandy. No, Meyer. I feel foundered and wind broke in some other dimension of myself. I feel sick of myself, as if the prospect of me in action would turn me off, way off."

"How?"

"Everything I thought I believed about making love to a

woman sounds very stale. I hear myself talking to too
many of them. There has to be affection, dear. Respect for
each other. We must not hurt each other or anyone else,
darling. There has to be giving on both sides and taking on
both sides, honeybunch. Oh Meyer, God help me, it all
sounds like a glossy sales talk. I was kidding them, and I
was kidding myself. Look. I was holding out a package
deal. And on the bottom of the package in small print was
the guaran-goddamn-tee. Mary Dillon picked up the package. I didn't force it on her. I just left it around where
she'd see it. She picked it up, enjoyed the product, and
then married Harry Broll, and now she's buried in a wash-
out behind a seawall under transitmix concrete. So something is wrong with the small print or the service contract
or the damned sales force, Meyer. I just can't . . . I can't
stand the thought of ever again hearing my own sincere,
manly, loving, crap-eating voice saying those stale words
about how I won't ever hurt you, baby, I just want to
screw you and make you a more sincere and emotionally
healthy woman."

"Travis, Travis, Travis."

"I know. But that's what's wrong."

"Maybe there is some new kind of industrial waste in
the air we breathe."

"Fractionated honesty?"

"Don't suffer all over me, McGee. You are a good man.
There is no man alive who is not partially jackass. When
we detect some area of jackassery within ourselves, we feel
discontent. Our image suffers."

"What should I do?"

"How do I know what you should do? Don't make me
an uncle. Go get lost in the Out Islands and fish for a couple months. Go hire onto a tug and work yourself into a
stupor. Take five thousand of what was in that brown bag
and lease the *Hell's Belle* all by yourself for ten days. Take
cold showers. Study Hindustani."

"Why are you getting sore?"

He bounded off the bench, whirled, bent over, yelled
into my face, "Who's getting sore? I'm not getting sore!"

And he ran down to the water, bouncing hairily along, and plopped in and swam out.

Everyone was not acting like himself. Maybe there *was* some new kind of guck in the air lately.

By the time we had finished our swim, Meyer had gotten over his unusual tizzy. We walked slowly back across the bridge, and as we neared the *Flush,* I could see a figure aboard her in the shade of the sundeck overhang, sitting on the shallow little afterdeck.

I did not recognize her until we were within thirty feet. She lay asleep in the deck chair with a tidy, boneless look of a resting cat. There was a big red suitcase beside the chair and a matching red train case, both well scuffed by travel. She wore a little denim dress with white stitching. Her white sandals were on the deck under the chair. Her sleeping arm clamped her white purse against her.

Suddenly her eyes opened wide. There was no sleep-stunned transition. She lept back into life and up onto her feet in the same instant, all smiling vitality. "Hey! McGee! It's me. Jeannie. Jeannie Dolan. I should have looked over on the beach, huh?"

I introduced them. Meyer said he had heard nice things about her. He seemed to approve of the lively mop of red-brown hair and the quick glinting of the gray-green eyes.

I unlocked the *Flush,* and we went in. She said, "Leave my stuff right there, unless you've got thieves. Hey, can I look around? Say, this is a great kind of boat, Trav! Look, is the timing bad? Am I in the way or anything? If you guys have something all lined up . . ."

"Nothing," Meyer said. "Nothing at all."

"Wow, what a great kitchen."

"Galley," I said.

She looked at me blankly. "Galley? They row those with big oars. And a man walking around with a whip. Do you row this thing, for God's sake?"

"Okay, Jeannie. It's a kitchen," I said.

"Does it have engines in it? I mean, it will cruise around and so forth?"

"And so forth," Meyer said, looking happier.

"Wow, would I ever like to go someplace on a boat like this."

"Where's your friend?" I asked her.

"Betsy? We got tossed out of that Casa de Playa by the bank that took over. Not we, just me. Because she was gone by then. She went back to cleaning teeth. For a widower dentist in North Miami."

"Vodka tonic for you?" I asked her.

"Exactly right! It's wonderful when people remember things, isn't it? What I'm going to do, I'm on my way back to Columbus. No, not back to Charlie, that creep. But I called my old job, and I can make enough money so I can save enough to fly to the Dominican Republic and get a quickie divorce, instead of beating my brains out down here."

"Won't you sit down, Jeannie?" I asked her.

"I'm too nervous and jumpy, dear. Whenever I impose on people, I get like this. I've got the bus schedule and all, and then I thought, oh, what the hell, I wanted to see that McGee guy again and never did. A girl sometimes has to brassy or settle for nothing, right?"

I looked at Meyer. He was wearing a very strange expression. I handed Jeannie her drink and said, "Sometimes a girl gets brassy at just exactly the right time, and she gets invited on a private cruise. What would you say to that?"

"Aboard this wonderful ship! Wow! I'd say yes so fast—"

"HOLD IT!" Meyer roared, startling her. He trotted over to her and with raised finger backed her over to a chair. She sat down on command, staring up at him with her mouth open.

"I am going to ask you some very personal questions, Mrs. Dolan."

"What's the *matter* with you, huh?"

"Have you been in a lot of emotional turmoil lately?"

"Me? Turmoil? Like what?"

"Are you at a crisis point in your life?"

"Crisis? I'm just trying to get myself a plain, ordinary, divorce-type divorce."

"Mrs. Dolan, do you feel like a pathetic little bird with a busted wing who has fluttered aboard, looking for patience, understanding, and gentleness and love which will make you well and whole again?"

She looked at me with wide, round eyes. "Does he get like this a lot, Travis?"

"Pay attention!" Meyer ordered. "How do you relate to your analyst?"

"Analyst? Shrink? What do I need one for? Chee! You need one, maybe."

"Are you in love?" he asked.

"This minute? Hmmm. I guess not. But I sort of usually am. And pretty often, I guess. I'm not a real serious kind of person. I'm just sort of dumb and happy."

"One more question, and I must ask you both this one."

"You answer him, honey," Jeannie said to me.

"Would either of you two happy people mind too much if I spend the next few weeks in Seneca Falls, New York?"

"Speaking for the two of us, Meyer, I can't think of a serious objection, really."

He trotted to the doorway to the rear deck and opened it. He picked up the two pieces of red luggage and set them inside the door, gave us a maniacal smile, and slammed the door and was gone.

Jeannie stood up and sipped frowningly at her drink. Then she looked at me. "McGee?"

"Yes, dear."

"Everybody I know is acting weirder all the time. Have you noticed that too?"

"Yes, I have. Meyer isn't often like that."

"It's pretty weird and pushy for me to barge in on you like this. I'm not like this, really."

"It does have engines."

"That's nice. But do you feel like you've been maneuvered into something you'd just as soon not do, huh?"

"The more I think about it, the better I like it."

She put her drink down and came over and gave me one quick, thorough, and enthusiastic kiss. "There! Now it's just a case of getting acquainted, huh? Want to start by helping me unpack?"

We carried the luggage back to the master stateroom. She asked me what Meyer had meant about her having a broken wing. I said he was one of the last of the great romantics. I said there used to be two. But now there was just the one left. The hairy one.

SUSPENSE...
ADVENTURE...
MYSTERY...

John D. MacDonald's
TRAVIS McGEE SERIES